VICTIM
WITHOUT
A FACE

STEFAN AHNHEM grew up in Helsingborg,
Sweden, and now lives in Stockholm. He is an
established screenwriter, whose credits include
adapting Henning Mankell's Kurt Wallander
series for TV. He also serves on the board of the
Swedish Writers Guild. *Victim Without a Face*
is his first novel. It won Crimetime's Novel
of the Year in Sweden in 2014, and it has
been published in ten countries to date.

RACHEL WILLSON-BROYLES is an experienced
translator of Swedish fiction. Her recent
credits include the translation of *The Girl
Who Saved the King of Sweden*
by Jonas Jonasson.

VICTIM WITHOUT A FACE

STEFAN AHNHEM

Translated from the Swedish by Rachel Willson-Broyles

HEAD
ZEUS

First published in Sweden as *Offer utan ansikte* in 2014 by Bokförlaget Forum.
This translation first published in Canada in 2015 by House of Anansi Press Inc

First published in the UK in 2016 by Head of Zeus Ltd

This paperback edition first published in the UK in 2016 by Head of Zeus

9 7 5 3 2 4 6 8

A catalogue record for this book is available from the British Library.

Paperback ISBN 9781784975500
Ebook ISBN 9781784975470

Typeset by e-type, Aintree, Liverpool
Printed and bound by CPI Group (UK) Ltd, Croydon, CR0 4YY

Head of Zeus Ltd
Clerkenwell House
45–47 Clerkenwell Green
London EC1R 0HT
WWW.HEADOFZEUS.COM

VICTIM
WITHOUT
A FACE

PROLOGUE

Three days from now.

THE CROW LANDED ON his naked belly and pressed its sharp claws into his skin. The first few times it happened, the weight of the bird on his body had woken him up. He had managed to scare it off and make it let go. But this time the crow wasn't frightened as easily; instead, it stood unflinching, walking around on top of him, becoming more and more impatient and hungry. It was only a matter of time before it would start picking away at him bit by bit. He screamed as loudly as he could, and the bird finally let go, cawing as it flapped away.

At first he'd thought the whole thing was a nightmare and that all he had to do was wake up to make everything okay. But once he had opened his eyes, all he could see was darkness. He was blindfolded. The light, warm breeze indicated that he was outside and he could feel that he was lying naked on something hard and cold, splayed out like one of da Vinci's anatomical drawings. That was all he knew for sure. Everything else was just a series of questions piling up in his mind. Who had put him here, and why?

He tried to yank his limbs free again, but the harder he tried the further the barbs from the straps dug into his wrists and ankles. The sensation cut into him like a piercing treble tone. It reminded him of the excruciating pain he had experienced as a nine-year-old during dental surgery, after he'd failed to convince the dentist that the novocaine wasn't kicking in.

1

But then again, that was nothing compared to the pain he was in now. It usually came once a day and often lasted for several hours, penetrating him like a welding flame as it moved slowly across his naked body. Sometimes it would stop suddenly, only to return just as abruptly, and sometimes it didn't come at all. He had spent hours trying to figure out what caused the pain. Was someone standing there torturing him? How was this happening? Now he had stopped trying to make sense of it and was directing all of his energy toward trying to withstand the agony.

He cried out for help as loudly as he could. He was struck by how puny his voice sounded and tried a second time, making an effort to use more force. But as the echo died away, he could hear his own shrill notes of desperation stubbornly coming through. He gave up. There was nobody listening. No one except the crow.

He reviewed the sequence of events in his mind, though he had lost count of how many times he'd done so already. Maybe he was missing a small detail that could give him some answers. He had left his house just after six in the morning, more than forty-five minutes before his shift started. He left the car at home, which was his habit as soon as the weather permitted; his walk through the park never took more than twelve minutes, so he had plenty of time to get to work.

Immediately after leaving the house, he had felt that something was off.

The feeling was so strong that he stopped to look around, but nothing stood out as unusual. There were only two people out that morning: a neighbour struggling to start his rusty old Fiat Punto, and a woman pedalling by on her bike, her skirt and beautiful blonde hair fluttering in the breeze. He remembered that her bike basket was decorated with plastic daisies. It was as if she were out for a ride solely to put smiles on the faces of the people she passed by. He hadn't been receptive to it in the least.

His anxiety had a hold on him, and he walked with nervous footsteps to the other side of the street even though the walk sign was red, which he never usually did. But that morning was different; his whole body was wound tight as a spring, and by the time he had gone partway through the park he was certain that someone was following him. The footsteps on the gravel behind him sounded like tennis shoes.

He'd realized that he was walking very quickly, and he tried to make himself slow down again. The steps came closer and closer and he fought the urge to look back over his shoulder. His heart was pounding and a cold sweat washed over him like a wave. He felt like he was about to faint. He finally gave in and turned around. The man walking behind him was indeed wearing tennis shoes—a pair of black Reeboks. All of his clothes were dark and he had a lot of pockets. He had a backpack on and was carrying a rag in one hand.

But it wasn't until the man had looked up and met his gaze that he was able to see his face.

After that, everything happened so fast. The pain shot out through all his nerves as a fist struck him in the abdomen. He had to fight to breathe and immediately fell to his knees and felt the rag pressing into his face.

His next memory was of waking to claws sinking into his belly.

HIGH ABOVE HIM NOW, a lone cloud was hiding the sun, a moment of deliverance as ephemeral as a sand castle. When the cloud finally drifted on and disappeared, the sky was the perfect blue only seen on a Swedish summer day. The sun was shining with all its strength straight at the carefully placed lens, which in turn directed the beams to a focal point next to the strapped-down man. The earth's rotation took care of the rest.

The last thing he heard was the horrid crackling of his own burning hair.

3

PART 1

June 30–July 7, 2010

In the autumn of 2003, psychologist Kipling D. Williams performed an experiment to test social exclusion. He had three test subjects participate in a game of Cyberball—a virtual ball game where the players pass a ball around. After a period of time, two of them started to pass the ball between themselves. The third player, unaware that he was playing against two computerized test subjects, immediately experienced strong feelings of exclusion and rejection. The feelings were so powerful that an MRI was able to register enhanced activity in the very same part of the brain that is activated during physical pain.

1

FABIAN RISK HAD DRIVEN this route more times than he could remember, but it had never felt as easy and uplifting as it did right now. His family had left Stockholm early in the morning and rewarded themselves with a long lunch break in Gränna.

Fabian's anxiety about moving back to his hometown was already starting to dissipate. Sonja was happy, almost bubbly, and had offered to drive the last stretch through Småland so he could enjoy a beer with his herring at lunch. Everything was almost too perfect, and he found himself wondering if it was all just for show. If he were to be totally honest with himself, deep down he had been hesitant to believe that running away from their problems and starting over again would truly work.

The children had reacted just as expected. Matilda saw it as an exciting adventure, even though she would have to start fourth grade at a new school. Theodor hadn't been quite as positive, and even threatened to stay behind in Stockholm. But after their lunch in Gränna, it seemed that even Theodor was willing to give it a chance, and to everyone's surprise he had taken his earphones out and spoken with them several times during the car ride.

But best of all was that the shouting had finally stopped. The shouts and screams of people begging and pleading for their lives had hounded Fabian for the past six months, both in his dreams and during the better part of his waking hours. He had first noticed their absence around Södertälje, southwest of Stockholm, but he'd assumed it was just a figment of his imagination. Not until they'd passed Norrköping was he totally sure that with every kilometre the voices were losing strength. Now that they had arrived, 556 kilometres later, the voices were silent altogether.

It was as if their life in Stockholm and the incidents of last winter were deep in the past. They were starting out fresh, Fabian thought, inserting the key into the lock of their new home, an English red-brick terrace house on Pålsjögatan. Up to this point Fabian was the only member of the family who had been inside, but he wasn't at all nervous about what everyone else would think. As soon as he had seen that this house was for sale, he was sure that it was the only place for them to begin their new lives.

Pålsjögatan 17 was in the Tågaborg neighbourhood, a stone's throw from downtown and just around the corner from the Pålsjö forest. Fabian had plans to jog in the woodland each morning and start playing tennis again on the clay courts nearby. The seaside was also very close: it was a quick walk down Halalid hill to get to Fria Bad, the public beach where he had gone swimming all the time as a boy. Back then he used to pretend that he lived in this very neighbourhood rather than the yellow tenement buildings up in Dalhem. Now, thirty years later, his dream had come true.

"Dad, what are you waiting for? Aren't you going to answer that?" Theodor asked.

Fabian roused from his daydream and realized that the rest of his family were down on the pavement, waiting for him to pick up his ringing phone: it was Astrid Tuvesson, his new—or rather, future—boss in the criminal investigation department of the Helsingborg police.

He was still part of the Stockholm police department on paper for another six weeks. Outwardly, it had been his own decision to quit, but Fabian had no doubt that most of his old

8

colleagues knew what really happened. He would never be able to set foot in that police station again.

Now he had six weeks of involuntary vacation, which was starting to seem more and more appealing. He couldn't remember the last time he'd had this much time off — it must have been when he'd finished school. The plan was to use the six weeks to get settled in their new house and city. Depending on the weather and their mood, they might even take a trip somewhere warmer. The last thing they wanted to do was stress out. Astrid Tuvesson was undoubtedly well aware of this fact. And yet she was calling.

Something must have happened, but Fabian and Sonja had made a promise to each other. This summer, they would be a family again and share their parental responsibilities. Fabian was hoping that Sonja would have the energy to finish her last few paintings for an exhibition this autumn.

Weren't there other police officers in Helsingborg who weren't on vacation?

"No, the call can wait," he said, putting his phone in his pocket. He unlocked the front door of the house and opened it for Theodor and Matilda, who were fighting each other to be the first one in. "If I were you, I'd check out the backyard!" He turned to Sonja, who was coming up the stairs with an iPod speaker in her hands.

"Who was that?"

"It wasn't important. Come on, let's look at the house."

"It wasn't?"

"No. It wasn't," Fabian said. He could see in her eyes that she didn't believe him, so he got out the phone to show her who had called. "It was my future boss, who I'm sure just wanted to welcome us to town." He guided Sonja into the house with his hands in front of her eyes. "Ta-da!" He removed his hands and watched as she looked around the empty living room with its fireplace, and the connecting kitchen that looked out onto the small backyard, where Matilda could be seen jumping on a big trampoline.

"Wow. This is…absolutely fantastic."

"So it gets a passing grade? You like it?"

Sonja nodded. "Did the movers say anything about when they'll be here?"

"Only that it will be sometime this afternoon or evening. We can always hope they're delayed and don't get here until tomorrow."

"Why would we hope that, may I ask?" Sonja said, placing her arms around his neck.

"We have everything we need right here. A clean floor, candles, wine, and music." Fabian pulled out his old, scratched iPod Classic and placed it in the speaker, which Sonja had put on the kitchen island. He chose Bon Iver's *For Emma, Forever Ago*—a favourite album of the last few weeks. He'd been late to hop on the Bon Iver bandwagon. He had initially thought the record was boring, but upon giving it a second chance had realized what a masterpiece it really was.

He put his arms around Sonja and started dancing. She laughed and did her best to follow his improvised steps. He looked into her hazel eyes as she loosened her hair clip and let her brown hair down. The exercise her therapist had prescribed had certainly brought results, both mentally and physically. She must have lost about ten pounds. She'd never been fat, quite the opposite, but her facial features were sharper, and it suited her. Fabian swung around suddenly and dipped her. She laughed again and he realized how much he'd missed that sound.

They had discussed a number of solutions before settling on Helsingborg. Everything from moving out of their apartment near Södra Station and buying a house in one of Stockholm's many inner suburbs, to buying a second apartment and having a trial separation, taking care of the children in turns. None of these alternatives had seemed right. Whether it was because they were too afraid they might get divorced or because deep down they actually still loved each other was still unclear.

It wasn't until he found the house on Pålsjögatan that everything fell into place. He was offered a job as detective inspector with the Helsingborg police, there were open spots at Tågaborg School, and Fabian had found this perfect house, with its large, sky-lit attic that would make an ideal studio for Sonja. It was as if someone had taken mercy on them and decided to give them one last chance.

"What do we do about the kids?" Sonja whispered in his ear.

"I'm sure there's some room down in the basement where we can lock them up."

Sonja was about to respond, but Fabian interrupted her with a kiss. They were still dancing when the doorbell rang.

"Are the movers here already?" Sonja pulled away. "Maybe we'll get to sleep in our beds after all."

"And I was so looking forward to the floor."

"I'm sure the floor is still available. I said *sleep*. Nothing more." She resumed their kiss, letting her hand run down his stomach to find its way under his waistband.

Everything is going to turn out fine and we will live happily ever after, Fabian thought as she removed her hand and went to open the door.

"Hi, my name is Astrid Tuvesson. I'm one of your husband's new colleagues." The woman in the doorway extended her hand to Sonja. With her other hand, she pushed her sunglasses up into her curly blonde hair, which, along with her colourful dress, thin brown legs, and sandals, made her look a decade younger than fifty-two.

"Oh? Hello?" Sonja turned to Fabian, who walked over and shook hands with Tuvesson.

"You mean *future* colleague. I don't start until August sixteenth," Fabian said, noticing that her left earlobe was completely missing.

11

"Future *boss*, then, if we're going to be that nit-picky." She laughed and adjusted her hair to hide her ear, and Fabian found himself wondering if it was an injury or something she'd been born with. "Sorry. I really don't want to bother you in the middle of your vacation, and you both must be tired after your trip, but—"

"No problem," Sonja interrupted. "Come in. Unfortunately we can't offer you anything because we're still waiting for the movers."

"That's quite alright. All I need is a few minutes with your husband."

Sonja nodded mutely and Fabian showed Tuvesson to the deck out back, closing the door behind them.

"I gave in and bought my kids a trampoline, too. They had to bug me for several years before I agreed to it, and by that time they were too old," Tuvesson said.

"I'm sorry, but why are you here?" Fabian had no desire whatsoever to spend his vacation making small talk with his new boss.

"There's been a murder."

"Has there? What a shame. I don't mean to interfere, but wouldn't it be better to talk to one of your colleagues who isn't on vacation?"

"Jörgen Pålsson. Sound familiar?"

"Is he the victim?"

Tuvesson nodded.

Fabian recognized the name, but he wasn't tempted to try and place it. The last thing he wanted to do was work. He was beginning to feel like a fully loaded oil tanker that had just been hijacked by pirates and forced to turn away from an island paradise.

"Maybe this will jog your memory." Tuvesson held up a plastic sleeve with a photograph inside. "It was on the victim's body."

12

Fabian looked at the photo, and knew immediately that there would be no island paradise for him. He recognized the image, although he couldn't remember the last time he'd seen it. It was his class photo from the ninth grade, the last year of compulsory school—the last picture of all of them together. He was in the second row, and Jörgen Pålsson was behind him—crossed out with black marker.

2

FABIAN HAD SPENT JUST one hour in the house—one hour—before the doorbell rang. He understood why Tuvesson had chosen to contact him: he might be able to remember something that could speed up the investigation, and even save a few lives in the long run. But Fabian hardly remembered anything about compulsory school and he had no desire to relive that period of his life.

Tuvesson led Fabian to her white Corolla across the street from the house. She had offered to drive him to the crime scene and back, so that Sonja could unload their car. "Just so we're clear, I truly appreciate you taking the time to come with me, even though you're in the middle of a vacation."

"Middle? It's hardly even begun."

"I promise this won't take more than an hour." Tuvesson stuck the key in the lock and turned it. "The car has automatic locks, but the door sticks, so you'll have to put some muscle into it." Fabian yanked the door open and noticed the passenger seat was covered with empty travel mugs, open packs of Marlboros, keys, scraps of food, used paper towels, and a box of tampons.

"Sorry. Hold on, I'll…" She swept everything but the keys and the cigarettes onto the floor. Fabian got in and Tuvesson started the car and pulled away. "Is it okay if I smoke?" Before he could respond, she lit a cigarette and rolled down her window. "I'm actually going to quit. People always say that but don't follow through. But I'm planning on it—just not right now," she

14

continued, taking a deep drag as she turned left onto Tågagatan.

"No problem," said Fabian, his eyes glued to the class photo with Jörgen's crossed-out face. Why hadn't he been able to recall Jörgen Pålsson? If there was anyone he should remember, it was Jörgen. Of course, he had never liked him, so that might explain it. Maybe he had simply repressed the memory of him. "Where was his body found?"

"Fredriksdal School. From what I understand, he was a craft teacher there."

"He was also a student there once."

"Not everyone has the opportunity to go all the way to Stockholm, Mr. Risk. What do you know about Jörgen?"

"Pretty much nothing. We never hung out." Fabian started thinking about his school days, how all the guys used to wear Lyle & Scott sweaters and how the TV would be rolled in to watch skiing sensation Ingemar Stenmark. "To be completely honest, I didn't like him."

"No? Why not?"

"He was the class bully and a general pain. He did whatever he wanted."

"We had a guy like that at our school, too. He disrupted all the classes and took other people's lunch trays. No one stood up to him, not even the teachers." Tuvesson sucked the last bit of nicotine from her cigarette and flicked the butt out the window. "That was back in the day before all the letter-combo diagnoses like ADD and ADHD."

"Jörgen also only listened to KISS and Sweet."

"What's wrong with KISS and Sweet?"

"Nothing. They're good. But I only figured that out a few years ago."

FABIAN STEPPED OUT OF the car and looked at Fredriksdal School, a two-storey red-brick building that loomed behind the deserted schoolyard. Two basketball hoops with ragged nets stuck up out of the asphalt—a reminder that this was normally a place for children. He let his eyes explore the long rows of narrow, prison-like windows and had a hard time understanding how he'd survived three years in this building.

"Who found him?"

"Before I get to that, his wife called to report him missing a week ago, last Wednesday, but there was nothing we could do at that point. He had gone down to Germany the day before to buy beer for Midsummer, and was supposed to have returned home that evening."

"Buying beer in Germany? Is that still worth the trip?"

"It is if you buy enough. Forty kronor a case, and you get reimbursed for the ferry trip back if you don't stay longer than three hours."

Travelling all the way down to Germany just to fill your car to the brim with beer? The more Fabian thought about it, the better it seemed to fit with the Jörgen he was starting to remember. Jörgen, and possibly his partner-in-crime Glenn. "Did he never make it to Germany?"

"He was definitely there. We checked at Øresund Bridge and he returned on Tuesday night, as planned. But that's where all traces of him end. Our next clue didn't come until yesterday, when a glass company requested the removal of a vehicle that was blocking its cherry picker."

"His vehicle?"

Tuvesson nodded and they continued around the corner to the back of the school building. About twenty metres away, a Chevy pickup truck was parked next to a cherry picker. Police tape was already up, forming a generous perimeter. Two uniformed officers were guarding the area.

A middle-aged man with thinning hair, who was wearing disposable blue coveralls, approached Fabian and Tuvesson. His glasses were perched low on his nose.

"I want to introduce the two of you," Tuvesson said. "Ingvar

16

Molander, our forensic investigator, please meet Fabian Risk, who doesn't officially start until August."

"Does it matter when you have an investigation like this to sink your teeth into?" Molander pulled his glasses even further down his nose, and eyed Fabian as he extended his hand.

"It does make you wonder," Fabian lied, shaking Molander's hand.

"You're right about that. I promise you won't be disappointed."

"Ingvar, he's just here to do a quick once-over."

Molander gave her a look that sparked Fabian's curiosity, albeit reluctantly. Then he showed them into the school building and gave them each a set of coveralls.

This was the first time in almost thirty years Fabian had been inside the school. It looked just as he remembered, with the red brick along the walls of the hallways and the sound-absorbing tiles that resembled compacted trash stuck to the ceiling. They made their way to the wood shop off the rearmost hallway. Woodworking had never interested Fabian in the least until he realized you could make your own skateboards. One term later he had heated, bent, and cut so many sheets of plywood that he had been able to sell them and save up for a pair of real Tracker trucks.

"Allow me to welcome you to a murder scene that without a doubt qualifies as one of the top-ten worst murder scenes I have ever seen." Molander showed Fabian and Tuvesson through the door. "As luck would have it, the perpetrator set the AC to its lowest setting. Otherwise this would have been in the top five, considering that the body has been lying here for over a week."

Molander was right: the wood shop was very cold. It felt like stepping into a fridge, even though the thermometer indicated it was between twelve and thirteen degrees. Three other people in coveralls were taking pictures of the room, examining the scene, and gathering evidence. The familiar smell of wood and sawdust was all mixed up with a rotten, sweet stench. Fabian walked over to Jörgen Pålsson's body, which was lying in a large pool of dried blood, right next to a door. The lock mechanism and the door handle were covered in more blood. The body was large and fit, dressed in a pair of loose, worn jeans and a bloody white undershirt.

Fabian didn't remember Jörgen being so big—tough and cocky, yes, but not this thick. He must have been as strong as an ox. And yet the perpetrator had managed to cut his hands off at the wrist on both of his tattooed arms. The stumps were bloody and ragged, and Fabian couldn't even imagine how much it must have hurt. Why the hands in particular?

"As you can see, the blood on the floor indicates that he made his way from the workbench over there to the door where we came in," Molander said. "It doesn't have a lock, but what he didn't know was that it was blocked with benches, chairs, and tables on the other side. After he tried that escape route he made his way over here and attempted to get out through this door. But how easy is it to turn a door handle when you don't have any hands?"

Fabian studied the bloody knob.

"Have you had time to inspect the lock?" Tuvesson asked.

"It's filled with superglue, which explains the state of the victim's mouth." Molander took out his medical pincers and lifted Jörgen's upper lip to reveal a row of broken top teeth.

"He tried to turn it with his mouth?" Tuvesson asked.

Molander nodded. "Talk about survival instincts. I definitely would have died with my teeth intact."

"I don't understand. Surely he must have put up some resistance?" Tuvesson said.

"That's a good question. Maybe he did, but maybe he was drugged. We don't know yet. We'll see what Braids comes up with in the lab."

"How long did he struggle for?"

18

"Three or four hours, I'd guess." Molander showed them across the shop to one of the workbenches; it, too, was covered in dried blood. "The killer fastened his arms in this C-clamp, and performed the amputation with this handsaw." He used the pincers to point at a bloody saw that had been tossed on the floor.

"Have you checked with the glass company who called to request removal of the truck?" Fabian said.

"Why? Are you suggesting they're involved?" asked Tuvesson.

"If you ask me, this doesn't look like the work of a person who relies on chance."

Tuvesson and Molander exchanged glances.

"I have the company's number here." Tuvesson took out her phone and called the number with speakerphone on. After an unusual ringtone, an automated voice told them that the number they'd dialled was not in service. "It looks like you may be right. We'll have to find out who rented the cherry picker. Ingvar, make sure to examine the crane for any clues."

Molander nodded.

"And the hands?" Tuvesson went on.

"We haven't found them yet."

Tuvesson turned to Fabian. "Well? What do you think? Is this ringing any bells?"

Fabian's eyes swept over the workbench, the bloody handsaw, the tracks of blood on the floor, and the body without its amputated hands. He looked Tuvesson and Molander each in the eye, and shook his head. "Unfortunately not."

"Nothing? Not even some inkling that it might be someone from your class, or an idea of why someone would do this to Jörgen Pålsson in particular?"

Fabian shook his head again.

"It was worth a shot. If you think of anything, promise me you'll call or come by the station. Okay?"

Fabian nodded and followed Tuvesson out of the wood shop

haunted by a question that wouldn't allow him any peace until he had found the answer.

Why the hands?

August 18

This is the first time I'm writing in you even though I got you for Christmas two years ago from Mum. She said it's always good to write down your thoughts so that you don't forget anything. Yesterday I cleaned my whole room and filled a black bin bag with rubbish. Mum was super happy, and I found my C-3PO figure that had been missing for over a year.

Everyone was back in school today, except Hampus. They were all happy about our new classroom and our new books, but not me. It's my turn now and it started as soon as we had Maths. Everyone looked at me even though I hadn't done anything. I tried to act normal, like I didn't notice but they just kept staring. I know what that means. Everyone knows. I knew this was going to happen. I knew as soon as Hampus said he was moving away. I kept hoping I was wrong, but I guess I wasn't. It was all I thought about for the whole summer.

I sat at the very front in English so I wouldn't see when they stared. They were passing notes but I pretended that wasn't happening either. I didn't turn around. Not once.

Jesper read one of the notes out loud and it said I was ugly and smelled bad. I don't know how that's possible. I always scrub really hard in the shower and I've even been using deodorant for the past year because my sweat smelled more. Mum said that happens to everyone. I've tried to smell my own BO. I don't think I smell. But I know I'm ugly—ugly as shit.

P. S. Tomorrow is Laban's birthday so I'm going to buy one of those wheels, a water bottle, and sawdust.

3

WHEN FABIAN RETURNED HOME, the movers were in full swing. He looked into the truck and saw that they had emptied a bit more than half of it already. There was still a wall of boxes, old lamps, hockey sticks, their stained Klippan sofas from IKEA and the Ellipse table with its imitation Ant chairs, the big old TV they had let Theodor keep for his room but he never watched, cross-country skis, bikes, the display cabinet, which seemed to have one broken pane, and a mountain of black bin bags to go.

Was this really all he had managed to collect in his forty-three years of life? A few shabby sofas and dusty lampshades? Fabian felt the urge to tell the men to stop carrying things in and just drive the whole load to the dump instead. This move was making him feel as if he'd just bought a fancy new computer and was transferring over all his old files, viruses and all. What he really wanted to do was start over again. Forget about money for once and buy all new things. He wanted to rip off the plastic and inhale the scent of unused objects.

He nodded at the movers, who were unloading the old avocado-green filing cabinet he'd been given when he turned twelve. It looked heavy, and it took two men to carry it. He tried to think of what was in the drawers and couldn't remember the last time he'd opened them. The cabinet had spent the last twenty years relegated to the attic of their apartment. Why did it weigh so much?

An hour later, he was helping Sonja empty some of the boxes

in the kitchen when he remembered what the filing cabinet contained and rushed to find it. Sonja had directed the movers down to the cellar. On his way there, Fabian realized he'd never even set foot in the basement, which should have been the first priority for any serious buyer. He had blindly trusted the estate agent, who'd guaranteed that the house was superb. He wasn't too worried. After all, this was an old house with thick brick walls and a natural draft, not like the new, externally insulated buildings in the Mariastaden neighbourhood—or "Moldstaden," as people had started to call it.

He'd never had the chance to meet Otto Paldynski, the seller of the house. Apparently he was a true perfectionist, and had taken care of his home as if it were his own child during the thirty years he'd lived there with his family. Paldynski had wanted to make a quick sale due to private circumstances, and had been prepared to bring down the price quite a bit: something the agent said was like winning the lottery for Fabian—a once-in-a-lifetime opportunity.

Fabian was willing to admit that he hadn't needed very much convincing. But he still couldn't help wondering what those "private circumstances" really were. He'd gone so far as to ask the agent, who said that he was not in the habit of involving himself in his clients' personal business and elegantly changed the subject to the benefits Fabian could expect as a buyer. Fabian had accepted the answer with a smile and a nod and decided not to dig any further.

He walked up to the avocado-coloured filing cabinet, pulled out the top drawer, and immediately found what he was looking for—his yearbook from the ninth grade. He sat down on the cabinet and paged through to his own class. The yearbook photo was the same as the one the killer had left behind at the scene of the crime, except in Fabian's picture no one was crossed out.

Their hairstyles were the most obvious indicator that it was

1982, since everyone had big, bouffant, heavily styled hair. He started to remember bits and pieces about everyone: Seth Kårheden and his velvety moustache; Stefan Munthe and Nicklas Bäckström, who lived on the same courtyard as him, and were just as into skateboarding. He found Lina in the photo, with her blonde curls. Even Jörgen had a pronounced 1980s comb-over. They looked like a gang of true nerds, especially Fabian. He began to scrutinize his own image. He was wearing a tucked-in shirt, high-waisted pants, and the home-cut hairstyle that refused to lie neatly.

He was struck by the fact that he hadn't been in contact with anyone in the class since he moved to Stockholm—not even Lina. It was as if he'd packed up his entire youth in a moving box and left it sitting behind in Helsingborg for all these years, full of spiderwebs and forgotten until now.

"So this is where you're hiding…"

Fabian was visibly startled when he saw that Sonja was standing in front of him.

"Sorry, I didn't mean to frighten you."

He closed the yearbook as if he'd been caught red-handed. "I just didn't hear you coming."

"What would you say to taking a break and going out for pizza? The kids are starving."

Fabian put the book down and stood up. "That's a great idea. There is—or at least there was—a really good pizzeria just a few blocks from here." He turned around to walk toward the stairs but Sonja took his arm.

"Darling, are you okay?"

Fabian looked back at her and nodded, but he could see in her eyes that she didn't believe him.

EACH MEMBER OF THE Risk family carried their own personal pizza from Tågaborgs Pizzeria as they walked down to the boardwalk and sat on the sun-warmed wall. There was a beautiful view of the Sound and they could see all the way to Denmark. It was much more beautiful than Fabian remembered. The boardwalk had been widened over the years and was full of people enjoying a stroll in the light evening breeze. The changing rooms down toward Fria Bad had been renovated as restaurants, and the entire area around the old train tracks had been replaced by a lawn for bocce courts and barbecuing. Even further in the distance they caught a glimpse of the palm trees that were first put out during the architectural fair in 1999. From what Fabian understood, the palm trees had now become a perennial tradition, and what had once been a forgotten little patch of sand was now called "Tropical Beach," one of Helsingborg's most popular stretches of coastline. He felt like he had moved to a totally new city.

"This is the best pizza I've ever eaten in my life!" Matilda exclaimed. Fabian was inclined to agree. Never had a pizza tasted so good.

They sat there for a while, watching all the boats en route from Helsingborg to Helsingør, where they could go to Kronborg Castle. It was the very proof that they were now closer to the rest of Europe. Fabian promised himself never again to move a single metre further north. He turned to Theodor, who was gazing out across the Sound with a vacant expression. "How was your pizza? Was it the best you've ever eaten, too?"

"No, but it was pretty good."

"A four or a five?"

"A three and a half."

"Then you have to taste mine. It was at least a six," Matilda said, handing him a slice.

Theodor took a huge bite. "Okay, I'll give it a four. But that's all."

"God, you're so picky. Mum, isn't he picky?"

Sonja nodded and met Fabian's eyes. He had done all he could to hide it, and thus far she hadn't asked what Tuvesson had wanted. Yet there could be no doubt that she knew something wasn't quite right. As usual, she had seen right through his pathetic attempts at appearing to be present, even if she had chosen, on this particular night, to play along with his charade and pretend that they were just sitting on the warm boardwalk wall, enjoying the red evening sun and the sound of the waves as they washed over the rocks.

That night they made love just as he had fantasized about earlier that day.

The floor.

Wine and candles.

For Emma, Forever Ago…

4

MATILDA WOKE UP FABIAN and Sonja by crawling around on top of them, wondering why they were sleeping on the living room floor. They helped each other improvise an explanation, telling her that the bed in their room had to be adjusted before they could sleep in it. Theodor came downstairs and helped set the table out on the deck while Sonja and Matilda rushed off to the grocery store to buy food for breakfast. Soon after, they enjoyed eating together in the morning sun. All that was missing was the newspaper, which Sonja claimed to have forgotten to purchase.

"What are we going to do today?" Matilda asked.

"I suppose we'll keep unpacking and..."

"Adjust the beds! So you don't have to sleep on the floor!"

"Yes, that too!" Sonja laughed. "And I was thinking that we could go for a swim this afternoon."

"Yeah!"

"Can we go and buy a snorkel beforehand, Dad?" said Theodor.

"I'm sorry, but you're going to have to swim without me today."

"What?! Why?" Matilda cried. "Aren't we on vacation?"

"Yes, but Dad has a few things he has to take care of," Sonja said. "And he is just as disappointed as we are. All we can do is hope it doesn't take very long." She met Fabian's gaze and he could tell that she had read the paper in the store.

27

FABIAN STEPPED INTO THE recently built, white police head-quarters, which were right next to the E4 highway and just a stone's throw away from the old, castle-like prison in Berga. He walked up to the reception desk. Four different newspapers were piled up: *Helsingborgs Dagblad, Kvällsposten, Dagens Nyheter*, and *Svenska Dagbladet*. He looked at the front page of the newspaper on the top of the stack: CRAFT TEACHER TORTURED AND MURDERED IN HIS OWN CLASSROOM.

Was this the headline that Sonja had read? Two of the news-papers used pretty much the same photo. It had been taken at a distance and showed the cherry picker and Jörgen's pickup truck parked behind the school. The truck's number plate had been blurred out, but the red building, with its long rows of cell windows, made it very obvious which school was in question. And how many craft teachers could possibly work there?

Fabian introduced himself to the man behind the reception desk and explained the situation: he wasn't actually scheduled to start work until August but that Tuvesson had brought him in on the case of the murdered craft teacher and told him just to pop by if anything came up. The receptionist, who was in his thirties and wearing a police uniform, began to tap at the keyboard in front of him. Fabian thought the man's hair evoked images of Germany in the 1930s and he couldn't help being impressed by his upright posture.

"What was your name again?"

"Risk. Fabian Risk. But I don't think you'll find me in the directory. Like I said, my position doesn't begin until August."

The receptionist ignored him, fought with the mouse, typed in commands, and stared at the screen, appearing increasingly agitated. "I'm sorry, but I can't find you."

"I said you wouldn't find me, but if you call Tuvesson—"

"Astrid Tuvesson is in an investigation meeting and does not like to be disturbed at such times."

"I'm supposed to be at that meeting! She's probably waiting

28

for me right now," Fabian lied, and then realized that he sounded overly angry. "Do you think it will help if I try to call her?"

"It's not up to me who you call, but I can promise you that she won't answer. She never picks up the phone when she's in a meeting."

Fabian knew that the man was probably right. He had already tried calling her without getting an answer.

"So how can I get in?"

"I don't know. Don't ask me. I can't let just anyone in whenever they want. Just imagine how that would look."

"You must be Fabian Risk," he heard a female voice say behind him.

Fabian turned around and saw a woman who he guessed was about thirty-five. She was in good shape and wearing a short-sleeved plaid shirt and a pair of cut-off jean shorts. Her dark hair was cropped and she had at least twenty earrings in one ear.

"Two-fer said you would probably be standing here trying to get in. I didn't think you were starting until August."

"Me neither," Fabian replied, wondering how much Astrid Tuvesson had actually found out about him.

They shook hands.

"Irene Lilja."

"Maybe you can convince this man to let me in," said Fabian, pointing to the receptionist.

"He's not in the directory and I have explicit orders to never let anyone in, under any circumstances, who isn't—"

"It's fine. He can come with me, and I'll make sure he signs in." Lilja gestured for Fabian to follow her through the glass door to the lifts. "Lucky for you I was late. Florian can be pretty overzealous."

They stepped into the lift and Lilja turned to him.

"Have you thought of anything yet?"

"I'm sorry, I haven't."

"Then what are you doing here? From what I understand you just moved back to the city and must be incredibly busy."

Fabian fumbled for an answer but was interrupted by the lift doors opening.

Lilja showed him into the meeting room. It was an amply sized space with an expansive view of Helsingborg, Øresund, and beyond. There was an oval table in the middle of the room and the walls were well lit and functioned both as whiteboards and as screens for the projectors mounted on the ceiling. Fabian had never seen such a fresh and modern conference room. He was used to holding meetings in windowless rooms with no ventilation.

"No, he hasn't figured out who the perpetrator is, so you can start breathing again," Lilja announced.

"I mostly wanted to sit in and hear what you've come up with, if that's okay?" Fabian said.

"Of course it is. Come in and have a seat," Tuvesson replied, and introduced him to the rest of the group.

There was only one person Risk hadn't met yet: Sverker "Klippan" Holm, a powerful man a bit over fifty. "We'll have to manage without Hugo Elvin. He just left for Kenya and won't be back for a month."

"Kenya," Klippan muttered. "So that's where you have to go to get some time off." He turned to Fabian. "Risk. That's your name, right?" Fabian nodded. "I'm warning you. If you so much as sit down on that chair you can kiss your vacation goodbye. If a vacation is what you want, head for Kenya—or somewhere even further away. I had to settle for my in-laws' house on the Koster Islands this summer, and look at where I'm sitting now." Klippan threw his arms in the air.

"It was your own choice to cancel your vacation and come in—which I am extremely grateful for, by the way," Tuvesson said, putting up a photo of Jörgen Pålsson on the wall above the crime scene photos.

"Choice? You think I could lie on a dock navel-gazing while someone capable of this sort of sick crime is on the loose?"

"On a positive note, you're always complaining about your in-laws' place, saying that it's more work than vacation to be there," Lilja said.

"One thing I can say for certain: I would definitely rather be with my family than here in this conference room with all of you, and that's why no one should be allowed to commit serious crimes during my vacation time, goddammit!"

"I guess you'll have to submit a motion to change the law," Tuvesson said in a tone that indicated the time for chit-chat was over. "And Fabian, you don't have to worry. No matter how much I want to, I can't cancel your vacation. You earned the time in Stockholm."

Fabian sat down.

"Don't say I didn't warn you, Risk," said Klippan.

"May I just ask one question before we jump into things—I don't suppose you've found Jörgen's hands yet?" inquired Fabian.

"We were just getting to that." Tuvesson motioned to Molander, who stood up and pressed a remote control button. A projector on the ceiling lit up, showing an image of two sawed-off hands on a bloody, white-tiled floor.

"This picture was taken in the boys' shower room that's connected to the gym."

"We're talking about the same school, right?" Klippan asked. Molander nodded.

"Have you started compiling a criminal profile?" asked Fabian.

"What did I tell you?" Klippan said. "He's already working! I can assure you, he's not even aware of it himself."

"We haven't worked up a criminal profile just yet," said Tuvesson. "The signs suggest we're dealing with the worst sort of criminal—a lone madman who wants to make a point, has a plan of action, and is likely smart enough to make it a reality."

"Why are you so sure that he or she is working alone?" Lilja said, pouring a cup of coffee.

"Because this is so extreme." Tuvesson gestured toward the crime scene photos with one hand. "At the same time, it's much too well planned and well executed for it to be more than one person. When a group commits this type of insane act, it's almost always on impulse and under the influence of heavy drugs. Mistakes are made and they leave behind a wide swath of clues and technical evidence. But there were no mistakes here. We haven't found any fingerprints or strands of hair. We have nothing. And Fabian was right about the glass company—it doesn't exist. The cherry picker had been rented to PEAB Construction, who had no idea it was missing. In other words, the murder of Jörgen Pålsson was not a crime of passion, but a meticulously planned offence: the killer took his or her time to decide where it would take place, how it would be accomplished, and when it would be discovered."

"But why?" asked Molander.

"That's a good question," said Lilja. "Why chop off his hands?"

"Maybe he stole something?" Klippan suggested. "According to Islamic law, that's the punishment for theft."

"You think the killer is Muslim?"

"Why not?" Klippan said, picking up a copy of the class photo and pointing to one of the boys. "This guy looks pretty Muslim. What do you think, Fabian? Do you remember him?"

"Jafaar Umar. We called him Jaffe. He was a pretty funny guy, a bit of a class clown. There was nothing he couldn't make into a joke."

"That description doesn't exactly sound like our killer," said Lilja.

"It so happens that cutting off people's hands is common in a number of cultures," said Molander. "Just take the war in Rwanda. Prisoners of war had their hands cut off so they couldn't fight."

"In some cases, they cut off the hands of everyone in entire villages," Klippan broke in. "Men, women, and children, just so that they couldn't identify themselves and vote."

"What do you mean?" said Lilja. "Voting is something you do anonymously."

"Yes, but in order to get a ballot in the first place you have to identify yourself, and that was done with handprints."

Fabian didn't think the murder was an Islamic punishment for theft. He didn't remember Jörgen Pålsson as a thief. Rowdy yes; thief, no. The hands had been cut off and placed in a shower room. What could it possibly mean? There was no doubt that the murderer was sending a message.

"Risk. What are you thinking?"

He looked up and met Tuvesson's curious eyes. "What is the killer trying to say here? Is it important that the murder took place at Jörgen's work, or is it just a coincidence because he happened to work at the same place where he went to school?"

"Are you suggesting that it might be a student?"

"I'm not sure. It could be a teacher. Maybe someone he violated."

"Violated? What do you mean? As in raped?" said Klippan.

"If avenging a rape were the motive, I doubt it would have been his hands that got cut off," said Lilja.

"Just one more thing," Fabian continued, wondering where he'd got the idea for the word *violated*. "If Jörgen Pålsson really did cross the Øresund Bridge, there should be pictures to prove it, right?"

"We know he went over," Klippan said, passing him a printout from a logbook. "You can see the exact times from the toll booth at Lernacken of both his exit and return."

"On the other hand, it wouldn't hurt to get a visual confirmation. Risk, you're more than welcome to follow up on this lead if you want," said Tuvesson.

"Sure," replied Fabian, realizing that Klippan had been

absolutely right. Thoughts of his vacation seemed more and more distant.

"Klippan and Irene, I want you to identify everyone in the class and find out as much as you possibly can without getting in direct contact. Since the perpetrator might be one of them, I want us to keep as much as we can under wraps until we know more. Is that clear?"

Lilja and Klippan nodded.

"What about Fabian? What do we do with him?" Lilja asked. "He was in the class, too."

The others turned to look at him.

"I'll handle him," said Tuvesson.

"And then we have the victim's wife," said Klippan. "Er... widow. Who will contact her?"

"You mean Lina Pålsson?" said Tuvesson.

"Lina? Is that her name?" Fabian asked. Tuvesson nodded. "Is this her?" he probed, pointing at the blonde girl with long curly hair next to the crossed-out Jörgen. "They were together even back then. Unbelievable. If you want, I'd be happy to contact her."

"I bet you would be," Klippan said, looking at the class picture. "She sure was a looker." He grasped Fabian's shoulder.

"The way they look in this photo presumably has very little to do with how they look now, unfortunately," said Molander.

"Yeah, just look at Fabian," Lilja said, and the rest of the team burst into laughter. They all gathered up their documents and left the room—everyone except Tuvesson.

"I'm not sure how you feel about this, but it goes without saying that if you do want to help with the investigation I would be very grateful, although I certainly understand if you would prefer to prioritize your family vacation. The choice is completely up to you."

"I'm happy to help," Fabian said cheerfully. But he couldn't stop thinking that Tuvesson had it all wrong. What choice did

34

he have, considering what had happened? It wasn't his first time working on a case where the perpetrator had been meticulously prepared. But this time was totally different. Someone from his old class had been brutally murdered and was discovered several days later, on the very day he arrived back in his hometown with his family. Sure, it could be a coincidence. But something told him it was about as likely a coincidence as the sawed-off hands.

"There's just one thing I want to make absolutely clear to you," she said as she met his gaze. "I don't know how you did things back in Stockholm. But we're a team here and we work together—that goes for you as well."

Fabian nodded.

"Good. I'll make sure you start getting paid as of today."

"It would be helpful if you added me to the directory, so that Florian guy will let me in going forward."

"Of course. You'll also be issued an access card. For obvious reasons we don't have your desk ready, but you can borrow Hugo Elvin's in the meantime. As we discussed, he's away for several weeks anyway. I'll show you to it now."

Fabian followed Tuvesson through the department, but he wasn't listening to a word she was saying. His thoughts were somewhere else completely. Ever since he'd found out that Jörgen Pålsson had been killed, something had been nagging at his subconscious, refusing to emerge. But this feeling had developed more firmly during the meeting. It hadn't been by chance that he'd used the word *violated* when discussing the motives for Jörgen's murder.

Memories of his school days were becoming clearer and intensifying. He had the distinct feeling that Jörgen Pålsson had got exactly what he deserved.

5

LINA PÅLSSON DIDN'T REMEMBER him at first, even though he introduced himself using his full name and reminded her that they had been in the same class all through their school years. To be fair, they were talking on the phone and not meeting in person, but she was totally confused, which left Fabian wondering whether she really was the Lina from his class. She couldn't place him until he used the nickname "Fabbe," but once he did she immediately invited him to come over for coffee at 1 p.m. that day, which gave him enough time to get settled at his new desk and contact the Øresund Bridge.

Hugo Elvin's desk chair looked like a cool experimental piece from the future. It had lots of knobs and levers, but unfortunately was not very pleasant to sit on. Actually it was decidedly uncomfortable, and Fabian started to adjust the levers while he tried to explain to an administrator at the Øresund Bridge's central office why he was calling. He was transferred to someone else. As the phone rang, he managed to find a perfect setting on the chair. He couldn't help wondering what Hugo Elvin's body type was.

"Are you like that Kurt Wallander guy?" a woman suddenly asked on the other end. Fabian, who hadn't had time to realize that the phone had stopped ringing, explained that Wallander outranked him. Well, he would have outranked him if Wallander weren't fictional.

"Are you all really that smart in real life?" she asked.

Five minutes later, Fabian had managed to redirect the conversation away from Kurt Wallander so that he was the one asking the questions and the woman was answering them. She told him that every vehicle that passed through the toll booth at Lernacken was photographed by two cameras: one at the front, to capture the number plate, and one above, to measure the length of the vehicle, which ensured that the correct toll was debited. The bridge's central office also used the pictures as evidence when someone skipped out on paying.

Fabian told her that they were looking for a Chevy pickup with the registration number BJY 509. It should have passed through the toll on its way to Denmark on Tuesday, June 22, just after 6:00 a.m., and returned later that same day at 11:18 p.m. The woman promised to find the images and she asked for his email address so that she could send them to him. Fabian gave her Tuvesson's email address, since he hadn't been assigned one yet, and thanked the woman for her help. He then left police headquarters to go and meet Lina Pålsson.

THE GPS TOLD FABIAN to turn off at Ödåkra; it guided him through the neighbourhood, which looked like any other suburb, until he came to Tögatan, where he stopped outside number nine. He got out of the car and walked up to the two-storey home, which was made of the same red brick as Fredriksdal School. Fabian couldn't understand how Jörgen and Lina had stayed together for more than thirty years. Back then he had been convinced they wouldn't even last a term.

He rang the doorbell and thought of the first time he rang the doorbell at Lina's family's apartment. He'd been in fourth grade, and wasn't brave enough to stick around—he ran off to hide on the next floor up before her father answered.

Fabian and Lina had agreed to walk to school together in the mornings and from then on he rang her doorbell every morning. The journey to school had been the high point of each day. He had her all to himself. They would talk and laugh, and he did everything he could to make the walk as slow as possible.

Klippan was right. Lina had definitely been the most beautiful girl in their class, and Fabian wondered if she was still just as pretty.

A large woman, bordering on fat, opened the door. She was wearing a baggy brown dress and her hair was black, except for the roots, which were grey. She looked tired and worn out. Above all, she looked considerably older than her forty-three years. *I guess Molander was right about ageing*, Fabian thought.

"You must be Fabian Risk," she said. Fabian nodded, shaking her hand. "Agneta. Lina's cousin. We're taking shifts, so she doesn't have to be alone. Come in."

Fabian followed her inside. His eyes swept the living room, which was more charming than he'd expected after seeing the outside of the house. Lina, however, was nowhere to be seen.

"Wait here, I'll bring the coffee out," Agneta said, vanishing into the kitchen.

Fabian walked over to the bookcase. Even in the age of digital downloads, a bookcase was still one of the places in a home that held the most secrets.

This particular shelf contained the usual books, cultural items, and objects. A collection of colourful liquor bottles and crystal glasses of various sizes, as well as souvenirs from Greece and the Canary Islands, filled the illuminated glass portion. The CD collection consisted of a few compilations, and the DVD collection was half Disney and half Swedish detective films. Novels by Jan Guillou, Henning Mankell, and John Grisham made up at least three-quarters of the extremely selective book collection; the rest were the obligatory volumes by August Strindberg, William Shakespeare, and Charles Dickens. The only titles that spoiled the picture of normality, or improved it, depending on how you chose to look at it, were Paul Auster, Cormac McCarthy, and Jonathan Franzen. Fabian decided those books must be Lina's. He also discovered a few photo albums on the bottom shelf. He picked up the first one: it contained pictures of Jörgen and Lina's wedding. Fabian couldn't help thinking that she had married down. The next album was more varied, containing pictures of everything from Christmases and birthdays to crayfish parties and baptisms. In some of the pictures, Jörgen was posing bare-chested, showing off his tattooed and beefed-up muscles.

"Find anything interesting?"

Fabian quickly looked up from the album and saw Lina. "Well, there you are," he said, putting down the album and wondering if he should give her a hug. He decided to put out his hand, even though his palm was already sweaty. "Hi."

"Don't I get a hug?"

"Of course, I'm sorry. I just didn't want..." He gave her a cautious hug.

"I hardly recognize you. I heard you moved to Stockholm."

"Yes, but I'm back now. And I definitely recognize you. You haven't changed a bit."

"Thank you."

Fabian realized he had no idea where to go from here or how to avoid the awkward silence. He felt like the boy who had just rung the doorbell, but he didn't have time to run and hide now. Agneta came back from the kitchen with a tray of coffee and placed it on the table.

"Lina, do you want me to stay here?"

"No, Agge, it's fine. I'll be okay."

Agneta vanished again, and Lina and Fabian went over and sat down on the couch.

"You're going to work on this investigation, as a policeman?" Lina said while pouring the coffee; her hand was unsteady, making it nearly impossible.

"Please, let me do that," Fabian said, taking the coffee pot and pouring for her.

"I'm so sorry." Lina burst into silent tears. "But I just don't understand. I don't understand how someone could do something like this to Jörgen. He was so well liked. It just doesn't make any sense."

He wanted to move closer and put a comforting hand on her shaking shoulder, but decided to stay where he was. He was here in his capacity as a police officer and nothing more. "Lina, I know this must be incredibly difficult, but can you think of anyone who might be behind this?"

Lina shook her head. "Absolutely no one. Like I said, everyone adored him. His students at school absolutely worshipped him. He knew how to deal with them, especially the problem kids."

"Yes, I can certainly imagine. After all, he was a little...how should I put it...rowdy in his day."

Lina looked up into Fabian's eyes. "What do you mean?"

Either she's repressed the memories or she can't deal with them right now, Fabian thought, putting his mug down on the glass table. "Lina, if we're to have any chance of catching whoever did this, I'm going to need to do some digging and turn over some rocks."

Lina glanced away and Fabian didn't do anything to break the silence; at last, she gave in and nodded.

"As I understand it, he had just been to Germany to buy beer. Do you know if he went with anyone?"

"He always went by himself."

"And there couldn't have been an exception this time?"

Lina shook her head. "If he had to share the space in the truck with someone else it wouldn't be worth the trip."

"Not even for the company?"

"Who would want to do that? Sit in a truck all the way to Germany and back, and not even be able to buy anything?"

She's right, thought Fabian, who still didn't get the point of going down there at all. "Maybe a friend wanted to go? Did he keep in contact with anyone from our class, besides you?"

"No, just Glenn. Glenn Granqvist."

Fabian nodded. Glenn and Jörgen had been best friends for as far back as Fabian could recall—they were cut from the same cloth. A talk with Glenn would have to be the next item on his to-do list.

"Judging from what I saw in your photo albums, Jörgen looked like he was in pretty good shape."

"Yes, he was always careful to keep fit. When the kids were little, it sometimes felt like he was at the gym more than he was at home."

"So he worked out a lot?" Fabian asked, thinking that from here on out it was sink or swim. "Do you happen to know if he was taking anything to help increase his muscle growth?"

Lina met his gaze, as if she had been expecting any question but this one. "I don't know what you're talking about. Anabolic steroids? Of course he wasn't."

Fabian was certain that Jörgen had used steroids, but that wasn't the point of the question. The important thing was the way Lina had answered and that she was lying.

"Did he ever hit you?"

This time Lina was better prepared. She was cool and collected. She snorted and shook her head. "I honestly don't understand what you're trying to get at. Jörgen was one of the nicest people you could imagine, and he would never have hurt me, or anyone else for that matter."

"Lina, I'm not out to ruin Jörgen's reputation. But you and I both know what he was like back in school, and all I want to find out is whether he—"

"I think you should leave now." She stood up. "Please, just leave."

"I'm sorry. I didn't mean to—"

"Agge! You can come in now! We're done in here!"

41

6

FABIAN GOT INTO HIS car and stuck the key in the ignition. There was no doubt that he'd got exactly what he'd been after, and confirmed the hunch he'd been walking around with since yesterday. He was sure Jörgen Pålsson had dug his own grave. But Fabian regretted that he had come on too strong, without any consideration for the fact that Lina had just lost her husband.

Was that what he couldn't seem to come to terms with? That Lina had ended up with Jörgen, and their relationship had endured? What right did he have to question her choices? As if he had any idea what was best for her.

He opened the glove box, pulled out the car's most recent inspection report, and wrote a note on the back for Lina. He apologized profusely for hurting her feelings and assured her that she was more than welcome to contact him any time she felt the need. He ended by writing down his address and mobile number, then signed the letter, folded it up, and put it in her mailbox.

Throughout the process he could sense her watching him from behind a thin curtain, and just before he got back in the car to drive off, he turned around and gave her a smile and a little wave.

It wasn't long before his phone rang. But it turned out to be Tuvesson.

"The pictures from Lernacken arrived."

"Can you see anything?"

"I think it's best if you come in."

THERE WERE A TOTAL of four pictures from the toll booth. Tuvesson had uploaded them to the police headquarters server so they could be projected on the wall of the conference room.

"Don't tell me we're out of milk again," Lilja said, a cup of freshly brewed coffee in hand.

"There's always cream," Klippan noted, putting a splash into his own cup. "Just a few years ago, no one had any problem with—" but he was interrupted by his ringing phone. He took it out and looked at the number.

"Aren't you going to pick up?" said Lilja.

Klippan sighed and answered. "Hi, darling. Listen, I'm in my meeting and...What? Not again!" Another sigh. "But Berit, I've told you over and over. You can't use tons of toilet paper because it..." By now the whole room could hear Berit's voice. "Okay. I'll take care of it. I'll call someone...No, not this very second. As soon as I have time...Darling, I have to go now. Bye-bye." Klippan put down the phone and threw up his hands without comment.

"Shall we get started?" Tuvesson said, turning on the projector.

The first photo was taken from the front, and showed Jörgen Pålsson's Chevy waiting to be allowed onto the bridge to Denmark. In the bottom corner was a time-stamp that read *10-06-22 6:23 a.m.*, and the man behind the wheel was clearly Jörgen Pålsson. The next picture was taken from above, and in it you could see Jörgen's tattooed arm holding out a credit card.

"Well, he still had his hands attached then, at least," said Klippan.

"This is where it gets really interesting." Tuvesson brought up the third picture, stamped *10-06-22 11:18 p.m.* It was considerably darker than the first two images, and Jörgen's face was hidden in shadow. But there could be no doubt that he was the person at the wheel. His clean white undershirt was glowing like reflector tape in the darkness.

Jörgen wasn't the only person in the photo to capture their interest. There was a man sitting in the passenger seat next to him, wearing dark clothes and a cap that was pulled down so low on his head that his entire face was in shadow. He was right there—the killer they were searching for, blending into the rest of the darkness like a shapeless phantom.

"I can try to manipulate the image and see if I can't make the contrast a bit more noticeable," said Molander.

"Do you think we can fix up the photo well enough to release it?" said Klippan.

Molander shrugged. "We'll see, but I doubt it."

"Are we even one hundred per cent sure this really is our guy?" asked Lilja.

"No, but there's a lot to recommend him," said Tuvesson. "And of course, we won't release anything until we're sure we know all the facts."

"That guy could be absolutely anyone," said Lilja.

"What do you mean, *anyone*?"

"He could be a hitchhiker, for example."

"Who picks up hitchhikers these days?" asked Klippan. "There's hardly anywhere to stop your car."

"I do. The world really isn't as horrible as those of us inside these four walls might think," replied Lilja.

"Even if it isn't the perpetrator, he's likely the last person who saw Jörgen alive. No matter who it is, we want to track him down," said Tuvesson. "Let's assume for a moment that the man in the picture really is our guy. The question then becomes: Why did Jörgen Pålsson pick him up?"

"And where?" said Lilja.

"Could they have arranged a meeting?" asked Tuvesson.

"No. According to Lina he always drove down by himself," said Fabian.

"So she thinks. But who's to say she's right?" Klippan said. "My wife doesn't know everything about me, anyway."

"That's awfully lucky for her," Molander muttered.

"But considering how carefully planned the murder was, we ought to assume that the perpetrator would have been very sure that Jörgen would pick him up," Fabian continued, while the others listened. "And, like Klippan said, the whole route is more or less highway where you can't stop. So I wonder if we shouldn't find out his credit card numbers and see what sorts of charges he incurred along the way."

"Good idea," said Tuvesson.

Klippan turned to Tuvesson. "He's not a dummy, this new guy. Unfortunately, it's going to be pretty damn slow finding all this out; the banks love to delay giving us this sort of information."

Fabian knew Klippan was right. But he had a solution, and her name was Niva Ekenhielm with the FRA (National Defence Radio Establishment). She could hack her way through the thickest of firewalls like no one else. Niva had helped him quite a bit in his last investigation, but her help had come at a price, and Fabian had promised himself he would never contact her again.

FABIAN CALLED THE WOMAN from the central office at the Øresund Bridge again. She recognized his voice immediately and asked him how the case was going and whether they had found the murderer. Fabian answered evasively and told her that the investigation was moving forward and that they were doing everything in their power to solve the case as quickly as possible.

"I get it. You have to keep it confidential and you can't reveal any technical details about the investigation," the woman said in a generic southern Swedish accent. "But it's the guy in the passenger seat, isn't it?"

"As I'm sure you'll understand, I can't reveal everything we know," he said, trusting that would be enough. He still needed her help and was hoping he wouldn't have to get unpleasant with her.

"I'll take that as a yes. But don't worry, I won't tell the papers—not yet, anyway."

Fabian realized that he might as well make her feel he was letting her in on some secrets.

"I don't think you should do that, either. You're smarter than that, and we certainly don't want the perpetrator to find out how much we know, do we?"

"No, of course not."

"And since you're already so familiar with this case, I need your help with another thing."

"Oh?"

"Do you think you can get hold of the number of the credit card he paid with?"

There was a long pause before she responded. "You know we can't release that sort of information. Not without permission from a prosecutor."

She's not stupid, Fabian thought, but he knew there wasn't enough time to wait for a prosecutor.

"But just because it's you, Fabian Risk, my very own little Wallander, I'll make an exception. On one condition."

"What's that?"

"That you come by and say hello next time you drive over."

FABIAN WENT TO FIND the break room, where there was a large coffee machine with lots of buttons, so that he could make a call. He pressed the cappuccino button and heard the machine start up while the phone rang at the other end. She knew he was the caller; he was sure of that. She was probably staring at her ringing phone right now.

"How the hell do you have the balls to call me?"

46

Fabian was flummoxed and fumbled for something to say.

"Hello? Did you think I wouldn't know it was you? So fucking—"

"Niva, I didn't mean to—"

"We are finished. Have you forgotten that already?"

"No, I haven't, and that's not why I'm calling."

"I suppose you're calling to tell me how you're such a happy nuclear family now that you've fled the scene and emigrated to Skåne?"

"I'm calling because I need your help with an investigation and it's important that we move quickly," said Fabian. He took her silence as a positive sign. "I'm investigating the murder of an old classmate that I'm sure you've read about in the papers—the craft teacher who got his hands sawed off."

"Oh right, how very Skåne. Was he one of your old school friends?"

"Not exactly a friend. We were in the same class. I need to find out what credit card purchases he made on June twenty-second."

"Text me his card number and I'll get back to you."

"Thanks. It's really nice of you to help. I really didn't mean to—"

"How are things otherwise?"

"Fine. We just moved, so things are a little bit topsy-turvy. But it feels...I think it will be good. You?"

"Really awful and lonely, as usual. My therapist says it will be a while before I can move on."

"I'm sure you'll start to feel better soon. Now that I've moved you can have Stockholm all to yourself."

"What kind of consolation is that if you keep calling me?"

Fabian was about to answer, but he didn't have time. She'd hung up. He took a sip from his cappuccino and poured the rest down the sink.

7

"DAD, GUESS WHAT WE DID!" Matilda shouted, rushing toward Fabian, who was coming through the door. "We went swimming! There were really big waves and it was super cold! And we're going again tomorrow. Mum promised I could get a new swimsuit!" She hopped into his arms. "Can you come with us, please?"

"What if it's way too cold for me?" He walked into the kitchen, still holding Matilda.

"Dad, please. Please."

Fabian went up to Sonja, who was setting the table for dinner, and gave her a kiss.

"Dinner's just about ready," she said with a smile. "How did it go? Did you finish what you needed to get done?" She took off her apron and looked into his eyes.

"Darling, it—" "Forget I even asked. Forget that you're actually supposed to be on vacation."

"Darling…"

"Let's not talk about it. Go and get Theo instead."

"Sure. Where is he?"

"In his room."

"He's been in there all day," said Matilda.

"He didn't go swimming with you?"

"No. He'd been hoping you would come along and help him choose a snorkel," said Sonja.

"Dad. Promise you'll come with us tomorrow. Please… Promise?"

"I promise. To try my very, very—"

"You're so silly." Matilda wriggled out of his grasp.

Fabian turned toward the stairs just as the phone rang. "Is that thing hooked up already?"

"Apparently." Sonja walked over to the phone and lifted the receiver. "Yes, this is Sonja Risk... Yes, he's here. For you."

Fabian knew who it was right away, thanks to Sonja's curt tone. *You treacherous fucking weasel*, he thought before he took the receiver.

"Yes, this is Fabian Risk," he said in his most formal voice.

"Hi, sweetie," Niva answered from the other end. "I thought it was best to call your home number instead of your mobile, so it wouldn't seem as suspicious. After all, we have nothing to hide about this conversation, do we?"

"No, absolutely not." Fabian said, shrugging at Sonja as he walked into the living room. "Did you find anything?"

"You're always such an eager beaver. To be honest, I don't understand how Sonja stands it. Everything's over before it even starts."

"Niva, we were just about to sit down to dinner."

"How sweet. There was a 739-krone charge to the card number you sent me from the OK petrol station in Lellinge at 10:22 p.m. He also used it at the BorderShop in Puttgarden, where he must have bought enough beer for the whole Oktoberfest."

"Thanks for your help."

"It was nothing."

Fabian hung up and sat down to eat. Sonja would obviously be wondering what the call was about. She had every right to ask questions.

But she would have to wait until he got home later tonight.

FABIAN MANAGED TO LEAVE the house at just after ten o'clock. He got in the car, and headed for the OK petrol station in Lellinge, which was about forty kilometres southwest of

Copenhagen. He estimated that he would arrive just before midnight.

Although Theodor had refused to open the door when he was leaving, and Matilda and Sonja were now both mad at him, he had decided not to put off the journey to the next day. He had managed to buy some time and couldn't afford to waste it by letting an entire night pass by.

Fabian considered the facts he knew about the case on the drive there. It would have been impossible for the perpetrator to know exactly where, and how many times, Jörgen would stop, but he must have assumed that Jörgen would stop at least once on the way down to fill up the tank. According to Molander, the petrol tank of the Chevy they'd found at the school contained 88 litres of 95-octane petrol. It could hold up to 120 litres total, which meant that Jörgen had used up 32 litres. The station he had filled up at was 144 kilometres from the school, including the bridge crossing. Using 32 litres in 144 kilometres meant that the fully loaded Chevy had used 2.2 litres per 10 kilometres—a fair estimate. It seemed reasonable to assume that Jörgen hadn't made any unnecessary detours, but had driven straight to the school.

Jörgen Pålsson used his credit card only once in Denmark, at the OK petrol station at 10:22 p.m. The 739-krone charge equalled about 75 litres of petrol. If he had started his journey in Ödåkra with a full tank of petrol and didn't fill up until Lellinge, 380 kilometres later, a 75-litre pump seemed just about right. Jörgen had passed through the toll booth at Lernacken fifty-six minutes later, at 11:18 p.m., but it shouldn't have taken more than forty minutes to go that distance. This meant that he had lingered at the petrol station for fifteen to twenty minutes.

Then he'd crossed the bridge with a passenger riding shotgun.

THE MAN IN THE booth at the Øresund Bridge handed Fabian back his credit card, and the boom in front of him lifted. He pressed the accelerator as the radio played one of his favourite songs. He turned up the volume until Kate Bush's voice filled the car, singing about making a deal with God to swap places with her lover. He started humming as she sang the chorus line "Running up that hill."

This was the first time he'd ever crossed the bridge and the view bordered on magical. The sky shimmered dark blue and gold in the glow from the shining half-moon, and far below him the calm waters of Øresund acted as a gigantic mirror.

GLENN GRANQVIST SAT AT the kitchen table, unscrewed the lid of the glass jar, and looked down at the pieces of herring swimming around in the cloudy liquid. The jar was left over from when Anki had lived here; he didn't even like herring all that much. There was something that irked him about the texture, so he had to swallow the pieces whole and wash them down with a cold beer to keep them from coming back up again.

But now the beer was gone. Most of the things Glenn liked were gone, and these days he was emptying jars whose best before dates were in the distant past — olives, pickles, mustard, remoulade, and all of Anki's damn herring. He fished out another piece, stuck it in his mouth, and washed it down with the juice from a can of pineapple.

He hadn't been able to relax since he'd heard the news about Jörgen. He was having a hard time sitting still and had to keep in constant motion. He felt like he was on tenterhooks and that his heart was beating in double time. His best friend was dead, not because of a tragic accident or a brief illness, but because someone had purposely taken his life in such a meticulously planned and terrible way that the very thought of it sent cold shivers through his body.

He thought of all the fun they'd had together over their thirty-seven years of friendship — almost a whole lifetime. They'd met in first grade. After just a few minutes they ended up in a fight.

They'd been best friends ever since and had stood by each other through thick and thin.

But they had done a few stupid things, too; quite a lot of them when he thought about it. They'd left most of that behind, convincing themselves that they hadn't done anything to be ashamed of—and it had worked. For all these years he'd slept peacefully at night with a conscience as pure and clean as a commercial. Until Lina called him more than a week ago to tell him that Jörgen was missing. He'd had an inkling that something was off right from the start, and since then the images had kept popping up in a steady stream: old, forgotten memories that he thought had been stomped down into a hard, unrecognizable crust—paved over so they would never again see the light of day.

And yet here he was thinking about them.

He wasn't surprised in the least that Jörgen was dead, or that he had been murdered. It was those fucking sawed-off hands that had scared Glenn out of his wits. If it hadn't been for that one little detail, he was sure he would be sleeping at night. He wasn't able to grieve for Jörgen or be there for Lina—he had hardly even dared to contact her.

Hands had been Jörgen's speciality. It didn't matter how bloody and wrecked they got, he only used his fists to hurt and abuse. He hadn't started using the brass knuckles until after ninth grade. Glenn's own speciality had been kicking with his red, steel-toed Doc Martens.

He didn't understand why they had kept it up for so long. It was one thing during their school days—they had been bored and needed something to pass the time. It had made him feel powerful at that age: their victim would positively tremble with fear as soon as he saw Glenn and Jörgen, and would do everything they told him to. But why did they continue? It was like they had become addicted and couldn't stop until he was dead. And they thought they had killed him at their last "meeting."

53

The get-together had lasted for over five hours. That was eleven years after they finished the ninth grade. Until then, they had left him alone after they finished school and messed with other people instead. The truth was, they'd grown tired of him and had more or less forgotten about him, until the middle of a drunken night in Copenhagen when Jörgen suddenly came up with the idea to get back in touch with him to have one last meeting.

Equations exist to calculate how much energy the body burns when you go for a run, have sex, or sleep. But there was no formula to tell them how many calories they burned during a fight. It must have been a lot, because after three hours both he and Jörgen were totally exhausted. Their victim had screamed, cried, and begged for mercy. He said they could have his money, and that he was willing to do anything as long as they stopped. But they wanted him to give up and die.

The bastard refused to die. Sure, they could have stuck a knife in him, but that would have been cheating. They only used their hands and feet—nothing more.

They left the apartment and went to Tre Häster for a while to have steaks with fries and béarnaise sauce and large Cokes. Glenn could still remember how good it had tasted. It was as if their bodies were crying out for more blood sugar. After eating, they'd played pinball. He managed to get several multiballs and he might have set a personal record if only the machine hadn't tilted. They didn't say a word about the assault while they played the game, but a silent agreement was hovering in the air. They would keep at it until he gave up—once and for all.

When they went back, it turned out that their victim had managed to drag himself into the hall and pull the phone down from the table. He couldn't have known they'd cut the line.

Two hours later, they were the ones giving up. It was the first time they had ever grown tired of beating someone. The last thirty minutes mostly felt monotonous and unexciting, and Glenn recalled that they'd rationalized quitting because he would surely die on his own within a few hours.

They spent the next several weeks poring over the newspapers for an obituary or an article about the murder, but they didn't find a thing. There wasn't even a police report. After two months they went back to his apartment and found it completely empty. He had vanished.

They both felt uneasy and the feeling grew stronger. Where had their victim gone? Was he planning his revenge? They had discussed it on several occasions and came to the conclusion that they probably didn't have much to worry about. After another few years passed, they no longer gave it a second thought.

But then Jörgen's body was found with both his hands sawed off.

Did this mean it would be his turn soon? Would he get his feet sawed off?

He lay down on the bench in the kitchen and closed his eyes. Exhaustion felt like it was eating him up from the inside, but he didn't dare fall asleep. The few hours of sleep he'd managed to get during the past week had been worse than being awake. His dreams were stranger than ever—repressed memories came to life and twisted into a horror-film director's wet dream.

He had once read about a researcher who managed to stay awake for eleven days. After four days he had started hallucinating and thought he was the Argentinian footballer Diego Maradona. But after six days he was back to normal and he even managed to beat his assistants at pinball before starting to sleep regularly again.

But he would never be able to manage eleven days.

He needed to think clearly and not lose focus. He sat up, rubbed his eyes back to life, and stuck another piece of herring in his mouth. He tried swallowing it, but it wouldn't go down. He had already finished the last of the pineapple juice and the piece of fish kept coming back up until he steeled himself and started chewing. He needed to eat for energy if he was going to have any chance whatsoever when it counted. He was certain he was going to have to defend himself. He would put up a fight.

At least no one could accuse him of being a lazy-ass. Almost all of his preparations were finished. He had armed himself, installed locks on every window in his house, and rewired all the lights so he could turn them off with a single switch on a remote control he carried with him at all times. He'd also run barbed wire across the lawn behind the house and attached it with fishing line to the wind chimes in the upstairs window, so that he would be able to hear anyone who went back there.

All he had left to do on his list was to install the peephole in his front door, but that would have to wait until tomorrow when it was light out again. There had been a peephole in the old door, but he'd considered it an unnecessary expense when the door had to be replaced, only to change his mind and buy one to install on his own a few weeks later. That had been three and a half years ago. But he would install it tomorrow.

It was a really stupid idea for him to be living in this house now that Anki had left him. He was only staying to spite her. He didn't even like the house. It was poorly built, with its thin plaster walls that smelled mouldy even though they were only ten years old, and he'd already had to replace the door...

The ringing doorbell interrupted Glenn's thoughts about his inadequate house. It was eleven thirty at night. Who the hell could it be at this hour?

The bell rang again.

Glenn had assumed his assailant would come through the backyard, which wasn't visible from the outside. He had set up the barbed wire so that the attacker would trip, giving Glenn time to get on top of him and manhandle him inside. If, contrary to all expectations, the assailant managed to get all the way up to the house, the large glass doors would be easy for him to force. But Glenn was ready for that, too. He would drive the attacker into his workroom, where the man would never be able to get out—at least not before Glenn calmly locked him up and called the police. He was already looking forward to being in the papers as the hero who'd caught the murderer. It would sure show Anki.

But the front doorbell ringing wasn't part of his plan. The killer wouldn't just walk up to the front of the house and ring the bell. It wasn't possible. So who could it be?

The wind chimes had given him his first false alarm the night before. He'd turned out all the lights and rushed out into the yard in no time, but it was just a dog that had wandered in and got stuck in the barbed wire. The dog had managed to tear itself free and run off before Glenn could help it.

Maybe it was the dog's owner at the door. Glenn wondered if there could be anything illegal about putting up barbed wire in your own yard. It was his land, after all.

He grabbed the baseball bat and cautiously walked down the hall. The bell rang again.

Why hadn't he installed that goddamn fucking peephole? He unlocked the door and opened it.

9

IT WAS 11:30 P.M. by the time the GPS told Fabian that he had nearly arrived at his destination in Lellinge. The trip had gone faster than expected. There was hardly any traffic and, after hearing "Running Up That Hill" on the radio, he'd listened to the entire *Hounds of Love* album. It had helped jog his memory about his school days.

He'd never liked Jörgen Pålsson and had made sure to stay as far away from him as possible. It wasn't because Fabian was afraid, but more out of faintheartedness. He wouldn't have to witness the abuse and be forced to take a side if he hadn't seen anything. It might explain why his memories were so fuzzy. He was so fucking pitiful.

At least he remembered enough to say that Jörgen Pålsson and Glenn Granqvist had spread fear throughout the class, but they'd picked on one person in particular: Claes Mällvik. Mällvik was bullied as soon as the names were read for attendance in first grade, all the way until he finished the ninth grade. Everyone in the class had been well aware of it, and surely the same went for the teachers. Yet no one had done anything but avert their eyes.

There was one incident that Fabian hadn't been able to ignore. An incident he had repressed—but the chopped-off hands in the shower room brought it back to him. His complacency made him feel as guilty as Jörgen and Glenn.

They had just finished gym class and were on their way into

the locker room. Claes never showered, a fact the gym teacher had recently discovered. He threatened Claes with a failing grade if he didn't start washing. The teacher told him that it was a matter of personal hygiene to shower after gym class, not only for yourself but also for everyone around you; he probably had no idea how these threats would affect Claes.

The white-tiled shower room had eight showers along two walls. Everyone could sense what was in the air, and hurried toward them—everyone but Jörgen and Glenn. *What the hell are you staring at? Are you a fag or something? No, he's a tranny! Check out his dick! It's so fucking tiny it looks like a pussy!*

Fabian could still recall the way Claes had looked at him with pleading eyes, and how he had pretended to get soap in his eyes to avoid opening them. Then he heard the first blow. When he opened his eyes again, Claes was lying on the hard tile floor in foetal position, trying to shield himself from Glenn's kicks, which were aimed at his genitals, and Jörgen's blows to his head.

Fabian had been a coward and sneaked out with the rest of the boys. Claes didn't make even the tiniest sound. He didn't cry out or say a word. He didn't even ask them to stop. He just took the blows and the kicks in silence. It wasn't until they turned the shower on as hot as it would go that he started screaming.

Now, more than thirty years later, the perpetrator had sawed off Jörgen's hands and placed them in the very same shower room.

If anyone had a strong motive, it was Claes Mällvik.

THE OK PETROL STATION consisted of one building. After doing a circuit around it, Fabian parked in one corner, next to a Dumpster, and stepped out of the car. He filled his lungs with the night air, which was still thick and warm. If this weather kept up, he would soon be reading about the warmest July in one hundred years in the papers.

He walked around for a moment and then realized that he hadn't the slightest idea what he should be looking for, although he had a feeling there was a lead somewhere close by, something that he needed to discover sooner rather than later. As he searched the area around the petrol station, the feeling grew stronger and stronger. He couldn't be sure, but he felt increasingly confident that this was where the perpetrator had made contact with his victim.

How could the killer have planned for Jörgen Pålsson to fill up his tank at this petrol station in particular? The only thing he could have counted on was that Jörgen had to stop somewhere on the drive home. He must have followed Jörgen in a car of his own, a car he would have been forced to leave behind. If he hadn't already come back to get it there was a chance the vehicle was still here.

As Fabian made his way to the back of the petrol station he tried to get a clearer mental picture of Claes Mällvik. He remembered him as incredibly shy and cautious, someone who had hardly dared to raise his hand in class to answer a question. Had he now gone so far as to take the life of his tormentor in a brutal and headline-grabbing way? Fabian didn't quite know what to think. There was no limit to what violence and mental terrorism could do to a person: it was probably the very way to create a monster.

There were five cars parked behind the building, and none of them seemed to belong to customers inside the store. Three of them were in the staff parking spaces, but there were no signs in front of the other two. One of the cars was covered in a thick layer of dirt and dried leaves. Fabian walked over to the last car in the row, a Peugeot 206, and studied it. It had Swedish number plates, and a thin layer of dust suggested it had been sitting there untouched for a few days—perhaps a week at most.

He ought to call Tuvesson, but there was a good chance she would be angry with him for acting on his own authority. Instead, he called Lilja.

"Hi, this is Fabian Risk, your new—"

"I know who you are."

"I hope I didn't wake you."

"Not at all. I'm still at the office, trying to help Klippan get hold of a list of students from your class, which seems to be absolutely impossible. It was 9C, wasn't it?"

"Yes, but with a little luck maybe we won't need it. I'm in Denmark and I may have found the killer's car."

"What? How the hell did you manage that? Does Tuvesson know?"

"I'll explain more later. This is still a bit of a long shot, and I might be wrong, but if you could look up the plate JOS 652, that would be—"

"I'll call you back."

Fabian took a deep breath, stuck his phone in his pocket, and walked toward the petrol station's twenty-four-hour store. If it turned out that Claes Mällvik was the owner of the Peugeot, Fabian's suspicions would be realized and the investigation would enter its final phase: locating the suspect and making the arrest. That last phase could certainly take some time, but he would have done his job and then some, and he could return to his vacation with a clear conscience. He could take Theodor to Väla tomorrow morning to buy a snorkelling set, and after that he could take the whole family to the beach at Mölle, where they could sunbathe and snorkel by the cliffs. Then he would treat them all to a fancy dinner at Mölle's very own Grand Hotel.

He walked into the store and carried a machine-made latte, a chocolate bar, and a bottle of Ramlösa water—or "Danish water," as the Danes stubbornly insisted on calling it even though it was bottled in Helsingborg—over to the cash desk. There was a young female clerk behind the register. She didn't look any older than twenty, and had a piercing in her lower lip. She was far too young to be working the night shift all by herself, Fabian thought as he set down his purchases.

"Is that your car?" she asked in Danish, pointing at the Peugeot.

"No, but do you know how long it's been here?"

"About a week."

"Was it here last Tuesday?"

"No idea." She shrugged and started scanning his items. "I don't work Tuesdays or Wednesdays. I saw it for the first time on Thursday. Your items will be seventy-eight kroner."

Fabian handed over his credit card, realizing that the Peugeot could very well have been sitting here since the previous Tuesday.

He was leaving the store just as his phone rang.

"Fabian, it's Irene Lilja. The car is registered to a Rune Schmeckel."

"Sorry? What did you say?" Fabian stopped by the air pump, which was dripping and hissing. He'd been so certain she would say Claes Mällvik that he assumed he'd heard wrong.

"His name is Rune Schmeckel. Unfortunate last name, isn't it?"

Fabian felt deflated. If only it had been a rental car or something, just to give them a clue to work from. He knew for certain that there hadn't been a Rune Schmeckel in his 9C class.

"Has it been reported stolen?"

"No. That's the first thing I thought of, too."

Dammit, Fabian thought to himself. Maybe it wasn't the perpetrator's car after all. Or maybe he was completely on the wrong track. Could this case be about something other than a victim's revenge?

"Fabian, are you still there?"

"Yes. You didn't give me the answer I was expecting."

"His home address is Adelgatan 5 in Lund. He works at the hospital there."

"I have to go now. We'll talk more later."

Fabian ended the call. He had no desire to keep talking. He needed time to think—to reconsider everything.

10

IT WAS JUST PAST two in the morning, but the sky had already started to get lighter. Fabian decided that the view of Øresund had outdone itself as he crossed back over to Sweden. But this time he couldn't take any real pleasure in the landscape. He didn't even feel like listening to music. He couldn't stop thinking about Claes Mällvik and everything the boy had been subjected to during their school years. More memories had come back to him, each worse than the last, and they helped bolster the possible motives. Yet there was no concrete evidence to point to Claes. All Fabian had were a few fuzzy memories from long ago.

Fabian slowed down as he came to the Lernacken toll booth. He handed his credit card to the man inside and thought about Sonja. He hoped she would be asleep when he got home. Otherwise the conversation about why Niva had called would keep them awake all night.

"May I ask you to back out and drive to that building over there," the man in the booth said as he handed back Fabian's credit card, pointing to a structure that looked like an army barracks.

"Is there a problem? I have another card, if there's an issue with that one."

The man shook his head. Fabian had absolutely no idea what was going on, not even when he saw the overweight woman coming toward him.

"Fabian Risk, you weren't thinking of just sneaking past

me, were you? You promised me a date the next time you came through," she said.

Fabian stepped out of the car, shook her hand, and wished he were anywhere but there. The woman introduced herself as Kickan and dragged him into the barracks, where she emptied an old pot of coffee and started brewing a fresh one. Fabian counted the number of scoops she dumped into the filter and realized that he wasn't going to get a wink of sleep. Though it wouldn't make any difference if Sonja were awake when he got home.

"Why, you sure are handsome—even more handsome than I imagined!" said Kickan, filling two cups with black coffee. "Are you single or is that too much to hope for? I enjoy long walks and romantic dinners. Although, to be completely honest, I probably prefer the dinners."

"Sorry, but I'm married," Fabian managed, wondering what he had done to deserve this.

"That's no reason to apologize. But good things come to those who ask."

"The phrase ends with 'wait' not 'ask.'"

"What?"

"Good things come to those who *wait*."

"Exactly my point! Would you like a cookie?"

"No, thank you, I'm fine," Fabian said, having forced down his coffee. "I have to get going, but it was nice to meet you, and thanks for the coffee."

"It was nothing. I hope I didn't frighten you with all of my babbling on the phone. It can get a little lonely in the booths, but people don't think about what it's like in our little boxes. Everyone is on their way somewhere else—everyone but us."

"I can imagine it gets a bit lonely. I hope you have a nice night." Fabian turned toward the door.

"Listen, I thought of something related to the case you're working on."

"Oh?" Fabian failed to hold back a yawn.

"Let's assume it was the perpetrator sitting in the passenger seat in the photo from the toll booth. And let's say he's Swedish. He would have also had to drive across the bridge on the way to Denmark, but in a different car, which means the car could have been left behind in Denmark, right?"

"That's true, but unfortunately there are still far too many unanswered questions for that to lead to anything solid," Fabian said in a tone that made it quite clear that he had no more to add, even though deep down he was impressed by the woman's powers of deduction.

"Just one more thing before you leave... If you believe that is what happened, wouldn't the killer have passed through this toll booth around the same time as the victim?"

Fabian realized that he had completely missed the perfectly logical conclusion Kickan was laying out. "You know, that didn't even occur to me, but you're right. Is there any chance you can find pictures of the cars that passed through before and after him?"

Kickan smiled and held up a brown envelope. She opened it and spread the black-and-white surveillance pictures across the table. "At first I thought he would have passed through right after the victim, in the same line, but I don't think it's any of those vehicles. So I checked the cars in the other lines. And this one caught my eye... I could certainly be wrong. But what do you think?" She pulled out the last picture, which showed a Peugeot with the registration number JOS 652.

"Why did you pick this one in particular?"

"Can you see how he's bending down here? That almost never happens. Normally people don't register that they are being photographed, but this guy is fully conscious of it and he really doesn't want to be captured on film. Not to mention, he paid in cash."

Fabian studied the picture. The driver of the car was definitely hiding his face. Kickan was right; she had done a big part of his job for him. He thanked her, took the pictures, and promised not to forget to stop for some coffee next time he drove through.

"Coffee? Please. Next time is our second date, so I think we can progress a little further than that!" She gave him an exaggerated wink and laughed.

Unsure whether she was really joking, Fabian got into his car and drove back across the bridge to Denmark.

IT WAS TWO THIRTY in the morning, but Tuvesson answered her phone after just two rings.

"Why didn't you tell me you were out on a solo tour of Denmark?"

"Sorry, but I didn't want to wake you unnecessarily."

"Unnecessarily?"

"Before I knew if we had any good leads." He could hear how ridiculous this sounded. "Didn't Lilja call you about the owner of the car? His name is Rune Schmeckel, and he lives in Lund."

"Yes, she did. The Lund police have already been there, but there was nobody home." He could hear her taking a drag of a cigarette.

"Did you call the hospital? Maybe he's on duty."

"He's on vacation. Fabian, I want you to tell me where you are right now."

"On my way home," he lied. "What should we do with Rune's car? It's still at the petrol station and should be examined. Have you told Molander about it yet?"

"We can't do anything with the car until our Danish colleagues give us the go-ahead. In big cases like this one they usually like to let a few extra days go by to make us sweat. You know how it is when big brother asks little brother for a favour."

"It might be too late by then."

"He's already left the car there for over a week. He probably won't ever go and pick it up."

66

"What about Schmeckel's house? When can we get in to look around?"

"It's the middle of the summer, but I'll put some pressure on the Danes."

"Okay. I'll see you tomorrow."

"Listen, Fabian, like I said before...I'm very grateful that you're willing to help even though you're on vacation. But, dammit, don't forget that we're a team!"

Fabian didn't have time to answer before he heard the click of her hanging up.

Forty minutes later, he turned off at the OK station in Lellinge again, and drove around it once to make sure that nobody else was there—no one other than the girl with the piercings in the store. He had thought through his plan and weighed the pros and cons, fully conscious of the fact that it went against every rule he could think of. Fabian knew he could get into serious trouble, yet he felt certain that this was the right thing to do.

He parked right next to the Peugeot, took the jack from the trunk of his car, placed it under the other vehicle, and cranked it until the back tyre was off the ground. Using the four-way wrench, he loosened the four lug nuts and took off the tyre.

The girl behind the counter looked up from a magazine when he entered the store.

"Hello again. My name is Fabian Risk and I'm with the Helsingborg police." He showed her his identification.

"Okay...?" Her eyes immediately looked curious, and worried.

It didn't matter what the circumstances were, as long as his visit was unexpected, all Fabian had to do was introduce himself to be met with the same "what have I done now?" gaze.

"It's about the Peugeot out there with the Swedish number plates. We're going to have to bring it in for a technical investigation in a Swedish murder case, as soon as all the paperwork is in order between our two countries."

"That's no problem," the girl said in Danish. She shrugged with a stiff smile.

"But until then, I need your help," Fabian continued, watching as her smile disappeared and her anxious look returned. "He's probably left the car here indefinitely, and I don't expect him to come and retrieve it, but if he does I would like you to contact me right away. Is that clear?" He wrote his name and number down on a slip of paper.

The girl looked at the paper and sucked the piercing in her lip. "How will I know it's him? What if he just takes off?"

"That won't happen because you'll have the back tyre." Fabian went outside and brought in the tyre. The girl reluctantly took it, and rolled it behind the counter.

"I'm going to have to call my boss."

"No problem. He can give me a call if he wants to."

Fabian stuck a note he had written in Danish into a plastic sleeve and secured it under the Peugeot's windscreen wiper. Then he got in his car to go home.

THIS VEHICLE IS ON PRIVATE PROPERTY
PLEASE CONTACT PERSONNEL

August 20

I hate school. I hate it! Everyone can see what's happening, but no one does anything. Or they laugh and look away. I wanted to stay in at break today but the teacher wouldn't let me. She said that everyone has to go out and get fresh air. I told her they were stupid. She said it takes two to tango. No it doesn't. I hid in the bathroom and heard them looking for me and yelling that I was gay if I didn't come out. I stayed there anyway because I know I'm not gay. I like girls. Even though I haven't been with one I'm totally sure. Almost everyone who comes out as gay says that they knew they were gay since they were little, so I would know by now. I definitely can't be gay.

On the way home they were standing in the playground. Hampus always said you shouldn't run because that's what they want you to do. I wanted to run but I walked normally. They blocked my way. I tried to go around them but they just kept stopping me. I told them to move but they said I was too ugly, and that I stank, and that I had to carry their bags. I stood up for myself and said I didn't stink. Then they punched me in the stomach and said it was my fault because I was acting too cocky.

I promise:

1. I will never be cocky again.
2. I will never say anything to anyone at school.
3. Ever again.

P. S. Laban hasn't even used his wheel once. Stupid fucking hamster.

11

THE HELPLESS, PATHETIC SCREAMS echoed through the warehouse that was more than a hundred metres long. The screams managed to find their way in among the tall shelves, even though he had chosen a spot at the other end of the building. It sounded like a goddamn stuck pig.

He didn't like screaming, especially not from a man. It was a sign of weakness and lack of self-control. By this point, he should have realized that it was all over anyway and that screaming wouldn't help. He was going to die, so why not do it with dignity?

It was three thirty on Friday morning. Åstorp Construction Supply, which was closed for the holidays, wouldn't open again until Monday. He had found a relatively isolated spot, squeezed in between two shelves, where he could lay a blanket down and sit with his McDonald's.

He hadn't slept or eaten in the past twenty-four hours—not for lack of appetite or because of an inability to sleep, he just didn't have the time. But he was still a whole day behind schedule. A minor incident had delayed him and risked the whole plan. After a thorough review of the situation, he realized that the plan wasn't in any great danger of being derailed. Luck was on his side, and by tomorrow order would be restored.

The following day, he would go retrieve the car from Lellinge and park it at the harbour at Ishøj, where it wouldn't be found for many days, likely long after he was finished. But he wanted to be cautious and saw this as an extra safeguard. It was all part of his plan.

In a little more than a week he would be finished. Then he could lean back and let everyone else clean up the mess. He would watch them gather up the pieces while trying to understand everything. They would be amazed by his aptitude—it would keep them busy for years. Everyone would be talking about him.

He tore at the damp, paper McDonald's bag and shovelled down the cold, spongy hamburger and the barely salted fries. He saved the apple pie for later; it would be his breakfast. He licked the oil from his fingers and set the timer for four hours. If anyone showed up unexpectedly before it went off, the noise would wake him up and he would have at least a minute to gather up his blanket and escape through the window. It opened upward, which was definitely a drawback, but he'd already loosened the hasps and propped it ajar with a stick that he could easily remove from the outside.

He was very organized. He had gone through every scenario imaginable, time and again, and he felt as focused as Björn Borg going into a big match. He was totally convinced that the key to success lay in his meticulous planning and absolute focus, which is why he had spent the past three years devoting himself solely to his preparations.

He had officially decided to follow through with his plan in spring 2007, though the idea had been percolating for considerably longer. He had been walking around full of rage for as long as he could remember, with a wound that refused to heal and became more infected with each passing day. He felt like a walking pressure cooker, holding his feelings inside, ready to explode at any time. He had tried to be friendly and do all he could to make people like him. Nowadays he was sickened by his old, fawning, treacly behaviour and couldn't understand how he had managed to keep up a happy face for so long.

But it would all be over soon. His wound would finally be opened, drained of its pus, and everyone who was to blame would be held accountable. Every single one of those bastards who thought they had nothing to be ashamed of and slept peacefully at night would pay.

It was time for them to pay the piper.

His thoughts turned to Fabian Risk, who had stepped into the plan unexpectedly. Risk was always a wimpy little bastard, at once decent but underhanded, always with his own agenda and constantly preoccupied with trying to please everyone. Risk had never dared to say what he truly stood for, so it was no surprise that he became a cop. It was surprising that Risk had moved back home again. He could have never foreseen that, and it meant he'd had to make a number of adjustments to the first part of his plan, even though it hadn't changed anything crucial. In fact, he saw it as an unexpected bonus.

After studying Risk's resumé from Stockholm, the last little bit of worry left him. He had worked on a few murder cases, some armed-truck robberies, and a network of paedophiles, all of whom had gone free due to lack of evidence. Most recently, he had more or less been fired after trespassing at the Israeli embassy last winter; that was as incomprehensible as it was illegal. Fabian Risk was no great threat, either to him or to what he was about to set in motion. As an added bonus, Risk's move to Helsingborg would save him the two days he had allocated for travelling to Stockholm.

Jörgen Pålsson, on the other hand, had been very predictable. For each of the past three years he had driven down to Germany to buy beer the week of Midsummer's Eve, and this year was no exception. The plan couldn't have worked any better. All he'd had to do was follow Jörgen's flashy pickup truck down to Malmö, across the bridge to Rødby, and then pretend to run into him when he stopped for petrol on the way home.

The only thing that had worried him beforehand was whether

Jörgen's size would pose a problem. Once they were standing eye-to-eye, Jörgen's body looked so pumped up that it might explode at the slightest touch, but by then it was too late for him to abort the plan. Besides, bodybuilders were seldom as strong as they looked.

Jörgen hadn't recognized him, and he didn't do a thing to jog the man's memory. Instead, he said that his own car had quit on him and that he had to get back home to Helsingborg. Jörgen took the bait immediately and offered him a ride.

The biggest problem then became Jörgen's insufferable, amoeba-level babbling, which he'd had to listen to all the way home. It had been an unparalleled ordeal, and at several junctures he'd felt the urge to take out the bag with the drenched rag early and shove it into his face just to get the damn guy to shut up. But he'd restrained himself and waited for the right moment: Larmvägen in Fredriksdal, where he had claimed to live.

Jörgen insisted on driving him all the way there. Once they arrived he was finally able to take out the rag, and the rest went like clockwork. Jörgen slept through the entire operation. If the newspapers were to be believed, he woke up at the planned time and failed to escape. The superglue in the lock had been his favourite touch—he still got excited every time he thought about it.

Glenn Granqvist hadn't been quite so easy. He had certainly expected the news of Jörgen's fate to make Glenn more vigilant—how else could he interpret those chopped-off hands?—and afraid that he was next in line, but it had come as a complete surprise that Glenn had gone so far with his security measures; they'd almost disrupted the entire operation. He had to admit it: he'd underestimated Glenn and fallen right into his trap.

He had originally planned to enter Glenn's Eksjö house—"Villa Harmony"—through the back patio door and make his way to Glenn's bedroom upstairs. The attack itself was supposed to be a piece of cake, but he never made it that far. Instead, he got stuck in the unspooled barbed wire in the yard that must have been connected to some sort of alarm.

Glenn was outside the house with a baseball bat in less than fifteen seconds. He had no choice but to drop down, hide behind some currant bushes, and do everything he could not to scream as the barbed wire sliced into his throat. In that instant he was sure it was all over and that his three years of work would come to nothing, which would have been the case if it hadn't been for the dog, who came out of nowhere and got stuck in the barbed wire too. Glenn went to help it, but it tore itself free and ran away whimpering.

Glenn went back inside five minutes later, which finally gave him the opportunity to pull the barbs out of his throat. He was bleeding heavily and was forced to retreat. Once he arrived home, he discovered that his wounds were so deep they needed stitches, which he took care of himself. It wasn't pretty, but he did a clean job and it stopped the bleeding. The lumpy stitches on his throat, which would undoubtedly scar, would serve as a constant reminder never to underestimate an opponent again.

He lay down on the blanket and realized that the screaming had finally stopped. Everything was under control here. Once he moved the Peugeot the following day, order would be restored, which would allow him to move on to the next step in peace and quiet.

He closed his eyes and thought of all the people who were struggling to solve his puzzle, to figure out how it was all connected. Little did they know he had only just begun.

One last thought washed through him like a soft, warm wave before he drifted off. Soon, the whole class would have sleepless nights.

12

FABIAN RISK CLOSED THE door behind him as quietly as he could, pulled off his Converse shoes, and went into the living room. It looked like a bomb had just exploded. Black bin bags were scattered all over the place, and there were open, half-empty moving boxes everywhere. It was almost four o'clock in the morning, and it was so far into dawn that it was more day than night.

He brushed his teeth and washed up in the kitchen to avoid waking anyone. After spending a few minutes searching for a towel, he gave up and dried off with his shirt before going upstairs.

Sonja was on the very edge of her side of the bed, turned away from him, which was a bad sign. She had still been angry with him when she fell asleep. He cautiously crawled under the duvet. Sonja turned onto her back and took a deep breath, a motion that could be interpreted as an extended hand; it was up to him to accept it.

He found her legs with one hand and carefully groped her thigh. She didn't react; she was still deep asleep. He led his hand upward, edging closer toward her hips. He quickly realized that she wasn't wearing any panties. Confident that he had interpreted her reactions correctly, he pulled the duvet off and spread her legs. She didn't help him, but didn't resist either. He dived down and ran his tongue along the inside of her thigh as lightly as he could, focusing on one side and then the other. He let his tongue get closer each time.

Her breathing started to change. He licked her labia and she pressed her crotch up against his face. He replied to her excitement by entering her with a finger as he continued to pleasure her with his tongue. Her body twisted and turned, and a few minutes later she buried her face in the pillow, moaning as she orgasmed.

She pushed his head away once she had recovered. Her breathing slowed as if she had never woken up. Fabian felt the frustration throbbing inside him, but he knew there was no point in trying and so closed his eyes.

THE IMAGES HE HAD repressed for so long were flying straight at him like a volleyball. He remembered one gym class where everyone was screaming his name to jump up and hit the ball. He whacked it as hard as he could. Claes, on the opposing team, was hit, and his glasses broke; blood streamed from his nose and everyone laughed, even the gym teacher. Fabian laughed too. Jörgen came over to give him a high five. *Nice one, Fabbe!* And he reciprocated. Claes cried and tried to go home, but the teacher kept him there. *Everyone has to shower after gym class!* They all headed to the white-tiled shower room. *What the hell are you staring at?* Claes's pleading gaze, and his betrayal as he pretended to get soap in his eyes.

"HI, DAD! MOM SAID you were super tired and needed sleep."

Fabian came down the stairs and took Matilda into his arms. The memories had haunted him all night. Ripped out of context, they had distorted into increasingly incomprehensible nightmares. He'd woken, drenched in sweat, to discover it was already nine thirty.

"Matilda, go and brush your teeth so we can get going," said Sonja.

"We're going to Denmark!"

Fabian released Matilda, who edged her way past him on

76

the stairs. He went to the kitchen, where Sonja was cleaning up breakfast.

"Good morning. Did you sleep well?"

Fabian nodded.

"As you heard, we're going to the Louisiana Museum in Denmark today."

"Oh—that'll be nice. Do they have an exhibit on?"

"Theo doesn't want to come."

"Why not?"

Sonja shrugged. "Apparently he doesn't want to do anything at all if you're not there."

"Sonja, no one wishes more than I do that—"

"I know. You have to do it." She looked straight into his eyes. "But if Niva so much as thinks of calling again, you'll have to live here on your own."

"Honey, it's not what you think at all." He walked up to her and took her hands in his own. "She was only calling because—"

"You have no idea what I think." She pulled her hands away and started loading the dishwasher.

Fabian knew exactly what Sonja thought, and he knew that he would never, ever be able to change it. After several failed attempts he had given up all hope of trying to tell her what had really happened. Or, most importantly, what *hadn't* happened.

"Sophie Calle."

"Sorry, what…?"

"You asked about the exhibit at the Louisiana. Sophie Calle is that Frenchwoman who made art out of a break-up email she was sent from her now ex-boyfriend."

TUVESSON, MOLANDER, LILJA, AND Klippan were already reviewing the case details when Fabian joined them. Judging by the nearly empty fruit bowl, Fabian guessed they had been there for a while already. He sat down in an empty chair, sensing

immediately that the atmosphere was heavy and serious—
something had happened.

"Now that you've finally decided to join us, perhaps an
explanation is in order?" said Tuvesson.

Everyone had turned to him with curious expressions. Fabian
realized that *he* was that something.

"I'm sorry, I'm not sure I understand."

"I'm talking about your little solo tour last night. Evidently
you have a number of ideas about the case that, for some reason,
you chose to keep from all of us, isn't that right?"

"I wanted to wait until I had more to go on, until I was sure."

"Fabian, as I've said many times, I don't know how you all
work up in Stockholm," said Tuvesson, pushing two pieces of
nicotine gum out of their crinkly packet. "But here, we work
as a team. It doesn't make a difference whether we are sure or
unsure." She stuck the gum in her mouth and chewed as if the
nicotine couldn't work fast enough.

Fabian felt like he was at school, getting a talking-to in front
of the rest of the class. "I thought I had a solid idea of the
motive, but unfortunately it doesn't hold up."

"Or maybe it does."

"And since we don't have anything else to go on…" said
Lilja.

Fabian realized it was too late to get out of this, so he stood up
and walked to the whiteboard wall, drawing a circle around the
picture of Jörgen. "I believe that in some ways, Jörgen Pålsson
got exactly what he deserved." He saw the others exchange
glances out of the corner of his eye. "I don't know what he was
like later in life, but when we were at school he was the worst
sort of bully. His speciality was hitting with his hands—or
rather, his fists."

"And why are you only telling us this now?" said Tuvesson.

"I wasn't one of his victims. I did what everyone else did; I
looked away and tried to pretend nothing was happening. I had

almost forgotten that it happened—it only came back to me last night that he used to beat someone up in this very shower room." He drew an arrow toward one of the images, which showed the sawed-off hands on the tile floor.

"Who did he assault?" asked Tuvesson.

"Claes Mällvik." He circled Claes on the enlarged class picture. The others came up to have a look.

"The only kid with glasses," said Lilja.

"I suppose that's all it takes," said Klippan, moving to take the last pear from the fruit bowl.

"So you're suggesting that his murder could be an act of revenge?" said Tuvesson. Fabian nodded.

"Would he attack just anyone back then?" asked Lilja.

"At first they picked on several kids, but in the end they settled for Mällvik."

"They? It wasn't just Jörgen Pålsson?" said Tuvesson.

"No. It was Glenn Granqvist, too." Fabian circled Glenn in the class picture. "They were thick as thieves, and Glenn always did exactly what Jörgen told him to."

"Did he have a speciality as well?" Molander asked.

"Kicking."

"So if your theory is correct, he's in danger too."

Fabian nodded. "I was hoping that the Peugeot in Denmark belonged to Mällvik."

"But it doesn't," said Molander.

"No, the registered owner is a Rune Schmeckel. As far as I know, there was no Schmeckel in our class."

"We'll have to look at that as another clue moving forward," said Tuvesson, draining the last few drops of coffee from her mug. "Irene, find out all you can about Mällvik and Schmeckel. Klippan, how's it going with the rest of the class?"

"So-so, to be completely honest. The whole country is off soaking up rays over the holidays, so we haven't even been able to get hold of an official class list."

"Fabian must have one..." said Tuvesson.

"Unfortunately, all I've found is my yearbook from ninth grade. I can check with Lina Pålsson to see if she has one."

Klippan laughed and grasped Fabian's shoulder. "I imagine you can, but I've already taken care of it."

"What did she say?"

"She doesn't have one. But at least I got a few names and numbers, most of which seem to be from the Cretaceous Era."

"She didn't give you any other information?"

"No...Like what?"

"I was just wondering if she'd thought of something else since I talked to her," said Fabian, realizing that he was about to paint his way into a corner. "The school must have a class list, I presume?"

"You would think," said Klippan. "But according to the secretary, their records don't go back further than 1988—at least when it comes to class lists and that sort of thing."

"Why 1988?" asked Lilja.

"They installed their computer system that year. Prior to 1988, class lists were stored as mimeographs in a physical file."

"And those no longer exist, of course."

"They do actually. The papers were sent to the city archive long ago."

"Have you been to the archive?" Tuvesson asked.

"No, but it's on my list."

"Good," said Tuvesson, turning to Fabian. "And I want to see you in my office in five minutes."

TUVESSON'S OFFICE LOOKED NOTHING like how Fabian had imagined it. After his ride in her smoke-impregnated car he'd expected anything but this sparsely furnished room with a large, neat desk right in the centre, a set of leather furniture in one corner, and a few framed posters from the Lund Konsthall's collections on the white walls.

He scanned the row of spines on one of the bookshelves. Besides a multitude of reference books, there was a solid collection of crime novels—everything from Josephine Tey's *The Daughter of Time* to Graham Greene's *The Third Man*.

He walked over to the window to check out the view. On the other side of the highway he could see the *Helsingborgs Dagblad* building, and a few kilometres past that was Fredriksdal School. He tried to figure out which of all the red-brick structures it was, but it was too distant and was hidden by closer buildings. Fabian looked at the clock on the wall. Tuvesson was one and a half minutes late, and he wondered if this was on purpose. Another thirty seconds went by before she arrived with two freshly purchased lattes, which she placed on the desk.

She smelled like smoke and Fabian wondered if his excursion to Denmark was to blame for her seemingly increased dependence on nicotine.

"Have you tried the coffee here yet?"

"Unfortunately I have," said Fabian, sitting down in the visitor's chair.

"That machine cost a small fortune. It must have thirty different buttons, displays, and God knows what else. The only thing it doesn't have is good coffee. For that, you have to go to Café Bar Skåne on Bergavägen."

Fabian tasted the beverage and could only agree that it was very close to the perfect latte, not too warm or too milky.

"Fabian, what didn't you understand in the meeting yesterday?" Her smile had vanished.

"I'm sorry? I don't know if I—"

"What part of *teamwork* did I make unclear?"

"Nothing."

"Apparently it was something, since you still don't seem to have grasped it." She went silent and left him time to respond, but he didn't know what to say. "I appreciate that you were thrown right into this case without any real introduction to the

81

way I want us to work. I can also grasp the fact that we hardly know each other, which can excuse quite a bit. But I had hoped, or rather I had *expected*, that you would take the opportunity to explain everything that you knew about this case in the meeting today. But you didn't. Even when we spoke on the phone last night, you said you were on your way home, but you weren't, were you?"

How does she know? Fabian thought.

"You went back to the petrol station. Why?"

"I found more reason to believe that the car is linked to the perpetrator, and I wanted to make sure that he couldn't move it from the station."

"How did you do that?"

"I removed one of the back tyres and handed it over to the store."

It seemed to take Tuvesson a while to figure out what he had just told her. "You're telling me that you took off the tyre and gave it to the petrol station attendant?"

"Yes. She promised to give me a call if anyone comes looking for it."

It looked like Tuvesson was having a hard time deciding how to react. They were at a crossroads. No matter which path she chose, it would end up affecting their working relationship in the future. "Okay. Let's hope he leaves the car alone until the Danes get their thumbs out of their arses."

"Have you been in contact with them yet?"

Tuvesson nodded. "Before I forget, here's your access card." She pushed the plastic card across the table to Fabian. "The code is 5618. Okay?"

Fabian nodded, took the card, and left the room.

"DID YOU GET A SMACKDOWN?"

Fabian stopped and stuck his head around the door of Irene Lilja's office. "A little."

"I'm sure you deserved it. I actually don't like female bosses, but just so you know—this one, she's good. If I had been in her shoes I wouldn't have let you get anywhere near this investigation."

"But fortunately you're not."

"Nope, I'm not," she said. "Come in, I have a present for you."

Fabian walked into her office, which was the exact opposite of Tuvesson's. The small room was filled with teetering piles of stuff so high he found himself wondering if they had been glued together so they wouldn't fall over. The window was covered in an orangey-yellow Indian fabric that had gold elephants and small mirrors stitched on it. An unrolled sleeping bag lay on a mat in the corner. One wall looked like a giant bulletin board, full of taped-up pictures and notes that were connected by strange symbols and arrows running in different directions. Lilja sat right in the middle of the room at an undersized desk.

"Why wouldn't you want me working on the case?" said Fabian.

Lilja gave a laugh.

"Isn't it obvious? Tuvesson is letting you work because she thinks you're sitting on valuable information. But there's nothing that makes you any less of a suspect than the others in the class—besides Mällvik, who is your theory."

"You're absolutely right," said Fabian as he searched for something to fix his eyes on. "You said something about a present?" Lilja lit up and clicked her mouse. A printer quickly started humming.

"There." She nodded at the printer, which was hidden among books and binders.

Fabian pulled out the paper as carefully as he could to avoid toppling the piles. He glanced through the document. "Glenn Granqvist?"

"Jörgen Pålsson's right-hand man, if you're to be believed.

There are only three people with that name: one lives in Älvsbyn and one in Örebro, so I threw all my eggs into the third basket, in Ödåkra. He doesn't seem to be God's most gifted creation. Last time he did homework was in the ninth grade; he plodded his way through compulsory military service and will soon be celebrating his twenty-five-year anniversary as a truck driver at a construction supply warehouse in Åstorp."

"Why am I not surprised in the least?" said Fabian, making a move to leave. "I'll see if I can get hold of him. Maybe you and I can have lunch later?"

"Yeah, maybe."

"If you can find anything like that on Rune Schmeckel, I'll even consider paying."

Lilja flashed him a smile and Fabian knew exactly what she was thinking.

"It's okay," he said. "You can still keep suspecting that it's me."

FABIAN SAT DOWN IN Hugo Elvin's fancy futuristic chair, which he had firmly decided was truly comfortable, and started dialling Glenn's number.

"I see you've made yourself at home."

Fabian spun around to see Molander standing in his temporary office.

"I wanted to invite you and your family over for a barbecue tonight."

"Today?"

"I understand it's short notice, but if you don't have plans I think it will be fun. Everyone else is coming. It's a beautiful Friday with not a cloud in the sky..."

"That sounds really nice. Let me just check with my wife."

"Sure. No problem. Hope to see you later," Molander said, and went on his way. Fabian wondered if he was being paranoid or if he was actually a potential suspect in Molander's eyes too. Was that the real reason for the invitation? Regardless of

Molander's intentions, he had to go to the barbecue.

Five minutes later, Molander came back with a full cup of coffee. "Well? Have you got the go-ahead from the missus yet?"

"No, but you can count me in."

"Great," he said, about to leave.

"Hey, listen ... What's Hugo Elvin like? The guy whose office I'm using."

"Hugo ..." Molander chuckled, "... is impossible to describe. You have to experience him in person, but if I were in your position, I wouldn't mess with his stuff too much, especially the settings on the chair. Elvin isn't the type you want to provoke if you don't have to. Anyway, see you tonight." With that, he disappeared.

Fabian lowered his eyes to all the knobs he had already twisted on the chair, realizing it was too late for him. He would have to deal with Hugo's wrath when Elvin came back to the office.

He picked up the phone again to call Glenn. Six rings later, he heard Robert De Niro's voice in the receiver.

"You talking to me?"

13

HE HAD THOROUGHLY ENJOYED every second of his four-hour sleep on the blanket before his alarm woke him. He had slept deeply, more deeply than he had intended, which meant he was relaxed and felt safe. Maybe too safe, he realized just a few minutes later as he packed up his things. He'd had a visitor.

The packaging of his apple pie was torn to pieces, and all but a few crumbs were gone and had been replaced by rat droppings. They'd been hungrier than he'd expected. Once more, luck had been on his side, and he had to remind himself that luck was not something he could count on.

He left the warehouse through the window and walked over to the car, which was hidden behind some bushes on the other side of the road. There was not a living soul in sight. It was just him and the morning. He pulled off his boots and removed his dark work clothes in the peace and quiet. He washed up with some water from the can in the boot, and changed into a pair of beige shorts with large side pockets, a light-blue polo shirt, a yellow cap from Bubba Gump Shrimp Co., and a pair of green Crocs.

He felt like a clown in his new clothes, but the point was to look like a typical Swede on his way to Denmark to drink beer. In his backpack he put an extra pink shirt, a bottle of water, a pair of gloves, a camera, a rope, the keys to the Peugeot, a torch, a utility knife, and a syringe full of Propofol. The last item was just a security measure and would likely not be used.

He made good time to Knutpunkten, Helsingborg's central station. On his journey across the Sound he indulged in a beer and a large shrimp sandwich with far too much mayonnaise. It was too much food, but it would be a long while before he had time to eat again. He took the 10:55 train from Helsingør and it arrived in Copenhagen at 11:41. The bathroom at the station was so disgusting that he nearly missed the S-train to Ringsted. He arrived at Ringsted Station thirty-four minutes later and made his way to the bus stop on foot.

The sun had kicked things up a notch, forcing the temperature all the way to thirty-five degrees; he was grateful for his light clothing. He was surprised to find the Crocs so comfortable. At 13:00 he climbed on board the bus and sat as close to the front as he could. He didn't like sitting at the back, especially when it was so warm and the bus was full of sweaty passengers.

At 13:28 he got off the bus outside Lellinge School, and was finally able to take a few deep breaths without smelling the stench of collective sweat. The petrol station where he'd parked the car a week and a half ago was less than 300 metres from the school, and it wouldn't take more than two minutes to walk there. But he chose to take a detour through a number of little streets, making a wide circle around the station to be certain that there were no police staked out nearby.

At first he felt relieved, but his anxiety set in a few minutes later. Why hadn't he run into a single person yet? Why did the whole neighbourhood seem unnaturally deserted? Had he missed something?

He wasn't able to put the pieces together until he passed a house with open windows and heard the sound of a TV inside. Unlike Sweden, Denmark had made it to the World Cup and were playing a game in South Africa today. In other words, this was an ideal time to retrieve his car. He walked by a yard full of garden gnomes and took out his camera in the shelter of a few trees. He zoomed in on the petrol station 50 metres away. He couldn't see anyone, and the Peugeot was just where he'd left it. The only change was a note under the wiper, which didn't seem odd.

He put away his camera and walked briskly toward the car. His pulse increased with each step, but he knew it would slow down again as soon as he turned the key in the ignition and was on his way out of there. His body was pumping out adrenaline and he was very focused.

But the closer he came to the car, the more strongly he felt that something wasn't quite right. The Peugeot was tilted strangely, as if it were about to tip forward. He couldn't figure out why until he reached the car and grabbed the note.

THIS VEHICLE IS ON PRIVATE PROPERTY
PLEASE CONTACT PERSONNEL

14

IRENE LILJA SUGGESTED THAT they meet down at Olsons Skafferi for lunch just after one o'clock. Fabian knew the place and had been there several times before moving to Stockholm. It had been a new, hip restaurant back then, but now it was an old classic.

On the way there, he called Sonja, who was eating lunch with Matilda at the Louisiana Museum's outdoor café, where the view alone was apparently worth the whole trip. He told her about the invitation to the barbecue at Molander's and, to his surprise, she thought it sounded like a good idea. She believed it was important that they get to know some new people. If he had some nice colleagues, why not start there?

Fabian thought she was being sarcastic at first. Sonja had never been particularly interested in meeting his friends, much less his colleagues. But maybe she was doing just as they'd agreed—giving their new life a fair chance. They decided to meet at home around five. He said he would pick up some wine.

He found an empty parking spot on Hästmöllegränden across from Systembolaget, where he scanned the shelves for a creative wine. He usually ended up with a few different Riojas, chosen at random from the more expensive shelves.

Up until a few years ago, his ignorance about wine had chafed like a stiff laundry tag against his neck. As soon as the wine list came around to him he would be struck by panic at the thought of making a decision. He tried to remedy his ignorance by joining a wine-tasting club, but after just a few meetings, during which he'd tried to muster up enthusiasm for gurgling wine and discussing vintages and varieties of grapes, he'd accepted that his knowledge would never be anything to brag about.

He stepped into Olsons and saw that Lilja was already waiting for him at the window table in the corner.

"What do you say to Skåne roe deer with chanterelles sautéed in butter, puréed parsnips, potato blinis, and veal gravy flavoured with lingonberries?"

Fabian nodded and sat down.

"Good, because I already ordered it for us both—it was the most expensive item on the menu," she continued, placing a file on the table.

"Schmeckel?"

Lilja nodded.

"And?"

"So far I've only looked online, but he's definitely of interest and he seems to have a number of skeletons in his closet. He was born in 1966, just like you. He's single, no kids, and he works at the hospital in Lund as—and this is where it gets interesting—a surgeon."

"A surgeon? Any particular speciality?"

Lilja nodded and took a bite of bread. "He started working at Lund Hospital in 1997, and quickly became one of the best surgeons in the country for prostate cancer operations. But in 2004 there was an incident and he was barred from working for twelve months."

"What kind of incident?"

"He left two plastic surgical clips inside a patient."

"He left them inside the…"

Lilja nodded, sipping her mineral water. "In the bladder. The patient, Torgny Sölmedal, had to pee them out and apparently said it was one of the worst things that ever happened to him. Ironic, given Rune's last name, isn't it?"

"Did it end there?"

"No. They opened a huge investigation, as I understand it, and made a pretty big deal out of the whole thing. In any case, it turned out Rune was suffering from sleep deprivation and downing as many pills as Michael Jackson just to manage his job, but it clearly didn't help. The hospital administration supported him throughout the entire ordeal and he was back with knife in hand one year later, but these days he mostly does hernias and appendixes."

"Any other incidents?"

"Not that I could find."

"What do you have on his childhood?"

"More or less nothing, which is why I think it's fishy. Everything after 1994 seems more or less typical: his education, work history, various home addresses, phone numbers, the cars he's owned, and so on. He runs the spring marathon in Helsingborg every year, for example."

"Since when?"

"Records show since 1994. But that's the thing—there's almost nothing on him before 1994. The only information I managed to find about his childhood was on Wikipedia of all places: *Rune Schmeckel grew up in Malmö, where he graduated from the natural sciences programme at secondary school with top grades. After that he did his compulsory military service as a non-commissioned officer in Kristianstad.* That's his entire early-life biography. Other than those two sentences, it's like he didn't even exist before 1994."

"So you don't believe that information?"

"Well, for one thing, I checked the records and he never did military service in Kristianstad. It seems he made up a few things to make himself sound good."

"Why would someone do that?"

Her face lit up and she leaned toward him. "To hide the fact that there isn't anything there."

Lilja's theory had something to it. The Internet had been in its infancy in the 1990s, but for the most part enough information

91

could be found to form a picture of the person in question. Holes had a tendency to fill themselves, but apparently not when it came to Rune Schmeckel.

"Did you find any pictures of him?"

"On the third page of the document." Lilja held the file out to Fabian, who felt something spark inside him when he looked at the picture of Rune Schmeckel. He had never seen this man before, yet there was no doubt there was something familiar about him. He tried to figure out what it was, but gave up once their food arrived.

A few minutes later, Lilja broke the silence. "Did you and your family move to Helsingborg for a change or were you running away from Stockholm?"

Fabian had to finish chewing the bite of Skåne roe deer he had just put in his mouth before he could respond. "I don't understand. What do you mean?"

"You and your wife."

"Sonja. Her name is Sonja."

"Are things okay between you and Sonja? Or are you like most couples?"

Fabian had no doubt about the answer to that question, but it was hard to figure out what to tell her.

"Sorry, I didn't mean to touch a raw nerve."

"No, it's okay, you just took me by surprise. We moved to Helsingborg for a change, but like most people, Sonja and I have our ups and downs. What about you? How long have you been living in your office?"

"Since last week. It's been completely nuts. He refuses to move out, even though it's actually my apartment."

"Maybe he's hoping you'll come back."

Lilja snorted. "He can forget about that. You have no idea what a fucking arsehole he is. It's *over* this time, dammit, even if I have to sleep in my office for the rest of the summer." She resumed eating in silence and then looked at him across the table. "Wasn't it your colleagues who were involved in the incident at the Israeli embassy last winter?"

Fabian had been waiting for this question. He nodded mutely.

"What *happened*?"

"You tell me. I really don't have any idea."

"I suppose it's still under investigation, but isn't it weird how little the newspapers have reported on it? I mean, two police officers died. Don't you think that's odd?"

"I don't know," Fabian said, shrugging. "By the way, I tried to get hold of Glenn Granqvist—"

"Doesn't it almost feel like the whole thing has been covered up?"

"Like I said, I have no idea."

"Sorry. What do I know? Maybe you're not even allowed to talk about it. Forget it...Coffee?"

Fabian nodded and Lilja left to go to the counter. He could certainly understand why she was curious. He probably would have been wondering about the very same questions if he were in her position, only he wouldn't have voiced them. But Lilja wanted answers, and she wasn't above asking for them. She was on him like a furious wasp—and he liked her.

"You were trying to get hold of Granqvist." Lilja set down two cups of coffee.

"I called but he didn't answer his phone, so I was planning to stop by his house."

"I was planning on contacting the national registration office to see what they have on Schmeckel," Lilja said, downing her coffee in a single gulp.

"We should take a look at Schmeckel's house as soon as possible."

"Agreed. Tuvesson has promised to do what she can, but holiday season is throwing a wrench into the investigation. Worse comes to worst, it might not be possible until late next week."

"Let's hope we can get in there earlier."

"What do you mean, *hope*?" Lilja said, standing up.

A POLICE OFFICER DOESN'T hope. A police officer takes action and works methodically until the perpetrator is caught, making sure there is enough evidence for a conviction. Going around full of hope is the job of family members, not the police. Yet here he was, having just expressed himself as having *hope*. He pondered Lilja's question, started the car, and pulled out onto Drottninggatan.

Had he already given up, thinking that the battle was lost? Did he feel absolutely powerless to change the outcome, believing the only ace he had left was the small hope that everything would probably work out in the end, as if this were a Sunday-night movie? In truth, he had no idea how this would end. All he knew for sure was that for the first time in a long while, something about this case frightened him. He was scared this was far from over and scared of what the consequences would be if he failed again.

Fabian hit the accelerator to make the very best of the wave of green lights that had followed him all the way from Hälsobacken. He passed police headquarters going 145 kilometres per hour. Tuvesson called as he was driving through Väla.

"I just spoke to Sten Hammar regarding a search warrant for Schmeckel's house."

"And?"

"Unfortunately, he does not consider there to be sufficient grounds. I'm not surprised. All we have is a car that crossed the Øresund Bridge at the same time as our victim and is now parked at a petrol station in Denmark, which is not enough. We need something more concrete."

Tuvesson was right. The problem was that something more concrete would likely not be found in Schmeckel's house.

He put Radiohead's *Hail to the Thief* into the CD player and turned up the volume. He turned off at Ödåkra as the last few bars of "2 + 2 = 5" petered out. Soon, he was slowing down on Jupitergäten outside Glenn Granqvist's house. He stepped out of the car and scanned the area with his eyes. The neighbourhood seemed as deserted as it might be after a nuclear accident.

Granqvist's house looked just like the others on the block: two storeys, a white plaster façade, a pitched roof, and a separate garage. The house sat at the very front of the lot.

Fabian walked up to the front door and noticed that the outdoor lights were on, even though the sun was still high in the sky. The same went for the ceiling light in the living room. Was this a sign that he had come too late? Had Glenn already received his punishment? Or would the whole bully idea turn out to be a dead end?

He rang the bell, holding down the button for a long time. He looked at his watch and followed the second hand with his eyes. He decided to wait for sixty seconds.

Although he hoped that Glenn would come to the door and prove himself perfectly healthy, he couldn't ignore the little part of him that was crossing his fingers for the opposite result, because then all his doubt about the motive would vanish.

The door remained closed.

He rang the bell again, and held it for even longer this time.

A woman walked by with a pushchair, casting a look of suspicion. He responded with a smile.

"Hi! Listen, the guy who lives here, Glenn Granqvist... You don't happen to know if he's home, do you?"

The woman shook her head.

"The lights are on. I don't suppose you've seen him here in the past few days?"

She shook her head again and hurried on.

"Well, fine then." He took out his phone and dialled Glenn's home number, which he had found in Lilja's notes. He could hear it ringing as clear as day from inside the house.

"You talking to me?"

This time, Fabian left a message introducing himself and asking Glenn to give him a call as soon as possible. Then he called Glenn's mobile phone and left the very same message as he walked around to the back of the house.

The yard consisted of a large lawn surrounded by a hedge that hadn't yet grown taller than a metre. An open field began where the hedge ended, perfect for anyone who wanted to pay a surprise visit. But that wasn't what caught his attention—it was the barbed wire.

Fabian didn't understand. Why in the world would anyone lay barbed wire all over his backyard? He crouched down and cautiously touched the sharp wire, which twisted here and there across the lawn in long spirals. He heard a distant clucking noise and turned around, but wasn't able to locate the source of the sound before it stopped. He grabbed the barbed wire between his index finger and thumb and yanked at it. Once more he heard the clucking—this time loud enough for him to figure out that it was coming from one of the slightly open windows on the second floor. He stood up, taking a few steps toward the house so that he could get a better look, and walked straight into a piece of fishing line that was strung between the barbed wire and what turned out to be a wind chime made of bamboo, hanging inside the window.

So Glenn had come to the same conclusion as Fabian: now that Jörgen had been taken care of, it was his turn next. But Glenn clearly had no intention of being as ill prepared. Was Glenn's paranoia justified? And if so, was he able to defend himself?

Fabian was jolted out of his thoughts by his ringing phone. He took it out and looked at the screen: *0765-261110*. He repeated the number to himself before realizing that it was the very same number he had just called.

"This is Fabian Risk." He tried to sound as composed and neutral as he could, but there was no response on the other end.

Instead, there was an expectant silence. He could only just hear the sound of someone breathing.

"Hello? Who is this?"

"You were trying to reach me."

"Is this Glenn Granqvist?"

"Yes."

"I don't know if you remember me, but we were in the same class at school."

"Fabbe? Is that you?"

"Yes, that's right. How are you?"

"I can't complain. How about you? I heard you became a cop and moved to Stockholm."

"Yeah, I did. But I've actually moved back home now and I'm working for the police here in Helsingborg."

"Well, how about that! Guess I better behave myself."

Fabian laughed and decided to guide the conversation toward the topic at hand. "I assume you know why I was trying to get hold of you."

"Jögge."

"Right."

"It's just awful. I read about it in the paper and...damn. Do you have any idea who's behind it?"

"We're working on...a number of parallel leads." Fabian had been about to answer more fully, but he'd stopped himself. He couldn't put his finger on what it was, but for some reason he felt uncertain and on guard.

"Am I one of them or something?"

"In a manner of speaking. You were best friends after all, at least as far as I can recall from school. Were you two still in contact?"

"Jögge was my very best friend."

"I'm sorry, you must feel terrible. But I was thinking, could we meet? I have a number of questions you might be able to help me out with."

"Of course we can meet, but now is not a good time. Not unless you want to come down here."

"And where is *down here*?"

"Sunny Beach, Bulgaria. It's pretty fucking sweet. I've never seen so many horny chicks on one beach."

This damn holiday season was making it impossible to work. He might as well take a holiday himself, as planned, and hold off on solving the case until August 16, when most people would be back at work. On the other hand, maybe this trip to Sunny Beach was what had saved Glenn's life.

"When did you leave?"

"Just yesterday—July first. I'm staying for two weeks, until the fifteenth."

They had only gone to the newspapers with the murder yesterday. If Glenn read about it down there, as he'd claimed, he wouldn't have had enough time to string barbed wire all over his lawn.

"When did you first hear about the murder?"

"Lina called to tell me about it a couple days ago. Why?"

"Did you feel threatened when you heard about the murder? Was that why you left?"

"Why would I feel threatened?"

Either Glenn was lying or Fabian was speaking to someone else on the phone, he decided. "I thought the nature of the murder and the choice of location might make you feel a bit nervous." He had revealed more than he should have, but he couldn't help it. He wanted to provoke a reaction, to force whoever it was on the other end of the line to show his true colours.

"Excuse my French, but what the fuck are you talking about?"

Fabian decided to put the screws on.

"Why else would you have laid out barbed wire behind your house and connected it to the wind chime on the second floor?"

There was an uncertain silence, long enough for all of Fabian's doubts to scatter. The call ended.

98

October 18

I didn't listen to what the teacher said today, just saw her mouth moving. Jonas sits behind me and he tapped me on the shoulder. At first I wasn't going to turn around and I wanted to pretend that nothing was going on, but then I did anyway because I know he's usually one of the nice ones. He spat in my face and said it was from "you know who." I could see in his eyes he didn't really want to do it. I would have done the same thing if I were him.

Today Mum asked why I had bruises. I said I fell down in gym. I think she believed me.

But they did it again today at recess. They said I told on them even though I didn't. I got a bloody nose, then they took my hat and peed on it and made me put it on again. When I got home I showered and washed my hat and dried it with Mum's hair dryer. I don't think she noticed. At least I hope she didn't.

I should fight back but I'm scared. There are two of them and one of me. Plus they hit with their fists even though it's not allowed. It works in the movies, but not when it's for real.

About me:

1. A wuss.
2. Useless.
3. Weak.
4. Ugly.

P. S. If I were in my own class I would tease me, too. I'm the lowest of the low. I'm a fucking monster. I hate myself so goddamn much.

15

FABIAN WAS SUPPOSED TO have run home to pick up Sonja and the kids to go to Molander's barbecue more than half an hour ago. But he couldn't go home yet; there was no time to lose. He called Tuvesson and left her a short message about his conversation with the killer. She was probably busy fighting the Danes so they could go and pick up the Peugeot from the petrol station. There was no way for her to know that the information he now had would make her job much easier.

As Fabian waited for Tuvesson to return his call, he entered Glenn's house through the back door and searched it, but didn't find anything of interest.

Even though he didn't find any leads in the house, Fabian was absolutely certain that the motive he had suggested earlier concerning Claes was accurate. Glenn Granqvist wasn't on a sunny beach in Bulgaria; Glenn Granqvist was dead. Fabian was equally certain that the man he had spoken with was the perpetrator. Both he and Fabian had played their roles well, even if there could be no doubt that both had understood exactly what was really going on.

Fabian parked outside the police station and hurried in. The lobby was empty and he had to use his access card for the first time. He was surprised to find he remembered the code, and he used the time in the lift to call home.

"Hi, Dad. Mum says you should have been here more than half an hour ago."

"Yes, doll, Mum's absolutely right." He stepped out of the elevator. "A few things have come up at work and Dad has to take care of them."

"That's exactly what she said, too. And when the phone rang, she said it was you calling and that we probably wouldn't be going to any barbecue tonight."

"Did she? How could she know all of that?"

"I don't know. But you and that lady who isn't allowed to call are the only ones who have our new number. If you really wanted to talk to Mum, you would have called her mobile. By calling home, you hoped that me or Theo would answer instead."

She would make a good police officer, Fabian thought, and he asked his daughter to report that the barbecue would surely be cancelled, since Molander would also be tied up with things to do all night at the police station.

Fabian walked into the department offices, which were also empty. Where was everyone? He understood it was Friday, but they were in the midst of an investigation that might very well develop into one of the Helsingborg police's worst cases ever. He opened the door to Tuvesson's office, which was just as empty and desolate as the rest of the department. He walked over to the panorama window and took out his phone to call her again. Instead, it started ringing in his hand. It was Molander.

"Hello there. Where are you?"

"Huh? I'm at the station."

"What the hell are you doing there?"

"A number of things have come to light in the investigation, so I think we're going to have to cancel tonight and—"

"What do you mean, *cancel*? The barbecue is lit. There's no sign of a cancellation on our end," said Molander, without even a shred of interest in what might have come up.

"I'm sorry, Ingvar, but I'm afraid I have to work. We'll have to come over another time. By the way, do you happen to know where Tuvesson is?"

"Here. Where else would she be?"

Fabian pulled the phone away from his ear, and started at it as if it had come from another planet.

"WELL, HELLO AND WELCOME! You must be the new people," exclaimed a woman who seemed mighty proud of her extreme tan. "You're the only ones we're still waiting for. My name is Gertrud Molander. Come in! What would you like to drink?"

Sonja and the children followed Gertrud into the house and Fabian felt an immediate sense of relief. The car ride had only taken fifteen minutes, but it had been painfully silent, almost unbearably so. He'd asked about the Louisiana Museum and whether it was as beautiful as everyone claimed, and if they would like to visit again.

Sonja hadn't bothered to answer a single one of his questions. But now they were here, and he could tell already that she was in a better mood. Apparently someone like Gertrud was just what she needed.

As they walked through the house, Fabian observed that Ingvar Molander was married to a true collector. One of the largest plate collections he'd ever seen hung on one wall of the living room, and a lighted display cabinet contained crystal owls of all imaginable shapes, sizes, and colours.

"Aren't they beautiful?" Gertrud exclaimed, moving toward him.

Fabian nodded, although he had never understood the fascination with crystal decorations. "Are you the one who collects them?"

"No, but I started buying them when I was on my first trip around Europe."

"So they're Ingvar's?"

"Ingvar? You think he could stand collecting crystal?" she said, as if this were the most ridiculous thing she had ever heard. "To be completely honest there isn't one person behind it, but

102

most of my friends have contributed to it. Now and then a new little owl just shows up."

"People buy them and put them there without telling you?"

"Don't ask me. Come on, you need a drink."

Gertrud showed him out to the backyard. It looked just as Fabian had expected when he'd toured the inside of the house. The lawn was so meticulously mowed that it looked like a computer-generated image: there were garden gnomes, little windmills, and fountains in the background. There was even a little pond with a bridge across it. Matilda thought it was sheer paradise and ran around the yard as if she wanted to be everywhere all at once.

"Dad! The pond is full of fish! Come look!"

"I can't right now! Do you mind showing Theodor instead?" he called back, receiving a tired glance from Theodor, who was apparently capable of taking his eyes away from his phone for once.

Everyone from the police station was there, even Florian Nilsson, the receptionist, who had dressed up in a red shirt that buttoned up the side in honour of the evening. It made Fabian think of Midge Ure and how long it had been since he'd listened to "After a Fashion."

Molander was standing at the grill, looking as if his duty was a matter of life and death.

"Fabian, there you are! Come over here and say hi," Irene Lilja called. She was standing next to a muscular man with close-cropped hair, worn jeans, and a pink shirt. His lip bulged with a large packet of *snus*. Fabian walked over to say hello.

"We were starting to wonder what had happened to you," said Lilja. "Hampan, meet Fabian, my new colleague."

"Are you a police officer too?" Fabian asked, shaking hands with the man.

"No, I'm a boyfriend," the man replied, with a smile so broad that it revealed more than half of his *snus* packet.

"Oh. I see." Fabian gave Lilja a look but received no help whatsoever.

"So keep your hands off her, otherwise you'll get a taste of this," Hampan continued, flexing one of his biceps.

"Wow," Fabian said with a chuckle, but he could hear how hollow it sounded. "Maybe I'll go find something to drink." He walked over to the serving table, opened a beer, and wondered whether one would really suffice. Sonja already appeared to be on her second glass of red wine, and was in the midst of discussing her own art with Gertrud. Fabian took the opportunity to walk over to Tuvesson and Klippan, each of whom had a gin and tonic in hand, to explain the call from the person he believed to be the killer.

"And what makes you think that?" Klippan asked.

"He called from Glenn Granqvist's cell phone, and I'm convinced Glenn is dead."

"You mean he's been murdered?" said Tuvesson, as she took a fair-sized gulp of her drink.

Fabian nodded. "His yard was full of barbed wire and alarms, as if he'd prepared for our guy to come after him, which is exactly what I think happened."

"My God. What did he say when he called?" Tuvesson asked.

"I was the one who called him, and then he called me back."

"From Glenn's cell phone?" Klippan said.

Fabian nodded.

"He claimed he was in Sunny Beach in Bulgaria on vacation, and that he'd left yesterday—the same day the papers broke the story of Jörgen Pålsson's murder."

"It seems pretty pointless to put energy into laying out a bunch of barbed wire and then taking off for Bulgaria," said Klippan.

"We'll have to contact the airlines to confirm your theory that Glenn didn't leave the country," said Tuvesson.

"I can deal with that first thing tomorrow," said Klippan.

"Shouldn't we give the house a thorough look?" said Fabian.

"Absolutely," said Tuvesson, draining her glass. "I just have to contact Högsell and get permission first."

"Anyone besides me want a refill?" Klippan asked, holding up his empty glass.

"I wouldn't say no to another splash," Tuvesson replied, and they walked off together.

Fabian didn't know whether he should laugh or cry. Here they were, in the midst of a case with any number of leads to follow, yet barbecued meat and alcohol were the top priority.

"Just standing here alone, philosophizing," Lilja remarked as she handed him an open beer. "Come here, I want to show you something."

"I don't know if I should."

"Don't mind Hampan. He's just kidding around. Plus, he never gets too far away from the grill."

"At any rate, I take it you two found your way back to each other at some point in the last few hours."

"You would be reading too much into it. Don't ask me why, but for some reason Molander invited Hampan. He was already here when I arrived. But let's forget about that for now," she said, pulling Fabian into the house and down to the cellar. "If I didn't know Molander, this would totally freak me out." She turned on the ceiling lights and Fabian quickly realized what she was talking about.

They were in a room packed with shelves, display cases, and glass counters that were filled with various objects categorized in different groups, like a museum collection. Fabian was reminded of a place on Gotland island where someone had turned his own hoarded belongings into a museum. Molander's collection was more lavish and charming, though not as sprawling as the one on Gotland, which was made up of everything from magic wands to typewriters. Down here there was only one overarching theme: murder. He did have quite a few subcategories, such as hunting and fishing, poisonous substances, and various weapons—everything from firearms to knives and perfectly common tools.

After a closer look, Fabian changed his mind and elevated "Fishing" to a main category alongside "Murder." Almost half the collection consisted of fishing-related objects: trolling spoons and rods, different types of nets, and lots of mounted fish. There was even a display case featuring a collection of dried-up flies pinned onto a cushion in rows.

"He certainly has an eye for detail," said Fabian, studying a collection of scalpels.

"It probably explains why he's one of the best forensic investigators." Lilja pulled out a drawer lined with red velvet that was meant to display jewellery. It contained a collection of bullets, each marked with a number. "Each of these has killed a person." She pulled out another drawer of bullets. "These ones have only injured people."

Fabian looked at all the rows of deformed bullets. He counted thirty-eight extinguished lives in the first drawer, and an unknowable number of people left behind to deal with their sorrow.

"Aren't you going to ask if I've learned anything about Claes Mällvik?"

"Have you? I didn't know if I should wait until Monday. Everyone here seems to be on vacation."

Lilja gave him a snide smile, which was interrupted by her phone.

"Yes? What is it? I'm just with Fabian, showing him Molander's collection...Just come down here if you don't believe me." She ended the call and rolled her eyes. "Sorry, where were we?"

"Mällvik."

"Right. After compulsory school he did a four-year technical degree at Tycho Brahe School, where he got top grades. After that he studied medicine at Lund University, and in 1990 he started working as a general practitioner here in Helsingborg."

"Isn't Rune Schmeckel a doctor too?"

"Yes, but at a much higher level. Rune is a surgeon, one of the best in the country in his speciality. In any case, something happened in 1993. Claes went to the emergency room here in Helsingborg, and listen to this…" Lilja took a folded piece of paper from her jeans pocket, unfolded it, and read: *"Fractured mandible, serious head injuries from blunt force trauma — likely from being kicked. Five fractured ribs, internal bleeding,* and the list goes on. Look at this." She handed him a photograph that showed a beaten, swollen face that had been so gravely abused that it hurt to look at it.

"So someone assaulted him."

"I would probably label this as attempted murder. He underwent thirty-six operations. It's a minor miracle that he survived at all."

"Is there anything about where the injuries came from?"

"The doctors asked, but he refused to tell them."

"And then what?"

"Nothing."

"What do you mean, *nothing?*"

"The hospitalization and subsequent operations were the last things I could find out about him. I can certainly dig deeper to try and uncover more, but for now this is it."

"Could he have died?"

Lilja shrugged. "Maybe. Or left the country."

FABIAN SANK HIS TEETH into his meat, realizing how hungry he was.

"These cutlets are just about the best thing I've ever eaten," Sonja said, prompting agreement from the other guests.

"Thanks, Sonja," said Molander. "But just so you know, they're not cutlets."

107

"They're not?"

"No, this a butt roast."

"Ingvar, don't start with that again," said Gertrud.

"But it *is* a butt roast. Why not call it by its proper name?"

"Because it doesn't sound as appetizing." Gertrud turned to Sonja. "Don't pay any attention to him. His marinade is the secret to why it tastes so good. No one can make one like Ingvar. I think he should write a cookbook full of nothing but marinades!" She raised her glass. "Cheers, and thank you all for coming."

They toasted and proceeded with dinner. The more they drank, the more pleasant it was, and their discussions moved from one extreme to the next. One moment they were debating how much Michael Jackson's doctor could be blamed for the star's sudden death, only to then discuss the finals of the World Cup, which Sweden wasn't even playing in.

"It's such a relief!" Klippan exclaimed, noting this was the first time in a while that the knockout matches weren't giving him a stomach ache.

Even Sonja was having a good time. She smiled quite a few times at Fabian from across the table.

"What sort of paintings do you do?" Tuvesson asked Sonja.

"I mostly paint underwater images of schools of fish and crabs and things like that."

"I love fish," Molander said, raising his glass.

"No, you love killing fish," said Gertrud.

"And those sell well?" Tuvesson inquired. She seemed genuinely interested.

"A little too well, actually. I don't have time to develop anything new. Everyone just wants these damn fish all the time."

"I have an artist friend who ended up in the same situation," said Tuvesson. "He made a concrete bench with cut-out letters that spelled 'liars' bench' in the middle several years ago, and people loved it. Now he spends most of his time creating customized benches—buyers get to choose what the benches say. It's super smart, and it pays the rent. I think he even did a few for Princess Victoria and Prince Daniel's wedding. But is he an artist still, or a concrete worker?"

"It would take at least a long lunch to answer that question," Sonja said, holding up her empty wine glass. "And a little refill, please."

"That's a given," Tuvesson said, filling Sonja's glass.

"So why did you two move down here?" asked Lilja. "Stockholm is a fantastic city."

"Stockholm is a goddamn crap city, if you ask me," said Hampan. "I've been there three times and I can't think of a single reason why anyone would want to live there. Stockholmers are so fucking stressed out they can't even stand still on an escalator. Hell, I got run over by people just to get to the subway, even though another one always comes a minute or two later."

"Well, Hampan, I wasn't asking you—I was asking Sonja."

Hampan chugged his beer and everyone turned to Sonja, as if they were expecting a thorough yet concise answer, which Fabian was fully aware she did not have. He was the one who had put the pressure on, and she was the one who had given in. He started to take it upon himself to respond to the question directly, but Lilja stopped him; she obviously only wanted to hear from Sonja.

"Actually, I've always liked Skåne. Spring comes a month earlier and autumn happens a month later. And I'm hoping that the change of scenery will help me with my painting. As soon as this job opportunity popped up for Fabian, our minds were made up." She raised her glass. "Cheers to Skåne!"

They toasted, and Fabian blew a kiss to Sonja. It was a good answer—so good that he almost believed her himself.

"I'm not that easily fooled," Lilja said with a smile. Sonja's face looked quizzical. "And to be completely honest I think that goes for everyone here. We're police officers and we're used to hearing excuses—each more outlandish than the last."

"I thought this one was pretty decent," said Tuvesson.

"Definitely, especially that bit about the importance of a change of scenery. If she hadn't looked away at that very moment I would have given her a ten out of ten for sure. But she'll have to settle for a seven."

The others laughed.

"Okay, okay, okay!" Sonja broke in. Fabian could tell she was drunk. "Do you want to hear the truth?"

"Yes!" the others cried.

"Here's the thing: my relationship with Fabian started to seem more and more like a long-distance relationship these past few years, even though we share a bed." Sonja's eyes scanned the others as they sat quietly and waited for her to go on. "But since we still love each other more than anything else, we decided to make some major changes. Start over and try to find our way back...Cheers!" She raised her glass and was met by applause and cheering.

"That's what I'd call a fifteen," said Lilja.

Fabian felt how right Sonja had been about one thing: how much he loved her.

BY THE TIME FABIAN's phone rang, he had completely forgotten that he was in the midst of a complicated investigation, so his first impulse was not to answer it. Then he noticed it was a Danish number and immediately picked up.

"Hi, this is Mette Louise Risgaard...from the petrol station," explained the voice on the other end of the line. "The man is here right now," she said, and the line abruptly went dead.

16

KIM SLEIZNER FELT HIS phone vibrating in his pocket, but he didn't want to answer. It wasn't a good time; he had been looking forward to this moment all week and he wasn't about to let a stupid little phone call ruin everything. This moment was far too precious and life was far too short. He could say he was in a tunnel or a lift with bad coverage. This was his area of protection—his very own little bubble that no one had any business disrupting.

He thought of Viveca, and whether he ought to have a guilty conscience, but decided against it. All she cared about was her yoga and whether there was money in her bank account. Given how much had been on his plate recently, it was a wonder he could even get out of bed in the morning. Viveca wasn't the only one who depended on him to function and feel content—so did every citizen of Denmark.

The alternative was anarchy. He leaned back and enjoyed the prize he had awarded himself.

17

MORTEN STEENSTRUP WAS SITTING at the police station in the Danish town of Køge, tucking the shirt of his police uniform into his pants and adjusting the belt around his waist. The belt felt more uncomfortable than usual, as if it were crooked and chafing somehow. He had already made sure that his pistol, torch, and radio were attached in their proper places, so that couldn't be it.

In truth, he knew very well what was bothering him. Exactly a month had passed since Else left him, and no matter how much he wished, he could not trick himself into thinking he was starting to feel better. It was quite the opposite, in fact. The pressure in his chest hadn't subsided, and he had almost grown used to walking around with a constant sensation of breathlessness.

His doctor had advised him to find a friend to confide in, but there was no one he was close enough to who would understand. When he had tried talking to Niels, he had suggested that they visit a prostitute and even offered to pick up the tab, as long as he got to watch.

He had toyed with the thought of trying to win Else back but realized that would never work. She was on a completely different level, a fact they had both been aware of all along. They'd made a silent agreement to ignore that fact and pretend they were equals, and occasionally it had worked. At those times he felt like the happiest man on earth, but it usually only lasted for a little while. Each time, the realization of their inequality forced its way back to him, always crouching in the background like a distant but constantly rumbling threat. In the end he had started to get used to it, and had almost stopped thinking about it entirely. He'd let himself be lulled by the belief that there was no threat, that they were equal. They *loved* each other.

But there was no happiness in his life now. Everything was a strain, an uphill battle; even breathing took force of will. He would never be able to find someone new. Else was his soulmate. She hadn't even cared about his harelip or his fibrous skin. She had stroked his rough body as if it were baby soft, ignoring that it cracked and peeled. She had kissed him as though she wanted him and no one else.

He leaned back in his chair and thought about whether he should have coffee or tea. He decided on coffee and walked to the kitchenette to pour a splash into his dirty cup. Niels was at the table, still mourning Denmark's World Cup failure. Morten knew there was no point in trying to talk to him until he was over it. Morten had never been interested in soccer, much less Danish soccer. His only worry had been that the loss might lead to brawls. Statistics showed that sports defeats either cause people to get extra calm or encourage increased alcohol consumption, which leads to domestic abuse and, above all, vandalism. Contrary to what one might expect, a win usually led to a lot of the former.

He sat down at his desk with coffee cup in hand, unable to stop thinking of Else. She'd thought that he was too afraid of conflict, too timid. She said it like he was a coward. There was probably something to her opinion. He'd tried to stop avoiding conflict so much, but it was a fundamental part of who he was. He'd never liked arguments, and he didn't believe his own opinion was *that* important.

What made him get up every morning, take a shower, get dressed, and go to work? What was he waiting for? He unsnapped his holster, took out his pistol, and weighed it in his hands. It would be so simple—just a little pressure from his index finger and his suffering would be over. His loneliness, sorrow, and shortness of breath would be obliterated. But whichever way he looked at the situation, it would be nothing more than a pathetic end to a pathetic life—no one would do more than shrug their shoulders.

His phone started to ring. The call was from a Swedish number. As soon as he answered it, he realized that this was the very moment he had been waiting for.

SEVEN MINUTES LATER, MORTEN Steenstrup fastened his seatbelt, stuck the key in the ignition, and started the car. The engine roared to life and he wondered if he should turn on the siren, but decided it could wait until he was further away from the station. He didn't want Niels to come rushing out and ask what was going on. All Morten had told him was that he was going out for a bit "to show police presence." He put his favourite recording of Vivaldi's *The Four Seasons* into the CD player and turned up the volume. No one could conduct the piece as well as Carlo Chiarappa, especially the first allegro movement of "Spring," which always managed to fill him with positive energy.

The woman on the phone had been from Helsingborg. He had never been good at understanding Swedish, and thought the southern Skåne dialect was even more difficult to comprehend. He managed to understand that her name was Astrid Tuvesson, chief of the crime squad in Helsingborg. She told him that she hadn't been able to get hold of Kim Sleizner, her counterpart in Copenhagen, which was why she was calling the station in Køge. After that it became harder for him to understand what she was saying. She told him something about a car that was parked at the petrol station in Lellinge, a car that might belong to a Swedish criminal the police were after. A woman named Mette Louise Risgaard, who was the attendant at the petrol station, had called the police and claimed that the man was in Lellinge to pick up the car at this very moment.

He had no memory of the rest of the conversation, but that didn't matter. He didn't need to hear more to realize that this was his chance to stand out. He even knew Mette Louise because he often filled up in Lellinge when he was on the night shift and she was usually working. She'd pierced her lower lip a year ago, and he had summoned up the courage to ask her why she'd done it. What was the point of ruining such a beautiful lip? To this day he could recall the way she had responded with a look of disgust, and she hadn't so much as looked in his direction since, not even when he complimented her new hair colour.

And now she might be in danger. He couldn't understand why she had called the Swedish police and not him. He had even once left his business card to make sure that she had a direct line to the police station. How had she known the man was wanted in Sweden?

He was finally far enough from the station to turn on the sirens and speed up. He felt the adrenaline start to pump. Finally, he had the chance to show Else that he wasn't timid at all. He turned down the music, which had just transitioned into the largo movement of "Spring." He had arrived at the Lellinge petrol station, where everything seemed to be just as quiet as usual; some might even describe it as dead. He preferred the term *peaceful*, even if he did feel a bit disappointed that there was no action here. He slowly drove around the building and discovered it was pretty lifeless. All he saw was a man in sand-coloured shorts, a light-blue polo shirt, and a cap, kneeling next to a Peugeot that was propped up by a jack. He was holding a lug wrench and there was a tyre beside him on the ground.

Could this be the man who had put Mette Louise in danger by picking up his car? Morten couldn't see Mette Louise and the man didn't look particularly dangerous; in fact, he looked more like an idiot tourist. But if Morten had learned one thing during his years as a policeman, it was that it was better to be safe than sorry.

Morten calculated that it would be at least five more minutes until the man would be ready to leave, so he decided to make sure that Mette Louise was okay. He drove around and parked on the other side of the petrol station, so that he could get out of the car without worrying about being seen by the man. He adjusted his belt and made sure that his handgun and baton were where they should be, and continued toward the building on foot.

As soon as he stepped inside the store he sensed that something wasn't right. Nobody was there, not even near the register. He called for Mette Louise but didn't hear an answer, so he hurried behind the counter into the staff area. It was the first time he'd been back there, and it was much smaller than he had expected. There was a kitchenette, a table with a pile of dog-eared magazines, a few chairs, a Michelin wall almanac, and a bathroom with a locked door. He knocked and asked if anyone was inside.

The silence caused more alarm bells to go off. Where was she? He hurried back out into the store and searched around for a useful tool to turn the bathroom lock. He found a screwdriver, tore open the door, and discovered an empty bathroom. He tried to gather his thoughts, but felt a sudden thirst, as if his mouth had turned to sandpaper. He took a Coke from the cooler and let the sweet, bubbly drink fill his mouth before he swallowed and felt his energy return.

Mette Louise would never leave the petrol station unmanned, which must mean that she was with the man next to the Peugeot. He hadn't seen her there, but he had only driven by with a quick glance. He left the store and walked toward the man, who was still crouching beside the Peugeot with his back to Morten. As he got closer, he could see that the man was tightening the lug nuts with the wrench and didn't seem to have noticed his presence at all.

"Excuse me. May I ask you to stand up? Spread your legs, hands above your head," he said in Danish.

There was no reaction from the man, who tightened the next lug nut. *Is he deaf? Does he not understand what I'm saying?*

"Hello! This is the police! I want you to stand up immediately!" he said, trying to imitate the Swedish pronunciation he'd heard on TV. He was almost beside the man now. Morten looked into the car and observed that it was empty. Mette Louise wasn't there, either.

Morten Steenstrup had drawn his weapon three times in nearly twenty-eight years of service. He had fired his gun only once, at a man who was on drugs and threatening those around him with a knife. Morten had shot him in the leg and cuffed his hands behind his back. It was all by the book.

Right now would be his fourth. His body moved automatically, re-creating the action he had performed countless times at home in front of the mirror. His right hand moved back across his hip to open the holster without taking his eyes off the man in front of him. The gun slid out and he disengaged the safety with his left hand.

"This is the police! I order you to stand up right now!" he shouted in English.

After that, everything happened so quickly that he would have trouble remembering the exact sequence of events later on.

The man stood up suddenly and swung halfway around with his right arm extended. Morten didn't realize what was going on until he heard crunching in his right ear as the lug wrench struck him with full force. His vision went black; he felt a flash of pain and heard a loud, piercing noise. Just before his head met the pavement, it occurred to him that he would never again get to enjoy *The Four Seasons*.

THE HOWLING IN HIS ear persisted and he could hear his own pulse, which meant he was still alive. He felt his ear with his hand. It was wet and sticky. His sight was slowly returning, but it took a few more seconds for him to figure out just what he was looking at because everything was tilted ninety degrees. About twenty centimetres ahead of him he saw the inner side of a car tyre with a man wearing Croc sandals crouching beside it.

Out of the corner of his eye he could see the man's arm moving around and around. He quickly realized that the man was in the process of lowering the jack. He saw the wrench hit the pavement and the Crocs vanish from sight. The exhaust system of the car started to vibrate soon after that, and he could hear a dull rumble.

Protect your head, protect your head, he repeated again and again in his mind as the car started backing up.

The back wheel went first.

He tensed his chest and back muscles as best he could, but he still felt his ribs cracking one by one, the pain spreading from the upper part of his body to the lower, like red-hot lava.

Then it was time for the front wheel.

He saw the Peugeot moving away from him, turning left onto Ringstedvej. At least his head must have survived. Heartened by the realization that he was not dead yet, acknowledging that he could see and think, register information, and make decisions, he defied the pain in his chest and got to his knees. He reached for his gun, which was still lying on the pavement next to the wrench. Then he got to his feet and tried to make his way to his car.

His left leg refused to obey him, so he had to help it along with both hands. The burning pain in his chest was turning into a duller, pulsing sensation, and he could see more and more blood seeping through his uniform shirt. He really ought to contact Niels and let him take over and send an ambulance, but that would mean not only that the Swede would almost certainly escape, but also that Else would be proven right.

In one last burst of effort, Morten Steenstrup started the car, backed out of his parking spot, and headed east on Ringstedvej.

He pressed on the accelerator and thanked God for automatic transmission, otherwise he would never have been able to drive, considering the pain in his left leg. The aching sensation in his chest was almost entirely gone and he could feel only a dull throbbing. His shirt was red and sticky with blood. He decided not to look down again; it was better to focus on what was up ahead and think about which way the Swede had gone. The man had a little less than two minutes' lead, but he was already out of sight. Morten assumed he would have no reason to go toward Køge, so decided to bet on the E55 highway north, toward Copenhagen and the bridge to Sweden.

He felt like his entire body was about to go numb. He turned on the lights and siren to keep himself awake. The cars ahead of him slowed down right away and moved to the inner lane. Morten put the pedal to the metal and watched the speedometer pass 200 and push toward 220. He wasn't even the tiniest bit afraid any more; it was as if he had left his fear behind in Lellinge. He knew that he could handle anything that might happen. He wanted to show everyone that he was brave enough. Now he just needed to remain conscious.

The red needle was pointing to 230. If he could just keep going at this speed he would catch up with the Swede in a few minutes, assuming that he was sticking to the speed limit. Ten kilometres later, he could see the Peugeot, and he turned off the roof lights.

But it was too late; the Swede had seen him, and sped up to take the next exit. Morten steered after him. A wave of cold sweat came over his body as realized that this would soon be over. The car in front of him skidded right on Cementvej. Morten took the turn a bit more slowly. He didn't want to risk ending up in a ditch now that he'd come this far.

Out of nowhere, the Peugeot swerved to the left onto a gravel road. Morten looked at the GPS and saw that it led out into a field and up toward a cluster of trees, only to go around the trees and turn back again. Had the Swede painted himself into a corner, or had he seen the same thing on his own GPS and planned an ambush?

Morten cut the engine and rolled down the window. He could clearly hear the engine of the Peugeot on the other side of the trees. He defied the urge to close his eyes and just fall asleep; instead, he stepped out of the car and continued down the gravel path on foot, dragging his left leg and using a branch as a crutch. His shirt was sticking to his stomach and chest, but he resisted the urge to look down.

About fifty metres in front of him he saw the Peugeot, which looked like it had been deserted among some bushes with the engine running. Morten limped toward the car with his gun in his hand. He swung halfway around and couldn't see anything but trees and an open field. He took the last few steps to the car, bent down, and cupped his hands around his eyes so he could see inside. The car was empty. And then everything went black.

18

THE FESTIVE ATMOSPHERE VANISHED once Fabian received the call from Mette Louise Risgaard. The barbecue at Molander's quickly transformed into a regular police meeting, except this one included everyone's family members and quite a bit of alcohol in their bloodstreams.

Tuvesson immediately called her Danish colleague Kim Sleizner in Copenhagen. He didn't pick up, so she left a message on his voicemail to inform him of the situation and let him know that she was going to contact the local police station in Køge. Then she called the Swedish national police commissioner, Bertil Crimson, who in turn promised to contact his Danish counterpart, Henrik Hammersten, right away. She had to notify her superior because the Swedish police would be working with the police from another country.

The ball was rolling. All they could do now was to continue their dinner, and wait and see what happened. Sonja hadn't said anything, but it was obvious to Fabian that her mood had gone downhill. He could sympathize. He tried to come up with new topics of conversation, but only Gertrud Molander took the bait. Everyone else was waiting for Tuvesson's phone to ring.

One hour later, their wait was over.

It was Kim Sleizner on the other end of the line, and Tuvesson turned on the speakerphone so that everyone could hear the conversation.

"Henrik Hammersten said that you were trying to get hold of me, but I'm sorry to say I haven't received any calls from you," said the Danish voice.

"I definitely called you about an hour ago," said Tuvesson. "You didn't answer, so I left a message."

"If that were the case, I should have a missed call and a message waiting for me, shouldn't I? I'm telling you that I don't. Perhaps you forgot to dial the country code first—what do I know?"

Tuvesson shot the others a look and shook her head.

"But what I do know is that Morten Steenstrup, from my lot in Køge, took up the chase for the perpetrator."

My lot, Fabian thought. Sleizner did sound like the sort who considered his subordinates his personal property.

"And he did all this despite the fact that he was gravely injured and had lost a great deal of blood. If I hadn't been so quick to send a few cars out as soon as I heard what happened, he would be dead."

Fabian wondered whether this was all Sleizner had to say for now or whether he'd paused on purpose, to force Tuvesson to ask for the details. She didn't seem to feel the need to break the silence, which was bordering on painful by the time Sleizner gave in and continued of his own accord.

Morten Steenstrup had been run over by the assailant and was in intensive care, hovering between life and death. He'd clearly been a true hero, and against all odds had managed to get the Peugeot into police possession. The perpetrator, on the other hand, had gotten away. Other than the car, the only clue he had left behind was a pair of Crocs.

The fact that the Danish police now had the car was a great triumph in and of itself, and it was sure to be a large setback for the killer, but Fabian couldn't stop wondering what had happened to Mette Louise. There had been no trace of her thus far. Had the perpetrator taken her with him as a hostage? And if so, why?

IT WAS ALREADY PAST midnight when the Risks arrived home. Theodor, who had spent the entire evening sitting in a corner with his phone, vanished straight to his room, and Matilda claimed she was wide awake and didn't want to go to bed. She didn't even fall asleep after three chapters of Harry Potter.

"Dad, is the man you're looking for a serial killer or just a regular killer?" Matilda's bright, alert eyes met his own. He wished he could pretend he didn't know what she was talking about, but he thought she deserved an honest answer.

"I don't know, sweetheart. So far there's only been one murder, although I'm pretty sure that at least two have been committed."

"How can you be so sure about that?"

"Because it's my job."

"So does that mean it's a serial killer?"

"No, there would have to be at least three deaths for it to be the act of a serial killer, and I wouldn't categorize him as a serial killer yet."

"Why not?"

"A serial killer commits murders for the sake of murder. This killer's motivation is completely different," Fabian explained. He told her about the case and about how he had thought the original motive was revenge against people who had been mean to the killer, but now he was unsure about everything. Then he looked over to discover Matilda sleeping like a log. He left her, walked down to the kitchen, and uncorked one of the bottles of wine he'd forgotten to give to Molander.

Sonja was up in her studio, unpacking her current projects. She didn't even glance in Fabian's direction when he came in with the wine, two glasses, and his iPod. They really needed to talk, but both of them were too tired. Besides, there was nothing they hadn't said to each other already. Instead, he sat on the floor, poured the wine, and put on their song, Prince's

"I Would Die 4 U." They'd danced to it the first time they met. Tonight they made love in the studio.

THE NEXT MORNING, ASTRID Tuvesson gave Fabian the go-ahead to stay home over the weekend, as long as he promised to keep his phone within arm's reach. She promised only to call if it was an emergency.

They were able to spend all of Saturday morning in peace and quiet—unpacking boxes, emptying the last of the plastic bags, and putting up shelves. With Theodor's help, Fabian even managed to set up the stereo. They had a late lunch together on the deck in the shade of the umbrella and then went out in the afternoon. They bought a snorkelling set for Theodor, had coffee at Fahlmans Konditori on Stortorget, and then went for a walk by the new marina, stopping at Tropical Beach.

On Sunday they hung up their paintings, organized the books in alphabetical order, helped Matilda get her room in order, and, to Theodor's great joy, managed to get the wireless router up and running. Everyone helped out, and it finally started to feel as though they had really moved in. They went to Pålsjö Krog for a celebratory dinner in the evening.

Fabian's phone hadn't rung once all weekend; he hadn't received so much as a text message. But he hadn't been able to stop thinking about Mette Louise and about what Molander would find in the Peugeot. He thought about Lina, who still hadn't called, and questioned whether he should get in touch and apologize. He remembered dancing with her to "Rivers of Babylon" at his twelfth birthday party, sure that the two of them would spend the rest of their lives together.

The silence was broken on Monday morning.

"You have to come in. Right away…"

19

GUSTEN PERSSON LOVED EARLY mornings, and this one was no exception; the sun was shining as if it would never stop. But Gusten was already in a bad mood as he turned off Gruvgatan and drove into the employee parking area of Åstorp Construction Supply.

His holiday was over, and he had spent the entire weekend fixing the veranda without receiving so much as a smile from his wife, Inga. His old joke about "no kisses from the missus" had long since lost its lustre with her. He had heard from friends that menopause could be extra difficult for some women, but no one had said anything about how excruciating it could be for men.

He unlocked the door to Åstorp's large warehouse and walked inside, locking the door behind him. There was still more than an hour left before the store officially opened after being closed for the two-week holiday break. If he didn't lock the door, there was a risk that the building would be full of customers fifteen minutes before the store opened.

He started thinking about Thailand. Glenn had asked Gusten to join him there this coming winter. Apparently there were more willing—and, most importantly, cheap—girls than one could possibly imagine. Gusten had declined, feeling distaste at the thought of paying for sex. He had never done it and wasn't about to start.

But after this weekend, he wasn't so sure any more. Why shouldn't he get laid now and then? Weren't his urges just as natural as Inga's menopause? If things had been the other way around and men went through menopause while women just got hornier and hornier, prostitution would surely be acceptable. Yoga weekends would be replaced by sex weekends, and gossip magazines with porn. He wasn't even sure if Inga's issues were even related to menopause. Recently, it had felt more likely to him that she was using it as an excuse. As he went to turn off the alarm, he decided that he was definitely going to ask Glenn if he could still come along.

Employees had forty-five seconds to turn off the alarm after the door was opened. If you didn't make it in time, the alarm would sound, bringing with it a minor hell of phone calls and codes before order was restored. Gusten hardly dared think about how much such an ordeal would cost. In his early days at the company, he had always worried that he wouldn't make it to the box in time, so he'd run as soon as he opened the door. Over the years he developed a firm, instinctual understanding of exactly how long forty-five seconds was, and could now take his time getting to the box. It had almost become a game for him—to get as close to forty-five seconds as he possibly could.

But the alarm was already off today, which was unusual. Gusten wondered whether he had forgotten to turn it on when they'd closed up for the holiday, or if someone else had already been here and opened the door before him. He definitely hadn't seen any other cars in the car park. And the morning shift was not popular—in all the years he had been responsible for opening, the only time he had managed to get someone to cover for him was when he'd been off work for a month after a bypass operation.

Gusten walked further into the building and went on his usual morning rounds: turning on the ceiling lights, starting up the presentation videos, and putting merchandise back into place. He didn't understand for the life of him why it was so difficult for customers to put things back where they'd found them. It was almost as incomprehensible as Inga's grouchiness.

126

He stopped and looked at the window. It was definitely closed, but the hasps weren't secured. He walked over and felt the window, which opened upward. The cable that ran to the alarm contact looked okay. There had been a lot of break-ins at the store over the years, but not a single one since they installed the new alarm system, which had cost several hundred thousand kronor almost three years ago. Gusten had been very sceptical at the time, thinking that it would be cheaper just to have a few thefts now and then. But they had made up the cost last spring, and since then they had been in the black.

He interrupted his rounds and walked to the office. He turned on the coffeemaker while waiting for the computer system to start up. He signed into his computer with his personal security code and checked the log. Glenn Granqvist had turned off the alarm last Thursday night at 2:33 a.m. Gusten was bewildered. Glenn, of all people? He picked up the phone and called Glenn.

Gusten listened to the Robert De Niro greeting on the machine, but didn't leave a message. Glenn was probably still sleeping and needed a few more rings to wake up. He called again, but hung up after the sixth ring. Had he accidentally dialled the wrong number?

Gusten had Glenn's number programmed into his mobile, but he had called from the store's landline. After all, this was a work call and there was no reason he should have to pay for it. He dialled Glenn's number once more, checking each digit carefully. But he didn't make it to the last one. Instead, his eyes were on the monitor, which had come to life and was switching from one security camera to the next.

There was a forklift in the middle of the doors and windows department, blocking the entire aisle. What was it doing there? It belonged down in Aisle C. He couldn't put his finger on it, but there was something odd about the angle, too. He leaned closer to the monitor in order to get a better look but it quickly switched to another camera.

Gusten couldn't recall the last time he had run anywhere. The store had scooters to get around faster, but he always felt unsteady when he tried to balance on them, so he preferred to walk; he considered it his exercise. Now he wished he hadn't given up so easily. The doors and windows department was at the other end of the building, and he was already seriously out of breath.

A rat scurried past him on the cement floor. They had plenty of rats, he knew that, but they usually didn't show up in plain sight. Soon, another one appeared under a pallet of plasterboard, and went in the same direction as Gusten was running. What had happened? It occurred to him that he might be on *Candid Camera*, but he dismissed the thought almost immediately. This was no practical joke.

His heart was hammering like a machine gun and he was panting like a dog in forty-degree weather. He finally rounded the corner and could see the forklift, which was definitely in the middle of the aisle. Gusten assumed that this could have been what a burglar was after. And why not? Doors and triple-paned windows were some of the most expensive items the store carried.

Four more rats showed up from different directions and disappeared around the other side of the forklift. He could clearly see what he had suspected in the office: the forklift was reared back. The front wheels were hanging in mid-air, fifteen centimetres above the floor. The prongs were lowered, and he saw Glenn's squashed boots between the wheels and the ground. He would know Glenn's steel-toed, badass Doc Martens anywhere. But not even Doc Martens could withstand that much pressure. Gusten's mind was swirling; he was as confused as a compass at the North Pole.

He heard a sound and it helped him regain focus. It was coming from the other side of the forklift. At first he couldn't figure out what it was—a creaking or chirping? Then he realized the floor was full of rats, all running back and forth to something on the other side of the vehicle. He collected himself and walked around to take a look. The sight he encountered would haunt him for the rest of his life. Deep down, he had already realized that Glenn was dead, but what the rats had done shocked him.

November 26

When we showered after gym they said I was gay and that I was looking at their cocks. I didn't say anything but they just kept on talking, saying that I wanted to suck their cocks. I heard them laughing in the locker room, but I was scared to leave before they were gone. My coat was missing from my locker once I got there. My almost brand-new down coat that Mum said was too expensive. I found it in the toilet. It was disgusting.

I went to JC and found the same coat. I walked up to the register to pay and watched them take off the alarm, and stick the coat in a bag. They wanted the money, but I just ran out of the store without looking back.

I haven't been to school for a few days now. My fucking stupid teacher called tonight and told on me. Dad wasn't home but Mum got super mad. I didn't know what to say so I didn't say anything. She asked why I was being so quiet, but I still didn't say anything. I've got pretty good at being quiet.

Mum said she's going to come all the way to school with me next week and sit there for several of my classes because my teacher called. I told her not to come. Then she was the one who didn't say anything. If Mum comes to school, the guys are going to think I told on them and they will beat the shit out of me. I know it.

Tonight we had stuffed cabbage for dinner. I totally hate stuffed cabbage and she knows it. But Mum told me I had to eat it all. Then Dad came down and started yelling about how important it is to go to school. Jesus, I hate them so much. They don't understand a goddamn thing.

P. S. I put my own piss in Laban's water bottle. At first he refused to drink it, but then he did. It's so fucking nasty.

130

20

THE POLICE TAPE WAS already up when Fabian Risk arrived at Åstorp Construction Supply. Some curious onlookers, probably employees, were huddled together in a group, watching what was happening. Klippan was questioning Gusten Persson, who still hadn't recovered from what he had seen in the doors and windows department.

"Apparently he's the guy who opens every morning," Molander said as he took Fabian aside and showed him in under the police tape.

"Where's Tuvesson? Shouldn't she be here?"

"She had to go to Malmö."

"Malmö?"

"Crisis meeting about how to handle the conflict with the Danes. Apparently they're all pissed off because we went above the bosses' heads and sent out officers without telling them."

"We did call them. They didn't answer."

"Not according to them." Molander shrugged and walked into the building. Fabian followed him between the crammed shelves, which extended all the way up to the ceiling. They arrived at a long central aisle that ran through the entire warehouse. Molander stopped and nodded toward the far end of the aisle. "There you go."

The forklift was about ten metres away from them, its front wheels dangling in the air. Molander's assistants were walking around in blue coveralls, taking pictures and gathering evidence.

Glenn's body was lying face up, his feet caught underneath the prongs of the forklift. Fabian could tell there wasn't much left of him. The rest of the body was hidden behind the medical examiner and his assistants.

"How are things going for them?"

"Just fine, I'm sure, but it will probably take some time before he can be officially identified."

"I can identify him." Although Fabian hadn't seen any recent pictures of Glenn, he was sure he would have no trouble recognizing him.

"I don't think so." Molander placed a hand on Fabian's shoulder. "Anyway, I'd prefer not to have any more people than necessary over there before my men and Braids are finished. The rats have already made enough of a mess."

"The rats?"

Molander nodded. "But they also did something useful. Let me show you." Fabian followed Molander from the murder scene to the other end of the warehouse.

"Rats are drawn to food, and if we follow their tracks we'll find some real goodies over here." Molander turned away from the central aisle, walked between two shelves, and stopped at a hidden corner under a small, unlocked window. "I think he spent the night here, and — most importantly — ate something."

Fabian looked at the concrete floor, but couldn't see any traces of food. "Did the rats eat up all the scraps or something?"

"They left one thing behind." Molander held out an evidence bag with a McDonald's wrapper inside. "If I'm not mistaken, this is a Chilli McFeast Deluxe — really yummy, for McDonald's. It's only sold one day a week at select locations. With a little luck, he bought it at a McDonald's nearby."

"Hey, you pigheads! Full speed ahead," they heard a crackly voice say on Molander's two-way radio. Both men turned back toward the rearing forklift.

"What's he like? The medical examiner..."

"Einar Greide? He looks like a hibernating hippie who spends all his time chilling out and smoking up, but he's one of the best pathologists in the country. Even just the fact that he insisted on coming out here before we move the body speaks for..."

Molander stopped talking once he noticed Greide walking toward them. His long, silvery grey hair was styled in two braids, his beard in one. There were several different amulets hanging around his neck, and the colourful, crocheted pants beneath his protective plastic smock reminded Fabian of a Twister Popsicle.

"Well, anyway, he's one of the best." Molander vanished with one of his assistants.

"Hi! I'm Einar Greide. And you must be Fabian Risk." Greide extended his hand, which had at least one ring on each finger, and shook hands with Fabian. "We have an exciting time ahead of us," he continued, tugging at his beard braid. "This perpetrator knows exactly what he's doing."

"What have you come up with?"

"One thing at a time, and this is first on the list." Greide held up some crumpled blue shoe protectors and a hairnet. Fabian pulled the shoe protectors over his Converse, put on the hairnet, and followed the medical examiner to the other side of the forklift, where the lifeless body lay supine.

Both of Glenn's arms were bound to his thighs with straps. His shins disappeared under the prongs of the forklift, and there wasn't much more to the feet and boots than a whole lot of blood that had pooled onto the concrete floor and coagulated. Fabian let his eyes wander along the corpse, and understood why Molander kept talking about the rats, and why he didn't think Fabian could identify the body.

It wasn't just the feet that were gone—the face was, too. It had been eaten. Everything was missing: the eyes, the lips and mouth. All that was left was a meaty, red mass. Besides the hair, the protruding nasal bone, cheekbones, and teeth were the only other evidence that they were dealing with a human. The mass was so far from a face that it was hardly even repulsive.

Fabian stood up, feeling no doubt whatsoever that it was Glenn. Even if it was impossible to tell for sure, all the clues added up: they were at Glenn's workplace, he had been reported missing, and he had used his feet whenever he and Jörgen attacked Claes.

Einar Greide nodded at his men, who carefully rolled the body onto its side. He crouched down and pointed to a small head wound.

"As you can see, he received a powerful blow to the back of the skull, which almost always means an awful lot of blood." Greide pointed at the blood that had coagulated in the hair around the wound. "But if you look here at the floor under the wound, there's no blood at all."

"So he was hit there earlier?"

Greide lit up. "He's good, this new guy," he called out to anyone in the area who was listening, and he gestured at his assistants to lift the body into a cadaver bag. "Follow me. My doctor says I don't get anywhere near enough exercise."

Fabian followed Greide on a walk through the deserted building, its shelves full of dreams of new, more beautiful homes.

"So there's a chance he was dead even before he got here?"

"No, just that he received the blow to his head at an earlier juncture," Greide said, taking a whole fistful of sweets from a dish on the counter in the paint department. "But he died somewhere in the ballpark of three or four days ago."

"We're talking last Thursday or Friday?"

Greide nodded. "And even if it's not written in stone yet, it looks like the cause of death is blood loss from his face." He peeled the wrapper from a sweet and stuck it in his mouth. "He would probably still be alive if the rats hadn't kept his wounds open."

"So he should be grateful?"

"It depends on how you look at it."

"If we assume the perpetrator wanted the victim to die, the rats were no accident?"

"I need more time, but I wouldn't be surprised if his face had been covered in something that drew in the rats."

"Like what?"

"Honey? Kalles Kaviar? Liver paste? They'll eat practically anything."

Fabian's phone rang. It was Tuvesson.

"They found the girl."

21

WHY? ASK FABBE.

Fabian was sitting across from Tuvesson in her office, staring at the handwritten note.

The question was more than justified. How could he have been so stupid? He had dragged an innocent girl into the investigation and put her in mortal danger. Now she was dead, and the killer couldn't have put it more clearly: Mette Louise Risgaard hadn't been part of his plan.

"The Danes found her in the trunk of the car," Tuvesson said, struggling to hold back her rage.

"What about the note?"

"It was stuffed in her mouth."

Fabian closed his eyes and felt the effects of his decision weighing on him. The possibility he had been worried about all weekend was now a reality.

"Fabian. There's no doubt that this investigation has taken a large and valuable step forward. But the cost…is unjustifiable. The Danes now have an officer hovering between life and death, and a murdered young girl. They are placing the blame on us—the Swedish police."

"The Swedish police? This is my fault."

"You're certainly right, but I stand up for my team." She looked him in the eye. "Even when they run off on solo tours without getting my go-ahead or even letting me know. But yes, her murder is your fault, and that's something you'll have to live with for the rest of your life."

Fabian nodded. All he could do was agree with her. He wondered whether he would ever get better at predicting consequences.

"I just got back from Malmö, who received a complaint from the Danes. Bengt-Åke Persson and I have decided to hold the line and defend our actions. After all, we tried to get hold of Sleizner. And when Morten Steenstrup chose to act alone, he did so on his own initiative, against all the rules, which is something we can't assume responsibility for."

Fabian knew where Tuvesson was heading—she was going to demand his badge and access card and remove him from the investigation, which was only reasonable. But it was too late for him to stop. This was more than just another case. It had become personal: the note proved it...WHY? ASK FABBE.

"I should remove you from this investigation and let you go back to your vacation. But..." She stopped talking, as if she needed to think it over one more time. "Unfortunately, I think this investigation needs you." She stood up. "Everyone else is waiting."

KLIPPAN, MOLANDER, AND LILJA were already assembled when Fabian and Tuvesson entered the conference room. No one said anything, but it was clear that everybody was aware that there was a third victim, a young Danish woman who was only connected to the case through Fabian.

"Now that we're all here, I'd like to start by saying that Fabian will continue to participate in this investigation despite recent events."

Klippan and Molander nodded and shot smiles in Fabian's direction. Lilja's expression, however, did not change.

"Irene? Do you have any objections?" Tuvesson said. Lilja shook her head. "Good, because now more than ever it's important for us to work as a team and stand up for one another." She fixed her eyes on each person individually, except for Fabian, but she was making herself perfectly clear. Those words were meant for Fabian and no one else. "Okay, let's get going."

They went through the most recent developments, adding pictures of Glenn Granqvist as an adult, along with photos of the murder scene and the two suspects, Claes Mällvik and Rune Schmeckel.

"Ingvar, I know you're not finished yet, but did you find anything at the most recent crime scene besides that McDonald's wrapper?" Tuvesson asked.

"We did, actually," said Molander, holding up an evidence bag with a thick black marker inside. "Unfortunately it's perfectly clean. We should probably take it as evidence that the killer has quite the sense of humour, or that he thinks it's too taxing on the environment to print out a new picture for every victim." Molander took the marker out of the bag, walked up to the whiteboard, and crossed out Glenn on the enlarged class photo.

Tuvesson sighed and shook her head. "He's playing with us."

"How are things going with the Peugeot?" Fabian asked. "Is it on its way here?"

"That's going to take some time, I'm afraid," said Tuvesson. "If I know Sleizner, he's going to do everything in his power to drag it out so his own department can solve the case instead."

"What?! This is *our* investigation," said Klippan.

"In their eyes, the investigation is in their jurisdiction: a young girl was murdered and an officer is near death. Apparently *Ekstra Bladet* has already named him the hero of the decade."

"Which decade? The 2010s have only just begun," said Molander.

"I don't want to dwell on this...we don't have all day. How are things going on the McDonald's front?" Tuvesson asked.

"There are eight locations within a twenty-kilometre radius of Åstorp," Klippan said. "But only six of them do daily specials: one in Ängelholm, three in Helsingborg, one in Ödåkra, and one in Hyllinge."

"What days do they sell Chilli McFeast Deluxes?" Molander asked.

"On Thursdays, so that matches up."

"We should go around and check to see if any of the employees recognize Mällvik or Schmeckel. Can you take care of that, Klippan?" Tuvesson said.

"No problem."

Tuvesson handed a document over to Lilja. "I was thinking you and Fabian could deal with this."

"What is it?"

"A warrant to search Schmeckel's house."

"How did you manage that?" Klippan said. "We don't have a clear motive or any technical evidence. So far, the only thing that points to him is his car."

"Which was probably just stolen," said Molander.

"But why hasn't he reported it stolen?" asked Tuvesson.

"That will never hold up in court," Klippan continued. "And if I know Chief Prosecutor Stina Högsell, that's exactly what she said too."

"You're right, but apparently her ex-husband is Danish."

FABIAN SAT DOWN IN Hugo Elvin's chair, feeling absolutely out of ideas. He was confused; nothing in this investigation seemed to be connected. He had correctly predicted Glenn and his crushed feet. All signs pointed to Claes Mällvik; if anyone had a motive it was him. But where had he disappeared to? Lilja couldn't find any trace of him after 1993. It was like he had gone up in smoke.

And who was Rune Schmeckel? Had his car really been stolen while he was on vacation, or did he have some sort of connection to Jörgen and Glenn—a connection beyond the classroom?

139

Maybe the murders had nothing to do with their school days. What if the class photo was just an attempt to lead them in the wrong direction? Fabian leaned back in the chair and realized that the more he tried to figure out how everything fitted together, the further he got from solving it.

He decided to take a break and pulled out the top drawer of Hugo Elvin's desk, which was empty. Perplexed that the drawer didn't contain a single thing, he pulled out the next one. This one, too, was empty, and the same went for the third. The fourth and last drawer, however, was locked—a clear signal from Herr Elvin that he didn't want anyone snooping through his stuff. Fabian picked up his phone to call home.

"You've reached the Risks. Matilda speaking."

"Hi, Matilda. It's Dad. I just wanted to see how things are going over there."

"There's a ghost in the cellar." Matilda sounded as if this were a matter of life and death. "Me and Mum were down there looking for her paintbrushes, and one of the light bulbs went out. We changed it, but then that one went out too."

"I'm sure it's just a short circuit."

"No, we checked the fuses and there was nothing wrong. Mum says there really are ghosts."

"If there are ghosts, I bet they're nice ones. Is Mum at home?"

"Muuuuuuuuuum! It's Dad! He doesn't believe there's a ghost!"

"Hello?"

Fabian tried to interpret Sonja's tone, but it revealed nothing. He was calling to tell her the investigation was getting under his skin, and that he now had the death of a young woman on his conscience. He needed to talk to someone about how he was feeling. But it didn't sound like it was going to happen with Sonja right now.

"So you were visiting the ghosts in the cellar? Were they friendly?"

"I know you don't believe in the supernatural. On a different note, the cellar is too small."

"What do you mean it's too small?"

"It's smaller than it ought to be. It's like there's a hidden extra room, but no door to get in."

"Maybe it belongs to the neighbours?"

"It's possible, but we also found an oven. Did you know we had one?"

"No. What kind of oven?"

"A wood-burning bread oven, the kind with a hole that goes right into the wall. It's quite large. Matilda and I thought it might be fun to find out if it works."

"I'm not sure that sounds like a good idea. I might be mistaken, but I have a vague memory that the realtor said something about the chimney being closed off."

"Oh, that's too bad."

Fabian knew just what sort of oven Sonja was describing. There had been one at his grandparents' house in Värmland. It was so delightful when there was a fire in it. They baked bread and pizza in the oven and it warmed a big stone bench in the living room. His grandfather designed and built it himself so that the heat of the smoke conducted through the bench before it vanished up the chimney. It had been his great pride and joy.

Fabian had climbed into the oven once to hide when he and his sister were playing hide-and-seek. She didn't have a hope of finding him, and he just lay there enjoying the faint warmth from the fire the day before. He had even fallen asleep. His family found him by chance an hour later, when Grandma was about to light the oven. Fabian hadn't realized how dangerous it actually was until he was an adult.

"By the way, have you spoken with Theo today?" Sonja asked.

"I haven't had the time. We have another victim."

"From the class?"

"Yes. Glenn Granqvist. Jörgen Pålsson's best friend."

"Oh my God. Is there a chance that more—"

"Sonja, we don't know yet. Right now it feels like this case could go in any direction."

"I understand," she said with a sigh. "I really hope you solve it." "We have no choice."

"No, I suppose you don't. I know you have a lot on your plate today, but I think you should take the time to call Theo. Now that the Internet is set up, he refuses to leave his room; it's like he's nailed down in front of his computer."

"I promise to try and talk to him today."

"I love you."

"Love you, too."

They hung up and Fabian wondered what could be causing Theodor's behaviour. Sonja was right: he hadn't been very talkative, and stayed in his bedroom for the most part. When they had gone to the beach yesterday, Theo had sat and then snorkelled apart from the rest of them. But wasn't this perfectly normal behaviour for a fourteen-year-old? Hadn't he felt exactly the same toward his own parents?

Sonja completely disagreed with Fabian. She thought that Theodor actually missed his father and was in need of a male role model—one who came home before ten o'clock at night. Fabian knew she was right, but he didn't think his absence entirely explained Theo's behaviour. He suspected that the move had caused Theodor to close himself off even more.

He dialled his son's number while he paged through the yearbook he had brought from home. He noticed class after class of pimply students with hairstyles that made you wonder what sort of experiments they had been subjected to.

"Yo," came a tired voice on the other end of the line.

"Hi, Theo. What are you up to?"

"Nothing. Playing *Call of Duty*." Which was all Theodor ever seemed to be doing these days. He spent hours manoeuvring his players around bombed-out cities, hunting for other soldiers. Fabian was convinced that most kids could tell the difference between video games and real life, but Theo spent so much time in front of the screen, he couldn't help but worry.

"Listen, I know that it's a little rough with all your friends being back in Stockholm, but I guarantee that once you start school in August you're going to..."

"Did Mum tell you to call?"

"No, but she told me that you're cooped up in your room and don't want to do anything."

"There's, like, not much to do here."

"Sure there is! Helsingborg isn't exactly a Podunk town with only one hot-dog stand on a windy square."

"So what do you suggest I do?"

Fabian realized he had no idea what his teenage son should do for fun in Helsingborg. The city had changed so much since he was young. Helsingborg had shed its skin and gone from a grey Swedish Anytown to a little pearl with a beautiful waterfront, cafés, and boardwalks. But Theodor's interest in cafés and boardwalks was practically non-existent. What's more, Fabian wondered if Theo was still disappointed that he and Sonja hadn't allowed him to go to the Sweden Rock Festival.

"Why don't you and I go out and do something tonight? Just the two of us." Fabian felt like he had just jumped straight off a cliff without a parachute as the words came out of his mouth.

"Like what?"

"We could go out to eat and see a movie? We could see if there are any good concerts on?"

"I checked already. Sofiero is the only place with concerts nearby."

"Who's playing there?"

"No one, really, just The Ark, Kent, Robyn...people like that."

"We could go and see Kent. They've done quite a few harder

songs, too." Fabian heard how incredibly ridiculous he sounded and bit his tongue.

Lilja came into the room and indicated that Fabian should follow her.

"Listen, I have to go. Think about it, and we'll talk later."

"Sure," was all that Theo could muster.

Fabian hung up.

22

THE CYLINDER OF THE lock had been fitted with a tempered-steel locking mechanism to make break-ins more difficult, and the spring-loaded pins had been treated with extra-hard chrome. This was no average Chubb lock; it provided very high security. In order to open the door, a key had to raise the pins to the correct levels and turn them in a very precise direction. And they didn't have the key. Instead, the locksmith was using a six-millimetre, water-cooled diamond drill to precisely cut his way in, severing pin after pin, down to a hundredth of a millimetre.

A few minutes later, he was able to pull the bit out of the cylinder, stick a hook in the hole, turn it, and open the door. Fabian and Lilja stepped into a tiny front hall with a big pile of mail, flyers, and magazines on the floor. The July issue of *National Geographic*, with a chipped skull on the cover and the headline 4-MILLION-YEAR-OLD WOMAN, was on the top of the pile.

The floor plan was open-concept, with the living room on the right and the kitchen to the left. A staircase led to the second floor in front of them. The house was in the older part of Lund and had been built sometime in the 1700s. It had undergone a careful renovation that made it feel new and modern.

Fabian preferred to be alone when he visited the home of a victim—or, in this case, a suspect—for the first time. He wanted to be able to listen to the rooms, not the voice of another person. He didn't want to miss any clues that could help them move forward. The tiniest little detail might be the very puzzle piece they needed to see the case in its entirety.

Lilja seemed to feel the very same way. Without a word, she disappeared up the stairs to the second floor.

Just as Klippan had pointed out, Fabian knew they lacked concrete evidence that Rune Schmeckel was the killer. Now that he was standing here in the middle of Schmeckel's living room, he felt something nagging at him...something that didn't add up. Who *was* Rune Schmeckel?

The room was sparsely furnished with a pale-brown vintage Newport sofa, and a well-used Bruno Mathsson chair and ottoman over by the window. There was no TV in sight, only a Bang & Olufsen stereo. A few framed black-and-white photographs of rolling countryside and an old city with lots of houses hung on the walls. Fabian thought the photos had probably been taken somewhere in Spain, Italy, or Portugal—he couldn't tell exactly, but he did know that they definitely hadn't been taken in Sweden or Denmark. The windowsills were free of flowerpots and he couldn't see any sign of pets. Aside from a thin layer of dust, the room was clean and tidy, and everything seemed to be in its proper place. Had Schmeckel planned his disappearance, or was he just a neat person who cleaned up before he went on vacation?

Fabian walked over to the stereo on the wall and turned it on. A CD started spinning and soon classical music emanated from the small speakers. Fabian had almost no knowledge of classical music—every time he gave it a chance, he decided it just wasn't for him, like golf, hunting, and vintage wines. He found an empty CD case on top of the stereo and established the music was Berlioz's *Symphonie fantastique*. He cautiously sat down in the Bruno Mathsson chair, leaned back, and was struck by a broad, deep sound that couldn't possibly be coming from the small satellite speakers. He looked around and realized there was a large subwoofer behind the sofa.

Fabian had spent a frightening amount of money on his own stereo equipment throughout the years. He'd even managed to make Sonja burst into tears once when he showed her his new speakers—a pair of Bowers & Wilkins 802 Diamonds. After the fact, he agreed they weren't the most beautiful boxes ever, but they sounded fantastic.

He put his feet up on the ottoman and closed his eyes. This was just the way classical music should be enjoyed. A comfy chair, a good stereo, and above all: total solitude. As he opened his eyes, Fabian realized how isolated the entire room felt. Schmeckel probably didn't have any relatives or friends, and spent his free time reading, listening to music, and improving himself.

Fabian rose from the chair and walked to the opposite wall, which was covered by a built-in, floor-to-ceiling bookcase with roughly seven or eight shelves. One section was devoted to CDs—mostly opera and classical, and some jazz—but the majority of the shelves were taken up by books. Schmeckel was obviously a big reader. The literature portion filled two shelves, and the rest were full of non-fiction titles divided into various subcategories such as "Medicine," "Self-Defence and Martial Arts," and "Physics and Biology"—all meticulously labelled. Fabian noted a number of titles in the Psychology section: *I Don't Want to Die, I Just Don't Want to Live*; *It Wasn't My Fault: On the Art of Taking Responsibility*; *Offence and Forgiveness*; and *Anger Management: The Complete Treatment Guidebook for Practitioners*.

When Fabian had first walked into the house, he'd thought Schmeckel was a lonely but somewhat harmonious person, a man who took joy in the good things in life. But the more he scanned the bookshelves, the more he was beginning to form a completely different image, of a person with poor self-esteem, maybe even a victim of bullying.

He pulled out a photo album and opened it. The first few pages were filled with pictures of a trip to some southern

European country; then came pictures from a Halloween party at Lund Hospital. In one of the photos, Schmeckel was dressed up as a bloody butcher, chewing on a detached finger made of what looked like marzipan. Fabian doubted it was the sort of picture Schmeckel would want the general public to get hold of, considering the scandal with the forgotten plastic clips. Fabian flipped through the rest of the album, but there were no more photographs.

The problem with new technology was that no one ever got their photos developed any more; instead, they were put onto a hard drive. All you usually found these days were albums full of very old photos with handwritten captions.

And then it struck him. As his eyes swept around the room, he realized there was nothing in it that could be from Schmeckel's childhood or teenage years—no nostalgic records by KISS or The Who or, as in Fabian's case, Duran Duran. The only albums here were of "grown-up" music, for mature listeners with good taste. The same thing could be said about the bookcase: there was no *Hitchhiker's Guide to the Galaxy* or *The Secret Diary of Adrian Mole*. It was as if Schmeckel's whole youth had been erased, like it had never existed.

Fabian left the living area and went into the kitchen to have a look around. There was a wine cooler full of French wines sorted by region and year; Rune certainly was a pedant through and through. He opened the stainless-steel refrigerator to see what was inside. The stench came as a total surprise, hitting him right in the gag reflex. He had expected the fridge to be clean and empty, but the opposite was true. Besides rotten vegetables and old milk, there was half a crab on a plate. A crab that looked like it was capable of killing anyone, despite being deceased itself. Based on what Fabian had determined from the other parts of the house, leaving fresh crab to rot in his fridge wasn't Schmeckel's style. In other words, he had not planned to be away from home.

Fabian continued searching the kitchen for more clues, uncertain whether the rotting food really meant something or if it was just a false lead, planted intentionally. There was nothing out of the ordinary in the cupboards, pantry, or freezer. He went through the drawers last. The first one contained silverware; the second had various kitchen utensils; and the third was full of the random items people usually don't know what to do with: pens, rubbers, obsolete coins, rubber bands, a roll of tape, an empty notebook, and a few keys, one of which looked like a car key. He picked it up and looked at it. PEUGEOT was engraved on the head.

Fabian had an idea and stuck the key in his pocket.

23

THE COLD STEEL WALLS pressed against the left side of her body and there wasn't much more room on her other side, three or four centimetres max. The space she was lying in was bordering on too small and it was dark and cold—twenty-two degrees below freezing, to be exact. Even if someone turned on a light it wouldn't get brighter. But even though she was lying naked on her back in a freezing, dim space, she didn't feel cold in the least.

DUNJA HOUGAARD HATED when people were late. She thought it was the height of disrespect to waste other people's time, as if it weren't just as valuable as your own. Oscar Pedersen was late, as usual, so Dunja took the initiative and pulled out the box identified as METTE LOUISE RISGAARD from the wall of cold-storage boxes. She looked at the young, naked woman, her dark hair spread out around her head like a fan. She was beautiful, and aside from the piercing in her lip and the diamond tattoo on her right shoulder, she was somehow undisturbed. Life hadn't started to eat away at her and leave its marks; death had beaten it to the punch. Mette Louise somehow looked so alive, like she was just sleeping deeply. *What a waste*, Dunja thought. She couldn't understand what the Swedish police had been thinking when they had neglected to contact them. They were counterparts after all, and the Swedes must have been fully aware that a dangerous killer might come to the gas station.

The door behind her opened and Oscar Pedersen came in

with his usual superior smile, a smile that indicated he didn't care a bit about his tardiness.

"Hello, beautiful. I suspected that you wouldn't be able to keep your hands to yourself. Have you found anything?"

"Today isn't about my opinions. I want to hear from you."

"It's such a waste. She's definitely a ten, wouldn't you say? Think about how much joy she had left to spread around." He laughed at his own joke and lowered the sides of the box.

Dunja had never liked Oscar, and she was sure he had become a medical examiner for all the wrong reasons. As soon as a female victim landed on his table, he was in an extra-good mood, especially when they were young. Unfortunately, he was one of the best pathologists in Denmark, and had never missed a clue or failed to discover a cause of death in his nearly thirty years on the job.

"This criminal sure knows how to kill someone. Take a look at this." He bent the victim's head back to reveal the neck fully, and turned the head from one side to the other. "See that?"

Dunja nodded. There were two small bruises on either side of the throat.

"He strangled her with the so-called pincer hold, which only requires the thumb and index finger. I'll show you." He demonstrated the technique using his own fingers. "It's one of the most effective ways to strangle a person." Dunja had to force herself not to back away from his claw-like hand. "It's far better than squeezing the whole neck, the way amateurs do, which takes both hands and at least fifteen minutes for the victim to die. We would be spared a lot of suffering in the world if people did their homework as well as this guy did."

Dunja wasn't sure whether he was kidding, but she decided to take him seriously. "Do you mean to say that the perpetrator might have training in various killing techniques?"

"He might, but it really only takes a basic knowledge of anatomy and heartlessness."

DUNJA STEPPED INTO THE lift and pressed the green button. She could feel herself moving up and immediately found it easier to breathe. She had never liked to be underground, and couldn't understand why morgues always had to be in the basement. It made no difference to the deceased, but moving the morgue upstairs would improve the lives of everyone who worked at the hospital. She could never manage more than thirty minutes down there at a time.

She would have liked to go up a few extra floors to have a chat with Morten Steenstrup, but he was still unconscious on the operating table. At this point the doctors couldn't say anything about his prognosis. All she could do was hope—not just for his sake, but for the investigation as well. Morten was her only chance right now of understanding exactly what had happened at the petrol station in Lellinge.

She walked by Rigshospitalet's convenience store and saw Steenstrup's face on all the billboards. He had become a great hero over the weekend: the little officer from Køge who refused to give up and kept fighting even though he was alone and seriously injured. Dunja thought his actions represented the height of stupidity; not only did they go against everything they had learned at the police academy, they went against all common sense. But people wanted a hero, and the fact that he was currently hovering between life and death didn't hurt in this department. *Perhaps it would have been even bigger news if he were a baby hippo*, Dunja thought, walking out through the main entrance.

She was biking down Ravnsborggade past Nørrebro Theatre, turning left onto Nørrebrogade, when her phone rang. She answered without stopping.

"You were trying to reach me." It was Kjeld Richter, their forensic technician.

"Yes. How are things going with the Peugeot?" Dunja asked.

"I'm sure it's fine. The car should have arrived at the station

152

by now and I've contacted Peugeot to order a key, but that's going to take at least two weeks since it's vacation season."

"You haven't started examining it yet?"

"When would I have had time for that? I'm still in Lellinge. Have you ever been here? It's a fucking shithole. I couldn't work over the weekend since both Agnes and Malte have the stomach flu and Sofie needed help."

"It's fine. I get it." Dunja thanked God she didn't have any kids as she pedalled across the Dronning Louise Bridge over the Lakes, where people insisted on jogging even though one pass was equal to half a pack of cigarettes' worth of exhaust fumes. "Shouldn't we consider sending the Peugeot over to Sweden if you don't have time to examine it? I've heard that they can't wait to get their hands on it."

"I suggested that option to Sleizner, but apparently as long as the conflict with Sweden is unresolved, we're not going to let them have anything. You know how he is when he's in *that* mood."

Dunja knew very well what "*that* mood" meant. If you managed to get on Sleizner's bad side, you might as well emigrate. No one was more stubborn than him. He was like an angry badger that refuses to let go before it hears the sound of breaking bones. She had heard stories about him even when she was back at the academy, but she'd always thought those were just tall tales. Now that Sleizner was her boss, she knew better.

"But we can't just let it sit here untouched for two weeks. It would be better to let the Swedes come down and examine it themselves."

"I'm not going to get involved. If you feel like getting Sleizner worked up, be my guest. Just don't count on any help from me when the shit hits the fan."

By the end of their call, Dunja's bad mood had grown even worse, if that was possible. She wondered whether there was any reason not to co-operate with the Swedes, aside from Sleizner's obstinate personality. As she biked along Kultorvet, she decided to contact the Swedish police in Helsingborg the minute she got to the station. Surely there would be someone in their department who was in a situation like her own.

24

"FIND ANYTHING INTERESTING?" FABIAN Risk asked as he stepped into the bedroom upstairs. Irene Lilja was standing behind the twin bed, leaning over a stack of books on the nightstand, glancing through the titles. There was another Bang & Olufsen stereo here, and more enlarged photographs of the same countryside as on the living-room walls.

"I don't know." She threw up her hands. "To be completely honest, I don't get this guy. On one hand, he seems so—how should I put it?—level-headed and totally in control of his life. He has good taste, is well read, and is so meticulous it borders on a disorder."

Fabian nodded. Lilja had arrived at the same muddled conclusion as him.

"But then you find something like this and it throws off your whole assessment." She handed him a blue notebook with the handwritten title MY SLEEPING DIARY.

"Sleeping diary? What's that?"

"Open it up and you'll see."

Fabian opened the book. It was jam-packed full of handwritten entries. Not a page was empty from cover to cover. There was a date and time in the upper right-hand corner of each page. Fabian read a passage out loud.

"*May 20, 1994, 3:12 a.m. I ran as fast as I could, but I'm still in slow motion. They just kept getting closer and closer: wolves with razor-sharp teeth. I came to an elevator and pressed the* button, but nothing happened. I banged on it as hard as I could. The doors opened, far too slowly. They caught up with me. I didn't do anything. I wanted to, but I couldn't. It was like I was paralysed. I just stood there and took it. I wanted to spit in their faces, but I didn't dare. The littlest one, who was maybe eight years old, came up and shoved me. I was totally unprepared, lost my balance, and fell right down the cliff..." Fabian stopped speaking and looked up from the book. "So it's a dream diary?"

Lilja nodded, took the notebook back, and flipped to the end. "Listen to this one from September 12, 2001, 5:38 a.m.... He lay down. I hit and kicked him until my white Nikes turned red and kept going until his face was no longer a face." She met his gaze. "You heard it for yourself. He's definitely not of sound mind."

Fabian agreed with her, and told her about the self-help books he had found in the living room. They agreed to let Molander take over and perform a thorough examination of the whole house to look for any clues that they'd missed. On their way through the upstairs hallway, Fabian suddenly stopped. "Did you check the attic?" he asked Lilja.

"No, there doesn't seem to be one here. I looked in every room."

"But what else would need one of these?" Fabian lifted a long, narrow steel rod from the nail in the doorjamb it had been hanging on. It was painted white and had a hook at one end.

Lilja shrugged and Fabian started walking around the second floor to inspect the ceiling. Lilja was right: there didn't seem to be an attic hatch in any of the rooms. Fabian didn't find what he was looking for until he climbed up on a chair and examined the ceiling light, which resembled an upside-down umbrella. He used the rod to pull it down. A steep ladder unfolded.

They climbed up and found themselves in a dark attic with a ceiling so low they had to stoop. When Lilja turned on the light, Fabian realized his initial impression of Schmeckel had been way off the mark. The attic functioned as a studio, just like the one in his own house, although it was considerably smaller than Sonja's and it didn't have any skylights. The paintbrushes were clean and arranged bristles-up in jars. Tubes of paint were sorted by colour. The space looked completely different from Sonja's artistic chaos.

"Yikes. Look what I found." Lilja lifted one of the canvases and placed it on an easel.

Although the painting was abstract, with thick strokes of bold colour, they had no problem deciphering the battered head of a human. Sonja would surely have said that Schmeckel was talented and that the painting was interesting. Fabian found it repulsive. The head was floating free against a white background, severed from its shoulders. Sinews and blood vessels hung from the neck. The nose was crushed and the skin had been removed from large portions of the left side of the face, exposing tendons, bone, and parts of the left eye socket.

"Say what you want, but this guy obviously has a gift." Lilja held up a few of the other canvases. All of them showed battered and beaten body parts. One of the paintings showed a pair of severed feet next to a bloody axe; another featured a torso with roughly twenty stab wounds, the knife still in the body, twisted a quarter-turn.

"I don't know what you think, but I believe these creative impulses fit the profile of the kind of man we're looking for," said Lilja.

"How do we know it's the same person?" asked Fabian.

"What do you mean?"

"I'm not sure exactly. The man downstairs seems to be the very picture of harmony, but his house is so superficial and devoid of personal artefacts you can't help wondering who he is deep inside. And then we come up to the attic and find so much personality here, it almost feels like a different guy."

"Maybe he has a lodger? Someone who uses his car as well?"

"Isn't there only the one bedroom upstairs?"

Lilja nodded.

They grew silent and each looked around the attic separately. They both needed time to think and make sense of it all. They poked around the tubes of paint, the easels, and the bizarre paintings. There was a metal box behind the jars of paintbrushes; its blue paint had rubbed off along the edges. Fabian carefully lifted the box and opened it. It contained around fifty Polaroid pictures. As soon as he saw the battered, swollen face he knew exactly how everything was connected.

December 16

Yesterday I went to the hospital.

They were waiting for me in the courtyard of our building. I ran but they caught me and took me to the playground. I tried to protect myself but I fell and they just kept kicking me. At first it hurt a lot. Then I didn't feel anything. It was like I stopped caring. I heard them laughing and showing each other different kinds of kicks. A man came and yelled at them. They ran away.

I tried to get up but I couldn't. Everything was spinning. The man helped me and asked me my name. He told me my head was bleeding and that I had to go to the hospital. I never told him my name even though he kept asking. He finally left so I could go home but I was hurt and it took a long time.

Mum started crying when I got home. I've only seen her cry one other time, when she was fighting with Dad, but it wasn't like this. I said I got in a fight and it was my fault. She wanted to know if I was fighting with someone in my class. I just said it was some guys I had never seen before. I think she believed me.

The good part is that I have two broken ribs, a concussion, and a couple of deep cuts so I get to stay home until Christmas vacation!

P. S. When I came home Laban was lying in his cage like he was sleeping, but he wasn't sleeping. I stuck a needle in his back to get him up. At first he squeaked and tried to get away but I held him down super hard. Then he ran around in his cage like someone was chasing him. It was super funny.

25

"ARE YOU SURE?" TUVESSON looked at the Polaroids showing the battered face that were spread out on the table.

"Yes," Fabian said confidently. It had come to him the instant he saw the pictures up in the attic in Lund — Claes Mällvik and Rune Schmeckel were the same person. "We've got a clear motive and a link to both the car and the murders of Jörgen and Glenn. I don't know why I didn't think of it earlier."

It was just the two of them in the meeting. Tuvesson would tell the others the news as soon as they were done going over the details.

"Why would Claes Mällvik change his name to Rune Schmeckel?" Tuvesson looked up from the photos and met Fabian's gaze.

"I would assume to escape his tormentors once and for all, so he wouldn't have to go through it again. He was brought to Helsingborg Hospital in 1993 more dead than alive, according to the records. It took thirty-six operations to save him, and that isn't even counting the cosmetic surgeries."

"And by tormentors, you mean Jörgen and Glenn."

Fabian nodded and walked over to the two photos on the whiteboard that depicted Claes Mällvik and Rune Schmeckel. Now he could tell that they were the same person. Sure, Schmeckel had had plastic surgery and looked different, but once you knew, it was impossible to miss.

"He didn't even report it to the police?" Tuvesson asked.

"No. Instead of alerting the authorities, he went underground and changed his identity so that he could plot his revenge undisturbed."

"It certainly is a strong motive," said Tuvesson. "But is he finished? Or could more classmates be in danger?"

"Are you asking whether more people bullied him?"

Tuvesson nodded. Fabian thought about it, looking at the enlarged class photo with Jörgen and Glenn crossed out. Fabian had never done a thing to him, besides look away and pretend nothing was going on. He told Tuvesson that he couldn't think of anyone else who had messed with Claes.

Tuvesson looked out at Helsingborg through the panorama window. "I'm going to call a press conference. We'll put out an alert for the suspect."

FABIAN SAT DOWN AT Elvin's desk with his ninth-grade yearbook, looking through the old class pictures for the umpteenth time to ensure that he hadn't missed anything. Were Jörgen and Glenn really the only ones who had bullied Claes? The whole class, not to mention the teachers, shared the blame in some way since they'd let it keep happening.

Lina caught his eye in one of the photos. She still hadn't called him and probably wasn't going to. He thought back to when they both lived on Dalhemsvägen—he at 143C and she 141B, the apartment just across the courtyard.

He remembered meeting her for the first time. It was the summer before they'd started first grade. He was standing in the parking lot with his tennis trainer, trying to bounce the ball on top of his racket as many times as he could. He hadn't noticed Lina show up, but she was sitting on the kerb watching him. She looked like a vision, with long blonde braids, a green skirt, and knee socks. She even had a tennis racket with her.

Neither of them said anything to each other. He tried not to look; he wanted to make it seem like he didn't know she was there. It didn't even occur to Fabian to let Lina play with the ball. His attempt at setting a record suddenly seemed absolutely trivial, and all he wanted to do was try to hit as hard as possible to show off his strength.

He went to bash the ball, but the blue rubber string he'd tied together in several places broke and the ball flew in a great arc, landing far out in the street. They both stayed put for quite some time, neither of them saying a word. He could remember how silly he'd felt, just quietly standing there. He was still pretending she wasn't there, so he had no idea how to get himself out of the situation.

"Do you want me to help you find the ball?" she said.

He still remembered each word as if it was one of a string of lottery numbers that had made him a millionaire. The silence was broken.

"No. I was going to buy a new one anyway," he replied, turning his back on both her and the tennis trainer and walking away. He waited several hours to sneak back and grab the ball, but by then it was gone.

His phone rang, giving Fabian a start. He accidentally tipped over his glass of water. A small flood spilled across the desk and he was quick to shove the yearbook and his stacks of documents aside as he answered the call.

"Risk speaking."

A Danish voice responded. "My name is Dunja Hougaard and I'm calling from the Copenhagen police's murder squad. It's about the murder of Mette Louise Risgaard and the attempted murder of Morten Steenstrup. As I understand it, the two of us are looking for the same guy."

"Dunja, I appreciate your call, but I think it would be best if you spoke to my boss, Astrid Tuvesson."

"That is exactly what I'm hoping to avoid."

By this time, Fabian had managed to rescue most of his

documents from the flood, which was turning into a small waterfall at the edge of the desk.

"And why is that?" He crawled under the desk and rescued the day's edition of *Helsingborgs Dagblad*.

"Don't ask me why, but my boss, Kim Sleizner, has given clear orders to my unit not to contact you all."

"So, in other words, this is an informal conversation." Fabian watched the blurry image of the rearing forklift at Åstorp Construction Supply darken as the moisture from the water spread out over the newspaper.

"Exactly. I was hoping we could help each other out."

"How are things going with the car? Have you found anything in it?" Fabian was just about to get up again when he caught sight of a key taped to the underside of the desk.

"I'd rather not discuss it over the phone. It would be better if we could meet."

"I'll have to think about it and get back to you."

"Of course. You know where to find me."

Fabian ended the call and contemplated what Dunja had said. He needed to carefully consider the consequences of going over Tuvesson's head again. She had given him a second chance, and made it crystal clear that it was his last one.

He gently loosened the tape, took the key, and weighed it in his hand. He stood up, checking to make sure no one was watching, and stuck the key in the lock of the drawer he hadn't been able to open. The key slid in easily. He looked around again and cautiously pulled out the drawer. It was full to the brim.

On the top of the heap, there was a calendar beside a pencil box. He lifted up the box to see what lay underneath, and was surprised by its heavy weight. He wondered if he should give in to his curiosity and open the box, but decided against it. He closed and locked the drawer and taped the key back in its spot under the desk.

26

CAMERAS WERE CLICKING, CHAIRS were being filled, and microphones were aimed at Astrid Tuvesson, who was sitting with Chief Prosecutor Stina Högsell behind a draped table on a podium. Fabian was leaning against the wall on the side of the room, amazed at what a freshly ironed white blouse, a few swipes of lipstick, a quick hair brush, and powder to cover dark rings under the eyes could do for a woman's appearance. Few men could achieve such a quick turnaround.

"Take it easy! Everyone will get in," ordered a guard, even though the room was already bursting at the seams. Journalists and photographers had come from all over Sweden for the press conference; there were even quite a few from neighbouring countries. The national television stations, TV4 and SVT, were there, as were DR and TV2 from Denmark, and NRK from Norway. Fabian could understand the enormous interest in the case. It was absolutely spectacular: a well-planned and artful crime like no other.

"I'd like to start by welcoming all of you here today," Tuvesson shouted into the buzz of voices, which soon faded. "For those of you who don't know me, my name is Astrid Tuvesson and I am in charge of the crime squad here in Helsingborg. Chief Prosecutor Stina Högsell is with me."

"Is it true that one of your officers was in the same class as the two victims?" someone in the audience yelled out.

"There will be time for questions later," said Tuvesson.

"Since the initial murder of Jörgen Pålsson, and then that of Glenn Granqvist immediately following it, we have focused on finding a tenable motive and perpetrator. While we were working on several lines of inquiry at first, one now stands out as most interesting. Today we are publicly naming this man a person of interest." Tuvesson picked up a remote and aimed it at the projector mounted on the ceiling. A large picture of Rune Schmeckel appeared behind her. "This photograph can be found on our website. Right after this press conference, we will open up a twenty-four-hour telephone line so that the public can call us with tips. The man's name is Rune Schmeckel, although he only began using that name in 1993. He previously went by the name Claes Mällvik. He was in the same class as the two victims, who allegedly mistreated him throughout his school years. There are also a number of reports suggesting that this mistreatment continued for many years into their adult lives."

"Are you implying this is a revenge killing for being bullied?"

"That is one of several possibilities we are looking at."

"Do you think he might kill someone else?"

"We can't answer that question for obvious reasons, but for the moment we are working from the theory that he is finished and in hiding. He may have even left Sweden, so we are issuing his description internationally. I would also like to emphasize that he is extremely dangerous and will continue to take more lives in order to escape, something we witnessed in Denmark."

"But isn't it your fault the situation in Denmark ended that way?" asked a Danish journalist. "Wasn't it your responsibility to inform the Copenhagen police that the killer was in the country?"

"I do not regard our efforts in that matter to have been misguided, but I have no further comment on that point, given that this investigation is currently active. We are putting all our efforts right now into finding and capturing the perpetrator, and that is the focus of this press conference."

Fabian was impressed by Tuvesson's ability to keep a firm

hand on the wheel and to steer the topic away from the incident in Denmark. She had even managed to defend him without saying his name.

"I have a question for Fabian Risk. How well did he know the suspect?"

"Fabian Risk isn't here right now, so I'll have to ask you to direct your questions—"

"Yes he is; he's right there!" said someone in the crowd, pointing at him.

Tuvesson turned to Fabian, who nodded and waved. "Yes, I'm here! And I didn't know the perpetrator at all really."

"Did you know he was a victim of bullying?"

Fabian thought for a moment before he nodded. "I did. I believe the whole class was aware of it."

"But you didn't do anything about it? Shouldn't you have—"

"We can't get into details, as I'm sure you understand," Tuvesson interrupted. "But we have a strong suspect, who is currently at large—"

"It's okay. I don't mind answering," said Fabian.

Tuvesson leaned back in her chair.

"Of course we all should have reacted, but we were afraid of becoming their next victim if we stuck our necks out. I think that's something most people can relate to from their school days. I'm not proud of it. In fact, it's one of the reasons I became a police officer. I didn't want to see myself as the sort of person who turns his back and closes his eyes."

Tuvesson let Fabian's words sink in and then bent over the microphone. "Are there any further questions?"

"I have one about the automobile you found in Denmark," shouted someone in accented Swedish from the mob. It was clear that it was a Dane trying to speak Swedish.

"The car is currently in the custody of the Danish police, who are undertaking a separate investigation of the events that happened there. We can't comment on it."

"I'll ask anyway, and we'll see if you can respond. Was Fabian Risk under your orders to remove one of the automobile's tyres and hand it over to the young woman at the petrol station, who was later murdered?"

Fabian tried to see who had asked the question, but the man was hidden by the other journalists. He turned to Tuvesson, who looked confused.

"I'm sorry, I didn't see who asked the question."

"It was me!" A man stood up, waving his hand. "My name is Svend Møller and I work for *Sjællandske*." He was blond with a reddish beard, and was wearing round glasses and beige outdoor clothing.

"What was your question exactly?" Tuvesson continued.

"I have information that the back tyre from the suspect's automobile was removed and that there was a note on the windscreen telling him to pick it up in the petrol station," the man said in broken Danish–Swedish. "As I understand it, the plan was to force the killer to contact the petrol station attendant, who had orders to call the police. So I'm wondering if you sanctioned this, because it cost an innocent Danish girl her life."

The silence only lasted for a few seconds. Yet it was very clear that Tuvesson didn't have a response. Fabian had no idea how the reporter could be so well informed. Was there a leak in the police department? They were about to lose control of the situation, so Fabian decided to try and take the wheel.

"Excuse me, where did you get this information?"

The bearded journalist turned to Fabian, looking quite pleased with himself.

"I got it from Mette Louise Risgaard's two colleagues. They claim there was a tyre in storage from Thursday, July first, to Friday, July second, when the killer returned to the location. They gave me this as proof." The man held up a note encased in plastic for everyone to see:

THIS VEHICLE IS ON PRIVATE PROPERTY
PLEASE CONTACT PERSONNEL

Everyone's attention was on the journalist, who was displaying the note to cameras with a smile, answering his colleagues' questions with a recommendation to purchase the next issue of *Sjællandske*.

One of the reporters from *Helsingborgs Dagblad* turned to Tuvesson. "Can you confirm these allegations are correct?"

"I can't confirm anything when it comes to the various details of our police work at the present time. This is partially to do with our technical investigation, but also because of the ongoing investigation in Denmark. I would like to take this opportunity to emphasize that I take full responsibility for my officers' actions, which have led us to the identification of a suspect. It is deeply unfortunate that these actions cost an innocent woman her life. We must not forget that the perpetrator is the one who took her life, not the police."

"Didn't the killer blame Fabian Risk for Mette Louise Risgaard's death in his note?" asked the bearded journalist wearing the outdoor clothing.

The news that the perpetrator had mentioned Fabian Risk specifically hit the journalists in the room like a missile. All of them had caught the scent of blood and were drowning Tuvesson out with questions.

"No comment!" Tuvesson repeated, declaring the press conference over.

Fabian forced his way through the throngs of journalists who were each trying to shout their question loudest, toward the spot where the Danish reporter was standing. But when he got there, the spot was empty. He couldn't see the man anywhere. Fabian climbed up onto the man's empty chair and did a sweep of the room. Could he really have left so quickly? He turned to the podium and saw that Tuvesson was already on her way out.

27

DUNJA HOUGAARD WAS WAITING for the lift doors to open. Her heart was racing and she could feel sweat forcing its way out through her pores, making her shirt stick to her back, and yet she kept making the mistake of cycling too fast. It was as if she was in a rush every time she got on her bike.

Today she was hurrying to see Morten Steenstrup, whose condition had become a matter of national concern; the media were following it as if he had royal blood. Medical experts had been flown in from Germany and England, and they had managed to stop the internal bleeding after a long series of complicated operations. His condition was now listed as "somewhat stable." This gave Dunja a small window to speak with Morten before he was readied for the next operation.

The lift arrived and she stepped in, pressing the button for the fourth floor. The lift moved up, stopping at the second floor to allow two men in green scrubs with masks hanging around their necks to step in. One of the men pressed the button for the third floor.

"How old did you say she was?"

"Forty-two."

"Kids?"

"Three of them. I don't usually react to that sort of stuff, but given her age and the fact that she had three kids, I couldn't believe how perfect they were."

"Real?"

"I think so."

"You think so?"

"It was impossible to tell."

"You can always tell."

"Believe me, I took a very good look."

"There's only one thing to do." His hands squeezed at the air. "What room did you say she was in?"

They burst into laughter and left the elevator on the third floor.

Dunja was about to run after them to find out their names, but she stopped herself and let the elevator continue to the fourth floor. She was already late.

She stepped out of the open doors and shook off any negative thoughts about whether Steenstrup would be receiving the same care without his hero status. She had to focus and use her time well. After a lot of persuasion, the attending physician had agreed to give Dunja three minutes with Morten, and not a second more. Steenstrup had recently woken up and was in no condition to withstand a long interrogation. He was hardly aware of where he was, much less the excitement his efforts had caused. But that was no problem for Dunja—she knew exactly what she was after and it wouldn't take her more than thirty seconds to find out.

She made her way down a long corridor that opened into a waiting room full of journalists. A few were typing at their laptops and others were playing chess. She saw a reporter from *Jyllands-Posten* playing against a reporter from *Politiken*, and noted with disappointment that *Jyllands-Posten* was winning.

One of the journalists noticed her and ran up to carpet-bomb her with questions, which caused the other reporters to come to life. Cameras started clicking as if she were the perpetrator; questions flew through the air, hitting her like wet snowballs. No one seemed to hear her when she said she couldn't give any comment whatsoever at the current time.

After a lot of pleading from the journalists, Dunja finally told them that she was going to have an initial and incredibly brief meeting with Morten Steenstrup, who had just woken up. She showed her badge to the officer on guard and entered the unit. She didn't exhale until the door had closed behind her.

"Dunja Hougaard?" asked the attending physician. He looked at her without batting an eye.

She nodded.

"When I say stop, it's over. Do not keep going. Okay?"

Dunja already disliked him, and she continued along the corridor without answering.

"I hope you acknowledge the massive exception I am making for you. The responsibility for this patient's life rests with me and no one else," the doctor went on, taking a left into another corridor. "And I intend to fulfil that responsibility." He stopped at a door guarded by two uniformed officers, and fixed his eyes on Dunja. "I hope you understand the gravity of this situation and that I can count on you to spare my patient any unnecessary digressions during your questioning."

"I suggest you open the door before he gets Alzheimer's."

MORTEN STEENSTRUP WAS AT the far end of the room, looking like anything but a hero. Both of his legs were in casts, there was a brace around his neck, and most of his hair had been shaved off. He was hooked up to an IV and a lot of beeping machines that monitored his vital signs.

His mouth was half open and his eyes were aimed straight up at the ceiling. He didn't react when Dunja entered the room. She couldn't help thinking that Morten looked dead, and worried he had passed away the moment before she'd entered the room, which would mean she had missed her chance thanks to the irritating doctor, who had followed her into the room to monitor her visit. She pulled up a chair and sat next to Steenstrup's bed.

"Hi, Morten. My name is Dunja Hougaard and I work as a detective with the crime squad in Copenhagen." She waited for a reaction and ignored the doctor, who cleared his throat and indicated her time was counting down by tapping his wrist where a watch would be.

"I only have a few minutes and I don't want to exhaust you. All I want to know right now is whether this is the man who attacked you." She took out the wanted picture of Rune Schmeckel and held it in front of Morten's face, but she didn't get a reaction.

"Morten. Do you see the man in the picture?"

"Yes," the police officer replied in a slightly raspy voice.

"Is this the same man who attacked you?"

"No."

His response came as a total shock. Dunja hadn't even considered the fact that he might not recognize the perpetrator.

"Are you totally sure? I want you to look at the photo again, very, very carefully."

"I'm positive it's not him."

"I don't want to put pressure on you right now, so I'll come back in a few days. Then we can—"

"It's not him."

"Okay, Morten. Can you tell me what's different? Is it the hair, or something else that's easy to change? Take as much time as you need to think. There's no point in forcing an answer."

The doctor cleared his throat and poked at his imaginary watch.

"Everything," Morten hissed.

"What do you mean, *everything*? I'm not sure I understand what you're saying."

"Everything is different. You've got the wrong guy."

28

THE FRONT PAGES WERE all adorned with the image of Rune Schmeckel.

WANTED!

Fabian Risk tossed back his espresso, ate a spoonful of princess cake, and started looking at various newspapers' home pages on his phone. He had walked into town, where he'd found a corner seat in Fahlmans Konditori. He could sit inside in peace, while everyone else crowded under the awnings of the pavement café.

He'd gone straight up to Tuvesson's office after the press conference. She wasn't there, so he'd had to wait, sure that she would want to talk to him and likely remove him from the case. After sitting there for quite a while, he decided to leave the police station and take a walk. He noticed the fresh billboards, and increasingly felt that the whole situation was starting to look more and more like a witch-hunt. His own misconduct was almost as big a story as the killer's identity. Several of the papers had published pictures of Fabian, and a few had gone so far as to accuse him of the murder. He couldn't say he was surprised. The press conference had been a total mess, and all the focus had landed on him.

He thought about what he would do if he were removed from the case. Would he go back to his vacation as planned, or keep investigating on his own? He decided on the former, although he knew deep down that he would end up pursuing the latter.

Kvällsposten had devoted the most space to him. They had mapped out his past in an impressively short amount of time thanks to old pictures and interviews with people he used to know. The article reminded Fabian why he sometimes thought the police should recruit journalists: the newspaper had managed to track down an old, retired soccer coach who claimed to have taught Fabian. The man had told *Kvällsposten* that Fabian hadn't been a team player, and always tried to take the ball all the way up the field to the goal on his own.

Fabian had no memory of playing soccer for any great length of time. He had never been all that interested in ball games, but he couldn't deny that he wasn't a team player. He had always believed that the goal was more important than the way you got there.

IN LOVE WITH THE VICTIM'S WIFE

Aftonbladet's headline hit him like a fierce lash of the whip. The article claimed that Lina Pålsson had been his high school sweetheart, and questioned whether his love was still alive and could be blamed for the fact that he had lost his good judgement. How could the article possibly know any of that? He'd never told anyone how he'd felt about Lina. Until a few days ago he hadn't given it a single thought in years.

The newspaper must have been in contact with Lina; it was the only explanation. He couldn't remember if he'd ever told her about his feelings for her. She had chosen Jörgen, and Fabian had chosen to bury his emotions so deep that no one would ever be able to find them. Unfortunately his feelings were now on public view, beyond his control.

It was a sensational story, and Fabian wasn't surprised that *Aftonbladet* had chosen to make such a big deal of it. Could his

174

relationship with Lina have affected his work on the investigation? Was it even possible for him not to be swayed by the fact that the victim had been married to his first love? He took out his phone and dialled Lina's number, but hung up as soon as he heard the phone ringing. He had no idea what he was going to say.

When he was finished with the newspapers he resumed his walk past the Helsingborg City Theatre and north along the boardwalk. It was windy. Waves reached above the wall and sprayed his face with cool, salty water. He realized how much he'd missed this city.

Fabian climbed up and walked along the wall back home, becoming wetter in the process. It wasn't until he stepped into the hall and pulled off his damp clothes that he understood how tired he really was. The day, which had started with the news of Glenn's death, continued with a chaotic press conference, and ended with the papers hanging him out to dry, felt like it had lasted an entire week and it was still only seven in the evening. The house was silent and there were three empty pizza boxes on the counter. They had eaten without him, not that he could blame them. His schedule was unpredictable. He didn't even know if he was hungry. The princess cake he had just eaten was sitting in his stomach like a ton of bricks, keeping all of his feelings from coming out.

Fabian went upstairs and looked in Matilda's room. He was surprised at how far she had come in organizing it. *Grease*, *High School Musical*, and *Dirty Dancing* posters were stuck up on the walls and the bookcase was full of books and all the little plastic objects she collected. Her desk was organized with pencil boxes and rubbers, just waiting for school to start in August. Her bed was made, and on the ceiling above it she had made a Pisces, her Zodiac sign, out of glow-in-the-dark stars.

All that was missing was Matilda herself. He looked in his bedroom, but it was empty as well. After changing into dry

175

clothes he knocked on Theodor's door, but didn't get a response. He opened the door and saw Theo lying face-down on his bed, hardly moving, a harsh sound emanating from somewhere in the room.

"Theo? Hello? Theo, can you hear me?" he said without raising his voice very much. Theodor showed no signs of life. "Hello?! Theodor?" He walked over to the bed and placed his hand on his son's shoulder. Theodor turned over, obviously startled, and pulled out one of his earphones. Metallica blared into the room.

"What?"

"Didn't you hear me calling you?"

"No."

Theo shrugged and put the earphone back in. Fabian yanked it out again and did the same with the other one.

More angry lyrics poured out of the earphones.

"What the hell do you want?"

"Where's everyone else?"

"How should I know?"

Fabian knew the teenage years were supposed to be rough, but he had expected a lot more yelling, slamming doors, and late nights out. This silence was an entirely different beast, and he had no idea how to handle it.

"Hey … how are you doing, really?"

Theodor sighed and paused the music. The words from "Enter Sandman" still rang in Fabian's ears.

"Do you miss your friends from Stockholm? I understand if that's what you—"

"What friends?"

"I don't know. The ones you used to play with?"

Theodor rolled his eyes.

"Or hang out with, or whatever you call it," Fabian went on, feeling like a blind man on a tightrope. "But you'll make new friends here. Well, maybe not right here. You'll have to leave this room and go out and—"

176

"Are you done?"

Fabian nodded, realizing that he probably would have reacted just as Theodor did to a dad like him. He left the room and couldn't help feeling a certain amount of relief.

HE FOUND SONJA UP in her studio, where she was working on a big new painting with broad, aggressive strokes. He watched her from the doorway, well aware that she disliked people looking at her while she painted, but he loved it; he thought she was most beautiful in these moments—no makeup, splashes of paint on her face, and a complete focus that blocked out all her surroundings.

She had a brush in each hand, a couple of paintbrushes in her hair to hold it up, and she was wearing her overalls, which were covered in so much paint they looked like a piece of artwork. Fabian could see she was wearing the red bra he had given her for Christmas two and a half years ago.

"Hi, honey."

"Hi," she replied with a smile, but her eyes said it all. She went back to spreading paint over the canvas.

"May I come in?"

She didn't answer, so he walked into the room and stood behind her. "It's great that you're back to work."

The painting was unlike anything she had ever done. He appreciated that she had been searching for a new way to express herself, after all those years of working with fish motifs. The fish years had been a successful time, and Sonja's profits had far exceeded his own salary, no matter how much overtime he worked. Everyone wanted to have her escapist underwater portraits of schools of fish, octopuses, and crabs. It was every artist's great dream, but it had become a nightmare for Sonja in the end. During her peak, she'd had a waiting list of more than a year. Her customers got to choose the size and colours to match their home decor. Sonja had felt like anything but an artist and eventually found herself hitting a wall.

That had been a little over six months ago, and she had been experimenting since then. For a while it had looked like birds would take over where the fish left off; she'd painted nests, eggs, and flocks in the sky. But what he was looking at today was something completely different: a violent cacophony, each shade redder than the last.

"Please. I'm working."

"I assume you've read the papers."

"You shouldn't believe everything you read."

"The young girl was my responsibility and my fault."

"What about Lina Pålsson?"

Fabian had been waiting for that question. He couldn't blame her for asking. After what had happened with Niva, her trust in him was broken, barely hanging on by a fragile thread.

"Yes, I was in love with her, and yes, I wanted nothing more than for the two of us to be together. But, Sonja, that was in the past, at school. And it never *was* the two of us, which I'm happy about today."

Sonja turned and looked him in the eye. Paint was dripping from her brush to the floor. "So she doesn't mean anything to you now?"

"She's nothing more than an old classmate whose husband was just brutally murdered."

"Okay." Sonja went back to her painting. Fabian stood there, wondering if he should embrace her, when his cell phone rang.

"Hello?"

"How are you doing?" It was Irene Lilja.

"Well, you get what you deserve, as my mother would say." Fabian backed up a few steps to avoid being hit by Sonja's paint spatters. "But it's not a great time. Can I call you back?"

"Hold on. Is it really true?" she asked curtly. "The part about Lina Pålsson?"

"Yes."

Fabian was met with silence on the other end of the phone.

He could tell Lilja was thinking the same thing he was—how were his feelings for Lina affecting him during the investigation? He left the studio and walked down the stairs.

"Just so you know, I wasn't even fully aware of the feelings myself, at first. It's like I've repressed my entire upbringing." He felt the need to explain himself, to try and make her understand. "That's why I didn't say anything…"

"Listen, I think it would be better to bring this up with Tuvesson. I'm sure you have a great explanation." It was impossible to miss the sarcasm in her voice. "But that's not why I called. There's been another death."

Fabian quickly tried to figure out who it could be. Who had he missed?

"It's not a member of your class."

"It's not? Well, who…"

"Monika Krusenstierna. Your homeroom teacher."

All Fabian could remember about Monika Krusenstierna was that she always wore knee-length skirts, usually plaid, and she never, ever cracked a smile. She'd taught her classes as if they were just something she had to get through on a schedule. Maths problems had to be figured out, maps had to be labelled, and books had to be read out loud, chapter by chapter. Discussion and reflection were out of the question. The more he thought about it, the more his years with Monika Krusenstierna seemed like one long vocabulary quiz.

"The homecare aides found Monika seated in an armchair in her apartment. Apparently it took them some time to realize that she was actually dead, since there were no visible marks on her body."

"Have they determined the cause of death?"

"Heart failure. Braids just called to give me a preliminary report. Her blood vessels were more plugged up than an old coffeemaker."

"So it wasn't murder?"

"No. I just wanted to put it on your radar before it shows up in the papers. We know how they'll spin it. One juicy detail I thought you would like: she had the latest issue of *Kvällsposten* open in her lap."

"To which page?"

"The story where they describe how everything went so wrong."

Fabian knew exactly which article Lilja was talking about: THE TEACHER WHO TURNED A BLIND EYE? The article described how Claes Mällvik had been systematically bullied by Jörgen and Glenn and how no one had done a thing about it. Even the adults hadn't bothered to care. The journalist asked why Monika Krusenstierna hadn't raised the alarm, and suggested that she must have suspected that all was not right in her class. Fabian pitied her. The accusations in the article would have been terrible to read—and must have indirectly caused her death.

"Thanks for calling."

"No problem. See you tomorrow, Mr. Lover Boy."

29

IT WAS FAR TOO late by the time he realized how badly he had underestimated Fabian Risk. The incident in Glenn's yard had cost him a day and given Risk enough time to find the car in Denmark. He went over the events again and again in his mind, scrutinizing every detail, but he still had no idea how it happened. It was a complete surprise to discover that Risk had removed one of the tyres. He was turning out to be a much greater threat than he ever could have expected. He had to admit that deep, deep down, he was impressed.

He had failed to move the car. He'd been forced to give up, to run off and leave it behind. It was now in the hands of the Danish police, which was at least better than if the Swedes had it. The Danes wouldn't find much of interest. The only question was how long it would remain with them.

He had seriously considered aborting his plan and leaving on the boat that was fuelled up, well stocked, and waiting for him in Råås harbour. But instead he decided to look into changing parts of it. He would be delayed by at least another whole day, which he had to accept. Quitting would be such a monumental defeat that he wasn't even certain he could live with it.

Risk had played only a small role in the original plan; he was practically just an extra body. However, once he had discovered that Risk was moving back with his family, he had been given a slightly more active role. Things had got out of control and now Risk was taking up much more space than he was meant to. Risk needed to be put in his place before the plan derailed entirely. He still didn't know exactly how he could do it, but he had turned weaknesses into strengths before, and he had no reason to doubt that he would be successful this time too.

Most of the events of the last few hours had played right into his hands. His guest appearance as a Danish journalist had succeeded beyond his hopes. It had made Risk the centre of everyone's attention, which would hinder and probably also delay the entire police investigation. As an added bonus, the Danes had set up obstacles for both themselves and the Swedes, for which he was grateful. The fact that a car was pulling out in front of him, leaving an empty parking space right in front of Risk's terrace house, was just the cherry on top.

He fastened a little web camera to the inside of the side window with a suction cup, screwed on the antenna, and coupled the power cord to the cable he had run from the car battery. He turned it on and the diode started blinking like a car alarm. He took out his phone and sent a six-digit code to a specific number via text message. About ten seconds later, the video came to life on his phone. He aimed the camera at Risk's front door and adjusted the focus.

He got out of the rental car and locked the door. He had worn his gloves the entire time he was in the car; he wasn't about to make that mistake again. He headed left on the pavement and counted four doorways before he turned right onto Brommagatan at the corner. Just after he passed the illuminated shop window of Skandia Realtors, which was full of properties not even people moving from Stockholm could afford. He took a right onto a gravel path and walked past a number of waste containers and a sign informing him that the area was for residents only.

The small yards crowded each other behind the terrace houses, each one fancier than the next. He counted his way to Risk's and noticed that the previous owners had chosen to stay out of the great yard-furnishing race. He climbed over the half-rotten fence and hid behind a tool shed. From there he could see straight into the house.

FABIAN WAS HAVING TROUBLE keeping his eyes open, but he knew he wouldn't be able to fall asleep. His thoughts wouldn't grant him any reprieve, and he couldn't shake the sense that everything he was trying to accomplish was about to crack and collapse into pieces. He was sitting at the kitchen table with his laptop, clicking around Mette Louise Risgaard's blog. At first he'd thought it wasn't about anything in particular, since it mostly consisted of a lot of short, uninteresting entries about Mette Louise's daily experiences. Very occasionally she might offer a thought or reflection.

But the more entries he read about going to work at the petrol station, meeting friends, thinking about getting new tattoos, and watching DVDs, the more wrapped up in her life he got. A picture of an intelligent young girl developed, someone who was full of thoughts and ideas but couldn't do anything with them in the backwoods town where she had grown up. Mette Louise Risgaard hated Lellinge more than anything else, and would rather have killed herself than grow old there.

Fabian couldn't tell if she had a boyfriend from the blog, but he did get to read about himself: the Swede who had left her with a tyre. It was the most exciting thing that had happened to her that week. Only two more posts followed: one about a broken coffeemaker and one about a neighbour who bought porn videos. If you weren't aware of what had happened, it might take a few days to realize the blog was abandoned. She was dead.

Fabian went to another website, which informed him that the funeral would be held in two days' time, at one o'clock in the afternoon at Lellinge Church. He decided to attend, whether or not Tuvesson thought he should keep working on the case. It was the least he could do.

He closed the computer and was brushing his teeth in the guest bathroom when the doorbell rang. He looked at his watch—it was just past midnight—and turned off the water. Maybe he was hearing things. He had just rinsed out his mouth when it rang again. It was impossible to miss this time. Someone was standing at his door, ringing the bell.

Fabian dried his face and went to open the door. On his way there, he wondered who it could be, but he couldn't think of anyone who would visit at this hour. He made a mental note to put in a peephole as soon as he had time. Then he unlocked the door and opened it.

30

HE HAD TO READ the article a few times before he understood what had happened. He had been incapable of taking it in the first time. It felt like news from some parallel reality. But after reading it through twice, the news hit him like a bucket of cold water. Could it really be true? He had searched other news sites, watching as the story got bigger and bigger. It really had happened: Monika Krusenstierna was dead.

"Shit," he hissed to himself. Everything had gone as planned with Risk and he had just rented a second car to go pick up Monika when he'd glanced through the latest news on his phone. He stopped on the side of the road to read the article a third time. Could it be a different Monika Krusenstierna? He'd searched her name in the White Pages, and only got one hit. And that was in Helsingborg, at an address he'd unearthed during his research. He needed to see it with his own eyes to make sure it wasn't another trick set up by Risk.

Monika Krusenstierna lived at Dalhemsvägen 69, on the fifth floor of a high rise that had just received new steel siding: yellow had been discarded in favour of grey. He parked the car by Dalhem School and went the last little bit on foot. From the top of the pedestrian bridge across Dalhemsvägen he could see the flashing blue lights reflected on the façades—the parking lot was full of police cars. It definitely was his Monika.

Not only had it cost time and resources to prepare the space for the old homeroom teacher, but it was also to be the crowning glory of his plan, the last piece of the puzzle that would make everything else fall into place. Now none of it would work, and once more he would have to go back to the drawing board.

Time was his biggest problem. He'd already gone over his margins, and couldn't afford to spend any more days adjusting the plan. Tomorrow's schedule was already full — he had to go back to Denmark and finish what he'd started. Why he hadn't done so in the first place, he didn't know. He hadn't intended to take the lives of innocent bystanders, and had been taken by surprise: first by the girl, and then by the police officer. He hesitated, choosing to flee instead of finishing the job. He wouldn't make that mistake again. From now on, he would let nothing stand in his way.

His phone buzzed and the screen lit up. He saw that the camera in the rental car had come to life. He'd programmed a time delay into the motion detector so it wouldn't react each time someone walked by — only if someone went up the front steps. He entered his code and waited.

He saw Risk opening his door and letting in his visitor. Suddenly it all fell into place. Instead of Monika Krusenstierna, he would give Fabian Risk the main role. Going forward, he would play the central, most crucial part in the whole scenario. The solution was as simple as it was brilliant, and once he thought of it he didn't know why it hadn't been part of his original plan.

31

LINA PÅLSSON WAS SITTING on the sofa next to Fabian. Her face was swollen and her eyes were red. He gave her a handkerchief to wipe her face and poured some piping-hot tea. Considering Sonja's reaction to the article in the paper, he had been hesitant to let Lina in once he realized she was the person at the door, but she'd wanted to come in. Fabian had to ask her twice what she was doing there. She apologized and burst into tears. He couldn't help but give her a hug.

It was past one thirty in the morning, and they were both drinking tea in the living room. Fabian allowed silence to fill the room; he thought it was up to Lina to break it. Half an hour earlier he had heard Sonja coming down from the studio. She was on her way down the stairs, but she changed her mind and went back up again. Twenty minutes later, she had come down wearing only her Japanese robe, which she knew he loved. She greeted Lina, saying she was sorry for her loss, and then she kissed Fabian goodnight and went back upstairs. He called up that he would be in bed soon. She told him to take all the time they needed.

"To be honest, I don't even know why I'm crying. I don't think I ever really loved him."

"You must have loved him at some point," Fabian said, regretting his words immediately. This was not a discussion they should be having.

Lina shook her head.

"Actually, I don't really understand how Jörgen and I ended up together. To be totally honest, I always thought it would be you and me." She laughed and took a sip of the hot tea.

"So why Jörgen?" He didn't want to ask, but he couldn't help himself.

"Do you remember that class party? The one we had at the start of seventh grade in one of those places near where we lived?"

Fabian recalled it all too well. It had been a masquerade, and he and Stefan Munthe had struggled to sew their own prisoner costumes. They had taken old sheets and added stripes with spray paint and masking tape, and then spent hours sewing. It had taken up their evenings and all of Saturday. They were determined to have the best costumes, like it was a matter of life or death. Fabian had also finally decided to ask Lina out; the time was right for him to tell her how he felt.

Once he and Stefan got to the party, they were the only ones dressed in costumes, and realized that everyone was laughing at them behind their backs. Everything felt wrong and they decided to bike home to change into regular clothes fifteen minutes later.

"Jörgen kissed me that night," Lina continued, "and told me we were a couple. I had been hoping it would be you, but you didn't really seem interested in me. You took off and it was a long time before you came back, and…well, I ended up with Jörgen." She shrugged and stopped speaking.

Fabian nodded mutely, preoccupied by the memory of how much it had hurt. "Lina, is there anything you want to tell me that might help us with the investigation?"

Lina didn't initially react to his question; instead, she sipped her tea and took her time setting her cup back down. "Glenn and Jörgen did a lot of stupid things. To be completely honest, sometimes I was afraid of Jörgen."

"Did he hit you?"

"No, but he could be rather rough."

"In what way?"

"He would go pretty far when we had sex. I tried to talk to him about it, but he just brushed it off, saying that it was all in good fun and he could tell that I liked it. It was mostly just a game for him." She grew quiet.

"Lina, I understand that you need to talk about this stuff, but I'm not sure I'm the right person for it."

She nodded and placed a brass key on the coffee table. "This is for a safe at Glenn's house."

Fabian picked up the key and studied it. Molander and his men had already gone through Glenn's house. Nothing of great interest had popped up, so a more thorough search had fallen low on the list of priorities. Fabian would definitely know if they had found a locked safe.

"It's supposed to be in the kitchen, but I couldn't figure out where," Lina said, looking him right in the eyes. "I know it's in there though."

"How did you get this key?"

"Glenn didn't want to keep the key in his own house. He thought having the safe was risky enough."

"How do you know all this? I have a hard time believing that Jörgen just came out and told you."

"They weren't always sober and careful. This key was my insurance in case Jörgen ever went too far."

"Do you know what's in the safe?"

Lina responded with a tired smile and stood up. "Thanks for the tea and for taking the time to listen to me. I'll show myself out."

"Let me give you a ride."

"Please don't trouble yourself. I have the car."

"I'll walk you there. It's the least I can do." Fabian stood up and followed her into the hall.

"Fabbe, you really don't have to. It's pretty far from here."

"All the more reason I—"

"To be perfectly frank, I don't think your wife would appreciate it."

"I guess you have a point there," Fabian said with a smile, opening the door and accompanying her out of the house.

He took her arm as they walked along the empty pavement. Neither of them said a word and the silence felt totally natural. Lina turned to look at him when they arrived at her car.

"Do you remember the time we were playing marbles at recess and I let you borrow my last one after you lost all of yours?"

Fabian nodded. It had been one of the first great moments of his life. He had managed to knock down pyramid after pyramid with Lina's last marble. His hands had felt magical in that moment. Almost everyone from his class had gathered around to watch him. Soon students from other classes came to watch him, observing his exceptional skill, though it might have been luck. Luck or skill aside, he had won a big bag of marbles, which he'd given to Lina.

"I still have those marbles." She gave him a hug and a kiss on the cheek before opening the car door and climbing in.

FABIAN CRAWLED INTO BED as carefully as he could so that he wouldn't disturb Sonja, but she was already awake. She rolled over to embrace him; her body felt warm and naked. He couldn't stop thinking about how tired he felt.

"Fabian, do you love me?"

"Of course I do."

"Are you sure?"

He pressed his naked body against hers and leaned over to kiss her, but she put her hand over his mouth.

"Listen, there's something I've been thinking about."

He sighed and rolled onto his side. "Sonja, I know this is not what—"

"Please let me finish. I think it would be best if the kids and I go back up to Stockholm for a while, otherwise I'm just going to hang around here getting bitter, which is the last thing we need right now. I suggest we put our fresh start on hold until the case is finished."

He wanted to protest and promise that from now on everything would be so much better if she decided to stay in Helsingborg.

"I've already spoken with Lisen, and we can have the guest house out on Värmdö for the rest of the summer, which would give Matilda a chance to play with her cousins."

Fabian couldn't bring himself to do anything but nod.

"As soon as the case is finished and you have time for us, we'll come down and start over together here—the way we had originally planned."

"I think we should go somewhere far away together—just the two of us—after everything is finished," Fabian said.

Sonja agreed.

32

THE DRIPPING LEAVES BETRAYED the quiet rain, a reminder that the beautiful weather of the past week hadn't been typical in the least. Helsingborg was normally a windy, rainy city. On the other hand, few of the events of the past week could be considered normal, Fabian thought as he walked through Pålsjö forest with Astrid Tuvesson.

She had called him that morning to suggest they take a walk. So far they had spoken about everything but the real reason they were meeting. She'd asked if his family liked Helsingborg and how the children felt about starting at a new school. Fabian had answered all of her questions as honestly as he could, but he made sure not to reveal more than he had to.

The beech forest opened up as they approached Pålsjö Castle. They hadn't spoken in several minutes and Fabian felt as if the silence were about to take on a life of its own. They walked around to the other side of the castle park, passed the labyrinth, and crossed the wet grass over to the long avenue where the trees formed a dark tunnel. Fabian remembered how he used to play tag here as a kid, and how he'd thought it was so unusual that the trees grew so precisely that they formed that tunnel—until one day he saw a gardener with a chainsaw.

"Fabian, I'm well aware of the fact that if it hadn't been for your shortcuts, this case would be going nowhere. But the investigation is my responsibility and I can't continue to defend what happened in Lellinge, otherwise I will be removed from the case, too, and the whole investigation will be moved to Malmö. We both know how things end down there."

Fabian knew what she was insinuating: Malmö was famous for topping the "most unsolved cases" list year after year.

"I want to solve this case as much as you do, and as quickly as we can, but we can't afford to play such a high-stakes game any more."

"I understand what you're saying. You need a scapegoat."

"It's not very hard to find one in this particular case." She allowed herself to smile for the first time during their walk. "And that's without mentioning your alleged teenage crush." Fabian was about to explain, but he stopped talking when she held up a hand to ward him off. "Which I don't even want to address."

They emerged from the tree tunnel and noticed that the rain had stopped, the sky already brighter. Tuvesson paused at the scenic outlook and gazed out across the lively, busy sound, where Kronborg Castle was already bathed in light.

"I suggest you return to your vacation and start again on August sixteenth, as we originally planned. If I were in your shoes, I would take care of my family and be glad for the chance to enjoy myself. This weather won't last for more than a few weeks."

Fabian nodded and Tuvesson turned to walk away.

"If I'm going to be on vacation, it might be more appropriate if you took care of this." Fabian dropped the small brass key into her hand. "Apparently it's to a safe in Glenn's house."

Tuvesson looked puzzled.

"All I know is that it's supposed to be somewhere in the kitchen." She thanked him and left.

Fabian looked toward Denmark at the beautiful view, and reflected on what had been said. He'd been expecting Tuvesson to take him off the investigation—it was the only option she had, given what had happened—but deep down Fabian knew it would take a lot more than regular, by-the-book police work to solve this case.

December 24

Hello Diary, and Merry Christmas.

I've been trying to act normal but both Mum and Dad noticed that something was up. They thought I didn't like my presents even though I said I was super happy. I got a keyboard with a stand. Dad wanted to help me set it up, but I didn't feel like it. I told him I was tired and went to my room even though it wasn't even eleven o'clock yet.

I read about someone who jumped in front of a train. She was the same age as me and they went after her the same way they went after me. Everything she had written in her suicide note reminded me of my life.

I've never told anyone this before, but just so you know, I've thought about jumping several times. I'm not brave enough yet. I'm so fucking tired of being afraid. It's been going on for six months now. I'm afraid to eat in the cafeteria, afraid at recess, afraid of doing something stupid in class, afraid of people who used to be my friends, afraid of going home, afraid of what happens after Christmas break.

Mum came in my room even though I said I wanted to be alone and asked why I didn't want to play the keyboard. I didn't want to answer but she kept pushing. I started to cry. I tried to stop, but I couldn't and then I told her I didn't want to go back to school because everyone there is so stupid. She asked if someone was bullying me and I told her that wasn't it. She said she thought it could be and had met with my teacher to talk about it. The teacher hadn't noticed anything except that I've been more absent-minded and quiet and that my test grades have gone down.

I didn't have anything to say to my mum after that so she left. I can't believe they went behind my back, talking a lot of shit about me.

Stupid, shitty school starts again in two weeks. At first I thought about skipping, but decided not to. I've made up my mind to do something else. I've thought about it so many times and I'm totally sure now. I have nothing to lose. After all, it can't get any worse.

Goodnight.

P. S. I didn't buy Laban a Christmas present, but he didn't seem to care. His fur is falling out all over. Maybe it's all the piss he drank. He's so goddamn idiotic and ugly and disgusting. I fucking hate him.

33

LILJA, MOLANDER, AND KLIPPAN were already sitting in the conference room when Astrid Tuvesson arrived with a tray of fragrant lattes and a bag of croissants. The exhausted faces suddenly smiled, and Klippan started joking about how much weight he was going to gain if they didn't solve this case soon.

"I want to start by saying that Fabian Risk has been taken off this case, effective immediately," Tuvesson informed the team as she handed out the coffees.

"That's too bad. I thought he seemed pretty good," said Klippan.

"I would have liked nothing more than for him to stay, but it was untenable."

"That's obvious enough," said Lilja. "He was a member of the class, and we can't treat him any differently from all the others."

"You don't think he's a suspect, do you?" Molander asked.

"I wouldn't go as far as to suggest he is a suspect, but—"

"I think we'll leave it there," Tuvesson interrupted, staring firmly at Lilja. "Okay?"

Lilja and the others nodded, and started reviewing the new information. Lilja told everyone that she had contacted all the airlines, but none of them had a record of a passenger by the name of Rune Schmeckel on board in the last few days—or Claes Mällvik, for that matter.

"There's no reason he couldn't have kept driving through Denmark in another car, which would put him far beyond

Germany at this point," Klippan said, reaching for another croissant.

"We've put out an international APB, but for now we'll work with the theory that he's still in Sweden. Have you been able to identify everyone in the class yet?"

"It's more or less finished, wouldn't you say, Irene?" Klippan answered.

"It's as good as it can be," said Lilja. "I would have preferred to double-check it against an official class list, but that's been impossible to track down."

"Why? Wasn't there supposed to be a copy at the city archive?" Tuvesson asked, turning toward Klippan.

"I'm sure it's there, but the electronic catalogue for the archives crashed."

"What do you mean, *crashed*?"

"Do you remember that cyberattack on City Hall back in May that was in the papers quite a bit?"

"Of course. Weren't they bombed with emails?" said Lilja.

"Yes, and probably a ton of viruses and Trojan horses, too. The server containing the city's archives catalogue conked out, too."

"How convenient," Tuvesson sighed.

"A little too convenient, if you ask me."

"I don't get it. If class lists also exist in the physical archive, we should be able to go and get them," said Lilja.

"Without the catalogue, they don't have the archive number. And without the archive number it's like looking for a needle in a haystack, only harder. They've promised to give it a shot, but it will still take weeks—if we're lucky."

Tuvesson didn't say anything for a moment, and then shook her head. "This is totally pointless." She turned to Lilja. "How many of the students we've identified still live in Skåne?"

"All of them live here, actually, except for one who lives in Oslo."

"However, a lot of them are on vacation abroad right now," said Klippan.

"Let's draw up a list and rank the class in the order we want to contact them. Our priority is to identify if anyone else might be in danger."

"Already done. I've been in contact with a few of them," said Lilja.

"And?"

"So far everyone has described one another as sparkling, saintly little lights that did nothing but spread love and warmth around them."

Klippan laughed and shook his head.

"Let's hope Jörgen and Glenn were the only victims," said Tuvesson, turning to look at Molander. "Are you done combing through Schmeckel's house?"

"More or less. Aside from a few fingerprints and stuff, I haven't found anything of particular interest. I had been hoping to at least find an extra key to his car, but there wasn't one there."

"Maybe he has a place in the country?" Klippan said.

"Not one that's listed under his name," said Lilja.

"Speaking of country homes," said Molander, sending around a few copies of the framed black-and-white photos from Schmeckel's home. "These were photographs we found in Schmeckel's house. If it's a country home he owns abroad, it's not at all a given that it would be registered in Sweden."

They looked at the pictures of the hilly landscape and the crowded city.

"Do you know where the photos were taken?" Klippan asked Molander, who lit up.

"At first I thought it was Carcassonne. I've always wanted to go to that part of France. Not to mention, *Carcassonne* is one of my very favourite games."

The others looked thoroughly confused.

"Haven't you ever played *Carcassonne*?"

The rest of the team shook their heads.

"Oh my God, you guys don't know anything," Molander said in an exasperated tone.

"But then you determined that the photo wasn't taken in Carcassonne?" said Tuvesson.

"Exactly. I did some analysis and the landscape is definitely Grasse, which is also in the south of France, but more to the east. I've been there, actually. Have any of you ever heard of the film *Perfume*?"

"Yes," Klippan said. "Wasn't that the one with—"

"I'm sure it was, but perhaps we could discuss it another time?" Tuvesson interrupted. "Instead, let's try to figure out if he has a vacation home in Grasse. I would also mention another lead that has been brought to my attention." She held up the key she'd received from Fabian. "I got it from Risk, who told me it unlocks a safe in Glenn's kitchen."

"I've already gone through that kitchen and I can assure you there's no safe," said Molander.

"I want you and Irene to take another look anyway, to be on the safe side." Tuvesson slid the key across the table toward Lilja and turned to Klippan. "How is the McDonald's trail going?"

"I've contacted all the locations we identified, but so far nobody recognizes him."

"So far?"

"They work in shifts, so I haven't met with all of them yet."

"Okay. What else do we have? Has anything interesting come in from the public since we released the picture?"

"Not exactly," said Klippan.

"What do you mean, *not exactly*?"

"To make a long story short, nothing has come in that would be worth telling the grandkids about." Klippan glanced at the last croissant.

"That might be true, but at this moment I would prefer the long version."

"Aside from the usual callers, two of his patients have phoned claiming to have spotted him in Farsta, Bollmora, and Grums, just to name a few far-off places. One claimed that Schmeckel surgically inserted a GPS transmitter into his stomach so that Schmeckel could find him if he ever got a taste for human flesh."

"Lovely. What did the other patient say?"

"His story is pretty funny. He claims that Schmeckel raped him while he was unconscious on the operating table."

"Did you say *funny*?" Lilja asked, taking the last croissant right from under his nose.

"I'm not finished." Klippan's eyes followed Lilja's croissant. "He claims it happened sometime in 1998, a long time ago. When I asked why he didn't report the incident back then, he replied that he got haemorrhoids after the rape, which he thought were too embarrassing to tell the police about." Klippan cackled until his whole belly shook.

Lilja exchanged glances with both Tuvesson and Molander. All three of them tried not to laugh.

"What made him suddenly want to tell someone?" Tuvesson asked.

"As far as I could understand, they only just started to let up."

"Twenty-two-year-old haemorrhoids?" Lilja asked. When Klippan nodded, she couldn't hold back her laughter any longer.

"Hasn't Linkert Pärsson called?" Molander asked.

"Link? I was just getting to him. He claims to know exactly where the killer is."

"You don't say," said Lilja.

"Did he mention how he'd figured it out?"

"He sure did, and he has his very own special theory as usual. He believes Claes planned his revenge back in his school days, which he deciphered from reading the graffiti on the school walls. Link thinks we should let him collect and decrypt all the graffiti in all the bathrooms at Fredriksdal School."

No one seemed to know what to say. Everyone at the Helsingborg police station knew of sixty-eight-year-old Linkert Pärsson and his long list of acronym disorders. He was nicknamed "Link" or "Pärsson's Syndrome." Linkert Pärsson's greatest dream was to become a detective, but after five failed applications to join the police academy, he'd become a janitor at Fredriksdal School, where he had worked until he was accused of sexual molestation for drilling a peephole into the girls' shower room. Although the prosecutor had called for jail time, Linkert was only sentenced to a fine and mental health treatment. Almost everyone at the station had an opinion on how good the treatment really was.

These days, he called himself a detective and had his own printed business cards: LINKERT PÄRSSON — SOLVES THE UNSOLVABLE.

In the past five years, Tuvesson and her group hadn't worked on a single case without a theory from Linkert, each more far-fetched and ridiculous than the last. Despite his faults, everyone liked him, and occasionally invited him to share his theories over a cup of coffee.

But nobody was laughing today. In many ways, this was a typical Link theory—crazy and improbable—yet none of them could quite dismiss it, perhaps because they all felt that anything was possible in this particular case. The idea that the perpetrator might have left clues among graffiti seemed just as plausible as any other.

"What does he want?" said Tuvesson.

"The usual. Coffee and a Punsch-roll," said Klippan.

"Doesn't he usually request almond tarts?" Molander asked.

"That was before he got it into his head that the Feminist Initiative was poisoning them with female sex hormones to bring down the patriarchy."

"Shouldn't they have gone with the Punsch-rolls instead?"

34

HE HAD THE WHOLE car to himself when he first boarded the train in Helsingør, but as they approached Copenhagen, more and more passengers got on. By the time they got to Hellerup Station all the seats were full. Most people had headphones in and were flipping through the free newspapers, which had devoted pages to the Danish police's search for him.

HERE IS THE SWEDISH KILLER!
HIS NAME: RUNE SCHMECKEL.

He grabbed a discarded newspaper and flipped to the articles that described—in great detail—how he had killed Jörgen and Glenn and, most recently, Mette Louise Risgaard. He burst into such loud laughter after reading the two-page story on the continuing conflict between the Danish and Swedish police that the woman beside him looked up curiously.

He devoted all but the last fifteen minutes of the train ride along the Danish Gold Coast to developing and polishing his new plan. The more he thought about it, the more the pieces seemed to be falling into place. His new idea had come to him the moment Risk opened the door for Lina Pålsson. He couldn't explain the timing, since the plan had nothing to do with Lina at all. He had been preoccupied with two big and seemingly impossible roadblocks: Monika Krusenstierna's unexpected heart attack and Fabian's nerve-racking police work. It wouldn't be the first time he had found it advantageous to have two problems rather than just one, since it was more a rule than an exception that each could provide the solution to the other.

He came up out of Østerport Station and was struck by the large, wide streets of Copenhagen. There were three or four lanes in each direction, as well as broad bike paths and pavements. Not many streets in Stockholm were this wide, and yet the Swedish city had stolen the title "Capital of Scandinavia" right out from under the Danes' noses. No wonder those Danish bastards were angry.

He walked up Dag Hammarskjölds Allé toward Østerbro and saw that almost every single billboard was about the hunt for him, as well as Risk's love affair. He also learned that he was now wanted internationally. *Not bad, not bad at all*, he thought, sitting down at a free patio table at Dag H Café.

HE ATE THE LAST of his chicken salad and emptied his glass of water. The waiter cleared the dishes off his table, and he took the opportunity to order a double espresso. He couldn't complain. Right now, things were mostly going his way. He looked around the patio and listened. He was on everyone's lips, and yet nobody recognized him. He might have been satisfied with a few days in the limelight in the past, but not now. He wanted more. When he was finished, no one would ever be able to overlook or forget him again.

He knocked back his espresso and looked at his watch. It was almost two thirty. According to the GPS, it would take him fifteen minutes to get to the location on foot. He left a generous tip and headed for Rigshospitalet.

It was time to take another innocent life.

35

"AFTER YOU." INGVAR MOLANDER lifted the police tape and allowed Irene Lilja to walk ahead of him into the front yard of Glenn Granqvist's house.

"I'm not a hundred per cent sure, but I think this was where the killer got him."

Lilja looked around the narrow hall that led into the house. "Here?"

Molander nodded. "The perpetrator probably rang the bell and waited for his victim to answer. When he did, our guy knocked him out with a drug—"

"The same as he did to Jörgen."

"Exactly," Molander said, clearly irritated that she had cut him off. "Anyway, I think he collapsed and hit his head here," he said, pointing to the sharp corner of a cast-iron shoe rack. "Which would explain the wound on the back of his head."

Lilja leaned over but couldn't see anything but the shoe rack itself.

"I believe the perpetrator dragged him all the way through the house, and out the back, which is shielded from view."

"If he had a head wound and was dragged through the hall, wouldn't there be some trace of blood?" Lilja's eyes scanned the linoleum floor, but she couldn't see anything that resembled blood.

"Look here." Molander crouched down, ran his index finger along the corner of the shoe rack and held a clean fingertip up to Lilja, who was starting to become impatient with the demonstration. Molander ignored her behaviour and touched across another part of the shoe rack. He showed Lilja his fingertip, which was dusty. "See? He cleaned up after himself. There's a layer of dust everywhere in the house, except some of the hallway." He pointed along the hall floor, then rose and walked further into the house. Lilja followed.

"But why spend energy cleaning up a few traces of blood when there's a ton of it at the scene of the crime?"

Molander turned to her and smiled.

"I asked myself the very same thing. The only answer I've come up with is that Glenn's murder did not unfold as planned: the perpetrator hadn't counted on his victim to fall straight onto a shoe rack and cut his head. And I'm confident this guy would do anything to stick to the plan. It's interesting though, because finding traces of blood here wouldn't even give us much of an advantage, but the killer didn't have time to analyse the consequences, so he cleaned up the blood as quickly as he could."

"What did he use to clean up? Have you found that?"

"I think he used a floor cloth," Molander said, opening the door to a small cleaning closet under the stairs. "It looks like he even rinsed it and wrung it out afterwards."

Lilja looked into the closet, which contained a vacuum cleaner, a bucket, a few bottles of cleaning products, and a low, stainless-steel sink. She felt the rag, which was hanging from a hook, and studied the floor directly under it. Sure enough, there was no evidence that it had been wet enough to drip.

"I suppose we should get going before Two-fer calls." Molander moved on toward the kitchen. Lilja lingered, as if there were something inside her that wanted to stay in the closet and examine it more thoroughly. She tried to focus.

"Irene!"

She gave up and joined Molander.

205

"We can always check with Risk, but I'm pretty sure Glenn skipped his Home Ec classes." Molander opened the kitchen door. "After you..."

Lilja stepped into the kitchen and immediately realized that Molander had a point. There was a pile of dirty dishes on the counter, and a small mountain of pizza boxes and half-eaten pizzas—all Hawaiian—on the table. There were two pots on the stove: one full of fuzzy green pasta and another of old meat sauce filled with a few worms. A swarm of flies buzzed around in bustling ecstasy, as if they didn't know where they should start the party. Every breath of the thick air felt like a step closer to death, and Lilja tried to inhale as little as she possibly could while rushing to open the window.

"Let's reason our way through this mess," Molander said, scanning the room. Lilja cautiously opened the fridge but quickly closed it again.

"Since there's no immediately visible safe, we can safely assume that it's hidden away somewhere."

"No, *really*?" Lilja said sarcastically.

"I'm not finished. Even if the safe is hidden, he probably wouldn't want it to be too hard to access and open, wouldn't you think?"

"You're right. Let's start looking." Lilja dragged the fridge away from the wall so she could shine her torch behind it; there was nothing of interest.

"At least we know it's not behind the fridge," Molander said. "There would have been obvious marks on the linoleum if it had been there."

Lilja looked down and saw the scrapes she had just made in the floor. She gave up with a heavy sigh. Molander wasn't one of the best crime scene investigators in the country for nothing. He had never missed a clue for as long as she'd known him. Lilja had learned to interpret his very smile, the one that was now plastered across his face. The whole thing was just a game for him, a game at which he was brilliant. She was more than happy to allow him that joy, and she laughed.

"So where is it? You know, don't you?"

"I have no idea." He threw up his hands and paused artfully. "But remember what I just said: it would most likely be in a place that is as hidden as it is easily accessed."

Lilja looked around. There were no paintings to check behind, just a Thai Airways poster with a picture of a beautiful beach. She ripped it down, but there was no safe there, either. Then she had an idea and turned to the cupboards.

"Why not?" Molander said. Lilja hurried to the turntable in the corner, emptying the two carousels of various pots and pans, a colander, and a couple of baking dishes. She crouched down and shone her torch inside. She didn't know exactly what she was looking for until she discovered a small door, painted the same shade of white as the wall, with a black keyhole. Lilja reached between the carousels, stuck in the key, and opened the small but thick door.

The cubby was more or less empty, except for a dark, square box. Lilja put on a pair of gloves and carefully lifted the compact box out of the safe and held it up to the light. Molander removed the tightly secured lid to see what was inside.

The box was full of homemade DVDs. Lilja started picking up one after the other, reading the handwritten labels: THAILAND '97, DRUNK CHICK '01.

"Look at this," Molander said, holding up a disc. VISIT TO MJÄLLE'S '93.

36

"WHAT DID YOU THINK?" Fabian asked as soon as they left their seats. He regretted his question at once. He personally abhorred being asked that right after seeing a movie. He still blushed whenever he thought of the TV4 reporter who had shoved a microphone in his face to ask his opinion after the unsubtitled premiere of Quentin Tarantino's *Reservoir Dogs* at the Stockholm Film Festival. Fabian had told her that he'd hardly understood any of the rapid-fire dialogue but he'd liked the music at least, and he followed up with an *ooga-chaka-ooga-shaka*.

"It was fine," Theodor answered with a shrug. It was obvious that Theodor had enjoyed the movie, but Fabian didn't mention it. Fabian had liked *Inception* a lot and had been looking forward to it for more than a year.

He'd had a weakness for action movies for as long as he could remember. But he preferred those that went deeper than just thrills. Some of his favourite films fitted into that category—*Star Wars*, for example. He remembered seeing it for the first time, gasping during the opening scene as the nearly endless spaceship zoomed along. He had never seen anything like it. And the film only got better from there. When the final battle on the Death Star was over, twelve-year-old Fabian had staggered out of the cinema on shaky legs, forever changed.

Fabian looked around in confusion before he realized that they'd exited onto the back street of Smedjegatan instead of through the main entrance on Södergatan.

"How about a spin?"

Theodor looked at him quizzically, which was the very reaction Fabian was hoping for. He explained that a spin was one of the activities that made Helsingborg one of the best cities in the world. It involved getting on the ferry to Helsingør on a one-way ticket and then staying there, eating and drinking tax-free, until you didn't know which country you were in. Theodor shrugged an uninterested okay.

FABIAN AND THEODOR WERE shown to one of the window tables in the restaurant area, where the tables were set with white cloths and candles. Fabian let Theodor order whatever he wanted and they both decided on hamburgers with fries and large Cokes. He asked Theodor how it felt to move to a new city, but he received only monosyllabic, uninformative answers. They felt like nails in the coffin of their relationship, lifeless and beyond salvation.

Once they were done eating, silence lay across the table like a wet blanket, sucking up most of the oxygen in the air. The waitress came over, asked if they were finished, and started clearing their table.

"Would you like any dessert?"

"Theo? What do you think?"

"No, that's okay. I'm full."

"Nothing more to drink either? Another Coke?"

"No, I'm fine."

"I'm going to have a beer, please."

The waitress nodded and disappeared. *I'm sure she gets it*, Fabian thought, gazing out the window. Helsingør Harbour was approaching far too slowly. And they still had half the journey left.

He regretted giving in to Sonja's pressure to take out Theodor. This whole plan had been her idea — talk about making a chore out of something that should be fun. It was doomed to fail.

He probably would have refused to speak if he were in Theodor's place.

"You're not still upset about Sweden Rock, are you?"

Theodor rolled his eyes and appeared to be looking for somewhere to escape to.

"Just so you know, we only said no out of concern. I'm sure you can go next year or the year after."

"Sure." Theodor's eyes were glued to his empty Coke glass.

"So how does it feel?"

"What?"

"You know...the move and everything."

"You already asked me that question."

"I know, but I didn't get much of an answer. Are you happy with your room?"

Theodor shrugged mutely.

"Well, you've certainly spent a lot of time shut away in there recently, so it must not be *that* bad." He sighed and wondered what else he should say. "I know it must be tough with your friends and everything, but I'm absolutely certain that—"

"Oh my God, stop bugging me about that! Did I say it was tough? Huh? Did I?"

"Theo, take it easy. That's not what I meant."

"Then what the hell *did* you mean? You and Mum are the ones having a tough time, which is why we moved in the first place. You don't think I get that?"

The arrival of his beer three minutes later broke the silence and was like a slap in the face. It felt like definitive proof of his failure as a father, a role he apparently couldn't handle without alcohol. He decided not to touch his drink and prepared himself for a long trip home.

37

MORTEN STEENSTRUP, THE COP who refused to die, was easier to find than he had initially hoped. He overheard a journalist from *Politiken* asking the receptionist on the first floor where Morten was in the hospital.

He followed the journalist, took a seat in the waiting room with all the other members of the media, and waited for his chance. Three hours later, he had all the information he needed to complete his task: Steenstrup's room number, his condition and the treatment, and—most importantly—confirmation that he was under guard.

A female police officer arrived and preoccupied most of the reporters. No one even noticed when he put down the health magazine he had been pretending to read for the last hour and walked over to the bathroom as the journalist from *Politiken* came out. He went in, locked the door behind him, and quickly realized that the journalist was having stomach issues.

He took the opportunity to relieve his bladder and to top up his water bottle with a few cups of cold water; he was struck by how bad the tap water tasted as soon as you took one step outside of Sweden. He stuffed the legs of his pants into his socks, tightened his bootlaces, and took a rope with a hook on one end from his backpack. He then took out a pair of thin gloves, put them on, and smoothed them out until they fitted like an extra layer of skin.

He was ready.

He grabbed the toilet brush, which was leaning against the wall in the corner, closed the lid of the toilet with one boot, and climbed up on the handicap bars, balancing with legs spread wide. He pushed aside one of the tiles of the drop ceiling with the toilet brush, fastened the hook onto a wire duct, hopped back down to the floor, replaced the brush, and unlocked the door, well aware that he was courting danger with his actions. He had decided that a toilet cubicle locked for an excessively long time would attract unnecessary attention and as a result could pose an even greater risk than an unlocked door.

He had no trouble climbing up the rope, thanks to the heavy physical training regime he had been doing for the past two years. Fitting through the small gap at the top was more difficult; there was less space than he had counted on between the tiles and the actual ceiling, and he had to take off his backpack in order to fit on top of the air duct. He gathered up the rope and shoved it into his outside pocket, replaced the ceiling tile, put on a mask, and cautiously began to use his hands to pull himself along the duct, which showed no signs of giving way despite his weight.

He pulled himself out so he was over the waiting room. The ceiling height was much more generous here, and he could get up and crawl along the duct on all fours, passing humming air handlers. He heard the annoyed voices of the journalists below him as they protested about the scanty information they had received from the female police officer, who could do no more than repeat the response from her superiors: "In light of the ongoing investigation we have no comment at the present time, but we will hold a press conference as soon as we..." He knew exactly what that meant.

They didn't know a goddamn thing.

He crawled on top of a dusty section of the duct and arrived at a split going ninety degrees to the left and the right. He took out his Neofab Legion II, the world's most powerful torch.

Despite the swirling dust that reflected most of the light back at him, he could see about sixty metres to the right and thirty to the left. In other words, he had arrived at the corridor that led out to the exit on the right and into the guarded ward on the left.

He followed the duct toward the ward. When he was directly above the entrance, he took out a spool of fishing line, which he had marked with measurements down to a half-metre, using bits of tape. While he was attaching the end of the line to the wall above the door, he heard two police officers walking just underneath him.

"Hello? Where the hell did you go?"

"Shut your trap, we're on our way," a voice said through a crackly two-way radio.

He left the police behind and moved into the ward. At times he had to wriggle his way through a narrow passageway or heave himself over an air handler. He lay down fishing wire as he went, noting the tape marks. He stopped at the twenty-three-metre mark, turned on the torch, and was met by a tangle of cables, tubes, and pipes of various sizes that branched down through the ceiling like a climbing plant that had been allowed to grow unimpeded. Whether this was a sign that he had reached his destination, he didn't know. The air duct didn't branch off to the left, which it should have done if there was another corridor or an examination room in that direction. All he had been able to see through the glass doors in the waiting room was that the police officers and doctors turned left somewhere around this point. He had counted their steps, starting at the door to the ward, and calculated that the turn had to come around twenty-three metres down the corridor.

He turned off his torch and pulled himself over to an air handler, from which he could reach a fluorescent light. He tried to lift off the casing but it was firmly attached. Why hadn't he brought tin shears? He let out a long sigh and felt the moisture

213

in his mask turning to drops, which ran down his chin. He needed to think and go through his options. He made his way back to the duct, lay down on his back, and closed his eyes.

He didn't realize he had fallen asleep until he heard the voices of police officers beneath him. It was uncharacteristic of him. He followed them from above, discovering that he had misjudged the distance of the left turn by two or three metres. At that point, the duct branched off as well, and he could easily follow them another ten metres or so before they stopped. On the way he heard the officers discussing Morten Steenstrup's heroic deed; they were in agreement that it had been more foolhardy and stupid than anything else.

"Aw, shut up, he's going to get a ton of pussy when he's back. Hell, he could probably bathe in pussy if he wanted."

In all probability, the officers were on their way to guard the entrance to Morten Steenstrup's hospital room, but there were several rooms in the vicinity, and it was impossible for him to know exactly which one Morten was in. The duct split in several different directions. The only thing he could do was wait for a lead.

He overheard the policewoman from earlier standing outside one of the rooms. She was apparently going to Morten's room for the second time, against the doctor's wishes. The officers on duty asked for her ID, unlocked the door, and let her and the doctor in, unaware that by doing so they had just signed their colleague's death warrant.

38

IRENE LILJA WIPED AWAY her tears right before walking into the conference room with the rest of her colleagues. Who were they really after—the perpetrator or the victim? She felt like hitting something or someone, or maybe sticking her fingers down her throat and vomiting. But instead, she had to dry her tears and push her feelings aside and act like a professional. She glanced over her notes quickly before summarizing them aloud for the team:

VIDEO I: MID-1980S

- *Clearly been transferred from a videotape, poor quality. Handheld camera.*

- *Glenn and Jörgen are mostly having vanilla sex with various women. Not sure if they're girlfriends or prostitutes. All acting like porn stars.*

- *Some group sex with Glenn, Jörgen, and Jörgen's wife, Lina.*

- *Everyone's drunk and giggly.*

- *All for fun with different positions.*

- *Jörgen forces his member into Lina's mouth. She gags. A blow to the face. Glenn laughs and masturbates.*

- *More sex and violence.*
- *Better camera on a tripod.*
- *It looks like Thailand, and the girls look underage.*
- *Anal.*
- *Urine.*
- *A drugged young woman, confused and chained up. A bag over her head and a cigarette pressed to her nipple.*

"And that was just the beginning," Lilja said, looking up from her notes.

"So Glenn and Jörgen systematically raped and abused women?" said Tuvesson.

Lilja nodded.

"What sorts of women?" Klippan asked. "Prostitutes?"

"I don't know. In some of the videos from the early nineties, Jörgen's wife, Lina, is involved, but she isn't in them anymore after he hit her and forced her to have oral sex on camera. It looks like they would bring home pretty much anyone, drug them, and then leave them somewhere to sober up."

"They filmed everything?" Klippan asked, and Lilja nodded.

"And transferred the videotapes onto DVDs afterwards."

"It's just sick," Klippan said, shaking his head.

"What's so sick about it?" said Molander. "It's just a way to relive and remember events. The videos functioned as a collection of trophies for them."

Klippan looked at Molander in disgust. "Ingvar, the whole thing is sick."

"In any case, I want you to look at the footage from one tape," Lilja interrupted, holding up one of the DVDs. "It's different from all the rest."

"In what way?" Tuvesson asked.

"First, there are no women in it, only our victim...our killer." She inserted the DVD into the machine and pressed play. A shaky, grainy picture projected onto the white wall; it had been filmed with a handheld camera. The first shot showed a stairwell with bare, flickering lights on the ceiling and graffiti on the walls. There was a time-stamp in the lower right-hand corner.

1993-04-13 6:17 p.m.

Jörgen enters the frame. He is wearing jeans and a hooded sweatshirt and is obviously drunk. He has a beer in one hand, and lifts it toward the camera as he rings the doorbell of one of the apartments. His lips are moving, but the sound on the video recorder has been turned off. He drains the last of his beer and points at the floor. The camera follows his finger and zooms in on a blurry view of Jörgen opening his fly and taking out his penis. The automatic focus moves in and out between the label on the bottle and Jörgen's penis as he urinates into the bottle...

"What a goddamn pig," Tuvesson said, shaking her head.

"I'm sorry to say that it's hardly even begun."

"Why isn't there any sound?" Molander asked.

"I think they just forgot to turn it on, but they figure it out in a little bit."

They continued watching the video.

...Jörgen is holding the bottle toward the camera, grinning. Glenn's hand enters the frame. He takes the bottle while Jörgen puts brass knuckles on his fingers and rings the bell again; this time he holds the button down for a long time. After a few seconds, Claes Mällvik opens the

door. He talks as his eyes flick back and forth between Jörgen and the camera. He looks afraid. His mouth moves again. Jörgen responds by what looks like burping in his face and shoving him into the apartment. The shaky camera follows them, moving all over the place as the apartment door is closed and locked. The camera finally settles on a hall mirror. Glenn is visible from head to toe, filming himself. He raises the full bottle with a smile, and puts it down on the hall table. He presses a button on the camera. The sound kicks in...

The emotional distance Tuvesson and the others had been able to maintain up to that point in the footage diminished immediately. Now they were fully present with Glenn, Jörgen, and Claes. They could hear Claes's weakening voice, begging and pleading for them to stop, in between Jörgen's powerful blows, which sounded like a hammer striking a watermelon.

...Glenn takes the camera, moving further into the apartment to find Claes, who has been silenced. He's lying motionless on the floor, receiving blow after blow from Jörgen's brass knuckles. His face is red with blood and mucus, and it looks more and more like one big open wound. Jörgen is out of breath and sweaty. He stops hitting him and wipes his bloody hand on Claes's shirt. "Shit, he can't give up that easily," Jörgen says with a sneer. "I think he's thirsty. Give him something to drink!" The camera moves down until it's level with Claes's bloody face. Glenn's hand enters the frame, holding the beer bottle. He pours the urine into Claes's mouth. Claes comes to life and coughs. Quite a bit of the liquid ends up on his face. "There you go. Clever boy. Just drink up." He presses the bottle into Claes's mouth and empties it. "Have some more."

1993-04-13 8:03 p.m.

Claes is hanging from the lamp hook on the ceiling like a punching bag, his arms extended above his head. His wrists are bound with duct tape, and the duct tape is wound around the hook. He's fighting to hold up his battered head, but it gives in to gravity and drops to his chest over and over again. Glenn is bouncing from foot to foot in front of him, as if he were in the middle of a karate match. Now and then he jumps up and kicks Claes's head, which snaps sideways at full force. "Hold your head high, I said!" Jörgen screams from behind the camera. He walks up to Claes and cuffs his ear a few times. "Jesus Christ, you're so disgusting! You fucking little pussy!" Claes tries, but he can't hold his head up. His mouth moves, but no words come out at first. Then: "Please...just kill me...please," he says in a voice that's barely audible. Glenn enters the picture: "Come on. Let's go grab a bite."

1993-04-13 10:28 p.m.

Claes is lying motionless on the floor of the hall with the house phone beside him. His wrists are still bound with tape. "How the hell did he get over here?" The camera zooms in on Jörgen, who shrugs. "Well, it doesn't matter, since the line was cut." Jörgen holds up the severed end of the telephone cord. "But you didn't think about that, did you? You disgusting little bastard!" Jörgen grabs the phone and slams it into Claes's head again and again. "Hey! Only hands and feet," says Glenn from outside the camera frame. Jörgen throws down the phone, lifting Claes's feet and dragging him back into the room.

Lilja pressed pause and turned to face the others. "It continues on like this for another hour."

None of the others spoke.

"Jesus fucking Christ," Klippan managed at last. "I'm starting to wonder whose side I'm on."

"I don't understand how he survived," Tuvesson said, standing up. "You'll have to excuse me, but I need to take a break."

"Should we decide on a time to resume our meeting?" Lilja wondered.

"No," Tuvesson said, and left the room.

39

HE WOKE UP FROM a pain that felt like a serrated knife was being pushed into his chest. He reached for the button to increase his dose of morphine and pressed it—nothing happened, so he pressed it again. He had a faint memory of some men wearing white, probably doctors. They were discussing his case. As far as he could tell, they were saying that he would survive, but it would take years of physical therapy if he were ever to walk again. Or was it the other way around—that no amount of physical therapy would get him back on his feet?

He tried to count the days he had been awake, but it was difficult. Everything had a tendency to melt together into a haze of days, nurses, examinations, and meals. He understood enough to know that he was seriously injured and in a hospital, probably Rigshospitalet in Copenhagen, given his injuries.

He remembered some of the details of what had happened that night: how he'd walked toward the perpetrator as he was putting the tyre back on the Peugeot; the way he'd grabbed his pistol but didn't draw it in time; and being surprised as the lug wrench struck him in the ear. But the memories were only fragmented images.

A woman had dropped by today. He was hoping it would be Else, but as the woman came closer, he realized she was definitely not who he was hoping for—she was nowhere near as beautiful. No one was more beautiful than Else. Else was the first thing he thought about when he woke up every morning in the hospital. He wondered if she knew what had happened to him and if she missed him? Did *anyone* miss him?

The woman was a police officer but she was dressed in civilian clothing. She said she had initially visited him two days ago. She was on the hunt for the person who'd injured him and she claimed to know his identity. She showed him a photograph, but it wasn't him. At least, he hadn't thought it was him. But now that she was gone he felt unsure all of a sudden—unsure of what he'd said and what he had seen.

He tried to concentrate on what he knew for sure, hoping that various small details might spark the rest of his memories to return. But all he could come up with was that he couldn't be absolutely certain of anything.

What if none of it had really happened? What if it was all just a dream, a dream that might come to an end at any moment when his alarm went off? His alarm made a horrible sound. If this turned out to be just a dream, he decided he would finally get a clock radio instead.

He pressed the morphine button again. The acute, sharp pain was almost completely gone, but there was still a pulsating, dull ache everywhere. A shapeless sea of questions floated around inside his head. Maybe he would stop breathing if he held his breath for long enough? Was that possible? Else, his beloved Else, did she know what had happened? Was she sorry she left him? Did she think about him? Did she even care?

He looked up and noticed one of the ceiling tiles was moving, revealing a hole above him. Maybe the tile had never been there? His thoughts moved to his colleagues. Had he made a fool of himself in front of them? He took a deep breath and felt the knife twist in his chest again. A figure in dark clothing came down a rope through the hole in the ceiling and walked up to him. For the first time in as long as he could remember, all of his doubts vanished. He didn't even need to see the man's face. He was totally certain that the man currently injecting a syringe into his IV bag was the same man who had struck him with the lug wrench and run him over in the Peugeot with Swedish plates. What was the registration number again? The man pulled out the syringe and massaged the IV bag.

JOS 652, Morten thought. A wave of peacefulness washed through him. The last thing he remembered was the sound of blaring alarms from the machines. They howled like crazy monkeys crowded into a tiny cage.

40

THE BELLS OF LELLINGE Church were already ringing when Fabian Risk arrived, a reminder that everything comes to an end. He hadn't been able to find his black suit, so he was wearing black jeans and a dark-grey wool jacket that felt far too warm. The church was full to capacity and he had to push his way through to find a place to stand along the side. Fabian was surprised Mette Louise had thought she had no friends.

The pastor who led the service had both christened and confirmed Mette Louise Risgaard. He spoke of her as a fantastic girl, full of life and joy. Many people were crying openly, and even the pastor had trouble keeping the tears at bay. He spoke of how Mette Louise had cried, or rather screamed, so loudly during her christening that not even the church organ had been able to drown her out. But she'd grown quiet as the consecrated water touched her little head and had given the congregation a smile that could have melted the polar ice caps.

The pastor was certain that Mette Louise and God had seen each other and he wanted this knowledge to act as an extended hand to help all of them through the sorrow that lay ahead.

"There is purpose in all of God's actions, even this one. We don't always understand it, but it can be helpful just to know that it exists."

If the purpose was to make the lump in his throat grow, God had succeeded, Fabian thought. The killer was right: Fabian was the only person to blame for Mette Louise's death.

After the ceremony, the churchwarden showed everyone to the neighbouring hall for coffee and cookies. Most people seemed to know each other, and within fifteen minutes the hall was buzzing with conversation. Fabian stood alone with a cup of coffee, wanting nothing more than to leave as quickly as possible, but something told him it was important to stay, not to run away, from his guilt.

He struggled to stand still, and started walking among the mourners. A few children were grouped around a mobile phone, and a few older gentlemen in suits were sitting at a round table. He gathered that they were talking about the warm summer. One of the men claimed this year was nothing compared to the summers of the 1930s.

A short, round woman, roughly Fabian's age, kept looking at him from a group standing further down the hall. He acknowledged her stares with a smile and short nod, but she didn't respond positively. It was quite the opposite—the woman looked more and more upset as she spoke with the others in the group.

Fabian put the pieces together and realized that she must be Mette Louise Risgaard's mother. He thought about going up and saying hello, but he didn't have enough time to make a decision because the woman was suddenly walking toward him. He extended his hand, but she didn't take it. She asked his name. He introduced himself and promised to do everything in his power to catch the killer.

"The killer? You're the killer! It's your fault!" the woman shouted. "You're the one who murdered her, who sentenced her to death!" The woman beat his chest with her fists, screaming over and over again that he was a murderer and he deserved to burn in hell.

Fabian didn't try to resist. The rest of the congregation stopped talking and turned to watch the incident unfold. A man with short hair and braces approached them.

"What the hell is going on here? Are you the Swedish police officer?"

Fabian nodded. Before he could react, the man shoved him. Fabian lost his balance and spilled his coffee on his white shirt as he fell to the floor. The man straddled him and drew his fist back to hit him again, but Fabian was faster. He grabbed the man's arm, pulled him down onto the floor, and then pushed himself up, allowing him to lock the man's arm behind his back.

"Let's take it easy here, okay?" Fabian increased the pressure to show him that he was serious. Three other men quickly yanked Fabian away and advised him to make himself scarce as fast as he could. He heeded their advice and hurried out of the hall. He heard people shouting that it was important to keep Denmark clean and trail the Swedish bastards back to the border.

He got behind the wheel of his car, locked the doors, and tried to stick the key in the ignition. But his jittery hand refused to obey him, and it took a few deep breaths before he was able to insert and turn the key, using both hands. He was definitely shaken.

On the way out of the church car park, he thought about the pastor's speech. If Mette Louise's death had any point at all, it was to help them find the killer before any more innocent people lost their lives. Fabian couldn't put his finger on why, but something told him that no matter how hard his new colleagues worked, the whole case depended on him. He put the car in gear, let up the clutch, and aimed for Copenhagen.

41

DUNJA HOUGAARD WOKE UP to the sound of a flushing toilet. It took her several seconds to realize that she was in the bathroom of the violent crimes unit at the Copenhagen police station. She had been so busy over the past twenty-four hours that her only chance to get some rest was to lock herself in a bathroom at work.

Morten Steenstrup's death had turned everything upside down. She'd heard about it just after two thirty this morning. She always went out on Tuesday nights — it was her only night out all week — and last night had been no exception. It was a ritual she'd had ever since she left her ex-boyfriend Carsten, which she'd done on a Tuesday night almost seven months ago.

She had gone up to Stockholm to surprise him; he was at a trade seminar with lots of other Nordea employees. But she found her live-in boyfriend/fiancé/father of her future children in bed with one of his Swedish colleagues, just the way it happens in bad movies. She turned around without saying a word and walked straight into the Stockholm night, her desire for revenge on the brink of boiling over.

She ended up at Kvarnen, an old beer hall in the heart of Södermalm. She had no problem finding someone to fuck. She couldn't remember his name, and maybe he'd never even told her. All she remembered was that he had red hair and was bigger than Carsten.

A little over a week later, she felt like she was more or less over Carsten. She hadn't given him a single thought since the redheaded Swede. *A man would have done the exact same thing in my situation*, she thought, and it had worked. She'd felt happier and lighter than she had in a long time, and she decided to make it a tradition. She would go out every Tuesday to top up on validation.

She had only ever missed three Tuesdays. Two of them could be blamed on the flu, but the third was because her father's new wife died after a long battle with lung cancer. He'd called a bit later in the evening, when she already had a few drinks in her. As soon as she realized who was calling, she regretted picking up the phone, but she couldn't bring herself to hang up. She agreed to keep him company even though she had never even met his wife and she'd stopped speaking to him several years before. She arrived at Rigshospitalet, where he was keeping vigil, twenty minutes later. She sat beside him and held his hands. Neither of them said anything all night. When the sun came up, he pulled his hands away and told her she could go and that he wouldn't need her help from now on.

They hadn't spoken since. She knew he was still alive, and she knew where he lived. Sometimes she even wondered how she would react if he died. She hoped she would shrug with indifference, even though she knew deep down that she wouldn't be able to escape the grief—for everything they never had time to work out and for all the things she never said out loud.

She had spent this past Tuesday in Kødbyen, where she had met a black American who worked as a commercial director. His attempt at Danish put her in a good mood, and after a few mojitos her problems at work seemed as blurry as the mint leaves behind the condensation on her glass. She got the call from work just as the American was unhooking her bra and kissing her breasts.

The hospital was in complete chaos when she arrived twenty-five minutes later. No one knew what was going on. What was the cause of death? Had he taken his own life, or had someone

228

murdered him? And if so, who—and how? The whole ward had been under heavy guard. And to be totally honest, she'd still been a little drunk.

She looked down at her phone and saw that she had slept for forty-seven minutes. She got up from the seat of the toilet, and fixed her hair and lipstick before she left the bathroom. On her way back to her desk she wondered again how the perpetrator had managed it. So far, they hadn't been able to find any clues that might lead in any particular direction. Richter was still on the scene with his technicians. She emphasized, for the second time, that they would have to continue searching until they found something.

Her buzz was finally starting to wear off, and she mostly just felt hungover now. She cupped her hand over her mouth to smell her own breath. Just as she decided that she should probably avoid talking for the rest of the day, Jan Hesk caught up with her with an update: Oscar Pedersen in forensic medicine had just called with Morten's cause of death.

"It was suffocation," he said.

"Suffocation? How? There were no signs on his body."

"No visible ones, but he had high levels of botulinum in his blood."

Dunja was very familiar with botulinum toxin, which was basically the same neurotoxin used in Botox. In high doses it could paralyse the muscles of the chest and cause suffocation.

"Did they check the IV bag?"

Hesk nodded. "Apparently there was enough toxin in there to kill half of Denmark. And speaking of…" He smiled and held out a packet of Fisherman's Friends. She ought to have been insulted, but she took a lozenge without protest.

"Take another one. Or a couple."

She took two more and headed for her office.

"It might be best if you took the whole bag," he yelled after her. She gave him the finger over her shoulder without turning around.

She put all the lozenges in her mouth at once as she walked to her desk. A man was sitting in her visitor's chair. She had never seen him before, but she knew immediately who he was.

42

TUVESSON, LILJA, AND MOLANDER were sitting around the oval table, eating chicken salads out of plastic take-out containers and waiting for Klippan, who had called the meeting, to show up. Tuvesson couldn't believe three small pieces of chicken, dry iceberg lettuce, a little canned corn, and a few olives constituted a "gourmet chicken salad" these days. She decided to balance out the scanty contents of her take-out with a cigarette after lunch.

"Has anyone heard from Risk?" Molander asked.

Tuvesson shook her head. "No, why would we? He's on vacation."

Molander nodded mutely.

"Ingvar, what was I supposed to do? I had no choice," Tuvesson explained.

"I know. It's just a little...unfortunate."

"You're definitely not the only one with that opinion," she said.

"Just so you all know, I took the liberty of checking up on Risk," said Lilja. "Did any of you know he was fired from his previous job in Stockholm?"

Molander shook his head.

Tuvesson sighed. "Shouldn't your hands be full enough with this investigation?"

"I just wanted to know a bit about his background. I thought it would be helpful if we were going to be working together."

"Irene, what are you suggesting? Yes, he used poor judgement and went too far, but don't you think you might have done the same thing in his position?"

"You mean if I were in love with the victim's wife?" Lilja said.

"That was a teenage crush. We have no idea how he feels about her now."

"That's exactly the problem—we don't know. And it doesn't seem to have been a one-time thing. I've seen the Stockholm police department's investigation into him from last winter, and if you read between the lines he went rogue up there, too."

"What did he do?" Molander asked.

"For one thing—"

"Irene, let it go," Tuvesson said, deciding to have at least two cigarettes when she got the chance.

"But—"

"Great, you're all here already," Klippan said as he walked in.

Tuvesson secretly thanked Klippan for changing the subject. Lilja was right, of course: this behaviour was exactly what Stockholm had warned her about when she'd initially inquired about Risk. Most of his colleagues had been in agreement about him: Risk was a good police officer, one of the best, but he did things his own way, and you never knew what he was up to or what the consequences might be. Tuvesson had wanted those characteristics in a police officer. She thought the others had become far too comfortable, although she would never say it out loud. Her officers were certainly professional and dependable, but they acted like they no longer had anything to prove, and they'd stopped taking risks or thinking outside the box, which was where Risk came in. Their almost-zero margin of error might look good in all the reports, but the reality was another story—in certain cases, it was necessary to take risks and push the limits. Sometimes you ended up on the wrong side of the boundary.

Klippan told them a female employee from the McDonald's in Åstorp had contacted him about someone she thought could be the perpetrator. He passed around a composite sketch based on her description. "She was working last Thursday night and didn't recognize Schmeckel or Mällvik."

They were thinking about Schmeckel and Mällvik as if they were two different people, two different killers, Tuvesson contemplated. And now a sketch of a possible third perpetrator was travelling around the table. How many possible suspects would they have before they were finished?

"Who are we looking at here?" Molander asked, holding up the sketch.

"Apparently he went to the McDonald's just after midnight last Thursday. He ordered a Chilli McFeast Deluxe meal, which is only served on Thursdays, but Thursday had just become Friday at that point."

"So they refused to give him a Chilli McFeast?" Lilja asked. Klippan nodded.

"I suppose they were just following orders," said Molander.

"But this guy wouldn't take no for an answer," Klippan went on. "He argued that it was still Thursday when he got in line and insisted on being allowed to order his meal. The girl at the counter tried to explain to him that she didn't make the rules. She was already serving the next customer when he gave her a warning."

"What sort of warning?" Tuvesson asked.

"He warned her not to ignore him."

The others exchanged glances.

"He was angry because she skipped him and served the next customer instead?"

Klippan nodded.

"What happened next?"

"He got his Chilli McFeast."

"So that's how you do it," Molander said with a grin.

"She didn't think it was an empty threat. It was clear he was serious."

Tuvesson took the composite sketch and studied it. As usual, Klippan had asked Gudrun Scheele, a half-blind, wheelchair-bound art teacher who had retired more than fifteen years ago, to do the portrait. She lived in the same retirement home as Klippan's mother. He had seen some of her portraits once on a visit and asked if she could help them with the sketch of a rapist who had been going after jogging women in Pålsjö forest. The man was identified three hours after they published Gudrun's picture, and they were able to apprehend him soon after. Since then, the Helsingborg police had employed her regularly, and the officers helped each other ignore the fact that she might die any day now.

Gudrun usually worked in charcoal, and today was no exception. Tuvesson couldn't help being impressed by Gudrun's talent. It ought to have been physically impossible for her even to hold a pencil with those trembling hands, but she sure could draw, and most of the time it took only a few strokes of the charcoal for her to bring forth a personality from a few extremely vague witness statements. Yet there was something that differentiated this portrait from all her previous composite sketches. Aside from the eyes, which were staring straight at her and looked truly threatening, the face lacked a clear personality. The man was so ordinary looking that Tuvesson thought she wouldn't have been able to recognize him even if he were sitting right in front of her—a common problem with composite sketches. You could see almost anyone in a sketch if you tried hard enough because they were so vague, but this was the first time she had experienced it with one of Gudrun's pictures.

"Are you going to release the sketch?" Molander asked Tuvesson.

"I'll check with Högsell," said Tuvesson, "but I'm leaning toward holding off. This feels so nonspecific that it could match more or less anyone. And, besides, there are too many variables in the equation. The cashier didn't recognize Schmeckel or Mällvik; she came up with an entirely different person who happened to look threatening, which doesn't get us very far."

"It wouldn't have to be a different person," Molander said. "He's changed his appearance before, so maybe this is a new look?"

Silence descended over the table. A few minutes later, Tuvesson realized that the composite sketch perfectly matched the feelings she was having about the perpetrator: they were searching for a phantom, an evasive creature who seemed to be just an arm's length away one second, only to go up in smoke the next. He could be anyone: a Claes, a Rune, or whatever else he was calling himself.

43

"DID YOU SCOPE OUT the ceiling space?"

"Scope?" Danish Dunja hadn't understood his Swedish vernacular.

"Yes—inspect?"

"Are you suggesting that he pulled himself up on top of that air duct and came into Morten's room through the ceiling?"

"How else would he have got in, besides the door?"

Dunja Hougaard shook her head and tried to figure out how she could have missed something so obvious. She felt stupid and wished she could sink through the floor. She tried to think of something smart to say, but her mind refused to work. Could she be any more awkward? Sure, he was good-looking, but he was married and she hadn't decided what she thought of him yet.

She'd had a negative first impression of Fabian Risk, as was the case with most Swedes. He walked around as if he owned the whole world and, more specifically, this investigation. Even though he had been formally removed from the case, he intended to keep working toward solving it. He said he would consider giving her a hand in exchange for her help.

"Is someone a bit hungover? It looks like you could use a bite to eat," he said. Dunja realized that he might not be so bad after all. "And if I don't get some food soon, I'll be the next victim."

She laughed and said: "First and foremost, it looks like you need a new shirt, unless that coffee stain is part of a new trend."

THE FRESH AIR DID Dunja some good. After a visit to Illum, where an overly helpful salesperson sold Risk one of their most expensive shirts, Dunja decided to take him to Café Diamanten on Gammel Strand. It was a stone's throw away and usually wasn't too crowded, even though it was only a few blocks from Strøget, the main shopping street. For some reason, the tourists never found their way to Gammel Strand, although it got great sun and had quite a few restaurants. Diamanten was her favourite and was the least pretentious.

They sat down at a table in the shade of an umbrella. Risk ordered a Caesar salad and mineral water, and she got a hamburger and an extra-large Coke. A few sips in, she felt herself coming back to life. She and Risk had made mostly small talk about the weather, the Danish soccer fiasco, and why Danes had such trouble understanding Skåne Swedish. They were avoiding the real topic, and Dunja decided to take the first step.

"I hope you're aware that I'm taking a big risk by meeting with you right now. I'm under strict orders to keep the Swedish police as far from this investigation as possible."

"Then it's awfully lucky I'm off the investigation and only on vacation." They raised their glasses to cheers. Dunja couldn't help smiling. She didn't know why, but Risk had managed to put her in a good mood in some mysterious way.

"Did your boss Sleizner explain why we aren't supposed to collaborate?"

"Kim isn't the type who wastes energy on explanations. My guess is that he wants to give you all a slap on the wrist for stepping on his toes. He hates two things more than anything else in the world: people who go over his head, and Swedes. You should have called Kim before getting in touch with the station in Køge."

"We did. I was there when Tuvesson made the call. Your boss didn't answer."

"Are you suggesting that he's lying?"

"I'm not saying anything except that we called him and he didn't answer, so we left a message on his voicemail. It was an emergency and we couldn't spare the time."

Dunja didn't know what to think. Kim had come out swinging to defend himself, both internally and to the media. He had made a big deal out of the fact that no one had contacted him, and he blamed the Swedish police for Mette Louise Risgaard's death. It was his word against theirs.

"Here's Astrid Tuvesson's phone number," Fabian said, writing the number down on a napkin.

Dunja looked at the Swedish mobile number. "What am I supposed to do with this? If I call her, I'm sure she'll say the same thing you just did," she said, dipping a French fry into the puddle of ketchup on her plate.

"I don't want you to call her. You should get in touch with the operator who connected the call."

Of course, she thought to herself, feeling unusually slow on the uptake today. With this number, she could find out whether the Swedes really had called Sleizner, as well as the exact time and how long the call had lasted. At the end of the day, the outcome didn't mean much in her eyes: the girl and now the police officer were dead, and it would be best for the two countries to co-operate in order to find the killer.

"What will it cost me?"

"Access to the car."

"No, that's out of the question. We're still in the middle of examining it."

"I just want to take a quick look. Five minutes max."

"What will I get out of it?"

"Besides my boss's number?"

She nodded, and he laughed.

"Another Coke, and everything I know about the case."

She pretended to consider it for a moment before smiling. "What do you know about the killer?"

"We were in the same class all through school. Back then, his name was Claes Mällvik and he was bullied pretty badly."

"Everyone picked on him?"

"I didn't, but others did. Two people in particular."

"The two victims?"

"Yes, but I wasn't that much better. I ignored it, just like everyone else."

"Why did they pick on Claes?"

"To be completely honest, I don't know. He had glasses and his last name was easy to make fun of, but mostly I think it was just chance that he got picked on. They wanted someone to bully, and it just happened to be him."

"You're sure he's the killer?"

"Who else could it be?"

Dunja shrugged. "Well, Morten Steenstrup didn't recognize him from the picture you released."

"There are lots of reasons why he wouldn't be able to identify Claes. Was there morphine in his system? Did he even see the perpetrator's face? Could his memory have been affected by the accident?"

"He was very emphatic."

"Was he able to describe the man?"

"Unfortunately not. He was too tired. I was planning to have him do that today."

"So that means the perpetrator probably changed identities again."

"Which tells us something else."

Risk looked her in the eyes.

"He's not done yet. There are more people on his list," Dunja said, standing up.

Fabian watched her as she disappeared into the café, thinking about what she'd just said. A nagging feeling had been bothering him for the past few days. He had tried to shrug it off, but it had stubbornly returned. And now that Dunja Hougaard had said

239

it so plainly, there could be no doubt. Rune, Claes, or whatever name he was going by, was not finished—not by far.

Jörgen and Glenn, the two most obvious targets, were out of the way. But who was left? Had he been bullied by others? Maybe at work? Fabian had read that adults who were bullied as children were often bullied in the workplace as well. It was like those around them could smell their weakness, a characteristic they couldn't shake throughout their lives. He decided to call Tuvesson and ask her to send someone to question Schmeckel's colleagues about the atmosphere at Lund Hospital, especially after the scandal when he'd forgotten to remove the clips from that patient's bladder. Incidentally, the patient was another person Fabian should contact. But first, he needed to take a look at the Peugeot.

DUNJA HAD MADE IT clear to Fabian that it would be best if no one found out she had a Swedish police officer with her, so they entered the station through the back door. The Peugeot was four storeys underground. The storage area took up an entire floor of the police station and was full of confiscated items waiting to be examined or used as evidence in trial. There was everything from cars to torn underwear.

An older man was sitting in a wheelchair behind a Plexiglas window, which was perforated by holes at face level, fiddling with something made of dark plastic. Naked pin-up girls from the early 1980s were pasted on the wall behind him, revealing how many years he had been sitting there hidden from daylight. Dunja knocked on the window, but the man refused to look up. She knocked again, this time so hard that the pane rattled, and pushed her ID through the hatch.

"Hello! I don't have all day—I'm here to see the Peugeot that came in a few days ago."

"The Swede car," said the man. "I just have to fix my catheter."

240

Dunja nodded.

"And who's that?" The man pointed at Fabian.

"My name is Fabian Risk." He reached for his wallet to dig out his ID.

"He's a potential witness. We're here to see if he can identify the car," Dunja said quickly, shoving Fabian's wallet away.

The man's eyes wandered back and forth between Dunja and Fabian as if he were considering an all-in poker bet. At last he gave a long, heavy sigh.

They followed the man through the warehouse. He steered his electric wheelchair so efficiently that they had to jog to keep up, but he stopped now and then to unlock a gate. Fabian had no idea how the man could find his way through the apparently endless labyrinth of aisles, whose shelves were as high as those in an IKEA warehouse, or how he knew which key fitted which lock. But he obviously knew his stuff, and they were at last shown into a garage full of cars, some of which closely resembled piles of scrap metal, while others seemed brand new. The Peugeot was in the far corner.

Fabian pulled on a pair of vinyl gloves, got into the driver's seat, and closed the door. He wanted to be left alone. Dunja seemed to understand and kept her distance. She had said that the car was still being inspected, but he couldn't see any marks to indicate which surfaces had been inspected, or where prints or strands of hair had been found. The only possible explanation was that they hadn't even started their examination. Fabian didn't know Ingvar Molander well, but from the little he had seen he was convinced the man would have already completed his investigation of the car if he were in the Danes' shoes.

Fabian opened the glove compartment and emptied it out. It contained a ballpoint pen with the Lund Hospital logo, a few AAA batteries, an extra bulb for the car headlights, and the manual and insurance papers, which listed Rune Schmeckel as the owner of the car. Nothing seemed out of the ordinary thus far. He flipped through the service records and discovered that Rune had followed the recommended schedule of maintenance appointments to a tee. Schmeckel was a scrupulous man, not the sort to be careless or improvise his way through a situation. Fabian only took his car to the mechanic when a new, alarming noise surfaced, often when it was too late—at least for his wallet.

In the rear-view mirror he saw Dunja standing and looking at her watch, casting impatient looks around the garage. The old man, however, was gone. It was time for Fabian to do what he'd come here for.

KIM SLEIZNER'S HEADACHE HAD started to ease up, and he could feel his body settling into an inner peace. He was standing at the window of his office, looking out across the water. He could see Islands Brygge on the other side of the harbour, as well as Gemini Residence, the harbourfront's most spectacular building. The structure was composed of two large converted silos, attached like Siamese twins; the interior stairwells always reminded Kim of *A Clockwork Orange*. He lived there with his wife and daughter in a fantastic apartment—the largest in the building.

He hadn't been able to get enjoyment out of much in the past twenty-four hours. His old ulcers had felt on the verge of tearing open from stress, and he feared that they might not be able to afford their apartment if he had to resign. But that was then. Now his anxiety had vanished, and he could barely feel his ulcers. Even his neck and shoulders were starting to relax.

The murder of Morten Steenstrup had played right into his hands. In one fell swoop, the storm of questions about who was to blame for the murder of Mette Louise Risgaard had abated, and all the focus had shifted to the perpetrator himself. Kim wanted nothing more than to solve the case before the Swedes.

Suddenly MC Hammer's "U Can't Touch This" came on, echoing through the room. He picked up his phone from the desk. His daughter had stolen his mobile phone, adding the "U Can't Touch This" ringtone and deleting all the other options. It was one of his least favourite songs—just the sound of it put him in a bad mood—but he didn't know how to change ringtones. He had been suffering through it for almost a year.

He tried to answer it before the irritating "woo-o-oo"s kicked in. "Hello?"

"Hi, this is Niels Pedersen."

"Who?" Kim had never heard of Niels Pedersen, and felt a pure and unadulterated aversion to finding out.

"I work down in the warehouse."

"You'll have to excuse me, but I'm in a meeting—"

"This will only take a second. I just wanted to double-check that I have all the correct information."

"What?" Sleizner hissed, feeling his ulcer awaken.

"You mentioned that nothing related to the Peugeot case is to be released to the Swedish police without your permission."

"Hold on. *Who* am I speaking to?"

"Niels Pedersen, down in the evidence warehouse. We sat across from each other at the Christmas dinner in 2003."

"Has someone contacted you?"

"Yes. He's here right now."

"Who, dammit? The Swedes?" *Shit. How the hell could they have got this far without me knowing?* Kim thought to himself.

"His name is Fabian Risk and he's here with Dunja Hougaard."

Dunja. Of course it was Dunja. This wasn't the first time she had refused to follow his orders. He had made it perfectly clear the minute he took over as chief of the unit that he would be nice to her if she was nice to him. It was very straightforward. Someone like Dunja Hougaard would most certainly have understood his intention for a symbiotic relationship.

Kim had recognized the type of girl she was when they'd met nearly five years ago. He had seen it in her eyes right away, but his outstretched hand had yielded him no results. Back then, Dunja walked around like she just wasn't horny, but ever since she had broken up with her boyfriend things had changed. Everyone in law enforcement seemed to know about the new Dunja. The rumours had spread like a virus to every backwoods town with a police station: how she gobbled up guy after guy, fucking like bunnies.

Yet she had rejected Kim, even at the most recent Christmas party, which he thought was pretty ridiculous considering that he had been hitting the gym three times a week, had the body of a thirty-five-year-old, earned good money, and had the power to jump-start her career—or stop it in its tracks. Kim had been searching for a solution that would allow him to get rid of her for a long time. He wanted to move her to a Podunk town as far away as possible, but no matter how hard he tried, he was never able to argue for her relocation because she was too damn good a police officer.

"Should I stop them?" Pedersen asked.

"No, let them continue," Kim said, his eyes following a tugboat moving along the canal. "But keep an eye on them, especially if it looks like they've found something of interest."

FABIAN TURNED OFF THE headlights so they wouldn't flash on automatically, stuck the new-looking key in the ignition, and carefully turned on the car. He absolutely did not want the engine to roar to life. The dashboard panel lit up, revealing the GPS start screen—just what he was after. Seconds passed as slowly as cold honey until a map filled the screen. It was zoomed in on a spot about ten kilometres north of Køge, at the intersection between Cementvej and a strange little road that led straight out into a field and rounded a grove of trees. *So that was where the chase came to an end*, Fabian thought. A digression that had cost two innocent people their lives. But Fabian hadn't come all this way to learn where Morten had ended his pursuit. He

navigated to the main menu and pressed FAVOURITE DESTINA-
TIONS. A list of three saved locations popped up on the screen:

- *Home—Adelgatan 5, Lund*
- *Work—Klinikgatan 20, Lund*
- *Away—15 rue du Thouron, Grasse*

He made a mental note to ask Tuvesson if they had found
anything of interest in Grasse, and pressed RECENT DESTINA-
TIONS in the upper left-hand corner of the screen. This record
was the entire reason for his visit to Copenhagen. A list of
various addresses and times appeared on the screen. He glanced
through them, quickly discovering that most of the trips before
June 19 had been between home and work, with the occasional
side trip to buy groceries.

The pattern wasn't broken until Monday, June 21, which is
where things started to get interesting. On June 22, the day of
Jörgen Pålsson's murder, the car had been at the Øresund Bridge
toll booth and went down to Germany, only to stop at the petrol
station in Lellinge. The car GPS only confirmed the information
about June 22 that Fabian already knew; it was June 21 that
sparked his interest.

At 10:23 a.m. on June 21, the car stopped on a street without a
name. The GPS showed the location on the map. The car had made
quite the detour from its usual route, travelling up to Söderåsen
about a kilometre north of Stenestad—thirty kilometres east
of Helsingborg. The road appeared to stop in the middle of
nowhere. Several hours later, the car left the deserted area and
was driven to Tögatan, the street Jörgen Pålsson lived on. Fabian
jotted down the coordinates for the unnamed road: *56.084298,
13.09021*. He had found exactly what he was looking for.

DUNJA LOOKED AROUND TO make sure that none of her colleagues could see her sneaking into the sleeping room they had

been allocated two years ago but that no one ever dared to use. She lay down on the cot and closed her eyes. Risk had seemed very pleased when they parted ways, though he claimed to have found nothing of interest. Dunja knew he had found *something*. She'd managed to ascertain that he was going back to Sweden to check on a lead, and he promised to contact her if it turned out to be interesting.

She wondered if she should feel irritated about Risk's reticent behaviour, but decided that she probably would have done the exact same thing in his position. She never liked to reveal anything prematurely, preferring to remain tight-lipped until she was certain the information she had was solid. She was well aware that several of her colleagues found this trait annoying; in their perfect world, every single idea would be shared with the entire team so they could twist and turn it beyond recognition.

Her phone started to vibrate. "*Sleazeball*" appeared on the caller ID.

"This is Dunja Hougaard."

"You don't have to pretend like you don't know who's calling."

"Hi, Kim. It's always such a pleasure to hear your voice. What can I do for you?"

"Come over. I need to talk to you."

"I'm busy working on—"

"Now."

DUNJA CLOSED THE DOOR behind her and sat in the visitor's chair facing Kim Sleizner's tidy desk. His smile did not bode well for her. She always felt more at ease when he was angry or grumpy. It was a different story when he was boasting a self-righteous smile, which usually meant that he had come up with some plan or other that he thought was incredibly brilliant, and would ask his little minions to carry it out for him. Previous tasks included everything from some cold case they'd be forced to follow up on, to a new rule assigning each person a day he or she would be responsible for bringing treats to go with coffee— everyone but the Sleazeball himself, of course.

"You look a bit tired. Was last night a late one?"

"Not as late as I had hoped. As you know, we got saddled with another murder." She made an effort to look as indifferent as possible.

"Right. How's that going? Have you made any progress?"

"Not yet. But Richter is at the hospital, inspecting the ceiling space. There are quite a few indications that's how the perpetrator got in."

"So, in other words, you have nothing right now?"

"Correct."

"Anything else you want to share with me?"

Dunja wondered if there was any chance he knew about her encounter with Risk. She thought it was unlikely and shook her head.

"You don't think that the fact you spent half the day with a Swedish police officer, letting him examine the confiscated Peugeot, is important enough to tell me?"

How the hell does he know?

"Don't you think that's a bit strange?" He stopped talking and waited for a reaction that she wasn't prepared to give. "Let me put it this way," he continued. "What, exactly, was unclear about my instructions not to release anything related to this investigation, especially to the Swedes, without my approval?"

It must have been that old bastard. He was the only one who could have called to tattle on her. Dunja wanted to yank out his catheter and jam it into his mouth. "Kim, I understood your instructions, but I believe that finding the killer is the most important task at hand, no matter who—"

"I don't think anyone asked for your opinion. While I am disappointed in you, I have no reason to broadcast your little overstep any more than is necessary."

"I don't agree that I overstepped. In fact, I think it—"

"Shut up! It doesn't matter what you think. You have violated the confidentiality clause in your contract!"

Dunja had no idea what contract Sleizner was referring to until he placed the document she'd signed when she was first hired on the desk. He tapped his nicotine-stained nail on the clause in question and read it out loud: "*The employee is prohibited from disclosing, releasing, or exploiting confidential information. This prohibition is applicable to the employee to the same extent that it applies to the public authority he or she is employed by.*" He looked up from the contract and straight into her eyes. "I hope you are aware that this is more than sufficient grounds for me to fire you."

He has to be joking, Dunja thought, even though she knew deep down that wasn't the case. "You can't do this," she said, cursing herself for sounding so pathetic. Her façade had crumbled. "You just can't—"

"I can do whatever the hell I want. If we're out of toilet paper, I am well within my rights to use you instead. I'm sure you understand that I can't have a bunch of unreliable leaks on my team."

"All I did was let in one of our Swedish colleagues, who is working on the same case—"

"I know exactly what you did! You let in an unauthorized individual and allowed him to examine our technical evidence, without having the slightest idea of his true motive."

"For God's sake, he just wants to solve the case, same as we do! Or at least the same as I do!"

"As far as the case is concerned, the perpetrator could just as well be Fabian Risk as anyone else. After all, they were in the same class."

"You can't be serious."

"The only thing we know for certain is that Morten Steenstrup didn't recognize the man in the wanted picture, which I've heard that Risk himself made a big deal of releasing. Steenstrup was murdered shortly after that, the same day Risk just *happens* to be in town. We also know that he was—and may still be—in love with the first victim's wife. Perhaps those are only coincidences, but what if they're not? In any case, *you* don't give a crap. You rolled out a red carpet for Risk, giving him total access to the car, even before we'd had time to examine it. Do you even have an idea of what he was doing in the car? He could have been removing evidence!"

Dunja realized there was no point in arguing with Sleizner any more. She was already stuck in quicksand: the more she fought, the deeper she sank. They sat staring at each other silently, both well aware that Sleizner was full of shit. No one could make bullshit sound more logical and meaningful than he could, which was probably why he had got so far in his career: he had certainly never been a good police officer.

Sleizner put away the employment contract and forced a smile. "As luck would have it, I'm not that kind of guy. I'm willing to put this little mess aside, let it marinate for a while, see how things shape up. Perhaps you can offer me a little something in return?"

44

FABIAN EXITED THE E6 and continued eastward along Highway 110 past Saxtorp. He had programmed the coordinates for the remote area into his own GPS and was letting the car guide him through the Skåne countryside.

He passed Markhögsvägen and a few large farms. The female voice from the GPS directed him to take a right on Eslövsvägen and then turn left on Hedvägen after a few hundred metres. Fabian was having no problem getting to his final destination, but he wondered what awaited him there. On the map it mostly looked just like woodland.

Fabian had investigated the area on Google Maps and discovered a two-building farm on the property. He hadn't been able to find out who owned the farm, so he'd called Lilja, hoping she could help. Lilja wanted to know why he wasn't on vacation and what had spurred his interest in this particular farm. Fabian told her the truth: he had found an extra key to the Peugeot when they were at Rune Schmeckel's house, and he had gone to Copenhagen to examine the car, which, according to the GPS, had been at this very farm the day before Jörgen was murdered.

The other end of the line went completely silent and Fabian had been forced to ask if she was still there. "You call this a vacation?" she said, and then informed him of how stupid it was to go to the farm alone. He tried to reassure her by explaining that it was probably empty and deserted, but she saw right through him. "You're scared, and you want to make sure we know where you are. Isn't that your real reason for calling?"

Fabian had no idea what he was going to find at the farm.

The landscape changed after Kågeröd: forests were replaced by open sky, and the roads became narrower as they wound up along the Söderåsen ridge. Soon the road grew so thin that it was effectively one lane, with no noticeable turnoffs. Fabian didn't think it was much of a problem given that he hadn't come across a single car in the last fifteen minutes.

The road meandered its way to another farm. Fabian double-checked to see if the GPS had led him astray. According to the map, he had to go straight through this farm in order to get to his destination. He defied the feeling of being an uninvited guest and drove between the buildings, looking around from inside the car.

The barn door was wide open, but Fabian couldn't see any people. It looked like the farm was deserted. A collection of rusty lawn-mowers, a few old tractor tyres, a bathtub, and a pile of naked, dirty mannequins were strewn outside the barn. He thought of the famous Laurie Anderson quote—people in large cities all over the world have more in common with each other than they do with their own rural countrymen. Fabian believed that could definitely apply to him: he knew little about life in rural Sweden and the people who lived there.

He started driving again slowly and noticed something move in the mirror on his right side. A large, barking German shepherd ran alongside the car for about ten metres, only to suddenly vanish underneath the car. Fabian put on the brakes. The car skidded to a stop. He instinctively locked the doors and waited patiently for the dog to come out. After a while, he backed up a few metres, but there was still no sign of the dog. It felt almost surreal.

He wondered if he had in fact arrived at the coordinates from the Peugeot, but his GPS said he had a kilometre or so to go.

He cautiously continued down the road. His phone rang. He answered, keeping his eyes on the rear-view mirror. Where was that dog?

"Urs Brunner," Lilja said, on the other end of the line.

"Who's that?"

"The owner of the farm you're headed for."

"A German?"

"Apparently. He bought the place in 2001. Do you think it's another one of Schmeckel's many identities?" The call started breaking up and it grew more difficult to hear Lilja's voice.

"It could be," Fabian said, continuing his slow crawl around the corner of a building. "Does he have a real address in Germany, or is it just a PO Box? Irene, can you hear me?"

"And I'm supposed to tell you that Tuvesson wants you to stop... until we..."

The call finally dropped. Fabian threw the phone onto the passenger seat and kept driving, dog or no dog. There was a forest on the right side of the road, and an open field on the other.

"In three hundred metres, turn left," the GPS instructed him. Fabian turned onto the last stretch.

The road ended one hundred metres later. Fabian stepped out of the car and looked around. A few scattered clouds hid the sun, making the summer feel like autumn. Three loud, flying swans broke the silence, their enormous wings making the air howl. But soon silence descended across the area once again. There was no traffic noise, no distant buzz, no wind in the trees. It was unsettlingly quiet.

A small lake glittered behind some of the trees. He couldn't see a farm. He walked over to a lone mailbox that stood deserted in the shadow of some overgrown lilacs, the lid covered in green moss. Fabian picked up a stick and scraped the moss off. A faded blue label read BRUNNER.

A path led him onward from the mailbox through the lilacs. Once he was on the other side of the bushes, he could see a flash of something in the air above the trees. As he got closer, he realized that it was a large, round, gleaming lens mounted on a pole that was attached to the roof ridge of one of the buildings.

He didn't spend long trying to figure out what the lens was for and continued down the overgrown path to the farm, wondering what it would be like to live this far out in the middle of nowhere. He probably wouldn't last more than a few days before absence of city air drove him crazy. This would pretty much be the perfect place if you wanted to be left alone and undisturbed. There were no neighbours as far as the eye could see, no access roads, no one to watch you. Was that what Urs Brunner was after?

In any case, it had obviously been a long time since Urs had been here, maybe even several years. Fabian waded through the high grass toward a building with mossy-grey, fibre-cement siding. He walked around the corner, stopping mid-step to try and digest what was before him. Either he was dreaming, or the killer was a much bigger mystery than he ever could have imagined.

About twenty metres in front of him, there was an identical building to the one he was currently standing beside. But the area between the buildings was extremely puzzling. The grass had been neatly manicured, as if it were a golf green ready for Tiger Woods's most crucial putt. There was a hedge, a few inches high, in the middle of the lawn, which framed a rectangle of neatly raked gravel. Fabian thought it looked like a gravesite and estimated it was about three by four metres.

He walked across the lawn to the grave-like area. What he saw fundamentally changed the investigation in a single blow. Everything they knew had suddenly become useless and they would have to start over from the beginning. Fabian had no idea where to go from here.

The sun peeked out from behind the clouds, the air immediately becoming a few degrees warmer. Fabian stepped across the hedge, stood in the gravel rectangle, and looked down at the three-centimetre-thick plate of glass that was suspended a few inches above the ground on four metal legs. Rune Schmeckel lay face up on the glass. He was naked; his arms and legs sprawled out to the four corners of the glass. His limbs were bound to the plate he was lying on.

The man he had been hunting for the past few days was right here—exposed, vulnerable, and scorched. He had no hair left and there were severe burns on his scalp. His skull was exposed in certain places. Fabian tried to gather his thoughts, to figure out what had happened, but each time he ended up bewildered. Long burns extended all over Schmeckel's face and body, as if someone had tortured him with a welding torch, but the wounds were far too straight to have been made by hand.

Fabian felt dizzy and sick from all the thoughts that were buzzing in his head like flies around a cadaver. Sweat beaded on his forehead and ran into his eyes, which tingled with the salt. Why hadn't he thought to bring some water? He tried to swallow the sticky feeling in his mouth, but that only made him more nauseous. He needed a drink. Maybe there was a well of water around here. He began looking for one when something started crackling right behind him. He smelled smoke and felt something get hotter and hotter. He turned around quickly, but he couldn't see anything that might explain the smell. Could he really be dreaming after all? Was he at home, asleep in his bed? The crackling sound was now right behind his ear, which suddenly stung with a terrible, sharp pain. Only then did he realize he was on fire.

PART 2

July 7–July 11, 2010

"It's not death itself that scares us when we are dying, but the risk of being forgotten." —I. M.

January 8

As usual, everyone looked at me and laughed when
I came into the schoolyard. I could feel them rubbing
against my mitten. I wish I hadn't been so nervous
and afraid, but I was. I was afraid that they had
thought up some new way to hurt me for the start of
the semester. A really horrible trick that would make
the rest of the idiots laugh.

But like usual, they shouted about me being gay
and smelling like a urinal. I didn't say anything, but
I didn't run either. I just turned around, walked up to
one of them, and hit him in the face with the brass
knuckles under my mitten. It hurt more than I thought
it would, but I hit him again because I knew one time
wasn't enough. He tried to hit back, but he missed. I
grabbed his hood, yanked him down to the ground,
and started pounding his head on the pavement over
and over again. I don't remember if it was him or me
screaming. I think it was both of us.

It was the most awesome thing I've ever done.
Well, since the first time I went to Legoland. I could
see the fear in his eyes and it just made me madder
and madder, but I also felt stronger and stronger.
He just lay there underneath me and took it. No one
tried to stop me, not even his friend. I could have kept
going until his skull cracked if I wanted to. I swear.

P. S. Laban was dead when I got home. I don't know
why, but I started crying.

45

FAREED CHERUKURI HAD BEEN thinking about it a lot, and now he was sure. He had, without a doubt, one of the most boring jobs in the world. If he had a choice, he would have rather helped clean up Chernobyl than sit here at TDC customer services and be forced to answer questions, each more stupid than the last. *Why won't my Internet work? Can you help me use Google?*

Even though he was overqualified, he had accepted the position because he needed the money. When your last name was Cherukuri, finding a job was practically impossible in a country like Denmark. He had been promised the possibility of a promotion as soon as they had assessed his work ethic. *There's always a demand for good programmers*, they had told him. Three years had gone by, and he was still sitting down here in the bunker, feeling the heavy weight of the headset. *I dropped my phone in the toilet and now I can't use it to make calls. Can you help me?*

But today, for the first time, he had received a question that woke him from his boredom. Just a few moments into the conversation, he found himself sitting straight up. He was excited.

The woman introduced herself as Dunja Hougaard. She was a police officer with the crime squad in Copenhagen. She told him that she should have called TDC's special division for mobile phone searches, but the paperwork would take too long and she would prefer to avoid starting such a major process at this early stage in the investigation if at all possible.

His job was customer service, not wiretapping. Unless she was having a problem with her TDC subscription, he couldn't help her. No matter how much he might want to, there was nothing in his power he could do to find the information she wanted. At least, according to his job description.

In fact he had spent all those years exercising his brain and programming skills by hacking into TDC's systems, breaking through firewall after firewall, and even reaching the Holy Grail—calls, texts, and data traffic. For the past year he had been able to eavesdrop on any call that was connected through the TDC network: it didn't matter if it was Queen Margrethe, Casper Christensen, or Søren Pind.

Listening to people's phone calls had brightened his days for a few months, but soon he had sunk back into a brain-dead haze. He had been hoping to find out about some juicy scandals, but he hadn't discovered anything outrageous. It was like everyone knew someone was listening. But today was different.

The policewoman asked whether a specific number in Sweden had called a specific number in Denmark sometime during the evening of Friday, July 2. He asked whose numbers they were, but she wouldn't tell him. He promised to see what he could do and to call her back as soon as possible.

He immediately discovered that the Swedish number belonged to an Astrid Tuvesson, chief of the crime unit in Helsingborg, and that the Danish number belonged to Kim Sleizner, the head of the Danish police. Now he knew why she didn't want to put this inquiry on the record.

This just kept getting better and better. Sleizner was something of a celebrity. Any time the police had to make a statement, the responsibility fell to Kim Sleizner. Fareed had no trouble with the search, and he'd been able to call Dunja Hougaard back after only a few minutes.

"The Swedish number called the Danish number at 5:33 p.m. last Friday."

"Did the Danish number answer?"

"No, but a message was left on the voicemail. Do you want me to play it?" Fareed could hear the policewoman's hesitation, which he understood. What right did she have to go in and listen to her boss's messages?

"Okay."

Fareed Cherukuri pressed play.

"This is Astrid Tuvesson with the Helsingborg police. We have an emergency situation in your jurisdiction. There is an extremely dangerous criminal at a petrol station in Lellinge, and we are afraid that he may have taken one of the employees hostage. He is behind at least two murders in Sweden, and he must be stopped before he commits any more. Call as soon as you get this message. In the meantime I am going to contact the station in Køge."

It had happened just as Fabian Risk claimed it had.

"Did the Danish number call the Swedish number back?"

"No. He didn't listen to the message until the next day, after which he erased it."

"Erased it?"

"Yes, but we keep the sound files for a year."

He said "he," Dunja thought. She knew immediately that he had looked up the name of the Danish subscriber, but she had no intention of commenting on it. She had the answer to her question. Now she just needed to figure out how to proceed.

"I found something else," he said, just as she was about to thank him for his help and hang up.

"Oh?"

"I know the geographic location of the phone when the voice-mail picked up the call."

"Okay?"

"He was at the corner of Lille Istedgade and Halmtorvet."

Dunja knew the address very well. It was famous for being a corner frequented by prostitutes. "I'm sure it's just a coincidence," she replied, thanking him for his help and hanging up.

46

THE WHITE-HOT BEAM OF sunlight hit the man's bare stomach just below his navel. A thin column of smoke rose from the point of contact and there was a faint bubbling sound, as if someone were frying a tiny egg. It was already past six in the evening, but the sun was still shining like it was midday. The air vibrated. It smelled burnt.

So this is what burning human skin smells like, Fabian thought, glancing up at the roof-mounted lens. *It's closer to fried pork than burning hair.* He had smelled that earlier, too, when his jacket and then his hair had caught fire.

Several precious seconds had passed before he'd realized that his body was on fire. He had thrown himself to the ground in an attempt to smother the flames, but they refused to go out. He nearly panicked when the hair on the back of his neck wouldn't stop burning. Now that it was over, the stench was nearly as unbearable as the pain; the fire hadn't gone out until he'd managed to pull his jacket up over his head.

Nearly an hour had gone by since then. Fabian noticed that the same ray had burned a centimetre of Rune Schmeckel's abdomen. He wondered if he should move the body, but the pain in his back made it almost impossible for him to move. He also didn't want to touch anything until Molander and the others arrived. He didn't want to give Lilja more reason to suspect him. Instead, he ignored the pain, stepped back over the hedge, took off his shoes and socks, and gingerly lay down on the grass.

The silence was nearly unreal. He couldn't hear any distant birds or the wind in the trees. It seemed as if this whole place was holding its breath, and he was the only thing still alive. He couldn't keep his eyes open a moment longer, and finally gave in to sleep, which surrounded him, pulling him deeper and deeper into a dreamless black hole.

47

DUNJA HOUGAARD STEPPED INTO the elevator and pressed the button for the third floor. Her back was still tender from her half-hour on the acupressure mat. She had decided to sit on the information she had received from the man at TDC. For once, she was going to avoid acting rashly. Before she did anything, she wanted to be sure that all the information was accurate.

It was clear beyond all doubt that the Swedes had called Kim Sleizner, but Dunja wasn't sure if Sleizner really had been at the corner of Lille Istedgade and Halmtorvet at the time of the call—and if he was, she didn't know what he had been doing there. It wouldn't surprise her at all to find out that the Sleazeball visited prostitutes. But if it turned out that he did it during business hours, all hell would break loose.

The elevator doors opened and she walked into the traffic enforcement unit, although that wasn't where she was headed. She was going to the IT department, way back in the far corner. There was one last thing she wanted to check on before she went home.

"Hey sexy! You look like you sold yourself and lost the drugs," hollered Mikael Rønning, whose outfit of the day consisted of tight white jeans and a very low-cut T-shirt with shiny silver appliqué.

"Well, I'd say that's about how I feel."

"What is it this time? Did your computer catch herpes again from all that porn you've been watching?"

"In a manner of speaking." She leaned toward his desk. If Mikael were straight, his language would have definitely pissed her off. For some unknown reason, she had so much more patience for gay guys. Mikael could say more or less whatever he wanted to her and she didn't mind—a fact he always liked to make the most of. He always found something wrong with her: if it wasn't her clothes, it was her hair, or her breath. *Did you forget to brush your teeth again? How many times do I have to tell you, you always have to brush after a blow job. You know they swim in and get stuck between...*

"I need a printout of the personnel log for July second."

"Last Friday?"

Dunja nodded with an expression that indicated she didn't want to say any more.

"May I ask why?"

"Ask away, but don't expect me to answer."

Mikael muttered something unintelligible, sat down at his computer, and entered a few commands. Soon after, the printer started spitting out page after page of logins and logouts for every employee in the building. Dunja took the pages before they even had time to cool off, and glanced through them as quickly as the machine could print them.

She found Sleizner's clock-in on the fourth page. At 11:43 a.m. he had swiped his key card and entered his code at the south employee entrance from the parking lot. From there he went up to the crime unit, where he logged into his computer. She didn't see anything until 10:46 p.m., when he logged out and left the building.

According to the TDC guy, Sleizner had been on Lille Istedgade, not far from the police station, at 5:33 p.m. But according to the log, he had never left the building. Either she'd been given false information, or Sleizner had managed to leave the building without having to log in and out.

"I'm taking this home with me," she said, hurrying off.

"You owe me!" Mikael Rønning shouted at her.

"You can get me into bed whenever you want! Just say the word!" She slapped her own arse before vanishing out the door. Mikael laughed, thinking that if he were ever going to do something as hopelessly stupid as crawling back into the closet, it would be with Dunja.

48

HE WAS SITTING IN "The Heart," his control room. "The Brain" would have been a more fitting name, but he preferred the former; he thought it sounded cosier. The Heart was just one of several rooms he had spent several years secretly excavating under his one-storey house, two and a half metres below ground. He had spent the past couple of months turning this subterranean space into his permanent abode, and only occasionally did he go up into the house. He could live underground and survive for more than a year if he had to.

He had a small kitchen with running water and a pantry that was well stocked with canned and dried food. There was a warmed waterbed in the bedroom that was even more comfortable than his regular bed. Since there were no windows, he'd spent a lot of time working on the lighting before he was satisfied. When he was finished he could brag that on a cloudy day, he had more daylight underground than there was outside.

His biggest problem had been the ventilation. The easiest solution would have been to put the inlet and outlet somewhere in the yard, but the noise from the fans would have been too obvious. Instead, he'd attempted to channel the air up through the house and out of a new chimney, but no matter how much insulation he used, the humming sound broke through, revealing that there was more than just a one-storey house there. He ended up staging a little bit of roadwork outside the house to "repair a water leak," so that he could move the ventilation system all the way over to the corner of the plot next to the electrical box. Yes, it had been complicated, but it was well worth the effort.

He was still the most pleased with The Heart. It was the shape of a hemisphere, just over two metres in diameter. It functioned like a cockpit, with everything he needed within an arm's reach. He had painted the concrete walls red, and used gold spray paint on the semicircle of the control panel and his chair. A recessed cabinet to his right held three custom-built computers. They made the most expensive computers on the market look about as advanced as a Commodore 64. He also had two NAS servers that held eight terabytes each. Everything was cooled and soundproofed. Each computer had a dedicated connection of one hundred megabytes per second in both directions. When he was online he used several proxy servers so that no one could trace his actual IP addresses.

He could see the police standing around staring at Rune Schmeckel's body on one of the six screens in front of him. Everyone was there except Fabian Risk, who had been taken to the hospital to have his burns treated. He had burst into wild laughter when he saw Risk catch fire. It was too good to be true. He hadn't even planned it. If he believed in God he would have taken it as a clear sign that God was with him in this mission. Although, as far as he was concerned, chance was just as good. Chance was absolutely perfect.

Whether it was chance that had helped Risk find Rune Schmeckel several days ahead of schedule, he didn't know. But a nagging worry told him that chance had nothing to do with it and that Risk was quite simply a dangerous adversary. He had already realized this a while ago, but this was further confirmation.

He had suspected this very thing might happen when he'd been forced to leave the Peugeot behind. And Rune was just the beginning. If his luck really went sour, the car could become a much bigger problem than he'd counted on. But for every problem, there was usually a solution. All he had to do was anticipate the problem in time—and for him, the solution's name was Risk.

It would have been simplest just to kill him now. But who said it would be simple? He had poured so many years and so much money into it that he wasn't about to settle for half-assing anything. He had already implemented the biggest changes in his plan: Risk was going to be the crowning glory of Plan B, so he had to be kept alive a while longer. All he had left was some recon to get the last piece of the puzzle to fall into place, which he would do tonight while Risk was in the hospital.

He pushed up one of the faders on the soundboard so that he could hear the police, who were standing around discussing Rune Schmeckel.

"It would be best if we could keep this internal for as long as we can. The longer it takes for the killer to learn that we've found Schmeckel, the better," said the female chief.

"So you're saying we're sure Schmeckel isn't the killer?" the cute one said, looking down at the dead body.

"Are you suggesting he might have taken his own life?"

"Why not? It's a spectacular suicide. Look around—the gravel has even been raked. The whole point of all this must be that we're meant to see it."

"Yes, but I'm sure we got here earlier than he'd planned. He couldn't have expected Risk to sniff this place out so quickly. And to be completely honest, I still don't quite understand how he did."

"Not to mention it would have been impossible for him to fasten himself down like that," the crime scene investigator added, kneeling down and pointing at the strap, which had cut into Schmeckel's wrist. "Look at these marks: clear signs that he tried to get free."

"How long could he have been here?" the fat one asked.

"Hard to say right now. But the burn marks will help us out."

268

"How?"

"The earth's rotation around the sun makes each burn unique. So the burn would have started in a new spot each day and slowly moved across his body."

He couldn't help being impressed with the investigator's deductive reasoning. Not everyone was capable of putting their emotions aside, but this particular guy seemed to be undisturbed by the naked man in front of him—a man who had obviously been forced to endure indescribable suffering before death took over and dulled the pain. A man they had been on the hunt for until now. A killer turned victim.

None of this seemed to affect the investigator in the least. Instead, he was totally absorbed in interpreting the burns and finding out how long Schmeckel had been bound to the plate of glass. *Impressive*, he thought. He was sure that he would have also made a good crime scene investigator. It certainly would have been fun. He had actually thought about pursuing it before, but that would have to be in another life now.

He had chosen to be self-employed, and he loved his job. He enjoyed nothing more than spending time in his workshop and working out new, innovative solutions. Sometimes he worked non-stop for several days, without pausing to eat or sleep. His work made him lose track of time and space. It helped him to forget what a pathetic guy he really was. He was sure that it was just the same for the investigator he was watching on the screen.

"LOOK HERE, FOR EXAMPLE," Molander said, pointing at a line of burns that ran from the left hip and up across the chest and face, with a few gaps in between. "This is one day."

"But if that's only one day, why isn't he burned here or here?" Lilja pointed at the empty spaces in the line.

"Those are probably from a tree or cloud that was blocking the sun." Molander looked annoyingly smug, Lilja thought.

"So all we have to do is count the lines?"

"Exactly."

"But you've already done that, haven't you?"

Molander nodded and adjusted his glasses. "Seventeen."

"Seventeen days? He's been lying out here for over two weeks?!" Tuvesson exclaimed.

"That can't be right," Klippan said. "The decay would be more advanced, especially with this heat."

Molander took off his glasses and polished them slowly and ceremoniously. "Just because he's been lying here for seventeen days doesn't mean he's been dead for seventeen days. A person can survive for several months without food, and ten days without water."

"Yes, but not in this heat."

"Agreed. He must have had access to water in some form or other," Molander continued, bending down and looking under the glass plate. "Just as I suspected." He pulled out an empty drum with a transparent tube that led up through a small hole in the plate under Schmeckel's neck.

"So, when did he die?" Tuvesson asked.

"Braids will have to take a look, but my bet is two or three days ago, max."

Tuvesson and the others stood around the burned body looking at it in silence. It seemed that they had just now realized how much pain Rune Schmeckel had been forced to endure in his last few days of life. The case was completely baffling. They were now more puzzled than ever.

THE AMBULANCE STAFF APPROACHED with a stretcher and asked if they could remove the body. Tuvesson nodded mutely. They cut the straps with their forceps and lifted the body.

Some sort of moss was growing under the glass plate, following the exact contours of the body. The moss had flourished in Schmeckel's shadow. It was shrivelled and burned in all the places that the sun had been able to reach. Rune Schmeckel was

270

on his way to the ambulance in a body bag, but it almost looked as if he were still lying in the moss.

"What the hell is that supposed to mean?" Klippan asked.

No one had an answer, not even Molander.

49

FABIAN RISK RECOGNIZED HIMSELF from the flames that shot up from the man's back and neck. There was a black-clad man holding a pistol that was disproportionately large in comparison to his body. A bullet was flying through the air. It couldn't be the first one, Fabian thought, because the black-clad man across from him had already been hit and was lying down with a gaping, bloody wound in his stomach, forming a considerable pool on the ground.

"That's the murderer," Matilda said, pointing at the bleeding man. "And that's you."

"But I'm still on fire. How am I supposed to—"

"There," Matilda interrupted him. "You can just run over and jump in. Easy peasy." She pointed at the deep blue sea in the corner of the drawing.

"Easy peasy," Fabian repeated, putting down the drawing. His eyes moved to Sonja, who was sitting on a chair beside his hospital bed.

"How are you feeling?" she inquired.

"Okay, considering the circumstances. The doctor says I only have second-degree burns, so they don't need to do grafts or anything."

"That's good."

"Does it hurt?" Matilda asked.

"Not too bad," Fabian lied, meeting Sonja's gaze.

"I burned myself once and it hurt a lot. Here, look."

272

Matilda pulled up her shirt and showed them the scar on her stomach.

Fabian had hoped the scar would fade with time, but instead it seemed to have grown along with Matilda. She had been two years old when it happened. She and he were alone at the time, and he was boiling her pacifiers on the stove. She had been absolutely obsessed with pacifiers, or "pacis," as she'd called them. She would whine and beg for a paci; she obviously didn't care about any old bacteria. *Want paci…please, paci now… Dada…Dada, paci now! Want now!*

He hadn't been able to take her whining any longer so he'd closed the bedroom door to make the bed in peace and quiet. It had come as a total surprise to him that she was capable of moving the stool, climbing onto it, and reaching the pot of boiling water.

"According to the doctor, I might be able to come home tomorrow or the day after."

"That's great."

"And I was thinking we could get started on that vacation, and—"

"Please stop."

"Sonja, I'm off the case." He looked her in the eye. "I didn't say anything earlier, but Tuvesson took me off it yesterday."

"And yet here you are in the hospital."

She was right. It didn't matter that he had been removed from the investigation or was incredibly burned out. He wouldn't be able to let it go until they had caught the killer, even though he was further from closing the case than ever at the moment.

"Where's Theo?"

"He didn't want to come. How was your trip with him yesterday, by the way?"

Fabian shook his head. "All he wanted was to get back to his computer and close himself off in his room."

Sonja smiled for the first time since they'd arrived at the

hospital. "You're so good at solving cases; you'll probably manage to solve that mystery too."

Fabian laughed. "No one's that good."

Her smile faded. "Matilda and I are taking the night train to Stockholm tonight."

"What about Theo? What does he think?"

Sonja shrugged. "You tell me. I asked if he wanted to come, but his new thing is to not respond when I ask him a question." She sighed and shook her head.

"Have you tried texting him? He usually has headphones on, so he can't hear you yelling, but he won't let his phone out of his sight. Honey, he's a teenager. Theo and most kids his age think we're just about the most annoying, embarrassing people in the world. Of course they don't want to talk to us."

"If he absolutely doesn't want to come I guess he can stay in Helsingborg, which might give you a chance to solve two things at once." She stood up, leaned over, and kissed him. In the midst of their worst crises, a kiss could remind them how much they still loved each other, deep down.

"See you later," she whispered into his ear, turning to Matilda. "Say goodbye to Daddy now."

"Bye."

"What, no hug?"

"Nope," Matilda said, taking Sonja's hand. "If you forget what to do, just look at the drawing."

They knocked on the door. A uniformed officer opened it and let them out.

50

DUNJA HOUGAARD GLANCED OUT the window at the dark-pink sky that was scattered with a few feathery, golden clouds. She was lying on the couch in her two-bedroom condo, which was above Blågårds Pharmacy on Blågårds Plads. It confirmed her belief once again that this very place by the window, in this very apartment, lying on this very worn-out sofa that she had inherited from her grandmother, was likely the best place in the world. Sunlight streamed in on sunny days, and she could listen to raindrops patter against the window when it was raining.

She was slowly and systematically reviewing the personnel log for the second time. She marked everyone who had logged in with a coloured pen as soon as she noted their log-out time. If Sleizner had logged out using someone else's ID, she would figure it out, but so far she hadn't found anything that didn't match up. Sleizner had arrived at 11:43 a.m. and left the building at 10:46 p.m. It was certainly a long day for a Friday, but there was nothing particularly strange about it, which was too bad.

She put down the stack of papers and looked out the window. She could see a blinking aeroplane far up in the sky and wondered what it would be like to go skydiving, to just tear open the aeroplane door and throw yourself out into the unknown. She had promised it to herself as a thirtieth birthday present, so she definitely needed to try it someday. She was almost thirty-five now.

Dunja vaulted out of her daydream. Could he have used

one of the emergency exits? She grabbed the paper pile again, flipping to the hours before 5:33 p.m., when he was allegedly on Lille Istedgade. She went through the list a third time, and found what she had been looking for all along.

- *Time: 4:27 p.m. — Emergency Exit 23A*
- *Time: 4:28 p.m. — Emergency Exit 11A*

The Sleazeball had left through the emergency exits in stairwell A. He had probably made sure that the doors didn't close completely, so he could come back in the same way and then log out with his card at 10:46 p.m. She now had confirmation that he had left the police station to run an errand on Lille Istedgade, an errand that as few people as possible would know about and one that was likely the very reason he hadn't answered his phone.

Her mobile started ringing: an unknown number was calling.

"Yes, hello...?"

"Hi, it's me. I just wanted to see if it's okay if I come over and get you into bed," said Mikael Rønning in his most heterosexual voice.

Dunja burst out laughing. "Of course! If you can get it up, that is."

"No problem. I'll bring a fake moustache, bald cap, and baseball hat."

"It sounds like you'll be right at home."

"By the way, did you see *Ekstra Bladet*?"

"No, why?"

"See for yourself."

Dunja turned on her iPad and went to *Ekstra Bladet*'s website.

COPENHAGEN POLICE CHIEF CAUGHT IN LIE!

Kim Sleizner was lying when he claimed that he did not receive a call from the Swedish police. Ekstra Bladet *can now reveal that he was on Lille Istedgade when the Swedish police tried to get in touch with him! According to our source, the Swedish police attempted to call Chief of Police Kim Sleizner at 5:33 p.m., but the call was picked up by voicemail. This report directly contradicts Sleizner's own claims that he was never con-tacted. Ekstra Bladet's source also claims to have proof that Sleizner was on the corner of Lille Istedgade and Halmtorvet at the time in question. Ekstra Bladet has not been able to reach Kim Sleizner for comment.*

Shit.

"Are you still there?"

"Ugh, yes…"

"That's what you were looking for, isn't it?"

"Yes."

"Wasn't very smart to take it to *Ekstra Bladet*, darling."

"It wasn't me."

"Who was it then?"

"No idea," Dunja said, but of course she did. It couldn't have been anyone other than the guy from TDC. But she had been wondering how she could use the information to put Sleizner in a downright embarrassing situation and indirectly blame him for the deaths of Mette Louise Risgaard and Morten Steenstrup. And she knew the Sleazeball would assume the whole thing was her doing, just as Mikael Rønning had believed.

51

HE'D WATCHED FABIAN RISK'S wife and daughter leave the house at thirteen minutes past ten that night via the wireless camera in the rental car. They were each carrying a suitcase, and jumped into the waiting taxi. Now it was just past midnight, and the lights were still on in the son's room. Regardless of where the others were going, he had chosen to stay at home.

He had not intended to go into the Risks' house after the son went to bed, but he couldn't wait much longer. He had a long night of preparations ahead of him, and it was important that nothing went wrong. The time had come to shift into high gear. He wanted to increase the pace and the level of confusion, above all.

He planned to throw out some bait—two delicious little morsels for those media hyenas to sink their teeth into, and which would indirectly assist in elevating his actions from a national matter to one of worldwide importance.

He walked around the block and turned down the small gravel path that led to the back of the terrace houses. He climbed over the Risks' fence and passed the trampoline, which took up more than its fair share of the small yard. There was no need for him to conceal himself or sneak up: Risk's son was the only person home, and it was clear that he was practically glued to the computer in his bedroom, which faced the street.

He peered into the kitchen window from the deck. It was dark, except for the light on the stove. The back door was locked, as expected, but it was no match for his picklock. Thirty seconds later he was inside. He didn't have to worry about making noise because death metal, or whatever you would call that blasting sound, was thundering down from the second floor. He could just about make out a man's voice yelling about being an animal and not himself.

He took out the video camera and started filming. He wanted to capture every detail because he didn't know exactly what he was looking for yet. The only thing he knew for sure was that this was the final piece of the puzzle, the Kryptonite that would put Risk exactly where he wanted him.

When he was done in the kitchen he moved to the living room, which still contained several boxes that hadn't been unpacked. He opened a few of them, filming their contents, and walked up the stairs to the second floor with his camera still on. The further he went up the stairs, the louder the distorted guitars and rumbling percussion became.

The lyrics were clearer now. Something about the victim being the one who put the stick in his hand.

The door to the master bedroom was ajar. He opened it with his foot and turned on the bare ceiling light with his elbow. He noticed an unmade bed, a few open and half-empty boxes along one wall, and clothes tossed here and there. The chaos made him want to vomit.

The daughter's room, however, was more orderly. The bed was made with red heart-shaped pillows on top, and there were a few drawings on the desk, which depicted the same scene in different ways. A burning man shooting another man. He picked out the one he liked best, turned on the desk light, and took a picture.

He returned to the hallway, where he had two doors left to explore: one led to the bathroom and the other to the son's room—it was open slightly.

The music spilled out of the crack, thundering about raping

279

the raper and hating the hater. He approached the door and opened it all the way.

The son was leaning over his desk at the window, his back toward him. The speakers stood on the floor; their size explained the volume. This teen had obviously spent his entire allowance on the sound system. He took a step into the room and looked around. Although they'd moved in just a week ago, the room was so messy it looked like it hadn't been cleaned in years. The walls were plastered with posters of Metallica, Slipknot, and Marilyn Manson. The bed was unmade and functioned as a general dumping ground for everything from dirty laundry to dumb-bells and scraps of pizza. His parents were clearly quite lax about the rules. It looked like he hadn't been under the watchful eye of an adult for a while—until now.

Satisfaction washed over his body like a wave. He felt high. The last piece of the puzzle had just fallen into place.

He walked toward the son, who was singing along, full of feeling, as he frantically wrote something in a book. He was writing as if it were a race against time before someone would come and rip the pen from his hand.

The song reached its climax with a chain of expletives.

The pen stopped moving and the ink spread out into a fat spot. Theodor had stopped singing along. He looked up from the book, straight into the pitch-black window, where he saw the reflection of a shadow that was coming up behind him. Someone was in his room.

He whirled around.

52

FABIAN RISK WAS FEELING restless and bored. He'd always been terrible at being sick. A fever was never enough of a reason to stay home, and the few times he'd been afflicted by a stomach flu that forced him to stay in bed, he'd complained so much that Sonja had threatened to divorce him. He was well aware that he should follow the example of the rest of his hospital ward and get some rest, but he couldn't fall asleep. Talking to Molander would be the only thing that would help him relax. Fabian needed to find out if they had arrived at the same conclusion. He had been taken away in an ambulance before he could hear everyone's theories about the crime scene.

He decided to call Molander, even though it was quite a bit past midnight. He dug out his phone only to discover that the battery was dead. He looked around the hospital room. There was a phone on the wall not far from him, which was probably only for internal calls, if it was connected at all. He ignored the pain and extended his arm as far as he could, but he couldn't reach it. With the help of one of the crutches leaning against the wall, he managed to unlock the brake on the bed and drag himself toward the phone.

He put the receiver to his ear and heard a dial tone, but soon discovered that his prediction was correct. He pressed zero and was put through to an operator at the hospital, who surprisingly agreed to place his call without asking any questions. He dialled directory assistance to request the mobile number for

Ingvar Molander in Helsingborg and was immediately connected: "*Hello. You have reached Ingvar Molander's voicemail. I can't take your call right now, so leave your name and number after the beep, and I promise to call you back. Or, even better, you can send a text. Thanks. Goodbye.*"

Fabian hung up. It was pretty late, but Molander couldn't possibly have gone to bed already. The crime scene at Söderåsen would likely keep them busy all night long and part of tomorrow, at least. He closed his eyes and realized that maybe his body was ready to give in to exhaustion after all.

HE WOKE UP TO Tuvesson standing beside his bed. He lurched forward and felt his pain level shoot from zero to one hundred. "Sorry, I didn't mean to wake you. I didn't actually think you were capable of sleeping."

"I didn't either, until . . . What time is it?"

"It's early — seven thirty. I brought you some breakfast. Hospital food isn't usually all that great." She put a bag from 7-Eleven down on the bedside table. "I wanted to see how you're doing."

"I'm okay. Besides forgetting to apply sunscreen, I don't have much to complain about."

Tuvesson laughed. "The sun is always stronger than you think."

"So, how are things going for the unit?"

"Well, we sure aren't lacking evidence to examine. By the way, Molander mentioned you tried to call him."

"I did, but he didn't answer. Where is he?"

"It was his and Gertrud's anniversary yesterday. They were going to stay at Marienlyst in Helsingør."

Anniversary. Fabian savoured the word. It had been a long time since he and Sonja had celebrated their own. For the first few years, they hadn't let anything get in the way of their annual celebration: they would hire a babysitter, dress up, and go out. One of them always surprised the other with an activity, anything from going out to the theatre and a restaurant, to having a picnic and taking a ride in a hot-air balloon. Fabian decided that as soon as this case was solved, he would surprise Sonja and make up for all their lost anniversaries.

"Have you come up with anything?"

He opened the 7-Eleven bag and was delighted to find that Tuvesson had treated him to a brownie, and a fresh roll, and was carrying a cup of good coffee.

Tuvesson pulled up a chair and sat down beside the bed. "Please allow me to ask the questions instead. I want to remind you that I took you off the case for a reason. You were supposed to let us handle this and take a vacation."

"I was kicked off the case because you needed a scapegoat. What I do on my vacation is my business—as long as I don't do anything illegal."

Tuvesson sighed heavily and threw up her hands. "The truth is that we haven't come up with much at all. And now that your theory about Rune being the killer has turned out to be totally wrong, we're feeling mostly confused and like we're back at square one."

"You haven't come up with a new theory yet?"

"Not exactly. It looks like it could be absolutely anyone—someone else from your class or one of the other classes in the same year, a teacher you were all a little extra-awful to, or even a parent."

She took out a cigarette and ran it under her nose.

"I'm not going to light it, I promise. Klippan and Lilja have contacted everyone in the class who isn't off travelling somewhere, and none of them have come up with any suggestions besides Claes Mällvik. So now I'm asking you . . . Do you remember if there was anyone who came in contact with the class in some way or another and—"

"Hold on. I don't understand," Fabian interrupted her. "How is it possible that you haven't come up with anything?"

"Can you please just answer my question?"

"The crime scene at Söderåsen must have given you a few new leads. You must have found *something*!"

Tuvesson stuck one hand in her pocket to reassure herself that she had a lighter. "All we know for sure is that Rune Schmeckel lay there burning for more than two weeks, and he didn't die until a few days ago. There was a drum of water hidden under the glass plate, and he had access to a straw so he could drink from it." She stopped talking and shook her head. "I can't even imagine how much he must have suffered, that poor man."

Fabian thought about what Tuvesson had just said and realized that it only strengthened his theory. He met her gaze. "I think the killer set up the whole place to present himself and his motives."

"I don't understand. What do you mean?"

"The place itself—he wanted us to find it. Maybe not right now, but in time. He put so much time and energy into the presentation; it couldn't just be about taking Schmeckel's life. There's more he wants to say."

"But the murders of Jörgen and Glenn were committed as punishment for their crimes."

"Right, and presumably the very same thing is happening here."

"But what is Schmeckel—or Claes Mällvik—guilty of, besides being Jörgen and Glenn's victim?"

"I don't know. That's why I wanted to ask Molander what you've found."

"Not much more than what you already saw...Actually, there is one thing. We found it when we lifted the body off the glass plate. The moss all around the glass was dead, but the moss that grew in the shadow of his body was alive and healthy. It formed the shape of a person, so it actually looked like there was someone lying under the glass, but really it was just moss. Do you follow me? It's kind of hard to explain."

Fabian nodded. He understood. "That must be him."

"Who? The perpetrator?"

"He created a self-portrait. That's how he wants us to see him."

53

HER HEAD WAS POUNDING with pain more intense than she'd ever felt before. Was this what a migraine felt like? She had never had migraines, but knew they were supposed to be horrible. This feeling had to be worse—much worse.

For once she had been really looking forward to her evening with Mona and Cilla. Most of the time these outings felt like a chore, but it gave her something to do. Really she just wanted to sit at home in front of the television all the time, even though she knew it wasn't healthy. She had no idea why she felt like going out tonight. She just wanted to get drunk and crazy, and forget about tomorrow.

As usual, they'd ended up at the S/S *Swea* down by Kungstorget. A group of guys had been watching them on the dance floor, and Mona disappeared with one of them. Mona, who had a husband and a family—everything she had dreamed of for herself, but had realized she would never have. Not long after, Cilla hooked up with someone and took off for the sofas, just as a guy was trying to get with her. By then she was already feeling sick, and all she wanted to do was go home.

She had fragmented memories of trying to find her friends and eventually giving up. Everything was spinning, and she had trouble finding the door to leave. The last thing she remembered was someone helping her into a car.

And now she was lying somewhere, head pounding, with no idea where she was. She tried to open her eyes, but only her left eyelid obeyed. The other was stopped by something moist that was pressing against the right side of her face. She tried to figure out what it was and realized that it was damp dirt. She guessed she might be outside—maybe in a park or in the woods?

She tried to turn her body so she could lie on her back, but was forced to give up after a sharp pain stabbed through her lower belly. She whimpered. What had happened to her? She cautiously felt herself with one hand and realized that she wasn't wearing any clothes and that something down there wasn't quite right.

She gathered as much air into her lungs as possible and screamed.

54

KLIPPAN, LILJA, AND MOLANDER were sitting around the table in silence, waiting for Tuvesson. The investigation had been going on for more than a week now, and the lack of sleep was starting to wear on them. No one had any energy to waste on words; instead they took the opportunity to close their eyes. The silence was finally broken by Klippan's ringing phone. He glanced at it quickly, but then closed his eyes again.

"Aren't you going to answer?" Molander said, but Klippan didn't even look in his direction.

After a while, the caller hung up. Molander's phone started ringing a few seconds later.

"Yes, this is Ingvar Molander. I see...Sure, no problem." He handed the phone to Klippan. "It's Berit."

Klippan heaved a long sigh and took the phone. "Hi, dear... Because I'm at work, in the middle of a meeting...Yes, he's working too and if he had known it was you he wouldn't have answered, either." Klippan shot Molander a look. "No, dear, I don't have time right now. Did you check to make sure it isn't just a blown fuse?"

Tuvesson entered with a travel mug in one hand.

"No, it's not difficult at all," Klippan continued, rolling his eyes. "Just check to see if the little red metal discs are still there or not. They're not? Anyway, I have to go...Molander needs his phone."

"No, I'm fine," Molander said, receiving a threatening look from Klippan.

"Can't you ask the neighbour or something? Bye." Klippan hung up, sighed in relief, and handed Molander his phone. "Thanks so much."

"No problem."

"Shall we get going?" Tuvesson said. "As you know, we have another victim."

"Have we identified the body?" Lilja asked.

"Her name is Ingela Ploghed, and she's forty-four."

"Is? Does that mean she's still alive?" Molander wondered.

Tuvesson nodded, taking a sip of her coffee. "She's being kept under sedation for the time being. As far as I understand, she's in a critical condition. She was found in Ramlösa Brunnspark around eight o'clock this morning, without any clothing on. She was seriously hypothermic and she'd lost a lot of blood."

"Had she been stabbed?" Klippan asked.

"No, that's the strange thing. She had no obvious external wounds—the blood was coming from her genitals."

"Do we know why?" Molander asked.

"Not yet, but I'm going over to meet with the doctor as soon as we're finished here."

"Ploghed...Wasn't she in the same class as everyone else?" Lilja asked.

Tuvesson nodded and walked over to the enlarged class photo to point at one of the girls. "This is her."

"Do we have a more recent picture?" Klippan wondered.

"I was hoping you could find one."

"What do we know about her?" asked Lilja.

"Not much at this point, except that she lived alone—no children or husband," Klippan said, browsing through his notes. "In 2002 she had her stomach pumped after overdosing on sleeping pills in a suicide attempt."

"If she survives this attack, we'll have a witness for the first time, which is exactly what we need," Tuvesson said, circling Ingela Ploghed's face and marking it with a question mark. She looked at the photograph, her eyes roaming from student to student until she came to Fabian Risk. "I stopped by to see Risk this morning."

"And how is the private eye?" Klippan asked.

"He's probably going to be stuck in bed for a little while longer."

"Did you ask him if..."

"Yes, and he couldn't think of any other suspect besides Claes Mällvik, but he had a theory." Tuvesson turned to face the others. "He thinks the entire crime scene was somehow staged to depict the killer and his motive." She took out one of the pictures of the human-shaped moss under the glass plate and held it up for everyone to see. "I think he was suggesting that the impression is the perpetrator's self-portrait."

Klippan burst out laughing. "Wow! What kind of drugs do they have him on? It must be something stronger than Tylenol."

None of the others laughed, and Klippan soon grew quiet as well. A resigned silence took over. There seemed to be a collective realization that the perpetrator was not just a few steps ahead of them—he'd lapped them. Tuvesson's eyes wandered aimlessly among the pictures on the wall, which ranged from Jörgen's sawed-off hands on the shower floor to the half-metre sun lens to the moss in the shape of a human. She felt tired and worn out, and was well aware that it showed, but she was too exhausted to care. All she was worried about was making sure they couldn't see that she had accepted defeat. Deep down she had given up hope that they would ever solve the case in front of them, even though hopelessness was a mortal sin in her line of work and she would never admit it. She had always believed in her team and had felt absolutely certain that they would figure it out in the end; after all, they had succeeded in solving most of the cases assigned to them. But right now she completely lacked trust in her own and the others' abilities—a lack of trust that would bring total destruction on the rest of their work if she allowed her doubt to show.

On her way in to the police station, she hadn't been able to stop thinking about how she would eventually have to make the decision to close the investigation. She knew she would spend the rest of her life looking back on this case as the most abject failure of her career. It would be her fault that they never fulfilled their objective; she was the one who had made the fatal error of removing Fabian Risk from the case. She had even toyed with the idea of bringing him back on board, but decided that would be tantamount to declaring the rest of the team incompetent. All she could do now was live with the consequences and hope for the best.

"I don't know how you're feeling," she said, mostly to break the silence, "but this is the most difficult and frightening case I've ever worked on, and it feels like we're still so far from even getting close to solving it. But I don't believe we *are* so far away. I'm sure that we're closing in on him." She looked into Lilja's, Molander's, Klippan's eyes in turn. "However, we have to be prepared to think outside the box if we're going to have even the smallest chance of solving this case. There are no dumb ideas any more. Fabian's suggestion that the moss could be a self-portrait might be the key to understanding the killer and discovering his motive." She let her words sink in.

"Are we even sure it's a man?" Lilja asked.

"No. As things stand it could just as easily be a female perpetrator."

"Speaking of thinking outside the box," said Molander. "Has anyone followed up on Link's idea about the graffiti at Fredriksdal School?"

"Come on, that was almost thirty years ago!" Lilja said. "The school must have been renovated several times since then."

"Apparently not," Klippan said. "According to Link, the school is set to undergo its first true renovation next summer, so there's a chance his theory could be true. How do we know for sure?"

"I suggest you go over to Fredriksdal and take a look," said Tuvesson. "It seems like we don't have anything to lose."

Klippan nodded mutely.

"Irene, you're coming with me. Ingvar, go to Ramlösa Brunnspark to investigate our new crime scene."

They all gulped the last of the coffee from their mugs and stood up.

"There's one thing we haven't discussed," Lilja said. "Jörgen and Glenn, the two class bullies, were the first victims. But now we've added Claes and this Ingela person to the list. How do they fit in? Does that mean everyone in the class is a potential victim?"

Tuvesson didn't know how to respond. The same thought had occurred to her, but she had dismissed it, perhaps because it felt as frightening as it was impossible to answer. Or maybe she was just too tired.

"I suppose we ought to put everyone under police protection," said Klippan.

"We don't have the resources," Tuvesson said. "We already have four men stationed at the hospital with Risk and Ploghed, and we'll have four more working the next shift because they need twenty-four-hour security. I'll call Malmö and see if they can help us out." Deep down she knew that they wouldn't be able to spare enough men. There was only one form of protection they could offer—capturing the killer.

55

ALTHOUGH HE DID ALL he could to move as slowly as possible through the hospital's seemingly endless corridors, the smallest movements stabbed at Fabian's back like a thousand needles. The two uniformed officers who had sat outside his door during the night had been switched out for two new cops, and they had reluctantly agreed to escort him to the emergency department, where he was hoping to find Ingela Ploghed. Neither of the officers had said a word during the slow journey, and Fabian wondered if they were playing the Quiet Game or if they were just angry at each other.

He had woken to the headline ANOTHER VICTIM IN THE CLASS OF EVIL forty minutes earlier. *I'm part of the class of evil*, he thought. He mouthed the words and tried to figure out why he had a nagging feeling that something wasn't quite right. For the first time, the perpetrator had failed to kill his victim. Was that his intention? Furthermore, he remembered Ingela Ploghed as one of the kindest people in the class. He couldn't recall her ever saying a mean word about anyone. In fact, she was the only person who had dared to stand up for Claes.

In one lesson they had presented their dream jobs to each other, and Ingela had said that she wanted to become a lawyer to help those who were weak and vulnerable. He had no idea if she had followed through with her goal, but he had got wind of a rumour that she suffered from serious depression and had even tried to take her own life.

When they finally arrived at the block of lifts, Fabian broke the silence and asked one of the officers not to press any of the buttons; he wanted to do it himself.

As a boy, he had loved playing with these very lifts. There were four of them in the middle of the cross-shaped hospital building—one for each point of the compass. The round lift vestibule had a large control panel in the middle and it felt like you were beaming right up into the command bridge of the starship *Enterprise* every time you got in. All the lift buttons were on this central podium—you even used it to select the floor you wanted to go to, rather than using buttons inside the lifts.

Fabian glanced around and realized that it still brought him the same sensation. The room had aged with similar plasticky dignity to *Star Trek*, and Christine Chapel's healing laser beam was the only thing missing. He pressed the green street-level button and the elevator doors opened soon after.

"YOU'RE ALREADY BACK ON your feet?" Lilja asked when Fabian shuffled into the emergency department.

"I don't know about that."

"I want to see how your burn looks." Lilja walked around and stood behind Fabian, looking down at his neck under his hospital gown. "Oh, shit."

"Thanks. Just what I needed to hear."

"I'm guessing you're here for the same reason we are, vacation notwithstanding," Tuvesson said. Fabian looked at her without responding.

A doctor joined them and pulled down his mask before shaking Tuvesson's hand.

"I understand you're here about Ingela Ploghed."

"How is she?"

"She's okay, given the circumstances. We've finally got the bleeding under control. It took some time before we figured out what had actually happened to her." The doctor stopped speaking and glanced around to make sure that no one else was listening. "Someone without medical skills tried to perform a vaginal hysterectomy on her."

"What does that mean?"

"He surgically removed her uterus."

Tuvesson turned to Fabian as if she were waiting for him to say something, but he was far too preoccupied trying to think of why someone would subject Ingela Ploghed to a vaginal hysterectomy — or anything at all cruel.

"How do you know he wasn't a doctor?" Lilja asked.

"The incisions aren't anywhere near where they ought to be, and he didn't bother to close up the wound. There were high levels of benzodiazepines in her urine, which is medication used for treating anxiety and insomnia."

"Someone drugged her and performed the operation while she was unconscious?"

"Yes, but someone raped her first."

"Excuse me?"

"I'll send you a written report, but first I have to continue on my rounds." The doctor took off before they could ask any follow-up questions. Tuvesson shook her head and turned to the others: the news of the rape seemed to overshadow the entire torturous operation. As far as Fabian was concerned, the rape removed all doubt.

"At least we've confirmed the killer's sex," said Tuvesson.

"And that we probably have conclusive evidence," added Lilja. Tuvesson nodded.

"This isn't our perpetrator," said Fabian. "It's someone else."

"Why would it be a different perpetrator?" Tuvesson asked.

"It doesn't fit with the previous pattern," Fabian said, suggesting that they take a seat in the café.

"I actually see quite a few similarities," Lilja disagreed as she cleared away the dirty coffee cups and saucers from the table and rubbed the dried spots with a napkin. "Besides the obvious ones, like the fact she was in the same class as the rest of the victims, we have the meticulously planned actions. Not to mention the timing. I was starting to hope he was finished."

"Yes. Many of us were hoping that," Tuvesson said, putting down the tray containing their order.

Fabian tasted what the hospital insisted on calling a cappuccino and realized that Lilja and Tuvesson had made the right choice by ordering tea. "Our perpetrator doesn't rape his victims."

"We don't know that with certainty. Ingela was the first female victim," said Tuvesson.

"Other than Mette Louise Risgaard, but point taken," Lilja added.

"Ingela Ploghed was one of the nicest people I've ever met," Fabian said. "She was more or less the only one in our class who stood up for Claes and always took his side. Why would anyone want to hurt her? And what does her uterus have to do with anything?"

"But Claes Mällvik isn't a suspect any more—he's dead," Tuvesson said.

"Maybe the perpetrator is planning on killing everyone in the class one by one? I'm sorry to be grim, but it's a possibility," Lilja said.

Fabian nodded. He knew exactly what she meant: he had been thinking the same thing for the past few hours—anyone from the class, including himself, could be next. "But why didn't he kill her? Our guy wouldn't have left her alive."

"Maybe he was just unsuccessful."

"It's possible, but if you ask me, he doesn't seem like the type to fail. He's in the process of building something up, I'm sure of it."

"Yes, I heard you had a theory that the moss we found underneath Claes's body was meant to be his self-portrait," Lilja said.

"More like his self-image." Fabian gave the brown sludge

another try, but gave up and pushed the cup away.

"What's to say that the removal of Ingela's uterus wasn't part of his plan? Maybe we just can't see the connection yet," Tuvesson said.

She had a point. It was certainly possible that this was the same guy, and that everything would be explained in good time, but Fabian had his doubts. Unlike Tuvesson, he had nothing to base his argument on except a strong suspicion that it didn't fit. He had a gut feeling that the person who had done this to Ingela was someone else entirely. On the other hand, he had been absolutely sure that Claes Mällvik was the perpetrator, so he couldn't be sure about anything related to this case now. All he knew was that whoever had done this would probably strike again soon.

56

KIM SLEIZNER HADN'T SLEPT a wink since the news had landed like a bombshell. He and Viveca had been out on the balcony drinking wine, looking out across the water and down at the crowds on Islands Brygge. They had been discussing the possibility of travelling somewhere other than Thailand this winter. Viveca had suggested Vietnam; apparently it was like an unspoiled Thailand. Kim had been receptive to all her suggestions because he was in an excellent mood: he finally had some dirt on Dunja, not to mention the newsworthiness of the conflict with the Swedes had finally started to cool off. Pretty soon, the record heat wave would dominate the headlines again. But Nanna had come running out just when they had decided to uncork a bottle of De Saint Gall Brut Rosé.

"Dad, you're in *Ekstra Bladet*! It says you're a liar!"

At first he'd had no idea what she was talking about. Why would he be in *Ekstra Bladet*? What could he have possibly lied about?

A few seconds later, panic started creeping in through his pores. He handed the champagne to Viveca and followed Nanna to her computer.

He had locked himself in the bathroom after he read the article so that he could splash water on his face and collect himself. He needed to figure out how to get himself out of this situation. When he had come back onto the balcony, Viveca was sitting in a chair, staring straight into the darkness with the half-empty bottle of Saint Gall in one hand and her phone in the other.

"Wow, you have to be quick if you want any champagne around here," he had said, adding a laugh to emphasize that he was joking. But the laugh was far too tentative, revealing that he knew exactly what had happened.

"You bastard. I want you to leave," she responded. There wasn't a trace of bitterness or anger in her voice. It was just a quiet statement, like a cashier at the grocery store telling you how much you owed. "You can get your things tomorrow while I'm at work."

It had dawned on him that she was far more prepared for this situation than he was. In truth, she had been waiting for something like this to surface. She had known all along but hadn't said a thing. She'd waited for him to embarrass himself. She'd wanted to catch him with his pants down.

He'd left the house without saying a word and checked into Hotel Kong Frederik, where he got a room looking out onto Vester Voldgade. Kim had lain on the bed, nervous about how big a story he was going to be, and waited for the next news segment to start on TV. But they didn't say anything about him or what had happened on Lille Istedgade. The news hadn't spread beyond *Ekstra Bladet* yet, which did not reassure him in the least. It was only a matter of hours before all hell would break loose. He'd turned out the lights and tried to sleep, but eventually gave up and opened the minibar.

The next morning he'd woken up on the floor with a pounding headache that only improved after drinking the last little bottle of Gammel Dansk. After a quick shower, he'd checked out and left the hotel. On the way to his car, he'd realized that the story had spread—his name was in all the papers. *Politiken* blamed him entirely for Mette Louise Risgaard's death, while *Ekstra Bladet* was focused on his Lille Istedgade activities, offering a 50,000-kroner reward to anyone who could clarify exactly what he was doing at the time.

The ride home to his apartment in Islands Brygge was fine, even though he was in no condition to drive. He didn't want to take a taxi and risk being recognized by some chatty driver. Once he got home, he went straight to his office and turned on his laptop so he could follow the latest developments. The most recent articles had been up for at least two hours already, a minor eternity in this type of situation.

During his drive home, he had wondered whether he should just turn his back on it all, go straight to the airport, and buy the first one-way ticket he found to somewhere warm. If he could empty his bank accounts fast enough—faster than Viveca's greedy fingers could, that is—he could last for a very long time in Thailand. He already had his diving certificate, so maybe he could learn to be a scuba instructor.

He took a deep breath, went onto *Ekstra Bladet*'s website, and immediately learned that the 50,000-kroner reward had already been paid out. Jenny "Wet Pussy" Nielsen had gone public, revealing that Kim had been in her apartment on Lille Istedgade at the time in question. She did not, however, wish to reveal exactly what they'd been doing out of consideration for her client, but she did mention he was one of her regulars.

This was all that fucking cunt Dunja's fault. It couldn't have been anyone else. Instead of taking his warning seriously, she had publicly spat in his face and declared war. He would give her a battle—one that he wouldn't quit even when she got down on her knees to beg and plead for forgiveness.

But first, Kim needed to think through the situation in peace and quiet. He wanted to weigh up his options, and evaluate the repercussions of each of them. There had been enough surprises. From now on, he would be back in control of the situation and stay a step ahead of everyone else. His phone started to ring, interrupting the calm—it was the national police commissioner, Henrik Hammersten.

DUNJA HOUGAARD SAT DOWN at her desk and turned on her computer. Her days with the Copenhagen police were numbered, so she had to work quickly. The Sleazeball would probably hide away a little while longer, licking his wounds. But there was nothing more dangerous than an injured lion, and once he emerged from his cage it would be her hide he was out to get.

She was aware of the consequences and had made up her mind: this case was more important than her career. She had lain awake all night, reviewing her options over and over again in her mind, only to realize that the choice was really quite simple. This was exactly the sort of investigation that had spurred her to become a police officer in the first place. She couldn't just back down.

She logged onto the police network with her name and password and clicked on the tab titled "Forms." Though she had never used an H3-49U, the form for special release of technical evidence, she knew exactly where to find it. She clicked on the PDF symbol and the form appeared on her screen. She filled in the information: *Peugeot, Swedish registration, JOS 652, archive number 100705-B39C, to be released to the Swedish police authority in Helsingborg for technical investigation.* She signed off as "Kim Sleizner" and clicked the print button. Then she placed the printout on top of her old employment contract and adjusted its position until Kim's signature was right where she needed it. She chose her best pen, tested it on a piece of scrap paper, and began falsifying the document.

She had everything to lose, but her hand didn't shake at all. She wasn't the least bit nervous. She blew the ink dry, folded the form, and left her office. *Maybe for the last time*, she thought as she walked through the hall.

The lift door opened the moment she pressed the button. She stepped inside, swiped her security badge, and pressed the button for sub-basement four. The lift doors closed and the car started to descend, feeling like it was moving slower than the usual free fall that caused her feet to feel light on the floor. This time it was practically plodding down, as if to mess with her. She took a few deep breaths, but she couldn't relax. The lift slowed down and stopped at ground level. The doors opened and the Sleazeball stepped in.

"Hello," she said, trying to sound as calm as possible.

He didn't respond; instead, he gave her a look and pressed six. The door closed and the lift continued its descent.

It felt like the walls were closing in on her. She tried to find somewhere to focus her attention and chose a small scratch on the door. Should she say something? *No*, she decided, *best to act natural*. But what was natural about this situation? She was sweating, and felt hot and sticky. She tried to swallow, but the lump in her throat wouldn't go away. *Don't take your eyes off the scratch on the door. Just keep focusing on it and wait out these never-ending seconds.*

Sleizner was standing less than a metre away from her and she could feel his eyes drilling into her side. *Has he figured out what I've been up to?* she thought. He was chewing gum, but it seemed to have no effect on his breath, which stank of stale alcohol and made the enclosed space feel even smaller.

When the lift door finally opened, it took great effort to avoid running out.

"See you," he said. She turned around, but only caught a glimpse of him smiling as the doors closed.

THE AIR ESCAPED FROM Kim Sleizner like he was a punctured tyre as he collapsed on the fold-down chair and put his head in his hands. Dunja was the very last person he'd wanted to run into at this particular moment, but he'd handled it with panache and turned it into a beneficial encounter. All his years of being the boss had paid off. He had immediately gone on the offensive and hadn't responded to her greeting or shown any signs of hesitation whatsoever. His gaze hadn't wavered an inch.

The same could not be said for Dunja. She had positively oozed uncertainty and guilt. If he'd been unsure who had tipped off the evening paper before, he wasn't any longer. He stood up with renewed energy, smoothed his hair back, left the lift, and headed straight for Henrik Hammersten's office.

"Well, this is quite the mess," Hammersten said as he greeted Kim, who always thought that stepping into the police commissioner's office felt like going back in time a hundred years. It had recently been renovated, but Hammersten had insisted on high, dark-wood panelling, hand-painted decorations on the ceiling, Chesterfield chairs, and an old globe that doubled as a cocktail cabinet.

"Have a seat." Hammersten nodded at the visitor's chair in front of the large mahogany desk, which had been bought at the Bruun auction house for the tidy price of 55,000 kroner.

So, not the easy chairs this time, Kim thought, bracing himself for a difficult meeting. He had to play his cards right if he were to have even the tiniest chance of coming out of this tête-à-tête with his job still intact. He threw up his hands and sat down. "Well, Henrik, what can I say? You sneak out the back door for a quickie and suddenly everyone's after you."

Hammersten nodded and walked over to the globe to get two glasses and a bottle of Gammel Dansk. Kim was pleased with his decision to get straight to the point instead of beating around the bush. Hammersten undoubtedly knew the value of a quickie now and again—he was the person who'd tipped him off about Jenny Nielsen and her extraordinary ability to provide for one's needs in the first place. But he wasn't about to open that door. It would be far too obvious.

"Do you know who leaked this to the papers?" Hammersten asked as he filled Kim's glass to the brim with amber liquid.

"Hougaard. Who else? She's had it in for me since the day I started working here."

Hammersten nodded and raised his glass for a toast. Kim

swallowed his in one big gulp, feeling the fire first in his oesophagus and then his stomach. It was just what he needed. He realized Hammersten's glass was still full when it was far too late. *Shit.*

Hammersten filled up Kim's glass again. He grabbed for it a bit too eagerly and spilled a few drops on the desk.

"I'm sorry, I've had hardly any sleep."

"No problem," Hammersten insisted, returning with a rag so quickly that Sleizner was afraid he had expected him to spill his drink. *Shit.* Of course that was why he'd filled the glass to the brim.

"It's too bad about Hougaard," Hammersten said. "She's a damn good policewoman."

"Sure she is," Kim said, not touching his glass. "But she's had her share of problems. On the other hand, who hasn't?"

"What kind of problems?"

"Obeying orders, for one. And I think she has a drinking problem. The other day she had what I would call a serious hangover."

Hammersten nodded, slowly sipping his drink. "As long as she does her work."

"And therein lies the problem." Kim took his glass and forced himself to take the smallest sip, although his body was screaming out for more.

"What did Viveca say?"

He shook his head. "She threw me out, and I don't blame her, to be honest."

"And that's how we ought to be today, isn't it?" Hammersten looked into Kim's eyes. "Honest."

"Why, I'm sure we always—"

"Kim," Hammersten interrupted. "I'm afraid I have to do the same."

"I'm not sure I understand."

"You know how much I admire you and everything you've done for the department, but this situation is escalating quickly and it risks becoming a stain on the entire police force. To be perfectly frank, I have no choice."

It had all been a charade. Hammersten got him to believe that they were in the same boat, when in actuality the old bastard had already made up his mind. Kim had nothing left to lose. He drained his glass and slammed it onto the mahogany desk. "What the hell are you saying? What do you mean *you have no choice*? Who the hell makes the decisions if not you?"

"Kim, I understand that you're upset. But—"

"Do you really?"

Hammersten sighed. "Kim, you and I both know what we're dealing with here. If the public loses confidence in the police, we're all in trouble."

"Henrik, this is nothing more than a groundless media witch hunt. Okay, so I wasn't there to take that damn call. So what?! That girl would have died anyway. What if I had answered? What then? There's no chance I would have been able to get a backup team down there in time, and that uniform from Køge would have still gone after the perpetrator himself. But sure, I can take the blame, if that makes people happy. No problem."

Hammersten considered Kim's argument in silence.

"Henrik, for Christ's sake. Give me a day or two and I'll right this ship again, I promise." At the last second, he stopped himself from pressing the most obvious button—Hammersten's weak spot. It lay there like a rolled-out red carpet, just waiting to be stepped on. But he didn't need it. They were both thinking about it anyway.

"You have until tomorrow."

57

HE HAD BEEN WAITING in the car for almost two hours when the right moment popped up. He could see the children playing outside the preschool through the small camera that was mounted on the rear window. They fought over the bikes, threw gravel, and cried with their snotty noses.

He didn't have any kids. He had never liked them, not even back when he was a kid. He'd done everything he could to fit in with them back then: he wore the right clothes and said the right things, but no one had noticed his desperate, tiny attempts, and his desire to be normal had turned into disdain for people his own age. These days, kids mostly just disgusted him. Their list of problems was never-ending: snot, pimples, scabs, warts, lice, eczema. Children were small, helpless reservoirs of infection that had no reason to exist, except to be mean. He had only truly understood the cruelty of children once he had grown up. In contrast to kindness, which had to be taught, nurtured, and developed, evil existed naturally from birth and grew more cunning through the years.

At 4:07 p.m., he left the car to pick them up. There were enough parents around by then that the staff wouldn't have time to pay much attention to him. He knew what Lovisa and Mark, three and five years old, looked like from Facebook. He found them straight away in the playground, and they swallowed his explanation without protest: he was a colleague of their mother's and she was stuck in a meeting she couldn't get out of before preschool ended. The promise of McDonald's helped to cement his story as truth.

It wasn't quite so simple with the staff. The heavy one was suspicious, and bluntly asked him who he was, making it clear that they couldn't hand the kids over to a stranger. He declared in an insulted tone that he wasn't a stranger but the children's father, feeling fortunate that the children weren't standing nearby. The heavy one grew flustered and embarrassed.

He explained that he travelled a lot for work and usually wasn't able to come pick them up. Today was a surprise. In the end, Fatso accepted his explanation but pointed out that he should let them know in advance if he was going to surprise them again.

Now they were in the back seat, deep in a drug-induced sleep. He waited for their mother to arrive. On the camera screen in the back window he saw Camilla Lindén slamming her car door and hurrying over to the preschool, late as usual. She came rushing back three minutes later and started poking at her phone, unaware that she was about to hear an automated message telling her that the number she was trying to reach was not in service.

He watched as she punched the number in again and listened to the same message. She threw her handbag into the passenger seat, got behind the wheel, and tore off, tyres screeching. He was more relaxed than she was—he turned the key in the ignition, began to follow her, and activated the camera's automatic face detection, which would guide the swivel-mounted laser with the help of the algorithms he had programmed himself.

If everything worked as he had planned, they would never be able to figure out what had happened.

58

A NURSE EYED ASTRID Tuvesson and pointed at the sign depicting a crossed-out cell phone.

"Okay, do that. I have to go now." Tuvesson ended the call and turned to Lilja. "That was Molander. They haven't discovered anything in Ramlösa Brunnspark."

"Nothing?"

"Just a few strands of the victim's hair in the bushes where she was found, but nothing useful for our purposes—no clothes, footprints, or tyre tracks. I've sent him back to examine the crime scene around Claes's body."

"But there's always *something*. Have you ever known Molander not to find anything?"

Tuvesson shook her head. "I guess the perpetrator has just done an unusually good job of cleaning up after himself. He's planted all of the clues we've found so far, right?" She turned to Fabian for a reaction just as the doctor arrived.

"You can follow me," he said.

The doctor updated them on Ingela's condition as they walked through the corridor. "She has recovered quite a bit, but she's still weak. In other words, this can't be a long visit, just so we're clear." He showed them to a door that was guarded by two uniformed officers. "I'll be back in ten minutes."

The doctor walked off and Tuvesson opened the door to go in.

"Hold on a second," Lilja said. "Is it really a good idea for Fabian to come in?" Tuvesson looked at her. "I thought he was off the case."

Tuvesson turned to Fabian. "She's right. What you do on your vacation is up to you. But if you want to see Ingela, you'll have to do it after we're finished."

"That's fine," Fabian said, turning back toward the lifts with his mute officers. He already had the answers he needed.

Tuvesson and Lilja walked up to the bed, which was propped up so that Ingela was half sitting. Except for the dark circles under her anxious eyes, she was as pale as the sheet she was lying on. Her hair was greasy and stringy, and her hands trembled like an old woman's as they rested on the blanket. *What can you expect from someone who lost that much blood from an involuntary, highly invasive operation by an amateur surgeon?* Tuvesson thought as she pulled up a chair and sat beside the bed.

"Hi, Ingela. My name is Astrid Tuvesson and I'm a detective superintendent with the Helsingborg police. This is Detective Irene Lilja."

Lilja greeted her with a wave.

"We have a few questions we're hoping you can answer."

Ingela shook her head. Her quivering chin let on that she was teetering on the edge of tears. "I don't have any answers. I'm sorry, but I don't remember anything."

"Ingela, I want to start by saying that we're terribly sorry for what you went through. It must have been utterly horrible. But unlike the other victims, you're still alive."

"Alive? You call this *alive*? If I had the choice, I would rather be dead. Someone was inside me...with a knife and...and..." Her face contorted and she burst into silent tears.

Tuvesson took her hand. "I know this is difficult. But all we want is to apprehend the person who did this to you. Any information you can provide will help us achieve that goal."

Ingela nodded. She calmed herself, dried her tears, and took a sip of water from the glass Lilja offered her.

"What's the last thing you remember from Wednesday night?"

"I was out with Mona and Cilla."

"Who are they?"

"Friends. We usually go out the first Wednesday of every month."

"And where were you the day before yesterday?"

"First we went out to eat at Haket, and…then we went to the S/S *Swea* and had a few drinks."

"What happened after that?"

Ingela shook her head and shrugged.

"Do you remember what drinks you had?" Lilja said.

"A caipirinha and a White Russian."

"This place, the S/S *Swea*, can you dance there?"

Ingela nodded. "I remember feeling dizzy all of a sudden, even though I'd only had two or three drinks. They were playing Lady Gaga and everything started spinning."

Tuvesson and Lilja exchanged glances.

"Did the same thing happen to your friends?"

"I don't know. I couldn't find them. It was so crowded, everything was spinning—I just wanted to get out of there, but I couldn't even find the door. Even though it's a pretty small place, it felt like a big maze."

"So you don't remember leaving?"

Ingela appeared to be making a very large effort to stay composed. The doctor came back into the room and pointed at his watch.

Tuvesson held up a hand to stave him off. "We're almost finished. Everything was spinning and you tried to find your way out but couldn't. What's the next thing you remember?"

Ingela thought about it, then shrugged. "I guess when I woke up and had no idea what was going on. I didn't know where

I was or even *who* I was." Her lower lip began to quiver and Tuvesson squeezed her hand.

"Did you feel any pain?"

Ingela shook her head. "I don't know. I don't think so."

"Do you remember how you were lying when you woke up? Were you on your stomach, your back, or—"

"I don't know. Please, I don't know. Aren't we done yet?"

"Ingela, this is important. Try to remember exactly what happened when you—"

"I don't know! I told you, I don't know!" Ingela started to cry. "Please, can you just leave me alone? I want you to leave."

"Ingela—"

"Just go away! Go!" Ingela cried, starting to hit herself in the stomach.

The doctor rushed over and tried to stop her from hitting herself and tearing at anything within reach.

"Just leave me alone!"

Lilja and Tuvesson each grabbed one of Ingela's flailing arms and held them down as the doctor filled a syringe and emptied it into her thigh. Ingela stopped resisting and looked at the doctor and the police officers with glassy eyes.

"Please...can't you just let me...disappear..." Her eyelids grew heavier and heavier.

"I think we're done here, wouldn't you say?" the doctor said, opening the door for them.

"When can we meet with her again?" Tuvesson asked as they walked down the corridor.

"As you can see for yourself, she's been through severe trauma and she's still in shock. She needs to rest."

Tuvesson stopped and turned to him. "So I'll ask you again. When can we meet with her?"

The doctor let out a long, ostentatious sigh. "To be honest, I don't really see the point. It seemed to me that she told you everything she remembers."

311

"I'd like to be the judge of that. When will she be back on her feet?"

He shrugged. "She should be able to at least sit up by tomorrow."

"Good. We'll come pick her up. I'm planning to take her for a drive, and it's totally fine by me if someone from the hospital wants to come along."

The doctor tried to protest, but Tuvesson and Lilja were already on their way out.

59

CAMILLA LINDÉN COULDN'T RECALL the last time this had happened: maybe two, three, or even four years ago. Although she'd solemnly sworn to herself that it would never happen again, she always made sure to keep a pack in her handbag, just in case she had an incredible urge and couldn't resist.

And who could blame me for needing one now, she thought as her right hand dug through her purse in the passenger seat. She knew it was somewhere among the lipsticks, keys, mobile phone, toothpicks, and tampons. Finally she felt the soft, crinkly pack with her fingertips and brought it up to her mouth. She bit off the plastic, grabbed a cigarette with her lips, and pulled it out. The lighter was already glowing, and she soon took a badly needed drag.

She always used to feel calmer as soon as she took that very first inhale. But it didn't have the same effect this time. *Dammit, I won't do this again*, she thought as she pulled into the left lane, hit the gas, and passed the burgundy Volvo that was lazing along in front of her. She inhaled as deeply as she could so the smoke would reach all the way to the tiniest capillaries, and the E6 highway flowed ahead of her like a 3-D computer game. She was going ridiculously fast, but she didn't give a flying fuck. *Let the police pull me over*, she thought. At least they could come along and give her a hand if they did.

This wasn't the first time that Björne had suddenly shown up and taken the kids somewhere without telling her first. Once he had driven them to Tivoli in Copenhagen, and another time he had decided to bring them on an outing to Ven Island. But this was the first time he had blocked his own number. *The first and the last time*, Camilla thought.

She'd had enough. She wouldn't settle for getting a little mad and letting it go. This time she would go all the way—a trial, revoked visitations, the whole goddamn shebang. She would make sure to put up a fight; he would get so badly burned he would never dare approach them again.

She stayed in the left lane, realizing her speedometer already read 150 kilometres per hour. Her speed didn't bother her, she just needed to make sure not to miss the exit for Strövelstorp, where he lived—that ass. She took one last drag on her cigarette, pushed it out the crack in the window, and lit another.

How could she have been so naïve? There had been so many warning signs throughout the years, so many chances to walk away. Instead, she had chosen to ignore them, and had turned the other cheek, pretending that nothing was wrong. As if he could stop drinking once he started. As if his bad moods were really her fault. This had all started before they'd even had any kids. If there were a championship in stupidity, she would win it without even trying.

She exhaled a big puff of smoke, which got caught in her throat and made her cough like an old woman. She noticed the burgundy Volvo passing her in the right lane. She glanced at the speedometer, which was down to 140 kilometres per hour, and moved into the right lane behind the Volvo.

More than ten years had passed, but she remembered the first blow like it had happened yesterday. They had been at her childhood friend Pavlan's for dinner. Her name was Elsa Hallin now that she was married to Jerker. The Hallins had invited them over for fondue after finding a fondue set while cleaning out the basement. During dinner they all talked about how unfair it was that such a delicious meal had been banished to the basement for who knows how long. Then they started talking about everything they liked about the 1980s, and she noticed that Björne had gone silent.

The Volvo's taillights flashed on and she had to brake hard so that she didn't rear-end the other car. She looked over her shoulder to see if she could drive past, but a truck was struggling to pass her on an incline. What was the point?

Björne hated everything to do with the eighties. It didn't matter that he had just gobbled down all that fondue as if he had a hollow leg. He despised anything eighties—full stop. The others discussed clothes and hairstyles, describing how much more fun it had been than the nineties. Pavlan commented that the obligatory nineties outfit—ripped bleached jeans, T-shirts, and flannel—was not a good look. She was apparently unaware that Björne was wearing a white T-shirt under an unbuttoned plaid lumberjack shirt. Or maybe she had been perfectly aware of it? It would have been so typical of Pavlan to want to stir the pot.

Camilla had tried to backtrack by saying that she thought plaid shirts could be pretty hot. Björne opened his mouth for the first time in twenty minutes. "The eighties were just for fucking faggots and homos with their goddamn shoulder pads and shit." Jerker had wondered what the difference was between faggots and homos, and raised his glass with a sneer.

The Volvo's brake lights flashed again and Camilla slowed down. Her speedometer was down to 125 kilometres per hour.

Everyone but Björne had drunk a toast. By all indications, his mood was way into the red danger zone. Camilla had tried to steer the conversation over to work. Pavlan caught on and said that her boss consistently under-prioritized children's literature.

"So, you're seriously saying you like that homo music they were making back then?" Björne had hissed. "Soft Cell and those Human League guys didn't even use real instruments. Fucking homos in makeup who couldn't even sing!"

If there was anything they *could* do, it was sing, Camilla thought as she noticed a green light come on in the back window of the Volvo, which was still right in front of her. Her thoughts quickly returned to that dinner. Jerker must have been super drunk because he really egged on Björne. "That's the kind of thing a closeted homo would say," Jerker had exclaimed and started singing, "*Don't you want me, baby? Don't you want me? Oh!*" as he got up, kneeled in front of Björne, and started rubbing his thighs. "*You were working as a waitress in a cocktail bar, when I met you. I picked you out, I shook you up, and turned you around...*" As Camilla tried to remember more of the details, the little camera in the car in front of her was in the process of locating her face and guiding the green ray up along her windscreen.

Pavlan had cracked up, and Camilla also had a hard time holding back her laughter. Jerker just kept singing and showing off at Björne's feet, "*Turned you into someone new,*" until she and Pavlan were howling with laughter. By the time she realized that Björne's expression had gone completely stony, it was too late. He stood up so fast that his chair tipped over and he informed her they were leaving. She had been stupid enough to obey him.

Once they got home, he'd locked the door with the deadbolt and a key. She'd watched him stick the key in his pocket, take a deep breath, and turn toward her.

She screamed as burning pain penetrated her left eye. It felt like someone had either thrown acid at her eye or stuck a needle into it. She closed both eyes and grabbed her face, but she couldn't detect any substances or objects. All she could feel was the intense pain that continued to burn into her eye socket. Her car was running off the road, but she managed to straighten out before it was too late. She stopped screaming and tried to calm down. What the hell was going on? Was she having a stroke or was it some sort of blood clot? Her eye still hurt, but the pain was dying down and becoming more manageable. She was soaked with sweat, but felt cold. Everything felt tight and sticky. She took the wheel with her left hand, and used her free hand to cover her right eye to establish if she could see out of the left one—she couldn't. What kind of sick nightmare was this? She just wanted to wake up.

She saw the green light again as it shot out from the back of the Volvo and hit her windscreen. This was no dream. The narrow beam travelled up across her chest. What the hell was it? Her thoughts didn't get any further than that before she felt the burning again: the same needle-like pain, but this time in her right eye. Everything went blurry and she could only see colourful spheres moving across her retinas. She screamed as loudly as she could while trying to keep the car in its lane, but her hands refused to obey and the steering wheel seemed to have a mind of its own.

Camilla's BMW veered into the side of a truck, only to pinball back into her lane and spin out into the grass, where it struck the STRÖVELSTORP 500M sign. One leg of the sign smashed the right headlight and caused the car to ricochet back onto the highway in front of an articulated lorry, which crushed the back of the car under its wheels like a tin can in a bottle-return machine. One revolution later, the car landed on its roof and slid across the road before coming to a standstill.

The cars around the BMW stopped, quickly creating a long traffic jam. The driver of the truck and a few other drivers got out of their cars and looked at Camilla's mangled BMW, which resembled a beetle on its back, wheels spinning in the air. A few people took out their phones and called for an ambulance. Others called home to tell their families how much they loved them. One of the men walked up to the BMW, opened the driver's door, and felt unsuccessfully for a pulse in Camilla's neck. He got back into his burgundy Volvo and drove off.

60

FABIAN HAD BEEN BEDRIDDEN for over twenty-four hours now and recognized that he would not survive another day of rest. A few more hours, and he would likely die of boredom. It didn't matter how much the hospital personnel nagged him about the importance of rest: the murder of Claes Mällvik—the latest twist in the case—would not give him a moment of peace.

Tuvesson also wasn't making it easy for him to relax. She had done all she could to hide her helplessness, but her eyes had given her true feelings away: deep down, she had given up hope of solving the case. It didn't matter to Fabian that he was officially off the investigation and stuck in hospital; it was now up to him to figure out how everything was connected—or if it even *was* connected.

He really wanted to leave the hospital, but his back pain was too severe. He couldn't even get out of bed. He was paying the price for his walk down to the emergency department. He gave in and took pills to alleviate the pain; a numbing calm spread through his body. With any luck he would now be able to focus on his work—because, pain or no pain, he was *going* to work.

A messenger had dropped by his house to pick up his computer, mobile phone charger, and some underwear. He had managed to convince the station receptionist, Florian Nilsson, to send over everything from his desk at the station to the hospital. One of the nurses helped him obtain a power bar, a shelving unit on wheels, a work lamp, and a foldable tray table that made an excellent bed desk.

He plugged the charger in and turned on his phone first. There was a message from Sonja: *On the train. Theo didn't want to come. Gave him 500 kr. so he doesn't starve while you're in the hospital. Please call and make sure everything's okay. Sonja.*

He called Theodor right away, but there was no answer. He called Sonja instead and tried to tell her how he was feeling, but she was only interested in knowing whether he'd spoken to Theo. He explained that he had only just got his phone charger, and promised to try again as soon as they were done talking. "Then I think we should hang up now," she said.

Fabian really didn't want to hang up and so he asked how she and Matilda were doing. Sonja said they'd been to the Gröna Lund amusement park with her sister and the cousins, and they'd had a wonderful time. "Listen, I have to go now. Call Theo."

"I love you," he said, and waited for her response.

"Call me as soon as you've talked to him."

Fabian dialled their new home number and listened to the phone ring again and again, echoing slowly into the ether. He tried Theodor's mobile again, but the voicemail came on after only three rings. He was probably playing video games in his room. Fabian promised himself he would try to get Theo to leave his room more, to help him do something other than imaginary killing.

An officer wearing a uniform that was at least two sizes too small opened the door.

"We have a delivery here for you—just a couple of things from the station."

The messenger came in with a box stuffed full of binders and documents, and handed him a sheet of paper to sign.

"I don't suppose you have the phone number of your colleague who was at my house about an hour ago picking up a computer and some other things?" Fabian asked while signing the paper.

"Pålsjögatan 17?"

Fabian nodded.

"Let me check," he said, looking up the information. "It was Jocke the Rocker." He found the number on his phone and showed it to Fabian, who punched the number into his own mobile and dialled it.

"Hello?"

"Is this Jocke?"

"Yes. What's this about?"

"My name is Fabian Risk. You picked up a computer and a few other things from my house earlier today...Pålsjögatan 17."

"Listen, I'm done with work for the day."

"I just have a quick question."

He heard an exaggerated sigh on the other end.

"Was my son at the house when you were there? He's fourteen and has dark, shoulder-length hair."

"No idea. But someone was blasting Marilyn Manson as loud as it's supposed to be heard."

"Thanks, that's all I wanted to hear." Fabian hung up and felt sudden relief, something he never thought Marilyn Manson at the highest decibel would ever bring him.

Twenty minutes later, his phone flashed with a new text message: *Hey Dad. Saw you called. I was out getting a kebab, just about to pay. When are you coming home?*

He typed a response: *As soon as the doctors let me go. My phone is back on now, so just let me know if anything happens, or even better, why not come visit* ☺. He sent the text and wrote another: *Honey, just heard from Theo. He's apparently eating kebabs 'til they come out his ears. Kisses. F.*

He put down his phone. Finally, he could get to work.

61

THAT WAS A CLOSE ONE, Tuvesson thought as she paid for the pizza and told Lilja, Molander, and Klippan that the food had arrived. Their focus had dwindled along with their blood sugar, and if they didn't eat something soon they might as well close up shop. The team had been working intensely all day and night, and their lack of sleep had long since passed a reasonable level. In an attempt to rid herself of the hopelessness she'd been feeling, Tuvesson had decided that no one was allowed to go home until the investigation had taken a big step forward. If the food served its purpose, they would get a second wind, which was Tuvesson's favourite. Everyone in the group was focused and committed to solving the case at any price during a second wind. Everything else was subordinate. Ordinarily, everyone would go home to his or her family, but for now they *were* the family. It reminded her of being a kid and sleeping over at her best friend's house, playing doctors or building with Lego all weekend. They were always in pyjamas because there was never any time to change. There was hardly even any time to eat— playing was the only thing that mattered.

Lilja and Molander rushed over and opened the two-litre bottle of Coke. They each poured themselves a glass. "If I had to choose between drinking only wine or Coke for the rest of my life, I would definitely pick Coke," Lilja said, chugging her glass.

"What kind of pizza did you get?" Molander asked, poking at the boxes.

"What kind did you want?"

"Oh…uh…maybe a kebab pizza?"

"Your wish is my command," Tuvesson said, handing him one of the boxes.

Although he never wanted to admit it, nine times out of ten Molander wanted at least half a kebab pizza. After a few slices, he usually got tired of the taste and wanted to try everyone else's pizza. Tuvesson had ordered on the safe side and got six different kinds of pizza.

"Where's Klippan? Doesn't he want any?"

"He locked himself in the conference room. He'll come out as soon as he's finished with that graffiti analysis," Lilja said.

"Oh right…that theory," Molander said disdainfully.

"I know it's a long shot," Tuvesson said. "But Klippan has put a lot of time and energy into it, so I want us to give him an honest chance. Okay?"

Molander and Lilja nodded, sat down, and started eating as though their survival depended on it. One-third of a kebab pizza later, Molander broke the silence.

"What else have we got on Ingela Ploghed?"

"More and more," Tuvesson said. "I've got a written report on her examination from the doctor, which is really just a repeat of what he told us earlier today."

"What did it say?"

"The operation definitely wasn't performed by a real doctor."

"How can he know that?"

"For one, whoever did this to Ingela used a standard scalpel, which isn't meant for performing a hysterectomy — not to mention it wasn't sterilized."

"Oh my God," Lilja said.

"The perpetrator also went in vaginally instead of an incision in the abdomen, which is considered the easier route."

"Let me get this straight…It's more difficult to do a hysterectomy vaginally?" Molander asked.

"Yes, but apparently the operation was impressively precise for a beginner."

Molander cut a bit of the kebab pizza. "Anyone want to trade?"

Tuvesson and Lilja shook their heads.

"How about you, Lilja? Have you come up with anything?"

Lilja nodded and washed down a bite of pizza with some Coke. "To be perfectly honest, I don't understand Ingela. She left Fredriksdal with a perfect grade point average. She also finished secondary school at the top of her class, studying natural sciences. Then she did two and a half years of law school in Lund, but then quit out of nowhere."

"What did she do after quitting?"

"Nothing—that's the weird part. She started working on the checkout at a grocery store, and is still there as far as I can tell. Talk about a waste of talent."

"Is there anything else?"

"Yes. She had an abortion in 1992. Ten years later, both parents died of cancer within a year of each other."

"Maybe the perpetrator took her uterus because she terminated a pregnancy?" Molander wondered, pushing away the kebab pizza. "Let's consider the pattern: he took Glenn's feet because he liked to kick, and Jörgen's hands because he used them to hit, so why not take the uterus of someone who had an abortion?"

"Your theory assumes it's the same guy," Tuvesson said.

Molander stopped chewing and turned to Tuvesson in confusion. "Of course it's the same guy."

"Not according to Risk," Lilja said. "He thinks Ploghed breaks the pattern."

"Breaks the pattern? How the hell can he think that? First he took the feet, then the hands, and now the uterus from people who were all in the same class. If that's not a pattern, I shouldn't have a job."

"But Ploghed survived—not to mention he raped her."

"So? She's the first female victim other than the Danish girl, who was obviously not part of the plan."

"True, but according to Risk she was the only one in the class who stood up for Claes."

"We all know that this isn't about Claes any more. Someone else…" Molander stopped speaking and looked back and forth between Lilja and Tuvesson. "Are you seriously suggesting that you think it's a different person?"

"To be honest, I don't know what to think," Tuvesson said.

"Me neither," added Lilja.

"But I suppose I'm leaning toward the idea that all the crimes were committed by the same perpetrator. I just want us to make sure we don't rule anything out at this stage. It could be absolutely anyone," said Tuvesson.

"Are there any double calzones?" they heard Klippan call from the hallway.

"Of course." Tuvesson pushed the fattest box down toward him.

Klippan cleared his throat and made an announcement: "I would like to take this opportunity to invite you all to the conference room." He had one arm out to welcome them, and appeared very pleased with himself.

Tuvesson and the others stepped into the room and looked around. Klippan had done a remarkable job papering all the walls with printouts of graffiti, starting at the floor and running two metres up. There was even a Post-it on each picture to note the location where it was taken.

"Wow!" Lilja exclaimed. "Is this all just from Fredriksdal School?"

Klippan nodded. "I thought this was the best way to get an overview of the graffiti."

"I feel like I've walked straight into a giant public bathroom," Molander said.

"Have you found anything of interest?" Tuvesson inquired.

"I haven't started looking yet." Klippan opened the pizza box and started eating as the others looked around at the walls. "I thought we could do it together. If we take a wall each, it shouldn't take too long."

As soon as Klippan finished eating, they spread out and got to work.

"How many 'dick in a pussy' do you all have?" Molander asked.

"I'm already up to three," Lilja said.

"Does 'suck my dick' count?" Klippan wondered.

"No—two completely different things," Molander objected. "One is penetration, the other is oral. Come on, we need to have *some* semblance of order here."

"I have two orals already," Tuvesson said.

"Which category does 'Alex likes toe sex' belong in?"

Fifteen minutes later, a focused silence had descended on the room. They all seemed committed to exhausting every possible lead. Klippan had done an enormous amount of work and they didn't want it to go to waste. He hadn't only photographed the most obvious public graffiti—the stuff on walls and lockers— he had also found the hidden messages under desks and on the backs of chairs.

Hope you have a Plan B was written on one of the toilet-paper holders; *Gays shit just like everyone else. They just have a little more fun* on the underside of a toilet seat. Most of the rest were along the lines of *Cecilia is a whore...HIF is best, fuck the rest!...Slipknot rules—Hellström sucks...Jörgen ♥ Lina...Rock is dead! Long live synth!*

Tuvesson scanned the graffiti; she felt like she was awash in teenage minds from past and present. Some of the images revealed several layers of graffiti, like growth rings left by years of students. It took some concentration to interpret the innermost layer.

Her eyes stopped at *Die, Mjälle*. The Post-it identified it as coming from the back of a bench in the boys' locker room. She shuddered and studied the picture more closely. The letters had been carved into the wood in a sprawling, angular style and looked like they had been made with a knife. The edges were smooth, meaning it could easily have been there for almost thirty years. But who would write such hateful words? Jörgen, Glenn, or the perpetrator?

"I found something interesting," Lilja said, reading the graffiti aloud to the others: "*I speak; no one listens. I ask; no one answers. The Invisible Man.* What do you make of it?"

"Where was it found?" Molander asked.

"Behind the fire extinguisher in the south corridor."

"I have a similar one," Klippan said. "*I hate every one of these fuckers, but who the hell cares? The Invisible Man.*"

"Do you think it could be him?" Lilja asked the others.

"Why not?" Tuvesson said.

All four of them took a few steps back and stared at the graffiti, as if they were hoping the killer would climb out of the walls.

HALF AN HOUR LATER, Molander walked up to his wall, took down one of the pictures, and sat at the table, examining the photo with a magnifying glass. The others continued to work on their walls, and gathered behind Molander as soon as they'd finished.

The graffiti he was inspecting was impossible to read. Over the years, the words had worn down so much that a few dots and lines of various sizes and angles were the only things legible; Molander was trying to restore them as letters. The Post-it said that the graffiti had been found inside locker 349.

"Don't tell me you unlocked every single locker," Lilja asked Klippan.

"They were already open — probably so they could be emptied and cleaned over the summer."

Tuvesson leaned over Molander's shoulder so she could see

parts of the text. *No one sees me...No one...* She couldn't make out the last few words. Molander's hand was covering the final section, and she didn't want to disturb him. When he was this focused, it usually meant the investigation was about to take a big step forward.

She secretly thanked the kebab pizza and looked out of the panorama window, which revealed a beautiful view of night-time Helsingborg. It was an unusually clear evening and she could see all the way across the Sound to Helsingør. She could even identify the blinking light on one of the towers of Kronborg Castle. Ven Island was evident in the distance, although she had never been there, like most people from Helsingborg. Then again, it was possible the lights she thought were Ven Island were just lights from a boat.

"Here he is!" Molander exclaimed suddenly.

Tuvesson turned around. "Are you sure?"

"If this wasn't written by our guy, I'll throw in the towel and change careers."

"What does it say?" Lilja asked, pouring the last of the Coke into her glass.

Molander read the graffiti, meeting the others' gazes. *"No one sees me. No one hears me. No one even bullies me. I. M."*

"He called himself the Invisible Man because no one ever noticed him, which is his whole motive, right there," Tuvesson said. "People say that constantly being ignored and left out is one of the worst feelings. You're not even teased. It must feel like you don't even exist."

"So that's what he's after," Lilja said. "He wants to put himself on the map; he wants to be famous."

Tuvesson nodded.

"So far, he seems to be doing everything he can to remain invisible," said Klippan.

"Either way, it means he was almost certainly in the same class," Molander said.

Tuvesson walked over to the enlarged class photo. Four of them were crossed out: Jörgen, Glenn, Claes, and their teacher, Monika Krusenstierna. There was a question mark over Ingela Ploghed. Tuvesson could feel her heart beating faster. They had finally got somewhere and narrowed down their pool of suspects to any one of the remaining students in the class. "We have to contact everyone who's still alive and check their alibis."

"Lilja and I already did that," Klippan said. "At least, those who aren't on vacation somewhere."

"And?"

"Unfortunately, they're all watertight."

"Every single one?"

"Yep. All of mine, anyway," Klippan said, turning to Lilja.

"Mine too."

"What about the people who are on vacation?" Molander asked. "Have you made sure they're really gone?"

"No, not yet," Lilja responded.

"Make sure to do that right away, and double-check the rest of the alibis too," Tuvesson said. "If his signature is 'The Invisible Man,' do we think we can assume the killer's a man?"

"Of course it's a man," Molander said. "He raped Ingela Ploghed."

"In that case, we're down to seven suspects."

"Does that include Risk?" Lilja asked.

Tuvesson's eyes narrowed in on Fabian in the class picture. His hair was parted down the middle and he was wearing the same uniform as the other students: polo shirt and wool cardigan. Tuvesson was considering the question when the door opened. A man walked in whom they didn't recognize.

"Are you the officers working on the class killer?"

"Excuse me, but who are you and how did you get in here?" Tuvesson said, as two of the building's night-security officers rushed in after the man and grabbed him.

"Sorry, we didn't have time to stop him and he blocked the

328

lift on his way up," one guard said as they tried to drag him out of the room.

"Take it easy, for God's sake! I only want to—"

"Report your wife missing. We know," said the guard. "But you don't do that here; you have to call the emergency number, which we will be happy to help you with...*downstairs*." The two guards, who had run out of patience, pushed the man to the floor and shoved his arms behind his back until he started to whimper.

"Calm down or we have to get out the handcuffs!" one guard shouted in the man's ear.

"Hold on, let him go," Tuvesson said.

The two guards looked at her quizzically.

"It's okay. I'll talk to him."

They exchanged glances and shrugged. "Okay, he's all yours." They let go of the man, who stood up and adjusted his clothing and hair, which was completely messed up. He looked afraid, as if he might be apprehended at any moment.

Tuvesson walked over and shook his hand. "My name is Astrid Tuvesson and I'm in charge of this investigation. How can I help you?"

"My wife, she...she's gone...missing. And I don't know what to do. What am I supposed to..." The man started crying. Lilja and Klippan helped him to a chair.

"Let's take things one step at a time. What's your name?"

"Jerker...Jerker Hallin."

"What's your wife's name?"

"Elsa Hallin."

"Hallin...What was her maiden name?"

"Pavlin."

"Elsa Pavlin. She was in the same class as..."

Jerker Hallin nodded. "That's why I'm here. It was her turn to make dinner so I could go and work out. By the time I was done I had a bunch of missed calls and texts from Bea, our daughter, who wanted to know why no one was home."

"And you've tried calling her, of course."

"It just goes to voicemail."

"Where does she work?"

"At the central branch of the library, downtown. I already talked to them. She's not there."

"Were they able to tell you when she left the library?"

Jerker trembled, ignoring the question. "Please...can't you put out a description or send out a search party? Anything."

"Of course we can do that," Tuvesson said, although she knew it was already too late.

62

DUNJA HOUGAARD HELD ONE leg above the surface of the water and ran the razor up her shin. She wiggled her foot, happy to see that the months of Pilates had already made her legs look several years younger. She definitely couldn't complain. People were seldom able to guess her true age. When she revealed she was thirty-five, they usually thought she was joking. And she couldn't blame them—she'd never looked better.

In the past six months, she had gone through a dramatic transformation. Some of her old friends hardly recognized her. She had a new hairstyle, had stopped shopping at H&M, and amped up her exercise routine, which had finally burned off the last of the baby fat she thought would follow her to the grave.

She put down the razor, slid her head down under the water, and rinsed out the hair mask. She was finally starting to relax. The warm bath and all the pampering had helped drive away thoughts of work, which had preoccupied her mind earlier in the day. She'd had to cut her workout short to go home and unwind because her thoughts were spinning so out of control: one second she thought she had done the right thing, only to decide a moment later that she'd made a fool of herself. But now she had finally made up her mind once and for all: she had made the right decision. If they wanted to fire her, so be it. All she wanted was for the investigation to move forward. If the car could help the Swedes, then a setback in her career was a reasonable price to pay.

She stood up, pulled the tub stopper out with her toes, and turned on the shower. After rinsing herself off, she stood on the bath mat, took the top towel from the freshly washed stack, and dried herself to the sound of the bathwater disappearing down the drain. She rubbed lotion on her skin and it burned where she had shaved.

Dunja listened to the prolonged slurping noise from the tub as it emptied. She knew the sound was the drain's cry for help, reminding her it needed cleaning. She had been meaning to do it for a while, but something had always got in the way. It seemed plausible that she wouldn't fix it until the water was flowing onto the floor and into the living room, with its recently refinished floor.

She was just wondering if her house insurance would cover that sort of damage when the doorbell rang. Her watch, which lay on the counter, said it was twenty minutes before midnight. Maybe someone had got lost? The bell rang again—long and insistent this time. Dunja put her kimono on and tied it at the waist as she walked into the hall. Could it be one of her more recent lovers? Although she'd always been careful never to bring them back to her place or to use her last name, three of them had managed to track her down. She hadn't had any problem with the first two, and had been more than willing to let them in. The third had come to propose to her and had broken down when she kindly but firmly said no. Two pots of tea later, he had finally agreed to take a taxi home. She realized that, somewhere inside her, she was hoping it was one of the other two men at the door tonight.

She leaned toward the peephole but couldn't see out into the stairwell. It was pitch-black. The doorbell rang again, this time at quick intervals, like a warning buzzer before an imminent blast. She turned the lock and opened the door.

"Mmm...just showered? Nice." Kim Sleizner took a sip of the half-empty bottle of whisky he was holding in one hand.

"Excuse me, but it's almost midnight. What do you want?"

Sleizner held up a warning finger and grinned. "You and me...we're gonna...have a little talk." He pushed past her into the apartment, and Dunja was left with the stink of alcohol in his wake.

He was standing at her iPod stereo when she walked into the living room, turning up the volume of Sade's "Your Love is King." Then he sank onto the sofa with legs splayed wide and took another sip from the bottle. "Perhaps you're wondering why I'm here? I would be, if I were in your shoes—or your kimono. It's pretty, by the way. Sexy."

"Kim, I have no idea what you want, nor do I wish to find out. All I want is for you to leave—now!"

"That's some tone to take with me when you're already down for the count. I really ought to be offended, but I can't help but think it suits you, especially in that kimono." He gulped down the whisky and wiped his mouth with the back of his hand. "Now, I want to know if you were the one who tattled to *Ekstra Bladet*."

So that's why he was here. He didn't yet know that she had forged his signature and that the Peugeot was on its way to Sweden. With a bit of luck, he wouldn't find out about the car until after he was forced to resign, which everyone was expecting in the aftermath of "Blowgate"—the name *Ekstra Bladet* had given to the affair.

Dunja took a few steps toward the coffee table and looked down at him. *Don't sit down. Don't invite conversation. And for God's sake, don't show any sign of weakness*, she said to herself.

"Kim, it's no secret that you and I haven't always got along, and that we tend to have different ideas about how an investigation ought to be run. But I would never sink so low as to contact the papers about your infidelities."

Sleizner considered what she had said, and then rose from the sofa. He walked past her into the hall. "So that's your statement?

It wasn't you? Interesting." He stopped, turned around, and looked into her eyes. "So you had nothing to do with it?"

He must have been able to smell the whiff of hesitation as she wondered how to respond, which was a microsecond too long. "Listen, Kim—"

He cuffed her ear so hard that she thought her neck had dislocated. She could hear him shouting, but she couldn't make out the words. Her cheek burned and throbbed in time with her heart. He grabbed her kimono and yanked her toward him. She felt his pungent breath encroaching on her. Then her hearing returned. It was as if someone had turned up the volume again.

"Don't you think I know you're lying? I know it was you!"

He knocked her legs out from under her and she fell straight to the floor. The recently refinished wood still smelled like varnish close up. He straddled her, clasping her arms above her head with one hand as he fumbled for her crotch with the other. His panting, stinking breath was right in her face. "Mmm...so smooth and shaven. How nice. Is that for my sake?" he rasped in her ear. "Maybe you could just feel that I was going to come for a visit? I know you want it. You just have to admit it. The first time I saw you I knew just what kind of woman you were, but you didn't want to sleep with the boss and reap all the benefits. Fair's fair, right?" His middle finger roamed about her clitoris. "But I have good news. Even though I'm your boss, I can guarantee that you will not reap a single benefit," he said, shoving three fingers inside her. "Just so you know. I'm going to be on you like a fucking leech." He moved his fingers up and tightened his grip on her pubic bone. It hurt, and she tried to twist out of his clutches, but he only pressed harder.

"And I'm not going to let go until I've sucked you dry." He pulled his fingers out. "And even if I'm not always around, you should be afraid that I might suddenly show up, because I will— when you least expect it." He tasted his fingers and wiped them on her cheek. Then he stood up and left the apartment.

63

FABIAN LOOKED AT THE clock. It was eighteen minutes past three. The hospital had long since gone to sleep, and all he could hear was a faint buzz from the ventilation system. He had heard the sound of distant sirens three times, and assumed this counted as an unusually quiet night.

He turned his eyes toward the yearbook that was sitting on the tray he was using as a desk. Aside from a few short minutes when he'd dozed off, Fabian had spent the last three hours studying his yearbook from the ninth grade in great detail. He had gone through it from cover to cover, calmly and methodically: class by class, student by student. With each new face, he'd tried to form a mental image of the person in question. He remembered most of them, although a few of his schoolmates took their time coming to life. People he had never had anything to do with turned out to be in there somewhere, like ghosts roaming his memory.

He had not, however, managed to come up with any suspects. Not one of those faces stood out more than any other. Just a few hours ago, he had been certain that the perpetrator would be in the yearbook somewhere, but now doubt had caught up with him. Was he on the wrong track?

He decided to flip through one last time. If he didn't find anything, he would turn out the light and try to get some sleep. At this point, the book more or less opened itself to class 9C. He didn't know how many times he had stared at this picture in the past week, but he couldn't get rid of the feeling that there was something he had missed. Something about the photo looked like it was hiding some sort of secret. Why else would the perpetrator have left this particular picture near Jörgen Pålsson's body with his face crossed out? It had to mean something, especially considering that nothing else seemed to have been left up to chance.

He went through the rows of faces and the names under the image, but no matter how hard he tried he couldn't manage to finger anyone as a potential suspect, except for Claes Mällvik, who was now dead. He put down the yearbook and rubbed his temples. What had he missed?

His thoughts moved to the sacrifice-like place where he'd found Claes. How could he have been there for more than an hour before the others arrived, and missed the moss under the victim? He had overlooked the moss in the shape of a human body—the true message—and the most important part of the entire installation. Fabian knew it revealed the perpetrator himself in the shadow of Claes.

In the shadow of Claes, he thought to himself again.

He had been looking at the class photo the wrong way. He and all the others had stared themselves blind at what was in the picture, when it was all about what *wasn't* in the picture. Fabian could feel his energy returning as he reached for the otoscope. It was meant for examining ears, but it would have to do as a magnifier for now. He turned on its light and held it up to the class picture. This time he knew exactly where to look, and sure enough he was there: the killer stood in the shadow of Claes Mällvik.

He was almost completely hidden behind Claes, so it wasn't possible to see any part of his face. Tufts of his hair were all that revealed his presence. Fabian and the other officers had thought it was Claes's hair, but looking at the photo through the otoscope made it very clear that the hair belonged to another person behind Claes. But who?

Fabian had no memory of another person in his class. Could he really have forgotten that there was one more of them? He double-checked the names under the picture: twenty names with no one listed as "not pictured." He had thought there were twenty people in his class. But in the picture, there were actually twenty-one. Someone had been among them all along, whom no one had noticed, whose name hadn't even been included under the class picture. Could this really be true, or was it just an optical illusion?

64

ASTRID TUVESSON WALKED AS quickly as she could through the hospital corridor, wishing that the doctor, who was following her like an annoying fly, would be paged and forced to leave her alone.

"This really isn't a good idea," he said for the umpteenth time. "Especially considering what happened yesterday."

"I promise to take it slow."

"Okay, but in my opinion she's not strong enough. It is therefore my duty to—"

Tuvesson stopped and turned to face the doctor. "I don't know how you could have missed this fact, but we are in the middle of an investigation, which has bodies piling up one after the other. For the first time, we have a survivor and if we can help jog her memory then that is *my* goddamn duty."

"But why can't it wait until she—"

"Because another victim could turn up at the morgue, any time. Maybe you'd like to take responsibility if that happens?"

The doctor sighed. "I want to ask her if she's comfortable with you coming in and questioning her. If she doesn't want to, it's a no, okay?"

Tuvesson chose not to respond and kept walking down the corridor. Her patience was gone, and she was bone-tired despite having managed a few hours of sleep while Klippan and Lilja made sure that everyone from the class who claimed to be out of town really had been. All but one of them had been able to provide proof that they were out of the country. According to information given to her team, Seth Kårheden was supposed to be in Spain, but thus far he hadn't answered his mobile. He was also divorced and a bit of a recluse. It was too early to tell whether this meant he was their guy, but either way, he was a suspect.

Tuvesson stopped by the two uniformed cops who were sitting on either side of the entrance. She nodded at them, and one stood up and opened the door to the hospital room where Ingela Ploghed was sitting up in bed, flipping through *Hemmets Journal*.

"Hi, Ingela, do you remember me? We met yesterday."

Ingela nodded without looking up from her magazine. Tuvesson took a seat on the chair next to the bed.

"You look like you're feeling much better today."

Ingela shrugged.

"Do you remember what we talked about last time I was here?"

Ingela nodded.

"You told me that you were out with some friends, having drinks on the S/S *Swea*, and all of a sudden you felt like you were under the influence of something other than alcohol. Has anything else come back to you?"

Ingela shook her head but didn't move her eyes from the knitting pattern in the magazine.

"How would you feel about coming along for a ride in my car? It might help jog your memory."

Ingela looked up and met Tuvesson's gaze. "I don't know." Her eyes moved to the doctor and back again.

"Ingela, right now you are our best, if not only, chance of identifying and apprehending the man who subjected you to this terrible cruelty."

"Is it the same person who killed the other people from the class?"

"We don't know yet. There's a lot to suggest it's all one person's doing, but there are also some things that indicate otherwise. Perhaps with your help, we can get an answer."

Ingela Ploghed looked down and appeared to vanish back into the world of knitting. Then she closed the magazine and looked up.

TUVESSON TURNED ONTO KUNGSTORGET and found an empty spot right in front of the S/S *Swea*, which was moored broadside to the quay. Ingela Ploghed sat in the passenger seat and looked out at the boat with an expressionless look.

"Are you okay?"

Ingela nodded. Tuvesson climbed out of the car, lifted a wheelchair out of the trunk, unfolded it, and helped Ingela get seated.

"I've never been here. Is it a nice place?"

"Sure, I guess it's…fine."

"Do you come here often?"

"No, only when I'm out with the girls. It's sort of become our place."

Tuvesson pushed the wheelchair across the gangway and into the restaurant. They were met by a man in chef's uniform, who informed them that the place was closed. She showed him her police badge and explained that they just wanted to look around. The man muttered something about making it quick and vanished into the kitchen.

Ingela pushed herself about in her chair as she looked around the room, which had walls panelled in mahogany and round, shiny brass portholes. Coloured spotlights and speakers were mounted on the ceiling: they were on the dance floor. There was a bar containing rows of liquor bottles along one wall, and a covered blackjack table stood in a corner. *This place is shabby and sad,* Tuvesson thought, *like all nightclubs in daylight.*

"Can you tell me a bit about what you remember from the night you were here?"

"I told you everything I remember."

"Okay, but maybe you can tell me again."

"We ordered some drinks, and after a while I felt weird and dizzy."

"Nothing else has come back to you now that we're here? It doesn't matter how small. Any little detail can help. Sometimes the tiniest thing is enough to jog all the rest of your memories. What were you wearing, for example?"

"Black jeans and a white blouse, the kind that you sort of tie around your waist."

"How about your shoes—high heels?"

"I never wear heels. I don't even know how to walk in them. I was wearing my regular old sandals, like I always do," Ingela said as she continued to look around.

Tuvesson studied her from a distance. Risk had said Ingela was one of the most well-liked students in his class, and the only one who had stood up for Claes, which must have taken courage and quite a lot of spunk—an image that didn't fit with the person sitting before her in the least. Aside from the effects of the recent attack, there was something heavy and grey about her entire personality. She looked okay, but her stringy, mousy hair, unfashionable shoes, and makeup-free face suggested that this was a person who had given up.

"Did you have fun? Before things went wrong, I mean."

"I don't know if I would call it *fun*." Ingela shrugged. "I mostly just go along with whatever my friends want. You have to hold on to the few you have left, after all."

"Have you lost many friends?"

"Not lost, exactly. But you know how it is: you drift apart, live different lives, and before you know what's happened it's been too long to just call and say hi."

Tuvesson nodded. She was familiar with the problem; she knew exactly what Ingela was talking about. The difference was that new friends showed up in most people's lives.

"We might as well go. I don't remember anything else anyway." Ingela rolled toward the door and Tuvesson helped her across the gangway.

"Do you remember anything about when you left?"

"No, I told you I...hold on..." She stopped the wheelchair in the middle of the gangway and looked down at the water. "It felt like I was going to fall into the water so I held on to the railing with both hands."

"Like this?" Tuvesson grasped the railing and Ingela nodded. "And then what? What happened next?"

Ingela considerd the question before speaking. "It was blue. The car was blue. A little darker than that one." She pointed at a blue car driving by.

"So a blue car stopped outside here?"

"No, it was already parked and someone came and helped me. At first he felt strong and safe because I was so scared of falling in the water, but then I got scared of him."

"Why were you scared?"

"He was holding me so tight. I tried to get away, but he was too powerful and he shoved me into the car."

"Can you describe him?"

"I never saw his face."

"What about his body? Tall, fat, or —"

"I don't know. Normal."

"His age?"

Ingela thought about it. "Middle-aged, or...I don't know. But I remember the blue car."

"You don't remember the model?"

"No—all cars look the same these days."

Tuvesson took out her phone and pulled up a relatively recent picture of Seth Kårheden that Klippan had found online, and showed it to Ingela. "Was this him?"

"That's Seth Kårheden."

"Yes, I know, but was he the one who helped you into the car?"

"How should I know? I never saw him."

Tuvesson gave up and wheeled Ingela back to her car. It was time for their next stop.

65

DUNJA HOUGAARD'S GENITALS STILL hurt, and Kim's thumb had left a big bruise just above her pubic bone. That was the extent of the physical injury; the real pain came from the degradation, which drilled deeper and deeper into her, even though it had been no more than a vulgar demonstration of pseudo-power by a fettered alpha male.

She had gone through her options. Reporting the sexual assault would mean his word against her own, not to mention she had voluntarily allowed him into her apartment. Forging his signature in a separate incident didn't exactly help her credibility. The alternative was revenge. She could contact his wife or *Ekstra Bladet* and tell them what had happened, or she could lure him into a trap.

She discarded each idea and decided that it would be best to bide her time and hold her head high. His goal had been to quash her and put her in her place, so the most effective strategy would be for her to show him that he hadn't succeeded. She needed to show him that she was stronger than that—stronger than him.

The problem was, he *had* succeeded. She felt broken, weak, and exhausted at the very thought of holding her head high.

The kettle whistled. She poured the water into the teapot, went to the living room, crawled onto the sofa with her tablet, and turned it on. His face was the first thing she saw: he was more or less staring straight at her; it felt as if he were still in her apartment.

So Kim had decided to eat humble pie, that smarmy bastard. She clicked through to the article, where he said in contrite terms that he wanted to apologize first and foremost to his family, but also to the Danish people. He blamed his misstep on being far too overloaded with work, which had led him to neglect his family and seek solace elsewhere. Asked whether he planned to resign, he'd responded:

> If they still want me, I'm willing to stay, but in the meantime I need to take a timeout. I'm not the only one having a difficult time with this; it is worse for my family. I'm hoping that you will respect our need to be left alone as we take care of each other. Everyone wants to be a superhero, someone who can handle anything and then some, but at the end of the day, we're all just humans who have faults and shortcomings. All leaders should remember this, but far too many forget.

Dunja turned off her tablet. She felt like throwing up.

66

"MAYBE SHE JUST GOT tired of the guy and took off," Klippan suggested to Lilja on their way to the central library through the shade-dappled city park. "I'm sure there are lots of frustrated women out there who want nothing more than to buy a one-way ticket so they can disappear; women who want to get as far away as they possibly can. Not to mention a lot of frustrated men."

"What about the daughter? Do you think she would have run away from her, too?"

"That depends on how desperate she was."

They walked into the library, which was dominated by a concentrated sense of order. Lilja took a deep breath and inhaled that unmistakeable scent of books, the smell that only exists in libraries. It took her back in time and felt almost like coming home. As a little girl, she had loved to spend time in this very library. Every Saturday, while her mother was working at Reflex—a high-end fashion boutique down on Järnvägsgatan— she had wiled away the hours here. She had gone to the children's plays and movies and read almost all the books for kids. The hours flew by, and she hadn't been bored for a second.

Now and then she would go on an adventure in the large library complex, which was made up of a number of connected buildings. You might find a door to a totally new, unexplored room when you least expected it. Once she had discovered a door in the middle of a shelf—a door she'd walked past many times without noticing. It was unlocked, and it led her into a study room that was empty except for two adults who had been far too busy with each other to notice her. That was the first time she saw it for real. Once she had heard her mum doing it after a drunken night out at the Charles Dickens pub. But *watching* was different.

She'd recognized both of them. The woman, who was leaning over a table with her panties around her knees, usually sat at the lending desk, and the man who stood behind her, pressing his crotch against her in hard, rhythmic jabs, was the library janitor. His big key ring jangled with each thrust. She'd been neither disgusted nor frightened—she was mostly just fascinated, so she sneaked further into the room to get a better look. Then the man turned around and caught sight of her. She didn't know if she should flee the room. His face cracked into a smile and he kept thrusting into the woman, harder and harder, and with every thrust her cries became louder and louder.

After a while, the man started groaning too. He pulled his member out of the woman and let it rest in his hand like a heavy piece of meat. His eyes were glued on Lilja the entire time. Even though something inside her told her she should run away, she hadn't been able to stop watching. To this day, she could still remember how large she thought his penis was. It was hard, veiny, and glistening with the woman's juices. He had used his free hand to turn the woman over, and he'd pressed her down and put it in her mouth, his eyes still fixed on Lilja.

"How may I help you?"

Lilja woke from her reverie and noticed that the librarian behind the lending desk was the same woman from the secret room, only twenty-five years and probably the same number of kilos later. As Klippan explained their business at the library, she wondered if the janitor still worked there too.

"Elsa Hallin," the librarian repeated. "Yes, she was here yesterday, but I actually haven't seen her today."

"How late did she stay?"

"Let's see…yesterday was Thursday. She works until four thirty that day, so she probably left around then. Her shift ends early on Tuesdays and Thursdays, and she probably went straight home as usual. Oh…actually, she had an appointment to get a facial before going home to fix dinner. She and her husband have a very strict schedule to divide their duties equally."

"Apparently she never arrived home to make dinner," Klippan said.

"You didn't happen to see exactly when she left?" Lilja asked.

"No, sorry."

"When was the last time you saw her?"

"Around three p.m. yesterday, I think. We were both on a coffee break."

"Did you notice if she was acting different in any way?"

"What do you mean?"

"Was she extra nervous or tense? Did she say anything about feeling threatened, or was there anything that seemed out of the ordinary?"

The librarian thought about it. She was just about to say something when a man approached the desk. "Where is your English-language literature?"

"Just go in and up the stairs to the right." The man vanished and the librarian leaned over the desk toward the police officers, speaking in a lower voice. "Elsa was in that class, you know, and the rest of us certainly wondered if she was worried, but she didn't want to talk about it and waved it off, like it didn't have anything to do with her. But if what the papers say is true—that those guys Jörgen and Glenn were bullies—then I would be worried if I were her."

"Why's that?"

"I'll put it this way: I don't have anything against her personally, quite the opposite, in fact." She looked over her shoulder. "But there are other people here who don't feel the same—people who have pretty serious issues with her. A few people have quit because of Elsa."

"What sort of issues?"

"How should I put this…she has a pretty sharp tongue, and at times it has bordered on workplace bullying. But I can't complain. She's never said a bad word about me—that I know of, anyway."

Lilja exchanged a glance with Klippan and realized that they were thinking the same thing.

"Do you have a staff break room or something like that?"

"Sure. Come with me and I'll show you. It's over here." She put an UNATTENDED sign on the desk and guided them through the library. It all felt familiar to Lilja. Aside from a room full of computers and the fact that the atrium garden had been given a large glass roof, she found that nothing had changed in the past twenty years.

"Here's our little nook." The librarian opened the door to the staff room.

It was smaller than Lilja had expected. There was a decrepit, striped green sofa in one corner, and a kitchenette with a cof-feemaker and sink in the other. A few easy chairs were scattered here and there with floor lamps to match, and two desks stood along one wall.

"Where does she keep her personal belongings?"

The librarian walked over to the furthest desk and pulled out one of the drawers. Lilja looked through the contents: a few lipsticks, dental floss, a tin of *snus* packets, a bag of gum, a few pens, and a phone charger. She sighed, feeling that they hadn't progressed at all. She had absolutely no idea how to move forward. She was too tired. She hadn't got more than two hours of sleep the night before, and all she wanted right now was to lie down on the ugly green sofa and close her eyes.

"Are any of these Elsa's?" Klippan asked, standing by the coat rack.

The librarian walked over to the rack, studied the coats, and held up a beige jacket. "This is hers, actually."

"Do you know if she was wearing it yesterday?"

"Yes, I think she was. And here are her outdoor shoes." She pointed with one hand to a pair of gold sandals, and put her other hand up to her mouth. "Oh my God! Does this mean he got her?"

"It's too soon to say," Klippan said as they helped the shocked librarian sit in one of the easy chairs. Once she had calmed down, he took out his phone and showed her the picture of Seth Kårheden. "Did you happen to see this man here yesterday?"

The librarian stared intently at the picture without saying anything. Only after thirty seconds did she look up at Klippan. "Is that him? Is that the murderer?"

"We don't know. All you need to tell me is whether you saw him here yesterday."

"I don't know. Maybe? I'm not sure." The librarian shrugged. "So many people come through here every day."

Klippan nodded and walked over to Lilja, who was at the coat rack, searching the pockets of the beige jacket. She found a wallet, which contained a few bills, a bus card, two Visas, an ID card, and a thick stack of various membership cards. Klippan fished an old Nokia mobile phone from the other pocket.

"Is this hers?" he asked, showing the phone to the librarian, who nodded and looked more and more anxious.

Lilja took the phone and pressed the buttons, making the screen light up. Elsa had eighteen missed calls and six voicemails. Lilja didn't need a PIN code to navigate to the call log: thirteen of the calls were from "Jerkan," two were from "Hollywood," and the rest were from "Home."

"I think we should leave," she said, casting a glance at the librarian. They left the staff room, dialled 222, and activated the speakerphone.

"*Welcome to your voice mailbox. You have six new messages...*"

Received July 8, 4:54 p.m: *"This is Freja from Salon Hollywood. I just wanted to check and see if you're on your way."*

Received July 8, 5:13 p.m: *"Hi, this is Freja again. I just wanted to tell you that I spoke to my supervisor, who says I will have to charge for this appointment. Just so you know."*

Received July 8, 6:07 p.m: *"Hi, Mum. It's me. Bea. Why aren't you home? It's scary to be home alone. And I'm hungry. You'll be here soon, right? Bye. Smooches."*

Received July 8, 6:11 p.m: *"Hello, where are you? Bea called and apparently she's home all alone? I'm still at the gym. Call me as soon as you get this."*

Received July 8, 6:36 p.m: *"Mum, where are you?* [Bursts into tears.] *Hello? Mum…"*

Received July 8, 9:46 p.m: *"I'm home now. We got a pizza and she's finally asleep…* [He sighs, it's clear that he is about to break down.] *Elsa, what the fuck is going on?"*

Received July 9, 1:03 a.m: [No voice, just someone gasping in uneven bursts, and eventually bursting into tears.]

"You have no new messages."

Klippan looked Lilja in the eye. "He either enticed her out into the park that surrounds the library, or overpowered her inside and carried her out without anyone noticing."

"Unless she's still here."

67

DUNJA HOUGAARD WAS TUCKED under the blanket on her sofa listening to The Cure's *Wish* on repeat. Her phone rang in the middle of "High," one of her favourite songs. She had turned off the ringer because she didn't feel like talking to anyone, but she couldn't help noticing that the display lit up with Kjeld Richter's face. She paused Robert Smith and answered.

"Where are you? It's really late."

"I have some things to take care of. I don't think I'll make it in until tomorrow. Is it important?"

"I just wanted to tell you that I'm finished, and you were absolutely right: we sure are dealing with a cold bastard."

Dunja's brain was working hard to get up to speed, but she couldn't think of what he might be talking about.

"He got in through the ceiling space, but unfortunately didn't leave any traces behind, except for the ones in the dust, of course. He must have had some sort of mask on."

Risk had been right again. He had mentioned his idea about the dropped ceiling without even batting an eye.

"Okay, but where did he enter the ceiling?"

"Through the bathroom by the waiting room. Like I said, he's a cold bastard. I think he even left the door unlocked, probably to avoid raising more suspicion than was absolutely necessary."

"If he didn't want to raise suspicion, he must have been sitting in the waiting room with the journalists," she said, thinking aloud.

"Probably."

She had an idea. "With a little luck, there'll be a picture of him."

"I thought of that too, but there are no security cameras in the waiting room, which there should be, given how much shit happens there—thefts and God only knows what else. Do you know how frequently people have sex in that room?"

"No."

"Me neither, but I can assure you that it's more common than you'd think."

"I'm actually hoping one of the journalists might have something for us; they were taking tons of pictures. He might have ended up in one."

"Of course. You're right."

"We'll talk more later. I'll come in this afternoon."

68

ASTRID TUVESSON WAS PUSHING Ingela Ploghed's wheelchair along the gravel paths in Ramlösa Brunnspark. Ingela was doing nothing to help, so it felt like she was pushing her up a steep hill. Tuvesson could feel herself breaking a sweat. She was also hungry and thirsty, and she was sure a headache couldn't be far behind.

Tuvesson had been hoping that returning to the scene of the crime would spark something in Ingela's memory, but she'd had no such luck. Ingela just sat in her wheelchair shaking her head; she couldn't even remember that this was the spot where she had regained consciousness. Other than identifying that the perpetrator had a blue car, this field trip had given them nothing of value. In fact, they'd lost an awful lot of their most valuable resource: time. Seconds had turned into minutes, which turned into hours. Soon, yet another day would slide through their fingers. And Tuvesson was out of cigarettes.

By the time they arrived back at the car, neither of them had said a thing for several minutes. Tuvesson unlocked the doors and helped Ingela into the passenger seat. She folded up the wheelchair and got into the car.

"You're not angry, are you?" Ingela asked.

"No, not at all. I'm just a little tired." Tuvesson turned the key in the ignition and put the car in gear.

"I'm sorry I can't remember anything or be of more help."

"Ingela, it's okay. It's not your fault, but if something does come back to you, no matter how tiny a detail, you have to give us a call. Okay?"

Ingela nodded and looked out the window at the old wooden building that had once housed the fine Ramlösa Wärdshus restaurant, but which had been converted into offices. Tuvesson turned on the car radio, but she couldn't find a good station and turned it off again.

Her mobile phone broke the silence. It was Molander, whose smiling face adorned the screen. The picture was from their most recent Christmas dinner—he had apparently had one or two drinks too many. She pressed the speakerphone button and placed the phone in her lap.

"Hi, Ingvar. How are things?"

"Oh, fine. Do you have a minute?"

"I'm in the car with Ingela Ploghed. But just a second, I'll find my headset." She leaned across Ingela. "Sorry," she said, opening the glove compartment. "Where are you?"

"At Söderåsen."

"I thought we were done there."

"I thought so too. But here I am. How's it going with that headset?"

"Take it easy…" She dug through the glove compartment with one hand as she steered with the other. "It should be here somewhere. Hold on, I'll have to pull over." She slowed down and stopped at the edge of the road, once again leaning across Ingela, who appeared increasingly nervous and crowded. "Sorry, Ingela, I just have to…Here it is." She pulled the tangled cord out and started undoing the worst of the knots. Meanwhile, she could hear Molander pretending to snore loudly. "I know, I know! I hardly ever use these things."

"Yeah, I think that's the —"

A train roared past them on the tracks that ran alongside the road, drowning out Molander's voice.

"What did you say? I can't hear you!"

"Ah, screw it. Just make sure you get that headset on before the world ends."

"God, just give me a second! Talk about impatient!" Tuvesson turned to Ingela, who was suddenly breathing in short, ragged gasps, her eyes glued to the bridge where the train was vanishing southward.

"What's going on? Ingela, are you okay?"

Ingela exhaled and seemed to calm down.

"Houston? Are we having a problem?" Molander said.

"Yes!" Tuvesson went back to the headset and managed to connect it at last. "Hello? Can you hear me?"

"Loud and clear."

"Tell me what's up."

"Well, I thought we'd searched the entire area."

"But you hadn't?"

"We definitely had, but what good is that when you don't know what you're looking for?"

"You found something new?"

"That's right. I went up there and measured the radio waves. There was no one else nearby, and I had my own phone turned off, but there was a lot of activity at 2.2 gigahertz."

"What does that mean?"

"That there was some form of mobile 3G unit in the vicinity."

"Did you find it?"

"Yup. We found a wireless pinhole camera with a microphone that was hidden in a birdhouse five metres from the grassy area."

"Oh my God," Tuvesson said, feeling a headache brewing. "That means he knows we found Schmeckel."

"In all likelihood, yes. It also explains why he's always a step ahead. If he had a camera at Söderåsen, he could have one absolutely anywhere. He's probably fully aware of exactly where we are in the investigation. For example, now he knows that I found —" Molander was interrupted by another train barrelling down the tracks, this time in the other direction.

"Hold on, I can't hear what you're saying," Tuvesson yelled before discovering that Ingela Ploghed was crying, her eyes on the tracks. "Ingela, are you okay? Did something happen? Is it the train? Is that what's making you..." She placed her hand on Ingela's leg.

"Don't touch me! I said don't touch me!" She batted Tuvesson's hand away as if it bore some deadly disease and tried to move as far away as possible.

"It's okay. You're okay. I'm not going to touch you. I promise." Tuvesson held both hands in the air, but panic refused to release its hold on Ingela, whose tear-filled eyes were moving from the open glove compartment to the headset in Tuvesson's ear to Molander's jovial face on the mobile phone screen. "Ingvar, I have to go. I'll call you back." She pulled the headset off and turned to Ingela, who was sweaty and out of breath.

"I want to go back to the hospital."

"Of course, Ingela. I promise to drive you there right away if you just tell me what's going on."

Ingela shook her head and burst into tears. "Please just drive me back. Please."

"Was it the trains? Is that what's upsetting you?" Tuvesson asked as another train thundered by.

"Drive! Just drive!" Ingela cried, banging on the dashboard.

Tuvesson realized that she wouldn't get any further and turned the key in the ignition.

69

THE TORCH ILLUMINATED ALL the CPUs that were lined up alongside the dusty fat monitors, printers, and keyboards. Lilja released the fabric that hung across the opening in the wall, which was several metres wide. This area had originally been intended to house an oil tank for the boiler, but the rise of district heating had rendered the oil tank obsolete, and these days the room was used as a graveyard for computers that couldn't understand anything more than Basic and MS-DOS. There was no Elsa Hallin here, in any case.

Lilja had been so sure that Elsa was still somewhere in the library, but they had almost finished searching the entire basement, and neither she nor Klippan had found even the tiniest piece of evidence to bolster her theory. Maybe the killer had decided it was entirely too risky to keep Elsa in the library: it was a public building with thousands of visitors each day, after all. On the other hand, this perpetrator seemed capable of just about anything. She couldn't remember the last time she'd felt this uncertain and confused by a case.

And then it hit her.

LILJA AND KLIPPAN RUSHED past the lending desk.

"Are you done?" the librarian called after them.

"Almost," Lilja said, hurrying into the main building with Klippan at her heels.

"Irene, can you tell me what you're up to? We've already been here," Klippan complained, all of his body language indicating that his blood-sugar levels had completely crashed.

Lilja didn't care; she went up the stairs to the second floor and into the non-fiction section. She felt her heartbeat quicken. She really hoped she was right this time.

It looked just as she remembered: the door, barely visible to anyone who didn't know about it, was in the middle of the shelf, surrounded by technical books for the nerdiest of technology freaks. She heard Klippan panting behind her.

She placed her hand on the cool handle, letting it rest there for a moment before she pushed it down. The door was unlocked, exactly as it had been back when she was a kid; it swung open silently, almost on its own.

The study room hadn't changed a bit. The same green-striped curtains hung at the windows, and the same desk was positioned in the same spot it had been twenty years ago. The only thing missing was the copulating colleagues.

Instead, there was a lone woman in a chair. Her head was bent toward her chest, and her long, dark hair hid her face and large portions of her white blouse. They approached the woman, whose legs and arms were bound to the chair with straps. A shiny, dark pool of blood had spread under the chair in a one-metre radius.

Lilja walked up to the edge of the blood. She stopped, crouched down, and felt the coagulated surface with one finger, which caused rings to spread through and wrinkle the glossy surface. Klippan grabbed a broom that was leaning against the wall, and held it to the woman's forehead so that he could carefully lift her head to reveal her face.

The woman in the chair was unquestionably Elsa Hallin, but that wasn't what made Lilja initially avert her eyes. A deep incision had been made from the underside of her chin down to the top of her rib cage. Something was hanging out of the open wound and over the white blouse, which had turned red — something that looked like a bloody fillet of meat.

"That fucker cut out her tongue," Klippan finally managed to say.

Lilja tried to make sense of it all, but she couldn't gather her thoughts.

"A Colombian necktie," Klippan continued. "This is the first time I've seen one in real life. Doesn't this corroborate what the librarian said?"

"What did she say?"

"That Elsa had a sharp tongue."

That's right, Lilja thought. Elsa Hallin had a sharp tongue, and the killer had pulled it right out of her throat until it hung down over her chest like a fat, bloody tie. According to Klippan, Colombian neckties had been a common method of execution during the Colombian Civil War. Their main purpose was to scare those who'd discovered the victim into silence. The method involved making a vertical cut in the throat while the victim was still alive and pulling the tongue out so it hung down over the chest. Death could take up to an hour, depending on whether the victim died of blood loss or suffocation.

"So she might have been sitting here trying to call for help for a whole hour?"

Klippan shrugged. "It's impossible to know exactly how long she was alive at this point, but it wouldn't have mattered how much she screamed, no one would have heard her because her vocal cords were shredded."

Lilja stood up. From now on, they would have to work according to the theory that the killer wouldn't rest until the whole class was obliterated. Her phone rang. It was Tuvesson.

"We have another victim."

"You mean Elsa Hallin?" Lilja said.

"No. Camilla Lindén. But, wait, did you find Hallin?"

Lilja felt her sense of balance vanish.

January 9

The first day of my new life. I had to meet with my
teacher and the principal. Mum and Dad were there
too. I confessed everything and said I was sorry,
but I wasn't. Not even a tiny bit. It was best to play
along, let them think I'm still the person I used to be.
I wanted to seem sorry even though I just wanted to
laugh in their faces. Spit on them! They said he had a
concussion and he would have to stay home all next
week. How could he have a concussion? He doesn't
even have a brain!

At lunch a few people stared at me but no one was
brave enough to do anything. As soon as I looked
back, they turned around. Fucking wusses. His buddy
was there and gave me cut-eye, of course. He looked
like he was thinking about doing something. I walked
over and punched him in the ear. He was just about to
hit back, but I threatened him with a fork. Soon it will
be his turn to carry my tray.

After school some of my old friends came up to me
and wanted to talk, but I told them to go to hell. I don't
have any friends any more. Instead I picked a fight
with Jonas. His ugly clothes have always annoyed
me. I hit him in the stomach until he fell down. I saw
the fear in his eyes. So fucking awesome.

To do:

1. Start working out
2. Get a switchblade
3. Visit the concussion

70

FABIAN RISK RAN AS fast as he could along the gravel path. The voices behind him were yelling, "Theo! Theo! Theo!" He turned around and saw Lina, Jörgen, and several of his other classmates running after him; they were all about fifteen years old.

He was in the middle of nowhere, his upper body naked, and the rays of the sun were burning the back of his neck. He could hear his pulse, and the smacking sound as he tried to swallow a sip of water, but he didn't have any left. Soon he wouldn't be able to manage any longer. The voices behind him grew louder and louder: "THEODOR!"

What would happen if he gave up? No, he couldn't. It was impossible. He couldn't give up at any price. He was approaching a rock wall and could hear other voices, begging and pleading for their lives. He started climbing up, higher and higher, as fast as he could. The higher he climbed, the steeper the rock wall became. He looked down and saw his two old Stockholm colleagues, Tomas and Jarmo, climbing up after him. They were shouting. If he lost his balance he would fall the whole way down and all would be lost.

A hand came out of nowhere, pulling him up over the edge and leading him into a large, underground cave. There were costumed people — or beings — everywhere, wearing large, round headdresses that looked like big balls. He bent down and allowed a boy with golden-brown skin to place a similar headdress on his head while someone else hung a thick, white, crinkly shroud over his shoulders. It felt nice and cool.

An older man approached, looked him in the eye, and said something—but he couldn't understand what. Yet he knew exactly what he was supposed to do. He held out his left hand and let the older man run an instrument with a beam of light across the back of his hand. The light penetrated his skin and bubbled through his veins, just as a peacock a few centimetres tall ran up his arm...

Fabian opened his eyes. Everything grew brighter, but not much clearer. He noticed two long, narrow lights on the ceiling. The protective casing of the fixture was missing, so the cables and the capacitor were visible. Not only did strip lighting shed ugly light, it was ugly to look at too, he thought as he attempted to sit up. The burning pain in his back intensified immediately and spread up toward his neck.

He reached for his phone to check the time, but he couldn't find it. It was gone. So were his computer and the yearbook. He was bewildered. Hadn't he found the killer hidden behind Claes in the yearbook? Or was that a dream too? He reached for the alarm button and jabbed it a few times, although he heard the alarm sound out in the hallway the very first time he pressed it.

The door opened. It was the brunette nurse, the one who was not exactly super helpful.

"So it's time to get up again?"

"Where are my things? My phone, computer, and..."

"Apparently you were up working until five this morning."

Was that true?

"And that is not what we would describe as resting. If you had followed the doctor's orders, you almost certainly could have been home by now."

"But I have to call—"

"No, you have to rest." She pressed him down into the bed. "Right now, your body is working overtime to heal, and it needs all the strength it can get. So, do you want tea or coffee with your breakfast?"

"I just want to know what time it is."

"It's just after two. Let me ask you again: Tea or coffee?"

Fabian wanted neither of the two options. The coffee was as watery as the tea, which he was sure they used the coffeemaker to heat the hot water for. "Juice...give me two glasses of juice instead. And I would be eternally grateful if I could get some toast and a boiled egg."

The nurse allowed herself a crooked smile. "With our current government, you can forget about the egg, but I'm sure we can offer you some toast."

By now, Fabian was sure he hadn't been dreaming about the connection between the crime scene in Söderåsen and the class picture from ninth grade. As soon as the nurse left the room he ignored the pain and sat up. He had five minutes—max— before she would be finished in the kitchen and back behind the reception desk, with a full view of the corridor. He slid onto his feet from the edge of the bed and tried to straighten his back as best he could. His pants, socks, and shoes were in the closet with his shirt and jacket, which had been far too damaged by the flames to be salvaged. He had no idea why anyone had put time and energy into hanging them up.

He opened the door and saw one of the silent officers flipping through a *Wheels* magazine.

"I'm just going to grab a few things from the reception desk," he said.

The officer nodded and went back to his hot rod article.

As usual, the nurses' station was unattended. He searched among the binders and stacks of paper but couldn't find any of his stuff. If none of it was here in the reception area, he had no idea where to look.

The brunette nurse walked into the corridor carrying his breakfast tray. Fabian bent down behind the desk and clenched his teeth. The pain in his back triggered sweat to start dripping from his forehead. He peered under the desk: his laptop case and a bag containing his phone and documents were stuffed in the corner. He let the nurse pass, took his things, and headed for the lifts.

71

ANOTHER VICTIM IN CLASS OF EVIL

Tuvesson, Lilja, Klippan, and Molander were standing around the table, looking at *Kvällsposten*; a picture of the wrecked car lying upside down on the E6 dominated the cover.

"Why didn't we know about this?" Tuvesson asked, wondering if she could allow herself to send Florian out for cigarettes.

"According to dispatch, it came in as a car accident and nothing more," Klippan replied.

"How did no one catch onto the fact that she was in the same class as the others?" Lilja said.

"Well, it's not their job to keep track of that—it's ours. And since we didn't even know she was dead..."

"How did *Kvällsposten* get wind of it?" Molander asked, paging through the paper.

"Either the perpetrator tipped them off himself, or they were just doing their job and put two and two together," Lilja said.

"But so far, we don't have confirmation whether it was an accident or not," Tuvesson said. "The car is on its way here, so we'll see if Molander finds anything, but in the meantime, I want us to work on the assumption that our guy is behind it."

"You're suggesting he committed two murders yesterday?" Klippan said. "And not just any run-of-the-mill murders. I'm not sure of the details of what happened out on the E6, but the library couldn't have been easy. It would have been difficult to just get her into that room without anyone noticing. The ritual itself..." Klippan grew flustered and shook his head. "He must be so cold-blooded."

"What do I know? Maybe this supports Risk's 'two different killers' theory," Tuvesson said.

"Hold on, let's try to look at this logically," Molander said. "All we know for sure about the car accident is that it took place yesterday at 5:38 p.m. on the E6. My investigation will show whether the killer was there or whether he sabotaged the car. And as for the library, has Braids come up with a time frame for when she actually died?"

"Between three and five yesterday afternoon," Tuvesson said.

"Suppose he cut her up around one or one thirty and that she died an hour or an hour and a half later, that gives him plenty of time to manage both murders."

"Well, in any case, we know he's started up again—and then some," Tuvesson said. "Let's compare these two incidents to Jörgen and Glenn's murders. What was Elsa Hallin guilty of, for example?"

"According to one of her colleagues, she had a sharp tongue," said Lilja.

"Maybe she was a bully too, but a verbal one? That would certainly explain her tongue being cut out." Tuvesson turned to Klippan. "Has anyone in the class mentioned something about that?"

"Not in so many words." Klippan flipped through his papers. "A few people said she was pretty cocky."

"Who said that?"

"Camilla Lindén."

Tuvesson sighed. "Typical. Didn't Elsa Hallin say something negative about Camilla, too?"

"Yes—Elsa said she stood by and watched Jörgen and Glenn tease Claes."

"So there's nothing that can be linked to the car accident?"

"Not as of now."

"And we still haven't heard from Seth Kårheden?" Tuvesson asked, checking to see if there was more coffee in the Thermos.

"No," Lilja replied. "But I was able to confirm that he was on a plane to Pamplona on June fifteenth, and he's booked on a flight back from Santiago de Compostela late tonight."

"Was he walking the St. James's path?" Klippan asked.

"Maybe that's what he wanted people to think," Molander said, "but he could have driven back up here by car just as easily."

"What was written in that locker?" Tuvesson said.

"*No one sees me. No one hears me. No one even bullies me.*"

"*No one even bullies me*...It fits with Risk's theory about the moss." Tuvesson stopped speaking and looked at everyone. "That it was his image of himself in the shadow of Claes Mällvik, who at least *did* get bullied."

"Right, there's a guy you'd really want to trade places with," said Klippan.

"Easy for us to say. Which is actually worse: being bullied, or being completely ignored and treated like you don't exist?"

"You think that's what he wants to change?" Lilja said.

"Yes, I believe that's the point of all his actions: he wants to be someone you can't just ignore; a person no one will be able to forget, ever again."

"So why not make his identity known?" Klippan said. "What's the point of being famous if no one recognizes you?"

"It depends on how famous he wants to be," said Molander. "Say we discover his identity or he reveals it now: it would definitely make headlines, but after a few years things would cool off and his name would be forgotten. By the time he'd served his sentence, no one would remember him any more, which is why he keeps killing."

"Agreed," Tuvesson reiterated. "He's building up his own myth, showing everyone how smart and invincible he is, and how no one—not even the police—has a chance of stopping him."

"He's killing his former classmates in order to immortalize himself," Lilja said, while the others nodded. "How many people do you think he will have to kill before he succeeds?"

"We all remember Columbine," Molander said. "Twelve students and one teacher died there."

"So you think he has to make it to thirteen?"

Molander shook his head. "Unfortunately, I don't think that would be enough to secure his place in history. Columbine was the biggest school massacre of its kind: all the ones that have followed in its wake are forgotten six months later. Even if this killer is in a completely different category when it comes to the murders themselves, he's still just another mass killer, which we've seen before. If he gets up to eighteen or twenty people, it will be a completely different story."

"He would have to kill the whole class to get up to those numbers."

Molander nodded. Silence descended around the table.

"Well, the mood sure seems cheerful around here."

Everyone turned around to see Fabian Risk in the doorway, stooping forward slightly and supporting himself with one hand on the door frame.

"Fabian? What are you doing here? Where's your police detail?" Tuvesson walked up to him, but he fended her off with one hand.

"I know who did it." He took a few steps into the room and looked at the printouts of graffiti all over the walls. "Wow, someone's been busy."

"Fabian, what are you—"

"I found him. Here he is." Fabian placed his index finger just above Claes on the enlarged class picture on the whiteboard. "He was there all along, right before our eyes."

Tuvesson and the others gathered around and looked at the photo.

"But that's Claes." Klippan turned to Fabian. "Fabian, Claes is dead."

"No, it's not Claes—there's a guy standing right behind him. Look closer, that's not Claes's hair."

"Let me see," Molander said, crowding his way in with a magnifying glass to study the picture. After a moment he turned around and nodded. "He's right."

"They forgot to add his name to the list," Fabian said.

"Maybe that's not too surprising," Lilja said. "He's certainly easy to miss."

"But shouldn't he still be listed as not pictured?" Klippan said.

"You'd think so."

"Not if you look at it logically," Molander said. "He clearly *was* there, so he wouldn't have been declared absent."

"So in other words he should be in some of the yearbooks from the other grades," Tuvesson said.

Fabian nodded. "And that's exactly why I'm here." He turned to Klippan, who threw up his hands.

"Everyone we've been in contact with has promised to look at their yearbooks, but so far nothing has turned up," he said.

"Maybe his name just ended up in the wrong place and is listed somewhere else in the yearbook," Lilja said as she started flipping through the pages.

"That actually happened to me once; or rather, to my entire class," Klippan said. "I think it was in fifth grade—all our names got switched with the names of the grade three students. Suddenly my name was Ragnar Bloom, and everyone called me 'Flowers' for the rest of my school days." Klippan laughed. "One of the other guys got stuck with the name Greta. He got that forever."

"Fabian, how are you feeling?" Tuvesson asked, grabbing him as he was about to lose his balance and looked like he might pass out at any moment. Molander came to her assistance, and they helped him over to a chair.

Fabian felt the exhaustion wash over him, and the cold sweats and nausea that came in its wake. "I'm fine...I just need some water."

Tuvesson placed a large glass of water on the table in front of him. "It's not okay. You're injured, and you should be at the hospital. According to the doctor you're supposed to stay in bed until the day after tomorrow."

"I have to go home...Theo, my son. He's all alone." Fabian picked up the glass and took a sip; he felt the water spread through his body like a cool caress. "They wouldn't let me work at the hospital, so I had no choice but to come here."

Tuvesson waited until he'd finished the glass, and then she sat down and looked him in the eye. "Fabian, listen to me. We are the ones working on this case. *We*, not *you*, okay?"

"I just have to call the school and find out the name of the person standing behind Claes."

"No, you don't, Fabian. You are no longer working on this investigation. You are on vacation, not to mention sick leave. All you should be worrying about is getting some rest. I'm sure we'll find your classmate's name somewhere; it can't be that difficult. The important thing is that you follow the doctor's orders. What's more, you and the rest of your classmates are clearly in danger. So I want you to go back to—"

"Number 349? Is that the locker number?" Fabian pointed at the Post-it note next to the picture of the worn graffiti from the inside of a locker door. Klippan nodded.

"Fabian, did you hear me?" Tuvesson asked.

"We think the killer might have written the message," Molander said.

Fabian held up the picture and tried to decipher the text.

"*No one sees me. No one hears me. No one even bullies me. I. M.*," Molander said.

Fabian looked at Molander. "I. M.?"

"The Invisible Man. He used that signature in a few other places, too."

371

"The invisible man who no longer wants to be invisible—he wants to come forward and be seen."

Tuvesson nodded. "But we don't think he's going to reveal his identity until he's killed more people."

"How many is that? The whole class?"

"We think so."

Tuvesson was right. A few clever murders wouldn't suffice if you wanted to be remembered forever. The media-fatigued public demanded at least two-digit totals for unforgettable killers. The perpetrator might as well try to wipe out the whole class as long as he was at it. After all, every one of them had been party to making him feel invisible, which was the very reason he couldn't stop killing and wait for Klippan and everyone else to *do their jobs*. If Fabian did nothing fast, it would all be over soon.

He stood up with renewed energy. He had an idea.

"Fabian, you have to let us take care of it."

"Okay," he said, leaving the conference room.

His idea couldn't wait.

TUVESSON WALKED UP TO the class picture and studied the hair behind Claes Mällvik that belonged to the boy no one remembered. All they needed now was a name—just one name.

If only they could identify him, the rest would follow, like solving one of the last words in a crossword puzzle. They would be entering the last stage of the case soon, so it was extra crucial to make sure that everything was handled properly. They had to follow the rules: an overlooked clause, a missing signature on a document, a piece of conclusive evidence that was collected in the wrong way—anything could become a potential obstacle in a trial, setting the killer free again before they even managed to take their lieu days.

Risk had already been in a similar situation. Tuvesson knew all about it; it had been during an investigation in Stockholm at least as big as this one, if not bigger. Risk didn't know that she knew, and she had no intention of ever bringing it up.

"Irene and Klippan, you'll have to contact everyone in the class again. Hopefully someone will remember him and can give us a name. And don't forget to remind them to look for other yearbooks."

"How are we handling the police protection?" Klippan asked. "Have you spoken with Malmö?"

"No, I haven't had time, but I'll do it right away."

Lilja and Klippan headed for the door. Tuvesson took out her phone, dialled a number, and looked at Molander, who had stayed behind. "You could get going on the wrecked car, so we can figure out what actually happened to Lindén."

Molander nodded and went to leave, but he turned around again. "Hey, how did your field trip with Ingela Ploghed go?"

"Oh right, that was today." She called Lilja and Klippan back in. "I'm sorry, I completely forgot to tell you all. I took Ploghed out this morning."

"How did that go?" Lilja asked.

"To tell you the truth, I don't know. I took her to the boat, and all she remembered was that she was picked up by a man in a blue car."

"Blue?" Klippan said. "She didn't remember what model it was? Or whether it was old or new?"

"No. Just that it was blue."

"Who *doesn't* have a blue car?" Molander said.

Lilja turned to him. "Isn't your car blue?" He nodded.

"Was that all you found out?"

"Yes. We went to Ramlösa Brunnspark after and nothing sparked her memory there either, although I sweated everywhere pushing that wheelchair through the gravel. On our way back to the city..." Tuvesson stopped speaking and walked over to the window to look out at Helsingborg. "I had to pull over and stop. Ingvar, it was right around when you called to tell me about the camera you found at Söderåsen. We were parked right next to the tracks, and as soon as a train went by..." She stopped speaking again.

"What?" Lilja said.

"She sort of flipped out, and had some kind of panic attack. She started flailing her arms and screaming at me to drive away. I tried to calm her down, but it was impossible." Tuvesson sighed.

"Maybe the sound of the train triggered her memory," Klippan said.

"Could the assault have taken place on a train?" Lilja asked.

"No, I doubt it—sounds way too complicated. But maybe it was near some tracks."

"Wasn't she drugged and unconscious during the operation?" Molander said.

"Maybe she registered the noise in her subconscious," said Klippan.

Molander snorted and shook his head.

"What? It's possible! Those trains are really loud," Klippan continued. "I go mushroom-picking near the tracks south of Ramlösa, and you basically have to cover your ears when trains go by."

"Can I interject?" Molander said. "I think you're on the wrong track."

"Why's that?" Tuvesson asked.

"What if she wasn't reacting to the sound, but felt trapped in the car?"

"Of course, you're absolutely right. Given how complicated the operation was, it's most likely he took her to someplace where he could be relatively certain he could work without interruption."

Lilja and Klippan nodded.

"Possibly a private home without neighbours close by," Tuvesson went on.

"Or some sort of workshop," Klippan said.

"Near the tracks," said Lilja.

Tuvesson added thoughtfully. "Yes, it's all possible. I'll take a look at the neighbourhoods around Ramlösa. After all, there's nothing to lose."

"Yes there is—time. I don't know about you, but I would say it's in short supply when it comes to preventing more murders," Molander said as he left the room.

Lilja watched him go and looked at the others. "What the hell is up with him? He's so freaking grumpy and negative."

"He's just tired," Tuvesson said. "Who isn't?"

"I think he's grumpy because he didn't think to look around Ramlösa himself," Klippan said just as Tuvesson's phone rang.

"This is Astrid Tuvesson... Yes, that's right... What? Suicide? Are you..." She got Lilja and Klippan's attention. "I don't understand. How? And where did you say?"

72

DUNJA HOUGAARD HAD NEVER tried so hard to appear unfazed as she did when she stepped out of the lift and headed for the violent crimes unit. She was only here to get work done. Sleizner was nowhere to be seen, but the door to his office was closed, which meant he was there—unless he had sneaked out through an emergency exit.

She logged onto her computer and checked her inbox: she had a response from nearly every newspaper she'd contacted. She had asked them to send her all the photographs that had been taken in the waiting room outside Morten Steenstrup's ward, and to her surprise they had complied with hardly any protest. Out of the big dailies, only *Jyllands-Posten* had grumbled about wanting a guarantee that they would get dibs on the news if their photos turned out to contain anything of interest. She started with their pictures for that reason and felt relieved when she recognized all the faces—she knew which journalist wrote for each paper. She looked at *Politiken* next, browsing through an abundance of pictures of herself looking like a total wreck: sweaty, no makeup, under-eye circles so dark they seemed to have been painted on. She came across as someone who needed all kinds of treatments.

The only bright side was that none of the terrible pictures of her had been published. Maybe even journalists had moments of compassion, or perhaps they'd realized they would never get a single interview or piece of advance information from her again if they so much as thought about publishing any of those photos.

She found him an hour and a half later. The picture had been taken from a bird's-eye perspective, as if the photographer had held the camera high above his head to snap a few pictures at random. From a publication standpoint, the photo was worthless—full of the partial, thin-haired heads of journalists and out of focus on the bottom edge. But for her purposes, the picture was nearly perfect. She knew she had unearthed a shot of the killer.

The chairs along the far wall were in focus. A lone man sat holding a magazine, observing the fuss from a distance. She zoomed in on him and the focus was almost perfect, although there was something unclear about his face. She knew in her gut it couldn't be anyone else.

There was no way Sleizner would agree to allow her to share the pictures with the Swedes, even if it was the right thing to do. They would have to manage without help. Kim Fucking Sleizner wanted to solve the case on his own, and would rather it remain unsolved than allow someone else to have the glory.

Every cell in her body was brimming with hatred for Sleizner. The thought she had toyed with so many times throughout the years was starting to solidify into a concrete decision. She had no choice. She had to get rid of him—not just for her own sake, but for the sake of this case and the whole Danish police authority. She had to do everything in her power to get him fired.

She picked up the phone and called National Police Commissioner Henrik Hammersten before she could change her mind. He answered and readily agreed to a confidential meeting with her later that day. She hung up and took a few deep breaths.

"There you are," she heard from a voice behind her. How long had that bastard been standing there? She turned around and looked him in the eye, but his expression was indecipherable.

"How about coming into my office and…having a little chat?"

"Is there any reason we can't do it here?"

"Not at all, but if I were you I'd prefer to have this conversation behind closed doors."

She followed Sleizner into his office. He closed the door behind her. Dunja ignored all the warning signs and took a seat in the visitor's chair. The Sleazeball walked around the desk and sat in his own chair. To her surprise, he wasn't wearing his usual superior sneer.

"I want to start by telling you how sorry I am for last night."

Was she dreaming or was he joking?

"To be totally honest, I don't remember exactly what happened, and maybe that's for the best. But what little I do remember is more than enough for me to realize that there is no excuse for the way I acted. All I can say is that I'd had a lot to drink and I lost control." He paused. "I just want you to know that I feel so terribly ashamed."

Dunja thought he actually looked like he meant it, and she wondered if she was supposed to say something, but she didn't want to make it easier for him.

"Dunja, I was totally sure that you were the one who tipped off *Ekstra Bladet*, but now I realize it wasn't you at all, and so I'm prepared to bury the hatchet. If you don't report me for the horrible things I did last night, I won't report you for refusing orders and falsifying documents."

He knew about her trick with the car.

"I know what you're thinking," Sleizner continued, "and the answer is yes. I have been fully aware of what you've been doing this whole time, but I'm prepared to wipe the slate clean, and even give you total freedom to work on this case however you see fit."

Was he serious? Had he really burned himself so badly that his only option was total retreat? Did he have no choice but to

378

ignore his own ego and let her do her job? Dunja knew Sleizner far too well to relax completely, but if he seriously intended to let her continue with the investigation, she didn't want to throw a wrench in the works. It wasn't her style to put herself before a case, nor would it ever be. She gave him a barely perceptible nod.

"Good. So that's taken care of," Sleizner went on. "How is the investigation going? Have you come up with anything I should know about?"

It would be a breach of duty not to mention the picture of the perpetrator, but Dunja knew that the photo should be sent to the Swedes straight away, a relationship Sleizner had forbidden thus far. She decided to test him. "I think I have a picture of him."

Sleizner's expression changed. "You do? How did you manage to find it?"

Dunja told him about Kjeld Richter's investigation, which proved that the perpetrator had reached Morten through the ceiling space. She explained that, based on this information, she'd deduced the killer must have been in the same waiting room as the journalists.

"Fantastic, Dunja. Well done."

"I suggest we send it to the Swedes and see what they have to say before doing anything else," said Dunja.

"If that's what you want, I'm okay with your decision." He walked around and sat on the edge of his desk in front of her. "Dunja, I truly meant what I said. You and I, we haven't got along from the start and that's my fault, for the most part. You've always been a fantastic police officer, and from now on I intend to allow you to excel. If you think we should send the picture to the Swedes, then that's what we'll do."

Dunja stood up.

"Just one more thing."

She turned around.

"If I've understood it correctly, you booked a meeting with Hammersten. If you don't mind, I thought we could meet with him together."

Dunja didn't know how to respond, but she found herself nodding.

73

THIRTY-SEVEN...THIRTY-EIGHT, she counted to herself before stopping to take a short break. She was already out of breath and she could feel the sweat soaking through her thin blouse. This was more difficult than she'd expected, even though she had crutches to help her along. She hardly felt any pain after swallowing four Tylenol 3s. The hospital had recommended she stay in bed for at least a week to lower the risk of bleeding, but she'd solved that problem with a hospital nappy and three menstrual pads. Her two police guards had initially insisted on following her, but after arguing about it for a bit they'd agreed to stay at the bottom of the stairs and guard the entrance.

She continued up the spiral staircase as she drank the last of the Brämhults Juice she had bought at the Pressbyrån down on Stortorget. She wished she'd bought a bigger bottle. She had wanted the larger size, but chose the smaller out of sheer stubbornness even though the price per litre was the same. It didn't matter anyway. Pretty soon nothing would matter.

Fifty-nine...sixty. She had eighty-six steps left before she was at the top.

Sixty-one.

This was the second time in her life she'd walked up Kärnan tower. The first time was on a class trip in the eighth grade: they'd had to go into the various rooms to look at paintings and hear about how the thirty-five-metre-high tower had been built by the Danes in the early 1300s to keep watch and defend the Øresund inlet, along with Kronborg Castle. All she and her classmates had cared about was counting the steps up to the top as fast as they could.

Glenn Granqvist had been the first one to finish and he claimed there were one hundred and thirty-nine steps, but he was wrong. She remembered it as if it were yesterday—maybe because she'd been the first one up to broadcast the right number. There were one hundred and forty-six steps; no more, no less.

Seventy-four.

She remembered her high school years as the best of her life. She'd been in her prime: top grades in all her classes and she'd still managed to be one of the most popular people in the class. Back then, Ingela Ploghed was the sort of person that people listened to. She'd wanted to become one of the best lawyers in the country and devote all of her energy to helping the weakest people on the bottom rungs of society. She'd had no problem getting accepted to law school in Lund and had loved the student life.

In retrospect, she had no idea how she did so well in school. There wasn't a night without an invite to a party, each one crazier than the last. She would dance herself into a sweat at Västgöta Nation, only to go to a Twin Peaks party dressed as the Log Lady the next day. Two and a half years later, the romance had ended.

One hundred and thirteen.

Late one night, she ran into Gerhard Kempe, her Civil Law lecturer, on her way home from Malmö Nation. He insisted on walking her to her door, and on the way they discussed the considerable differences in salary between male and female lawyers. Gerhard believed male lawyers earned more money because they were better at negotiating and realizing their own worth. She had argued that it didn't matter how much women negotiated, they would still receive lower salaries than men. Now, in retrospect, she would probably agree with him.

Once they arrived at Sparta, the student building she lived in, he asked if they could have a nightcap. She declined, explaining that the last thing she needed was more alcohol. After that, everything happened so fast that all she had left were sporadic memories.

One hundred and twenty-six. A hard blow to the face, falling.

One hundred and twenty-seven. Head hitting the asphalt. Hands everywhere.

One hundred and twenty-eight. Trying to claw her way free, screaming.

One hundred and twenty-nine. More punches. Her front tooth loose. The taste of blood.

One hundred and thirty. The sound of underwear ripping.

One hundred and thirty-one. Eager fat fingers, deep inside her.

One hundred and thirty-two. Giving up, letting him continue.

One hundred and thirty-three. Turned on her stomach.

One hundred and thirty-four. Hair pulled. Pain in her anus.

One hundred and thirty-five. A warning not to tell anyone.

One hundred and thirty-six. Scurrying footsteps, further in the distance.

She ran up the last few stairs as fast as she could and emerged into the daylight, the gentle breeze cooling her sweaty body.

The only visitors aside from her were a Dutch family with two adults and two children. She couldn't understand what they were saying, but she could make out that the daughter standing by the binoculars was begging for money and the son kept stubbornly trying to climb up over the edge.

She went to stand in the corner furthest from the family, struck by the marvellous view. She couldn't recall being this impressed when she was here with her class, which was unusual. As a kid, everything felt bigger, bolder, and deeper, but back then she'd had other concerns.

As usual, Jörgen and Glenn hadn't been able to leave Claes alone; they had lifted him up to the edge of the wall and threatened to throw him over. She could still hear his voice, begging and pleading with them to stop. Their other classmates emerged from the stairwell one at a time, each out of breath and armed with a guess on the number of stairs in the tower. As soon as they realized what was going on with Claes, they'd rushed to the other side of the tower and pretended to enjoy the view.

She had approached Jörgen and Glenn and ordered them to put Claes down. "He'll get down all right," Jörgen replied with a grin. Camilla and Elsa had been there, too. Camilla just stood there staring as they messed with Claes, like she always did. It was as if she'd enjoyed watching Claes suffer. Predictably, Elsa ran her mouth. "Come on! What the hell are you waiting for? The wind is blowing his fucking dandruff around like snow! Oh my God, it's so gross!"

It had felt like an eternity before Monika Krusentierna walked up, announcing the correct number of stairs. She had no intention of acknowledging that Claes was still sobbing, his eyes completely red.

The Dutch family vanished down the stairs and finally she was alone.

She rested her crutches against the wall, took off her sandals, and placed them beside each other along with her watch, headband, and necklace. She felt the pain return as soon as she climbed up and sat on the edge of the wall, but it didn't bother her in the least. She looked out at the roofs and trees far below and let her feet dangle in the air. She'd thought she would feel faint and nauseous, but she only felt a sense of freedom. Soon it would all be over.

She had considered taking her own life after the first rape, even giving it a few clumsy tries. She'd read somewhere that people who failed to take their own lives actually wanted to live, and that the attempt was just a cry for help. But that wasn't true for her. After the incident in Lund she'd started to hate herself until, deep down, she just wanted to die. It was no exaggeration for her to say that the last few years of her life had been nothing but a string of failures.

If she were to point her finger at the criminal who had assaulted her this time, it would only turn into another fiasco. She could identify him: the memory had come back to her in the policewoman's car. She didn't think she'd seen his face, but apparently she had. What did it matter now? No one would believe her anyway. If only it had been someone different, maybe she would have said something, but not him—not a chance. It would be her word against his. A drugged, half-conscious woman, or a...

Ingela Ploghed let go of the thought, closed her eyes, and leaned forward.

FABIAN RISK FOUND AN empty spot right in front of his house. He had found his car key on Hugo Elvin's desk along with a note informing him that his vehicle was out in the car park. Some kind soul had obviously driven it all the way back from Söderåsen.

He locked the car door and started walking toward the terrace house. It didn't feel like coming home—more like he was going to visit someone. Maybe that feeling wasn't too strange, considering he'd only lived there for ten days and had hardly even been in the house for most of them. He'd been gone for three whole days this time, and if he knew Theodor, it had been one long orgy of take-out pizza, computer games, and pounding metal.

He walked up the front steps and put the key in the door; he could already hear the rhythmic pounding of his son's beloved death metal. He had never understood the draw of all that racket: it was more anxiety-inducing than invigorating. But he had promised himself never to complain about his children's taste in music, even if he'd almost broken that vow several times already. His own parents had done nothing *but* complain. They couldn't tell the difference between Kraftwerk, Depeche Mode, and Heaven 17. It was all just "thump thump thump" and "not even real instruments."

"You must be the new neighbour," said a voice behind him.

Fabian turned around and saw a pear-shaped woman in shorts with large pockets, a T-shirt, and a sun hat. She was holding a glass jar full of redcurrants.

"Ulla Stenhammar...we live in number fifteen."

Fabian walked back down the steps and shook hands with the woman. "Hi. Fabian Risk."

"And what's your business, if I may ask?"

"My business?"

"Yes. What do you do for work?"

"So far I'm just on vacation, doing all I can not to think about my job." Fabian forced out a smile for the sake of neighbourliness and hoped that his first impression of this Ulla Stenhammar would turn out to be wrong.

"I just wanted to give you a warm welcome." The woman handed him the jar of redcurrants. "Everyone was always a little curious about who was going to move in here. I was delighted to discover it was a perfectly normal family."

"Oh? Was there something wrong with the old occupants?"

"Not *wrong*...but they were certainly a bit odd, if you ask me. They never came to the spring or autumn parties, and...well, you know how the backyard looks. It's a jungle back there and the bushes block the sun from our entire patio. Moss is the only thing that will grow there, which isn't so nice, if you ask me."

Unfortunately, Fabian was quickly learning that his first impression of Ulla seemed to be accurate. "I promise to do some cutting and pruning as soon as I have time."

"I don't want to interfere."

A silence followed, and Fabian turned back toward the door.

"The walls are pretty thick in these old houses, so you wouldn't think you could hear your neighbours all that much, but let me tell you, you can. Don't ask me how the sound gets through, all I know is that it finds a way."

"Is my son playing his music too loud?"

"I don't know if I would call it *music*, but if he would just turn it down a little at night, then it wouldn't matter. However, none of this noise compares to the Paldynskis...the old neighbours, that is."

"They played music loudly too?"

"No. Well...yes, some classical music, but that wasn't the issue. The fighting was the problem."

"Fighting?"

Ulla moved closer to Fabian, looking over her shoulder as if she were afraid of being overheard. "You can't imagine the way they screamed at each other. It sounded like *Friday the 13th* sometimes. It was so loud that when we were in our bedroom, it felt like they were in the room with us. I can't say anything for sure, but I'm pretty confident he beat her."

Fabian realized that he had to revise his initial impression: this lady was far worse than he'd initially suspected.

"Eventually she took off, and who can blame her? If you ask me, it wasn't the most pleasant way to leave, but that's none of my beeswax. There's nothing worse than a neighbour who sticks their nose in someone else's business."

"I agree. Thanks for the currants." Fabian made another attempt to go up the front steps.

"He had only left for the weekend—Berlin, I think? A strange city, isn't it? I went there on vacation once and we were so tired once we came back that we had to take another vacation right away. But when he got home all the clothes and toys were gone. She had taken the kids with full suitcases and vanished, just like that. It's not very amusing, if you ask me."

Now Fabian understood what the realtor had meant by "private circumstances."

"No, that doesn't sound very nice. Do they have any idea where she went?"

"That's just the point." She held up one index finger and raised an eyebrow as if to emphasize how strange a circumstance it was. "He didn't even seem to care. It was like he just shrugged and went on with his life."

"He didn't try to find them?"

"Not that I know of. He seemed almost relieved, if you ask

me." The woman was shaking her head. "I was just flabber-gasted; I didn't understand it at all. Imagine coming home and finding that the rest of your family had left."

"So no one knows where they went?"

The woman lit up with a big smile. "Well, I was so curious and couldn't keep my mouth shut, so I asked him directly. It turned out that he knew exactly where she had gone, which certainly explained quite a bit of his odd behaviour."

"I see," Fabian said, waiting to hear further details about the former homeowners, which Ulla didn't seem to want to supply. "Didn't he say where they were?"

"No, he only told me he knew where they were. I didn't want to keep prying. Even I have my limits." The neighbour burst out laughing. "But just a week or two ago I heard from the Wingårds in number thirteen that the wife moved to Denmark. As far as I understand she's living with another man there. I think she already knew him before, but that's only my opinion."

"And when did this happen?"

"A few months ago, in the spring. It was only a few weeks before he sold you the house. It makes sense; I'm sure he didn't want to stay here with all those memories."

Fabian walked up the front steps for the umpteenth time. He wondered how he would have reacted if Sonja had done such a thing. He turned the key, opened the door, and admitted to himself that a small part of him would probably feel relieved.

Upstairs, a voice was shouting about the dancing dead, backed by the sound of distorted guitars and rat-a-tat drums.

Even just being rid of this raging racket, which hit him like a wall of garbage as he came in, would be worth quite a bit. *Well, at least he's at home*, Fabian thought. He closed the door behind him and found the house just as he'd left it on Wednesday morning when he'd taken off for the funeral in Denmark. Three days felt like three weeks.

He walked into the kitchen, which bore several traces of Theodor, but not as many as he'd expected. The kitchen was almost pristine, aside from a few remnants of a kebab, a half-eaten pizza that was still in its box, some untouched coleslaw, and an empty Coke bottle. Had Theodor finally learned to clean up after himself?

Marilyn Manson was now screaming lyrics about the world spreading its legs for a star. He had been Theodor's favourite artist for the past few years, and was always on repeat. Fabian could hear why the neighbour had protested, but for now it was only quarter to five, so he wasn't about to go up and ask Theodor to turn down the volume. Instead, he sent him a text to say he was home and suggested they have some coffee out on the deck.

Two minutes later he received an answer: *Playing* Call of Duty *and in the middle of an assignment. Skipping coffee. See you later. T*

The exact response Fabian had expected, and also what he had been hoping for, deep down. Although it would have been nice to have a coffee break, he didn't have the time. He had to get that name before the day was over. A name he'd seen thousands of times but hadn't the faintest memory of—the name of a killer who would strike again if he wasn't stopped.

He had an idea about how to identify the man. It was a long shot, and he wasn't sure it would work, but given that he had nothing else to go on it was worth a try. But first he wanted to take a shower and change into clean clothes. On his way to the bathroom upstairs, he tried to remember the last time he'd gone for more than three days without a shower, and realized it must have been at the Roskilde Festival in 1995.

He could remember it as if it had been just yesterday, despite the buckets of beer and the constant difficulty he'd had keeping his balance. When he looked back, that had been one of the festival's very best years, with Oasis, Blur, The Cure, and Suede. This year's lineup, which included Prince, LCD Soundsystem, and Vampire Weekend, wasn't exactly anything to be ashamed of either. It was so tempting that he'd even suggested to Sonja that they begin their move by attending the festival as a family. She'd asked if he was having a mid-life crisis.

He locked the bathroom door, and carefully loosened the bandage wound tightly around his upper body. He hadn't thought about the stabbing, aching pain for several hours and it was only when he got down to the last few layers of gauze that he remembered how bad his injuries really were. Bloody pus had glued the bandage to his wounds, and he had to get under the shower and wiggle it free bit by bit. The pain went quite beyond his threshold, and he thanked Marilyn Manson, who drowned him out.

After he'd finished loosening the last piece of gauze, he turned the cold water on full blast and let it wash over his inflamed wounds. He enjoyed the sensation for several minutes before soaping up, washing his hair, and stepping onto the bath mat to air-dry.

He looked at himself in the mirror, which usually made him feel young. He was forty-three, but his body looked at least ten years younger. He wasn't carrying around any extra pounds like so many people his age did. He didn't even have the beginnings of a bald spot and hadn't started to go grey. But the man he was looking at right now appeared at least ten years older than usual. He was white as a sheet and his face sagged as if the force of gravity had suddenly doubled. He thought about turning around to get a look at his injuries, but he decided it was better not to.

The next track on Theo's playlist kicked in. Fabian tried to tune out the noise as he got dressed.

His clothes were still packed in the moving boxes beside his bed, and he dug around until he found a pair of clean underwear, socks, a loose red linen shirt to replace the gauze, and a pair of wrinkled linen pants...

He plugged his phone in to charge in the kitchen, and carried the remains of the pizza with him down to the basement. He needed to get to the green filing cabinet, but it was no longer where he'd last seen it. It had been left next to one of the walls in the middle of the cellar, but it wasn't there any more. He didn't know if Sonja had been down there to rearrange things, or if he wasn't remembering correctly. Somehow it felt different down here, as if everything had been moved around.

The basement was full of things that should have been driven straight to the dump, if only Sonja would have allowed it. She couldn't bring herself to throw anything away. She believed that something might turn out to be useful when you least expected it. Her own parents had never saved anything, which meant they had thrown away a minor fortune's worth of kitchen equipment that had gone out of fashion but later became super trendy. Fabian had no idea what he and Sonja were ever going do with broken bikes, sticky car seats, and boxes full of VHS tapes.

Twenty minutes later, he found the green filing cabinet behind an old brown sofa with three demijohns positioned on top. He pulled out the middle drawer, took out his old photo albums, then sat between the demijohns on the sofa and started flipping through them. Several of the pictures had come loose from their tape, leaving his misspelled captions hanging like forgotten ornaments on a discarded Christmas tree.

The pictures had been taken with the Instamatic he had received for his tenth birthday. Although the colours had changed and their sharpness had vanished, the pictures reminded him of when he'd glided further than anyone on his Ramprider skateboard with Tracker trucks and red Kryptonics; gone on a class trip to Copenhagen and eaten three cheeseburgers at the McDonald's across from Tivoli; and piled up the first snow to make Big Mountain, a little hill made of trash, so he could use his mini skis.

Almost all the photos had been taken during holidays between grades four and six. As soon as he started the seventh grade his camera had fallen by the wayside, except for one day in eighth grade when he took it to school and burned up a whole roll of film. He had taken thirty-six pictures of the same subject.

He hadn't thought of this series once in all these years. Klippan's picture of the locker door was the only thing that had sparked his memory. The thirty-six photographs were well hidden in one of the many albums from his school years. He had written the same thing under each photo—a single word:

Lina.

She was in every picture, not always in the centre, or in focus, but the obvious target of each image. You couldn't help but notice the photographer was in love, and Fabian remembered trying to get a shot of her any time Jörgen wasn't around. He'd done all he could to make sure Lina wouldn't notice; the last thing he wanted was to have Jörgen on his back. But now he could see how conscious she had been of his camera: her eyes, pretending to look away; her smile, trying to seem unaware. She'd liked it, and had never said anything to Jörgen. It was their secret.

All of a sudden Fabian looked up from the album. He thought he heard someone shouting, but he couldn't see anything around him to explain the sound. At the same time, he was sure he hadn't imagined what he had heard: somewhere, there was a voice. It was impossible to tell what it was saying—just that it was shouting.

Fabian stood up and followed the voice to the brick wall behind him and immediately relaxed. The wall faced the neighbours' house, so the voice was definitely the neighbour lady he had just spoken to. He went back to the photo album and found the picture he was looking for soon after. Just as he remembered, it showed Lina putting a few books into her locker. The door of the locker next to hers was closed, but the number on it was clear: *349.*

Lina's locker had been right next to the killer's.

75

THE SILVERY-GREY BMW I-SERIES M Coupé had gone from a shiny, top-of-the-line technological wonder to a pile of scrap metal in a matter of seconds.

Ingvar Molander had always loved all German cars, and he had refused to drive any brand other than BMW since the latter half of the 1990s. Examining this demolished vehicle was extremely painful for him. As if that weren't enough, he still hadn't managed to find the cause of the crash, leaving him no choice but to review his notes one more time to ensure there was nothing he had missed.

Left side: dents and severe scratches in circular patterns. The car drove into the side of a truck and struck its middle set of wheels. He had already located the silver paint on the truck's lug nuts. *Blades of grass and dirt are present on all four tyres, especially those on the right front and rear.* The car ricocheted toward the edge of the road and out onto the grass. *Right headlight shattered.* The right front bumper collided with the road sign and the car spun around a few times as it entered the highway again. *The majority of the rear half of the car is crushed.* The truck drove right over it. *There are several severe scratches and dents, primarily to the roof.* It rolled and came to an upside-down stop.

Molander was frustrated. He'd gone through all the information more times than he could count, without finding anything to suggest it was murder. He couldn't find any severed brake lines or loose lug nuts. There was nothing wrong with the steering-column lock or the servo, nor any indication that there had been another passenger in the car or any remote-controlled, foreign entity. The car looked exactly as it should after being run over by a truck and rolling over at 140 kilometres per hour.

He had spent three hours looking at the car — three hours with no results to show for it.

Molander had stopped smoking almost fifteen years ago. Since then, he only had a cigarette on special occasions. He didn't know whether this particular occasion could be considered special, but the smell of cigarette smoke in the car had convinced him that abject failures were also worth a smoke.

He opened the top drawer of his workbench, found the tin of Fisherman's Friend, took a cigarette from the pack of John Silvers, and sat on a chair outside the garage in the evening sun. He lit the cigarette and pulled the smoke as deep into his lungs as he could, trying to find pleasure in defeat.

His phone started to ring. He didn't want to answer it in the middle of a smoke break, with no concept of when he might be able to have another one. The annoying melody persisted; nothing would shut it up, not even limited battery life or a third world war.

"Yes...hello?"

"Hi, it's Irene. I'm just curious how it's going with the car."

"Badly."

"Aren't you finished yet?"

"I am."

"But..."

"I can't find anything that indicates there was foul play."

There was a brief silence. Molander took the opportunity to take another drag of the cigarette, away from the phone; he noticed a tow truck turning into the police lot.

He heard Lilja sigh on the other end. "Then it's probably even more important for me to be here."

"Where is here?"

"Forensic medicine. Braids is going to show Elsa Hallin's body to me. While I'm here I can try to convince him to take a look at Camilla Lindén's body too."

"Haven't they already looked at her?"

"Braids hasn't. She came in as a regular car accident victim."

Now it was Molander's turn to sigh.

"You don't think his autopsy will turn up anything?" Lilja said.

"I don't know what to think any more."

"Are you suggesting that Camilla Lindén wasn't murdered?"

"Car crashes happen. Maybe the perpetrator heard about the accident and told the press he was behind it. And while we're busy putting our resources into trying to find evidence that doesn't exist, he can continue his preparations for the next victim."

"You're thinking of Hallin?"

"Could be—or someone else. After all, our working hypothesis right now is that he won't be finished until the whole class is packed like sardines in the morgue."

"You might be right, but that doesn't change anything for us. All we can do is continue the investigation. I have to go now: Braids is here."

Lilja hung up. Molander stuck the phone back in his pocket, took one last drag, and stubbed out his cigarette on the asphalt. The tow truck backed in and stopped outside his garage. He hadn't realized until just now that it had Danish plates and was towing a Peugeot.

"Are you Molander?" the Danish driver asked.

Molander nodded, signing the delivery slip.

"This is also for you," the driver said, giving him a handwritten note.

Dear Ingvar Molander,

Fabian Risk has spoken highly of you. I hope you can find something conclusive in this car, since nothing is being done here in Denmark.

Best wishes,

Dunja Hougaard

Homicide Unit of the Copenhagen Police

Molander already knew of Dunja Hougaard: she was a competent detective sergeant. But she certainly didn't have the authority to send evidence to Sweden, which meant she had taken a great risk. He looked at the Peugeot, which slid silently to the pavement as the tow truck's cable let it down. He wondered what secrets the car might be hiding. The GPS had already directed Risk to the crime scene over at Söderåsen. Could there really be more?

The perpetrator had put a lot of work into trying to get rid of the car, which suggested that there was more for him to find. The crime scene had been designed to be discovered, with or without a GPS. Risk had surely found it earlier than planned, but the arrangement had been there all along. The killer had likely intended for them to find a planted lead when the time was right. He'd wanted the scene at Söderåsen to be a demonstration of power: to show them how far behind, and above all how helpless, they really were.

But it didn't explain the enormous risk the perpetrator must have taken during the chase with Morten. There must be something else in the car, something that the killer wanted to keep them from finding at all costs.

IRENE LILJA LET HIM have his way. Without interruption, Einar Greide — who was wearing four braids in honour of the day — showed her in great detail how the incision running from under

Elsa Hallin's chin down to her sternum had been done with surgical precision. She tolerated his overly exhaustive explanation of the way the perpetrator had avoided the aorta in order to keep the victim alive for as long as possible. She even let him demonstrate just how the killer might have pulled out Elsa's tongue and draped it across her chest.

She didn't drop the bomb until he was finished.

"Einar, I'm not here to discuss Elsa Hallin."

"Excuse me...what?" Greide looked like a well-trained dog that had just performed its best trick without being offered a treat afterward.

"I know the Colombian necktie is an impressive procedure if you want your victim to suffer as much—and for as long—as possible. And I know you've never seen anything like it; incidentally I haven't either. But I want to talk about someone else."

"Who the hell *are* you here to talk about, then?"

"Camilla Lindén."

"Who on earth is Camilla Lindén?" Einar reminded her even more of an angry mongrel.

"She died in an accident on the E6 yesterday. We suspect our guy is behind it."

"She was in the same class?"

Lilja nodded. Greide started fiddling with one of his braids, something he did only when life wasn't going his way. She knew the last thing she should do right now was pressure him. The slightest attempt to rush the process would have the opposite effect: he would dig in his heels and refuse to lift a finger.

She got the response she'd been hoping for two minutes later. Greide let out a melodramatic, tired sigh accompanied by a restrained shake of the head, and left the room, forcing Lilja to jog after him in order to keep up as they went through the long underground tunnel.

"Arne must have looked at her. You know what his motto is, don't you?" Greide spat. "'Why make things more complicated

398

than they have to be?'" he said, adding air quotes. "But in his case it actually means: Why do your job at all?"

"Einar, we're not even sure if it's true at this point. It's possible it was just an accident."

Greide shook his head. "How could it not be true? This isn't the first time Arne has missed something. His vacation doesn't start until next week, but two weeks ago he was already thinking about as clearly as a mouldy dishrag. Normally I double-check his bodies, but this time I was—"

"Full up with a Colombian necktie."

Greide gave her a look, stopped outside the morgue, and swiped his security pass. Once inside, Lilja went straight over to the wall of cold boxes, while Greide searched for a copy of the autopsy report.

"Here it is. Blah blah blah…*Substantial blow to the head, left posterior*…Blah blah blah…*Fractured skull, meningeal haemorrhage, cerebral swelling, cerebral haemorrhage, clear signs of increased cranial pressure*…Hmm."

"That doesn't sound totally out of left field, does it?" Lilja asked, pulling out the box identified as CAMILLA LINDÉN in scrolling letters.

"No, but it is Head Injury 101. If you're in an accident this violent and you manage to avoid becoming a hamburger, you're very likely to hit your head so hard that you'll die of a cerebral haemorrhage. This report could have been written without even examining the body and still be accurate in eight out of ten cases. The problem is that there's nothing else here." Greide held up the document between his thumb and index finger, waving it with disdain.

Lilja pulled back the sheet covering the naked body.

"There isn't even the smallest description of any distinctive marks on the body," Grede continued. "He's provided no insight or argument of his own. There's not a single observation here beyond the obvious."

"So you don't think he really examined her?"

"I don't *think* it, I *know* it." He let go of the report, which fell to the floor like a piece of trash. He walked over to stand on the opposite side of the body from Lilja.

The eyes were closed, and violent blows and impacts had left obvious marks on the face. Greide pulled on a pair of plastic gloves, rolled the stiff body onto its side and looked at the back of the head, revealing a severe wound and a ring of coagulated blood in the blonde hair. He released the body again, and started fiddling with one of his braids.

"Did you find what he missed?" Lilja regretted the question as soon as she'd asked, but it squeezed out like a mouse through a cracked door; she couldn't help it.

Greide let go of his braid and glared at her as if she deserved to be shot at daybreak. Then he laid his hand across Camilla's closed eyes and opened her eyelids.

Both of her eyes looked like someone had put out a cigarette on them.

76

"I'M GOING OUT TO hit a few balls at six thirty, so let's keep this as short and efficient as possible," Henrik Hammersten said as he took a seat at his desk.

Dunja nodded and sat down in one of the visitor's chairs, with Sleizner beside her. She wanted nothing more than for this meeting to be over so she could continue the investigation and contact the Swedes.

"Dunja, you requested this meeting. So I suggest you start us off."

"That's right." She cleared her throat, which was very dry. "I contacted you because I thought that the recent incidents in Kim's private life had overshadowed everything in this department and were keeping him from leading us in a way that moved our investigation forward."

Hammersten nodded, looking at Sleizner. "Kim? What do you have to say? Is there anything to Dunja's critique?"

Sleizner nodded. "Absolutely. The past few days have been overwhelming, to say the least. My private life has been turned upside down and I've been publicly hung out to dry. My wife left me and took our daughter with her. The fact is, my work is all I have left, and I intend to do my best to perform at the highest level. By the way, we haven't played for a long time. What's your handicap these days?"

"Eighteen point seven."

"Wow. You must have practised quite a bit."

No one can lick boots like Sleizner, Dunja thought. It didn't matter how much shit those boots had walked through, as long as he could benefit from it, he would lap away. Hammersten turned to Dunja. "How are things at the moment? Still the same?"

Dunja thought about it. She wanted to nod, but shook her head. She just wanted to get this over with and get back to work.

"Should I take that to mean you are retracting your statement?"

"As long as I can focus on my work, at least."

"And you're able to do that now?"

"I hope so."

Hammersten moved his gaze over to Sleizner. "And Kim? How do you feel? Do you have anything to add, or are we finished?"

Sleizner ought to have realized that her silence was a gift and the right thing for him to do was to bring the curtain down on their disagreements, sparing Hammersten any further spectacle. But he didn't. Instead, he shifted in his seat, raising one hand to indicate that he was going to start talking.

"Unfortunately, I have to say that my confidence in Dunja is as good as non-existent."

"And why is that?"

"Maybe she can answer that herself, because to be honest I don't understand it either. I've always considered her to be an excellent detective, and there's no question that she has been a great asset to my department. But, unfortunately, I can no longer trust her, and nothing good comes from not being able to trust your co-workers. I believe that wholeheartedly."

"Why can't you trust her?"

She knew it. She'd had a feeling, heard the alarm bells, and yet she'd walked straight into his trap.

Sleizner exhaled. "I don't know where to start. For one thing, Dunja bears most of the responsibility for this whole situation. She's the one who decided to do a search on my phone, and when it turned out to be in the vicinity of Lille Istedgade she called a tip in to *Ekstra Bladet*, which is not what I would describe as 'focusing on my job.'"

She wanted to protest and shout right back at him. But there was no point. It would only reflect badly on her and make her appear even more pathetic in their eyes.

"What's more," Sleizner continued, "when it comes to the work itself, she has gone behind my back on several occasions and acted in complete disregard of my orders. Not only did she forge my signature, she also sent important evidence off to Sweden before our own technicians had time to conduct their examinations. And to top it all off, most recently she tried to withhold the fact that we have a picture of the perpetrator. All things considered, I believe it is out of the question for Dunja to remain with my department."

"Dunja, is it true that you forged Kim's signature?"

Dunja nodded.

"What were you thinking?"

"It was for the sake of the case. Kim was doing everything he could to impede the Swedes' investigation." She could tell Hammersten wasn't listening. He had already made up his mind.

"And his claim that you had a search done on his phone records—is that true as well?"

Dunja nodded again. "But not for the reason Kim thinks. I did it to check whether—"

"That's enough." Hammersten held up his hand and looked at his watch. "Dunja, I'm sorry. I've always thought you were a fantastic police officer, but to be perfectly honest I have no idea what you thought you were doing. I have no choice but to take Kim's side."

He looked at Sleizner, who placed a completed form on the desk with a pleased expression.

"Here is your resignation. It gives you three months' severance. All you have to do is sign it—preferably with your own signature."

403

"And if I don't?"

"I've heard they need people in the Faroe Islands."

Dunja scribbled her name on the dotted line and left the office.

77

ASTRID TUVESSON COULDN'T STOP thinking about Ingela Ploghed and how she had jumped from the Kärnan tower. There were far too many questions, all crowding her brain to get to the front of the line. Was it her own fault? Had she put too much pressure on the woman? And had Ingela really been one of their guy's victims? Or was Risk's theory right—could an entirely different person be responsible? All these questions made it seem even more important for her to find out what had really happened.

She started by using Google Maps to look at all the buildings that might be secluded enough for the perpetrator to perform the operation on Ingela Ploghed undisturbed, but still close enough to the tracks for her subconscious to register the sound of the trains. In the several hours she'd been working the lead, she had managed to visit ten out of the twenty-seven places she planned to see.

Aside from three houses that she'd been able to cross off the list immediately, the rest were mostly offices and workshops, the majority of which were closed for the summer. As a result, she'd spent a lot of time climbing over fences, peeking into windows, and digging through rubbish bins, but all she'd ended up with were dirty fingernails, smelly clothes, and an itchy scalp.

Molander was right. The perpetrator was almost definitely in the midst of planning or committing yet another cunning murder, and here she was looking through the grubby windows of closed businesses.

She turned onto Gamla Rausvägen and took a left. The road was narrow and wound through thick vegetation; it would have been nearly impossible for two cars to pass. She parked the car and walked up to the closed gate to look into the lot. Google Maps had told her that it contained several ponds and separate buildings of various sizes, but she hadn't been able to decipher if they were private homes or if they belonged to some sort of company. Either way, she certainly got the feeling that she wasn't supposed to be there. The place reeked of "Do not trespass. Thanks, but no thanks." The fence was topped with barbed wire, and a sign on the locked gate said AUTHORIZED PERSONS ONLY. She got back in her car, and parked as close to the gate as she could. Then she climbed onto the roof of the car, jumped over the fence, and tried to land as gently as possible to avoid dislocating her hips.

There were three ponds as large as swimming pools to the left of the gravel road, which ran straight ahead, and a pond on the right that was as big as the other three put together. It almost looked like a small lake. An abandoned fishing boat sat directly on the ground beside the road, and she noticed old fishing rods, nets, and lures strewn about. She counted five separate buildings and decided to start with the furthest one on the other side of the three small ponds because it had initially caught her attention on the computer. It was right at the edge of the lot, only thirty metres from the train tracks. As she approached the building she could see it most closely resembled a barracks of about twenty square metres.

A white enamel sign on the green door read KRIGSHAMMAR. A green rectangle around the sign wasn't quite as sun-bleached as the rest of the door, and a few old screw holes revealed that the sign had recently been replaced, probably at the same time as the shiny new locks. She put on a glove and felt the door handle to make sure it was locked.

She walked around the corner of the building, shone her torch into the crawl space, and noticed that the building contained clean-water and wastewater pipes for both a bathroom and a kitchen. A rusty old Vespa was leaning under a window at the back of the building. She climbed up onto the seat and peeked in.

The curtains were drawn, but the gap at the bottom was large enough to see inside. On some sort of workbench, just below the building were a pair of transparent plastic gloves, a few jars and bottles, and a number of tools that would all be at home in the average toolbox.

All but the scalpel.

Her phone started to ring.

"Yes, it's me."

"Klippan here. I think you'd better come in."

"Why? Has something happened?"

"You could say so. I obviously wouldn't have called otherwise. I managed to get hold of eight of the class members."

"Could anyone identify him?"

"No, but they're at least trying to find their yearbooks now."

"How many do you have left to contact?"

"Five, if we're not counting Risk; Lilja's on top of it. Also, she had Braids examine Camilla Lindén again. Apparently she was on that Arne guy's table the first time."

"And?" She could hear the irritation in her own voice, but she brushed it off. She *was* irritated. If something were to happen to her, Klippan was the one who would replace her, and for the most part, there was nothing wrong with that. Klippan was both competent and experienced. He was careful and methodical and there was no task too big—or small—for him. Therein lay the problem: Klippan had a tendency to get caught up in minor details like no one else; they took up his time, and everyone else's too. "Klippan, I don't have time for this. What did Arne miss?"

"Her eyes. As far as I understand, they were completely burned up."

"What do you mean *burned up*?"

407

"I don't know. All Lilja said was that they were burned up."

"By fire?"

"I'm not sure, and for the time being I don't think Braids knows either. The point is her blindness probably caused the crash."

"Wasn't she the one who liked to watch when Claes was bullied?"

"Yes."

"And they're sure that this eye injury wasn't caused by the collision?"

"Yes ma'am."

Tuvesson didn't know what to think—a feeling that was becoming ever more frequent in this investigation. If Camilla Lindén hadn't already been blind when she got in the car, the perpetrator must have blinded her by burning her eyes as she drove, while managing to avoid the crash himself. The more she thought about it, the more confused she became—the killer seemed to have inexplicable supernatural powers. "Do you have more information?"

"If you have time."

"I don't, but go on."

"Camilla Lindén had sole custody of her two children, ages three and five."

"Children? But there weren't any kids in the car."

"Exactly."

"So where are they?"

"I wondered the same thing, so I checked with their pre-school. According to the principal, her ex-husband, Björne Hiertz, picked them up half an hour before the accident."

"Have you contacted him?"

"His number isn't working, and he lives out in Strövelstorp, just a few kilometres from the accident scene. I've sent two officers over, so we'll see where that gets us."

"Okay. Anything else?"

"Do you have more time?"

Tuvesson closed her eyes and put all her energy into keeping herself from exploding.

"Astrid? Are you still there?"

"Yes."

"The Danes finally sent the Peugeot over. Ingvar's working on it now, and won't stop until he finds something."

"Good. Let's hope he does."

"How are things at your end?"

"I don't know, exactly, but I think I found the spot where Ingela Ploghed lost her uterus."

"You think?"

"We can't be sure until we get inside, and we'll need a warrant from Högsell for that. If there's anything there, it has to hold up in court."

"Of course. Well, I'll count on seeing you here soon. We have to talk."

"Isn't that what we're doing now?" She heard a heavy exhale on the other end.

"We have to talk about what we're going to do with the members of the class. I don't want to do it over the phone. I think it would be best for Irene to be there, too."

"I've already told you, I'll check with Malmö to see if they can—"

"Astrid, I don't think we can wait for Malmö. Everyone asks questions when we talk to them, and we don't know how to respond, even though we know they're in danger. The question isn't *if*, but *when* he's going to strike again, and against whom. I don't know about you, but I have the feeling that..."

The deafening roar came out of nowhere and hit Tuvesson like a ton of bricks. She lost her balance and fell off the Vespa. The train came and went, and silence returned before she even had time to hit the ground. She brought the phone to her ear. "Hello? Klippan?" Her phone had dropped the call.

78

THERE WERE ALREADY SEVERAL cars outside Lina Pålsson's house, forcing Fabian Risk to drive past it and park two houses further down the street. He made one last attempt to call, but once again he was met with a voice that informed him that the number was disconnected. Directory enquiries had explained that she'd likely switched to an unlisted number.

He would have preferred not to show up unannounced, but he had no choice. He squeezed past the cars outside the house and rang the bell. A well-groomed man in a suit who was wearing too much cologne opened the door.

"It's open, come on in. Just don't forget these." Cologne held up two blue shoe protectors. "Just shout if you need anything."

Fabian didn't have time to respond before the man vanished back inside. So Lina was in the process of selling the house. That really wasn't so strange. This was her chance to move on. He couldn't say he blamed her.

He himself would never survive in a 1980s building out in Ödåkra. Even just coming for a visit put him in a bad mood. He'd never understood the point of living out in the country while simultaneously crowding into cloned subdivisions.

Some form of life insurance must have been released upon Jörgen's death, and if they didn't have too many loans she could start a new life without an abusive husband. Was that why she had got an unlisted number, or was she trying to escape the killer?

410

Fabian put on the shoe protectors and found the estate agent. "Excuse me, I'm actually here to see Lina Pålsson. Does she happen to be around here somewhere?"

The agent looked at him with a curious expression. "Is this the first time you've been here?"

"Uh, no..."

"Okay, I must have missed you last Wednesday. My bad. Ed Pärsson's the name."

They shook hands.

"Fabian Risk. But that's not—"

"Risk. Sounds like you might put in an exciting bid. But a word of warning might be in order. These days, no one knows where interest rates are headed." The agent clapped Fabian on the shoulder and thrust a prospectus into his hands.

"I'm not here to look at the house. I'm here to see Lina Pålsson." Fabian handed the prospectus back.

"Here's the deal. Lina and I have a reciprocal contract with each other. Which means that she can't have a deal on the side, even if she wanted to. So the bidding will go through me and no one else. All right?"

"Like I said, I'm not at all interested in the house. I just want to get her new phone number."

"And how may I help you?" The agent had deserted Fabian in favour of a middle-aged couple.

"Well, this house was built on a sill plate in the early 1980s. So what kind of shape are the joists in? Because in our house we've had to—"

"You can read all about that in the surveyor's report. But I can tell you right now, the joists have never been better. Do you smell any mould?"

The couple exchanged glances.

"Because I sure don't," the agent continued. "And I can promise you, with this schnoz I could get a job in Customs out at Sturup."

411

Fabian pushed between the agent and the couple. "Excuse me, but does the inspection report include the fact that this was where the Class Killer's first victim lived? Jörgen Pålsson, I think his name was."

"He lived here?" the woman said, at which the agent took Fabian aside and shoved a piece of paper into his hand.

79

IF INGVAR MOLANDER WERE to rank the days of his life, this one would have no problem landing very close to the top of the "worst day ever" list. The question was whether it would take first place, surpassing the day that Ljusne Kätting went bankrupt and he lost all of his savings.

He had received and examined two cars today: two cars that should have contained tons of evidence and clues, but so far he had come up empty.

Lilja had informed him that the BMW driver's eyes were burned, which could explain the crash. But it still didn't explain *how* her eyes had been burned. The same went for the Peugeot. He'd meticulously examined the car without finding even the hint of a clue. Given how much the killer had risked by trying to retrieve the car, it should have contained more than just what Fabian had found on the GPS. There should have been some Kryptonite, something so devastating that the perpetrator's whole plan would be at risk if the police got their hands on it.

He had one last small thing to check, an itty-bitty item he'd saved for last, mostly because it was so silly and obvious that he really didn't believe it would work. The guy they were after was intelligent, almost too smart for his own good—it would be far beneath him to leave such a trace behind. In fact, there was only one reason for Molander to inspect it: just so he could say he had and put an X in another box. He wanted to ensure that no one could come along and call his examination into question or criticize him later on because he hadn't done his due diligence and then some.

He got into the driver's seat and began to brush the steering wheel and the dashboard with white powder.

"How are things going here?" It was Astrid Tuvesson.

"To hell. I don't even want to talk about it."

"I won't make you. We can talk about my day instead."

Molander looked directly at her. "Did you find something?"

Tuvesson nodded. "I think so, at least. But you don't have to look so worried. I won't hold it against you."

"Against me?"

Tuvesson responded with a smile. "Weren't you the one who was so damn sure I wouldn't find anything, and that my search was a complete waste of time?"

Molander stepped out of the car, stretching his back. "Astrid, what did you find, exactly?"

"If I'm right—I think I found the place where Ingela Ploghed's operation took place. It's blocked off, totally isolated, and only twenty or twenty-five metres from the railway tracks. I actually lost my balance out of sheer panic when a train thundered by. I felt like I was right on the tracks. I'm sure that's what Ploghed was reacting to."

Molander considered what she was saying and scratched his stubble, evidence that he had been working non-stop for the past few days. "What's the address?"

"It's on Gamla Rausvägen. A really creepy place with several small ponds."

"I think I know where it is. I was there a few years ago."

"You were? What were you doing there?"

"Fishing. It was a fish farm and you could go rod fishing there."

He grew silent and Tuvesson looked over at the demolished BMW. "I heard she was blinded."

"Yes."

"Do you have any idea how it could have happened?"

"Not yet. There's nothing in the car that could have caused it, and I have a hard time believing that the perpetrator was in the car with her."

"So it must have come from somewhere outside the car, right?"

"Like I said, I have no idea right now. But let's get back to Gamla Rausvägen...Did you go inside? Did you see anything?"

"Just through the window. I didn't want to enter until we have Högsell's approval."

"We'll probably have to wait until after the weekend to get it."

"*Au contraire*," Tuvesson said, holding up a signed warrant, which Molander grabbed and read.

"Like hell."

"This is top priority. Malmö has offered to send their crime scene techs, but you're the only one I want. If you can manage, that is."

Molander smiled. "I've hardly had any sleep in the last few days, so what's another couple of hours? I just have one last thing to check here, and I'll stop by Rausvägen on the way home."

Tuvesson gave Molander a big hug that he didn't know how to respond to; he stood there as stiff as a board, totally caught off guard. "Thanks, Ingvar. What would I do without you?"

"I don't know. But if you don't let go soon, I'll have to report you for sexual harassment."

Tuvesson hissed like a cat and headed for the door, putting an exaggerated swing in her hips. Molander sat back down in the Peugeot's driver's seat and continued to dust powder anywhere someone might conceivably have put their fingers.

Most forensic technicians used gold- or silver-coloured powder and transparent gelatine lifters, but Molander preferred

415

good old white powder and the black lifters, even if they resulted in a negative image that had to be photographed in order to obtain usable prints. The prints were immediately visible, which was an advantage.

He didn't find any prints on the steering wheel or the dashboard. All he found were traces of a microfibre cloth. But he did find them on the gas-tank cover release, around the glove compartment, on the sun visor, and on the buttons that controlled the windows. The perpetrator had cleaned up under pressure, and missed the less obvious places. But this wasn't what caused Molander's heart to beat faster—that honour went to something else entirely. In order to confirm his gut feeling he would have to study the fingerprints under a microscope.

He removed the protective cover from the gelatine lifter cutouts, clipping a corner on each end so he could tell which way was up, and placed the lifter over the prints, pressing out the air bubbles and carefully peeling it back off. Then he reattached the protective cover to secure the print. He climbed out of the car ninety-eight minutes and twenty-two secured prints later; his back on the brink of a slipped disc.

During nearly twenty years as a forensic technician, Molander had seen his share of fingerprints, and had developed an eye that could tell at a glance which finger a print had come from, whether it was from a right or left hand, and whether the prints were all from the same person. Or, as was the case here, whether they were from different people.

Molander had discovered two different sets of prints.

His suspicions were confirmed under the microscope. Twenty of the prints belonged to Rune Schmeckel. The other two, a thumb and an index finger, both from a right hand and in all probability from the same person, belonged to someone else.

Were two fingerprints enough of a reason for the perpetrator to take such a great risk to retrieve the car? Could it really be his motive for killing an innocent woman and a police officer?

In Sweden, being linked to the car was not the same thing as being linked to the murder, so he must have had another motive.

The killer had to be in the database.

Molander put the secured prints in a folder and placed it in the usual spot. He finished by writing an email to Lilja asking her to search the registry.

He had too many other things to do right now.

80

FABIAN RISK TURNED OFF Tögatan onto Frostgatan. A few turns later he was speeding through Väla and accelerating onto the southbound E4. The estate agent seemed to have given him the correct number because Lina Pålsson picked up, which surprised Fabian. What had he expected? That Lina was behind the murders and had gone underground?

He asked why she'd changed numbers, and she told him she hadn't had a choice. Since Jörgen's death, the papers had hounded her day and night for interviews and statements, although she had made it clear she wasn't interested. She explained that she had moved to Norra Hamnen and invited him to stop by as soon as he had the time and desire. He told her that now was a good time, though it was clear from her tone of voice that he'd caught her off guard. After a few seconds, she'd told him to come over and ring the bell when he arrived.

He couldn't help feeling that something wasn't quite right: one moment she made herself inaccessible, only to be excessively hospitable the next. It was like she had been waiting for him to call and ask for her help, like she knew what he was after. She had changed her address and phone number. Could he be the only one who knew where she was, about to fall right into her trap? Should he call Tuvesson and the others and let them know?

But he knew it couldn't be Lina. He was confident the killer was the boy hidden behind Claes. Or at least he thought he was sure. Maybe it wasn't him. Why did he have no memory of this mysterious classmate? Maybe the boy in the picture was just another false lead; maybe the picture had actually been manipulated. Was it possible that someone had exchanged his yearbook for a different one? Maybe one of the movers did it.

Fabian's thoughts were darting in all directions, as wildly as free electrons. It wasn't until he was driving down Hälsovagen that he was able to regain control, thanks to Of Montreal's "Disconnect the Dots," and to determine that his paranoid thinking was likely the result of a lack of sleep. He found a parking spot behind the City Theatre and crossed in front of the old Sandrew cinema, where he'd managed to get into *Halloween* at age twelve but had to ask the projectionist to call his mummy to come pick him up after it was finished.

He crossed Roskildegatan and was delighted to discover that the Kafferepet bakery was still there. Not much had changed in this neighbourhood. It was a different story closer to the Sound. What had once been the city's backside — an industrial area full of railway tracks, shabby warehouses, and rusty silos — had been transformed into a charming marina with boardwalks, restaurants, and cafés during his years in exile.

There was a camera on the entry intercom for Lina's apartment. Fabian tried to look casual. The door clicked open, allowing him to enter. Her apartment door was open, and the scent of freshly brewed coffee wafted into the stairwell. He said hello, but didn't get a response, so he stepped onto the plastic that protected the floor in the hallway, closed the door behind him, and walked further along the crinkly plastic path to a large, unfurnished living room with an open kitchen.

A coffeemaker in the kitchen was sputtering out black poison, and the balcony door was wide open. Fabian walked out and looked across the Sound, busy with traffic, thinking that you couldn't live close enough to boats and the water.

Cars were a completely different matter. He wondered what this apartment must have cost and decided that the view would have gone for over a million kronor.

"Ah, there you are."

Fabian turned around a bit too quickly.

"Oh, I'm sorry. Did I scare you?" Lina put down a tray full of cups and a full coffee pot. Fabian took out the coffee bread he'd brought and laid it on its bag.

"Mmm…from Kafferepet?"

Fabian nodded. "What a fantastic view."

"Thanks. I've wanted to move here ever since they built up the area. But Jörgen refused to leave Ödåkra. *Over my dead body*, he used to say." She poured the coffee. "Milk?"

"Yes, please." Fabian took a sip, thinking it was unusually good for being drip. "Lina, how are you, really?"

She sat down, her eyes wandering out across the Sound. "To be perfectly honest, it's been a long time since I've felt this good."

"You know the killer is still at large, and that there are a number of reasons to believe that he—"

"Yes, but I was never one of the bullies. I never stood there egging them on like Pavlan, and I didn't watch like Camilla."

"But Lina, we no longer believe that his motive is—"

"Fabbe," Lina interrupted, turning to Fabian. "Jörgen's death was the best thing that could have happened to me—not that I wanted him to suffer the way he must have, but he's out of my life at the end of the day. You can't imagine the hell I've been through. It's like I can breathe for the first time since I don't know when. I've been walking around in fear for so long that I just can't handle it any more. Do you know what I mean? I can't keep being scared."

"Why didn't you leave him?"

Lina laughed. "Jörgen Pålsson isn't the kind of guy you just leave." She shook her head as if it were someone else's story she was telling rather than her own. "You needed my help, I believe."

Fabian took out the yearbook and his photo album. "I think I know who the killer is."

She looked him in the eye, her expression revealing that this was the last thing she'd expected to hear. He opened to their ninth-grade class photo and pointed at Claes's hair.

"Can you see how someone else is standing here behind Claes?"

Lina took the yearbook and looked more closely. "Oh yeah...God, who is it?"

Fabian shrugged. "I was hoping you could help me. I don't suppose you happen to have a yearbook? Preferably one from before ninth grade?"

"I'm sorry, I don't have any of that stuff. Jörgen burned it all."

"Burned it?"

Lina nodded. "It was a long time ago, sometime in the early nineties. He and Glenn were gone all night, into the early morning. I remember it clearly because Anki called to ask if I knew where they were. I had no idea, as usual, but they must have been up to some kind of shit, because once he came home I heard him drinking and ripping things off the bookshelf. I'd already gone to bed and I didn't dare get up, because it was never a good idea when he was in that sort of mood. The next morning I saw that he had burned everything from school: pictures, report cards, exercise books, and yearbooks. Everything was gone, turned to ashes in the grill."

"Do you know why?"

Lina shook her head. "I never dared to ask." She returned to the yearbook. "So he's been there all along."

"If it makes you feel better, I didn't see him until late last night, and I don't think anyone else in our class has either. Apparently the people who put the yearbook together didn't even notice him. Everyone is listed but him. See for yourself."

"I believe you. And you're sure it's him?"

Fabian nodded. "All I need is a name, and that's where you come in."

"I don't understand how I can help you. I had no idea there was an extra person in our class. Are you absolutely sure?" She picked up her coffee cup and tried to take a sip despite her shaking hands.

"Lina, his locker was the one to the right of yours."

"What? How—"

"We know which locker was his. Look at this photo." He opened the album and pointed at the photo of Lina with her back to the camera; she was putting books in her locker. Lina looked at the picture and then at the other photos on the page: they were all photos of Lina taken from various angles, more or less aware that she was being photographed.

"Did you take all of these?"

Fabian nodded. "Just so you know, you're the first and hopefully last person I've shown them to."

She met his gaze. "I don't know what to say. Fabian, I'm sorry."

"You don't need to be sorry. There was a time when I would have done everything for you. But that was then. Now I'm happily married, and I don't have any—"

"That's not what I meant," Lina interrupted him. "I just have no idea whose locker was beside mine. It was someone I obviously never spoke to. Was he really in our class?"

"Yes."

"I'm sorry, but I have absolutely no recollection of him."

"Are you sure? Are you absolutely sure?"

Lina nodded her head. Fabian felt the energy draining from his body. Maybe he hadn't been expecting Lina to rattle off the name as soon as he crossed her doorstep, but he had hoped that her memory would be sparked in some way and, in the best-case scenario, that she would have the name on the tip of her tongue. But instead nothing had happened. Lina's memory was just as empty as his own.

"Is it okay if I take a look?"

Fabian let Lina page through to another group of yellowed photos of herself. "I'll never forget that moment." She pointed at a picture where she was about to hit a tennis ball with a flat *brännboll* bat. Jörgen was standing next to her, holding out a round bat.

"What?"

"Don't you remember? Jörgen would get so pissed off. He always wanted me to use the round bat, but I could only ever hit the ball with the flat one. I got a fantastic hit right after this photo was taken. It went so ridiculously far. Don't ask me how, but everyone made it home and I even managed a double round."

"Of course," Fabian said, although he couldn't remember the event at all.

Lina looked at another photo, where she was sitting at a school desk, looking bored. "Oh yes, those German classes. God, I hated those more than anything else. *Aus außer bei mit*...what was it?"

"*Nach seit von zu.*"

"Right. German sure was your speciality."

"Oh, I don't know. It was more—"

"Don't even. I remember how you sat at the very front, always raising your hand and showing off."

"I wasn't showing off. I was just interested. I actually thought it was fun."

"German? Fun? You're kidding."

"*Nein, ich schämten nicht! Für mich war Deutsch immer viel spaß! Immer! Immer!*"

Lina burst into laughter. "What was his name again?"

"Whose name?"

"Our German teacher!"

"Helmut something, wasn't it?"

"That's right, Helmut...Krull...?"

"No, wait...Kroppen...Kroppenheim. That's it! Helmut Kroppenheim!" Fabian felt like he'd just won a lengthy game of Trivial Pursuit.

But Lina didn't give him any applause or hurrahs. Instead, she was looking out at the Sound. "That's right..."

"What?"

"It was so crowded around our lockers. Don't you remember?"

Fabian nodded. He could easily recall how crowded it was, and how you often had to wait your turn to reach your locker. But he didn't want to verbally agree; he knew what was about to happen, and he didn't want to risk disrupting her concentration for anything in the world. It was the very reason he'd come to see her.

"I accidentally backed into him a few times because I didn't even know he was there. And then I would do the very same thing again after the next class. God, it's really awful when you think about it." She shook her head and kept staring out into the distance.

The silence didn't last for more than a few minutes, but it felt like an eternity to Fabian. He started rummaging through his thoughts, trying to find something to say that might get her talking again.

"Oh, that's right...didn't he always sit with Claes?" she said suddenly, turning to Fabian. "After all, no one else wanted to sit with him."

Fabian nodded, although all he could remember was that Claes usually sat as close to the teacher's desk as possible. He had no idea who'd sat beside him. But Lina was right. It couldn't be anyone but him.

"Wait, I've got it. Torgny...wasn't that his name?" she continued, looking at Fabian. "Torgny Sölmedal."

Fabian repeated the name to himself and realized that this wasn't the first time his name had popped up in the investigation.

81

KLIPPAN DOLED OUT THE generic-looking hamburgers, fries, and Cokes to Lilja and Tuvesson, who were sitting in silence, trying to interpret the various *hmm*s from his phone call. They were alone in the seating area outside the grill on Rundgången, a stone's throw from the police station. Klippan had insisted on sitting outdoors: after what had happened with the camera at Söderåsen, he didn't want to take any chances that the perpetrator might be listening.

"Great. I'll call if that happens." Klippan stuck his phone in his shirt pocket and took a very large bite of his burger. Tuvesson and Lilja waited patiently for him to chew and swallow, only to watch as he took another bite.

"I don't suppose you were planning on telling us what was said," Tuvesson said.

Klippan pointed at his hard-working mouth. "Sorry, but I'm awfully hungry. Camilla's kids are with their father."

"Oh, thank God."

"So far so good. The problem is, he's not the one who picked them up from preschool," Klippan said, devouring another bite of the hamburger.

Tuvesson and Lilja had no choice but to wait for him to finish. "Let me get this straight: the kids are with Björne Hiertz, but he's not the one who picked them up, even though that's what the preschool says happened?" Lilja asked.

Klippan bowed his head in agreement and started speaking,

even though he wasn't done chewing. "Since their dad doesn't have custody of the children, I'm guessing he's probably never been to the preschool, or at most maybe been there once, which made it pretty simple for the perpetrator to pass himself off as their father. Remind me to send the preschool director a picture of Björne tomorrow."

Tuvesson and Lilja exchanged glances. "How did the kids get to their father?"

"That's the peculiar thing." Klippan filled his mouth with fries. "Our guy dropped them off at his house."

"What? The killer was there?"

Klippan nodded. "Apparently there was quite a bit of confusion, initially. Obviously Björne had no idea the kids were coming."

"How did the killer explain the situation?"

"He told Björne about the accident on the E6 and identified himself as a father with kids at the same preschool, which was why he was dropping his children off."

"I don't understand why he would have devoted so much time to picking up and dropping off the victim's kids," Tuvesson said.

"Or why their mum was on her way north on the E6 instead of heading for the preschool," Lilja added.

"She did go to the preschool, but the kids weren't there. The staff told her what they told us — their dad had already been by to pick them up," Klippan said. "Which means the killer probably knew she would drive to Strövelstorp to get them."

"So he tailed her from the preschool," Lilja said.

"It still doesn't explain how he managed to burn her eyes," said Tuvesson. They stopped speaking and went back to their food, which had grown cold and even more tasteless, if that was possible. Tuvesson gave up with half her burger left and pushed her paper plate away. "But I think we should put the cause of death on the back burner for the time being and focus on catching the killer. How many of the classmates have we contacted so far?"

"I've got a hold of eight," Klippan said.

"Four for me," said Lilja.

"So we've been in touch with all but one of them."

"Yes, assuming we're not including Risk."

"We're not. Who haven't we managed to get hold of?"

"Seth Kårheden," said Lilja.

"Right—the pilgrimage guy," Klippan said. "Isn't he supposed to land at Kastrup tonight?"

Lilja nodded and drank the last of her Coke.

"And so far nobody remembers any extra members of their class?" Tuvesson asked.

Klippan shook his head.

"Stefan Munthe and Annika Nilsson said they had a vague memory of someone else," Lilja said.

"Why are you just telling us this now? Do we have a name?"

"Unfortunately we don't."

Tuvesson sighed. She had lost her appetite for examining each clue from all angles, reasoning through every possibility, and trying to see connections that everyone else had missed, that might not even exist. It was all to catch a killer that no one could remember, but soon would never be able to forget.

"Astrid, we can't just give up," Klippan said.

"Of course we're not going to quit. Who said anything about giving up?" She saw Lilja and Klippan exchanging glances out of the corner of her eye. "But how do we move forward?"

"If I may, I believe we are obligated to provide some form of protection for the remaining members of the class. They are clearly in danger, and it would be irresponsible not to look after them," Klippan said.

"How many of them are abroad right now?" Tuvesson asked.

"Four of mine, but two are coming back tomorrow," responded Klippan.

"Just the pilgrim is away from my bunch but he'll be returning soon," Lilja said.

"Are any of them holidaying in Sweden?"

"No, but Christine Vingåker is renting a house with her family up in Lysekil."

"So we're down to eleven members of the class. Have any of them moved more than four hundred kilometres away from Skåne?"

"Lotta Ting lives in Oslo," said Lilja.

Klippan shook his head. "None from my group."

"Ten left. We'll need twenty men in place around the clock. If we count shifts, we're up to at least fifty officers," Tuvesson said. "How many people do you think we can scrape together from our office? Five officers? You can see the problem for yourselves."

"What about Malmö?" Klippan said. "Haven't you spoken with them yet?"

"Yes, but they can only spare ten, which is more than I'd expected. They'll be here on Monday."

Klippan released a long sigh. "We can't let him continue to pick people off one by one. He *will* keep going, and right now... dammit, right now they're sitting ducks."

Tuvesson could only concur.

"What if we gather everyone up?" Lilja said. "Collect the class members and put them all in one place. Then our five guys would be enough to protect them, don't you think?"

Klippan nodded. Tuvesson shrugged.

"What sort of place do you have in mind?"

"I'm not sure. What about getting some hotel rooms? It could be someone's house... or anywhere really?"

"I've got it!" Klippan said. Both Tuvesson and Lilja turned to look at him. He looked like he'd just hit the triple word score with both Z and Q. "I can't believe I didn't think of it sooner. The only question is whether we can convince them all to go along with it."

"*Where*, Klippan?" Tuvesson asked, but it was too late. He'd already taken a very large bite of her hamburger.

82

FABIAN RISK LOCKED HIS car and hurried across the street; his heart was pounding much faster than usual. He felt like he was finally starting to see light at the end of the tunnel. Lina Pålsson had remembered the perpetrator's name, just as he'd hoped. He had discovered the killer's name and now he wanted to pass the information on to his colleagues so they could do the rest. With a name like Torgny Sölmedal, the man's address shouldn't be hard to find.

It was already past nine when he unlocked the door to the house at Pålsjögatan 17. It was quiet, with no Marilyn Manson to greet him. Did he dare hope that Theodor had finally grown tired of sitting alone in his room, destroying his ears? Or had that neighbour lady come over to complain?

The kitchen looked just as he'd left it earlier that evening, which meant that Theodor probably hadn't eaten in several hours. He was most likely caught up in *Call of Duty* and hadn't had time to notice how hungry he was. Fabian didn't understand how computer games contributed to teens' weight gain; in his experience it was the other way around. He yelled that he was home, but didn't receive an answer, so he took out his phone and sent a text: *Hi Theo, I'm home now. Where are you? I was thinking we could go and have a nice dinner at Pålsjö Krog in about half an hour. Dad.*

In just half an hour, he would kick off his vacation by calling Sonja and asking her and Matilda to get the first train back.

Then he would drag Theodor out of his room and order him to experience their new hometown. On a warm summer evening like this, there was nothing better than a walk down the hill and through the woods to Pålsjö Krog.

He logged onto his laptop at the same time that Theodor's reply popped up on his phone. *I'm home. Still playing CoD. Headphones on. But Pålsjö Krog sounds good. Do they have burgers?*

Fabian laughed. *I'm sure they do, but am afraid they're about a hundred times better than McD's.*

Sweet, Theo replied.

Fabian focused on his computer again. He went to Eniro, the online directory, and typed "Torgny Sölmedal" into the search box. Just as he'd expected, there was only one person with that name, and he lived in Helsingborg—at Motalagatan 24 in Husensjö. A Google search, however, turned up 879 hits, which surprised Fabian; he had only been expecting a link back to Eniro.

There was a paid link at the top of the Google list: SÖLMEDAL ENGINEERING AB—INVENTIONS, DESIGNS, BUILDS—NO TECHNICAL PROBLEM IS IMPOSSIBLE FOR US!

Of course he owns an engineering firm, Fabian thought, scrolling down through the rest of the search results. Most concerned various patents on everything from small-machine parts to electronic operating systems. A few pages later he found a link that interested him: READ MORE ABOUT T. SÖLMEDAL, which relayed him back to Sölmedal Engineering AB.

> *Torgny Sölmedal was born in Ekeby on August 12, 1966. He stands 6'1" above the ground and burdens the earth with less than 160 pounds. He is ambidextrous and has an IQ of 131 and above, depending on the test. He has loved to build things ever since he received a Meccano set for Christmas when he was a child. In 1986 he started Sölmedal Engineering AB, with the motto*

that there are no problems that can't be solved; his
work has resulted in a number of patents as well as eco-
nomic independence. He continues to run his company
because—in his own words—"it's fun."

"Because it's fun," Fabian repeated to himself; he didn't know whether he should laugh or cry. A few results down he found a link to an article that piqued his interest. It was about the operation in which Rune Schmeckel had failed to remove two plastic clips from a man's bladder during an operation. *The patient, Torgny Sölmedal, is not planning to file suit at this time,* he read. Was that why he'd chosen Claes Mällvik as his main victim? First he had taken all the attention away from him in school, and then he'd supervised this catastrophic surgery.

Fabian's thoughts were interrupted by a strange sound coming from upstairs. It grew louder and louder, and sounded like someone was speaking through a megaphone. A minute later he heard an audience whistling and applauding. He realized Marilyn Manson was back on again, right before the drums and distorted guitars thundered to life at top volume, proclaiming the singer as all-American.

It was thirteen minutes past nine—not all that late. But considering that the neighbour had already expressed her displeasure, albeit in mild terms, and that Marilyn had probably been screaming at the top of his lungs all day, Fabian thought enough was enough and headed for the stairs.

The song was repeating a single swear word over and over again.

The volume was considerably louder on the second floor; it was nearly unbearable. He didn't understand how Theodor could even stand to be in the same room as those speakers. Was that why he was using headphones? Something seemed off. The door was ajar. Fabian was about to open it when his phone started vibrating in his pocket: it was Sonja calling. She was probably wondering how everything was going. He'd been meaning to call her but hadn't had the chance, so he hurried back downstairs, went out on the deck to shut out as much of the music as possible, and answered the phone.

"Hi darling."

"It rang for a while—am I calling at a bad time?"

"No, not at all."

"I mostly just wanted to check and see how you're doing."

"Oh, I don't know, about as expected, I suppose," Fabian said, realizing that he hadn't even thought about his burns for the past few hours.

"Are you still at the hospital?"

"No, I just got home. Sonja, I—"

"So you've seen Theo. Has he been okay alone?"

"Uh…yes, I think so. We've actually only texted so far, but at least he responds. His stereo is turned up so loud that it feels like my ears are about to—"

"Fabian, I met her."

"Huh? What? Who?"

"Niva Ekenhielm. We had coffee today. Lisen took Matilda, so we had time for a good long talk."

Fabian didn't know how to respond.

"She told me everything: every tiny, intimate detail. I wanted you to know."

She just doesn't give up, Fabian thought. Niva couldn't leave him and his family in peace. Was it because he had asked her for a favour? He wondered exactly what she'd told Sonja and how many liberties her active imagination and wishful thinking had taken this time. He wanted to protest—to tell Sonja that Niva had surely exaggerated her story to drive a wedge between them—but he stopped himself, realizing that it didn't matter in the end. He had lost this match long ago.

"Do you feel better?"

"I don't know. Maybe?"

"Is there anything you want to talk about?"

"Not right now."

He waited for her to say more, but she didn't. She obviously wanted him to say something, so he did: "I love you. Just so you know, I love you."

"Call me when you're finished. And can you tell Theo that he has to answer when someone calls him?"

"Darling, you can actually go ahead and book a ticket—"

He heard a click in his ear, stuck the phone back in his pocket with a disappointed exhale, and walked inside.

Marilyn Manson was still singing about raping the rapers.

As he walked back up the stairs to the second floor, he was overcome by a feeling that was growing stronger and stronger—a feeling he'd had since he stepped into the house. He stood outside Theodor's bedroom. He was sure that something was wrong, horribly wrong. He pushed open the door and stormed into the room.

The music was at fever pitch now.

He pressed button after button on the stereo, but it stubbornly continued to project a chain of expletives that assaulted his ears.

He finally yanked the entire stereo loose, cables and all, and threw it on the floor. The subsequent silence was anything but enjoyable. He knew it was pointless, but he still looked under the bed, behind the curtains, and in the wardrobe. Theodor was not in his room.

He shouted for his son over and over, as loudly as he could, even though he didn't expect a reply. He screamed until he had to stop, collapsing onto the edge of the bed to gather his thoughts, but he couldn't. Something inside him just kept wanting to panic and cry, as if he knew deep down that all was lost, that it was all his fault.

He closed his eyes and tried to force himself to take deep, slow breaths. A few minutes later he opened his eyes and looked around the room. Had Theodor even been here when he'd

434

returned home earlier? He had been welcomed by the same album of hellish noise then. He started to think about it, and realized that he'd last seen Theodor when they'd gone to a movie and taken the ferry to Denmark — on Tuesday. Now it was Friday. They hadn't spoken for three whole days.

Sonja had nagged him to call his son, which he'd done. But there had been no answer, except in the form of texts. He'd been satisfied with that response. He had never heard his son's voice, but had been content with his replies in writing.

He had only been thinking about the investigation.

Fabian put his head in his hands, hoping it would turn out that Theodor had just run away from home. It would be perfectly understandable: he probably would have done the very same thing himself. But Fabian was sure that wasn't what had happened. He was absolutely certain that something else was behind it, something much worse.

He stood up and started searching the room for clues. Most of Theodor's belongings were still in moving boxes. Aside from some clothes, only the computer and stereo had been properly unpacked. There was a black notebook he'd never seen before in the middle of the desk. A pen was stuck in the cord that held it closed. He pulled the pen out, loosened the cord, and opened the notebook.

This diary belongs to:

Theodor Nils Risk

If you are not the person listed above, and do not have permission from the person listed above, close this book immediately.

Did his son really keep a diary? He started flipping through it.

This is the first time I'm writing in you even though I got you
for Christmas two years ago from Mum. She said it's always
good to write down your thoughts so that you don't forget
anything...I've tried to smell my own BO. I don't think I smell.
But I know I'm ugly—ugly as shit...I hate school. I hate it!...
heard them looking for me and yelling that I was gay...they
punched me in the stomach and said it was my fault...spat
in my face...I hate them so much. They don't understand a
goddamn thing...they took my hat and peed on it and made
me put it on again...

Hate myself!...Laban was lying in his cage like he was
sleeping, but he wasn't sleeping. I stuck a needle in his back
to get him up. At first he squeaked and tried to get away but I
held him down super hard...super funny...walked up to one
of them, and hit him in the face with the brass knuckles under
my mitten...yanked him down to the ground, and started
pounding his head on the pavement...most awesome thing
I've ever done. Well, since the first time I went to Legoland...

July 7

It's been a week since we moved to this shithole. Dad's
fucking idea. Everything is supposed to be so fucking nice
and super-duper great here—like hell it is. He's good at
promising...this is like a slow, drawn-out hell.... I'm just
sitting here alone, hating...playing CoD...Dad took me to a
fucking piece of shit movie and tried to talk to me. So fucking
pathetic...I feel like hitting someone so goddamn hard. Just
dragging it out and

The last entry ended abruptly, as if he'd been interrupted
mid-thought. Fabian didn't know how to interpret the diary. It
was no secret that Theodor had had a difficult time at school
and that he'd been involved in a number of fights. But this was

something else entirely. Did Sonja know? He turned the page to make sure there was nothing more.

If you ever want to see your beloved little good-for-nothing son again I suggest you put on the baseball cap sitting on the moving box to the left and follow my instructions. I. M.

Fabian couldn't breathe. Deep down he'd known since he stepped into the room, but now he had proof. Everything was spinning and he was forced to sit down on the bed again before he lost his balance. The killer had been here—in his house— and taken his son. The pattern had definitely been broken. Until now, he'd only been after the people in his class—not their children. This was different. He took out his phone and sent a text to Theodor. *Come on down. Let's go. Your burger awaits…*

His hands were shaking so much that he had to put down the phone while he waited for a reply. It arrived much more quickly than he'd expected. *Nice try, but you'd better follow my advice.*

Fabian realized he had no choice and looked around the room for the hat. He found it quickly. It was black with a brim. He'd seen caps like it before: it had five LED lights on the front that could be illuminated at the push of a button. He'd thought about buying one himself the last time he was at Clas Ohlson, but had decided against it when he imagined Sonja's teasing voice in his head.

He picked up the cap—the eye of a camera had replaced the middle light on the brim. He hesitated, trying to think through the alternatives, but quickly realized he had none, and put the cap on his head. It fitted perfectly, as if it had already been adjusted for him. He received another text: *Log in at http://89.162.38.99:8099/cam12 password: aLmos1oVer*

Fabian did as he was told. A grainy image appeared on the screen showing Theodor lying on his back in a narrow space with his hands bound. He had obviously tried to free himself because he had bloody wounds on his arms and hands. He lifted his head and stared straight at the camera, completely terrified. He looked like he was screaming for his life.

"Theo, where are you? Tell me where you are and I'll come get you!" Fabian shouted at his phone.

He can't hear you.

"What about you? Can you hear me?!"

No one knows how long the oxygen will last. All I know for certain is that it's running out. It could be tomorrow, or maybe next week, or in two hours?

"Why bring my son into this? What does he have to do with anything? Take me instead!"

You have a task to complete if you ever want to see him alive again.

Fabian looked at his phone. He wanted to see Theo again and tried to type in the login information for the second time. But instead of seeing an image from the webcam, he received a message: Incorrect password! Unauthorized Entry Denied. He tried again but got an identical notice.

Get in your car, drive to the police station, park there, and don't let anyone see you.

Fabian didn't even have time to wonder what he could expect before another message popped up.

Tick tock, tick tock...

83

"ALL WE KNOW FOR certain right now is that it will take place at ten o'clock tomorrow morning, but speculation on the topic is already in full swing. Do you have any comment?" asked one striped tie to the other.

"Yes, this is absolutely the last straw. Considering what we learned yesterday, Kim Sleizner should have held a press conference right away, but gave an exclusive interview to *Ekstra Bladet* instead, which is far from sufficient to rebuild trust in the police. Tomorrow's press conference is absolutely crucial."

Dunja Hougaard wasn't surprised in the least. When it came to Sleizner, nothing would shock her any more. She felt like she had been drained of all her energy since his latest sneaky move. She pushed the button on the remote control and the ties were replaced by a young Julia Roberts, who was standing on Hollywood Boulevard next to a red Ferrari along with her prostitute friend. *"And remember, don't mouth off. They don't like that."* Dunja had watched the scene at least a hundred times and decided it must be the most frequently shown movie on TV ever.

As much as she didn't want to, she couldn't help flipping back to the news.

"And what do you think the topic will be?"

"It's likely that he'll announce his resignation and try to spin it as his own decision."

"Does that mean he's actually been fired?"

"Yes, in all likelihood. But a man with Sleizner's experience and competence will always be in demand. There's even talk that he could become our next Minister of Justice, so who knows what he's got up his sleeve."

"What if the press conference isn't about his resignation?"

"Then he'll have to have a tangible lead in the investigation—something to show that it's moving forward and that he's still a force to be reckoned with in the police corps."

"But you don't consider that likely?"

"No."

Dunja turned off the TV, then yanked the batteries out of the remote and threw it across the room so she wouldn't be tempted to turn it on again. She knew exactly what Sleizner's little press conference was going to be about: the picture of the killer.

Her picture.

Sleizner would beat his chest and hammer home the message that the department functioned very well while he was in charge—so well, in fact, that the Danes, not the Swedes, would soon solve the case and catch the killer.

As if Kim Fucking Sleizner gave a shit about the case.

It was all just a charade, a spectacle to take attention away from his private scandal. He had no interest in co-ordinating with the Swedes to find out what leads or theories they'd come up with, he was just taking the opportunity to toot his own horn. This press conference was about him and only him, no matter what it cost in the end.

He had lied straight to her face without batting an eye, sacrificing both her and her work. The ink on her resignation hardly had time to dry before he'd demanded her keys, badge, security card, and service weapon. He'd given her two minutes to gather her belongings in a box, watching over her shoulder the whole time like a hawk.

She had been tossed out in the cold like Fabian Risk, and just like him she couldn't let it slide. There was no chance that she would be able to keep herself from working on the case as long as it remained unsolved.

She didn't know what sort of ripple effect to expect from Sleizner's press conference the next morning, but she was prepared for the worst. The killer would probably go underground, becoming nearly impossible to find. The longer he remained uncertain about how much the police knew, the better. It increased the chances that he would eventually become overconfident and careless, and that he'd make a fatal mistake.

She had to do something. She couldn't stop Sleizner from publishing the picture, but she could make sure the Swedes got it first. She picked up her phone and called Fabian Risk. The phone rang, but no one answered. It was only twenty past nine, which wasn't super early, but also not exactly too late to call. She tried again, this time leaving a short message to say that she had something he needed to see and that she was on her way to Sweden to show him.

Since there was a possibility that someone had tapped his phone, she didn't want to specify what she had to show him. She hadn't initially planned to say she was on her way to Sweden, but now that she thought about it, it didn't seem like such a bad idea. She could send him the photo via email but, just like his phone, she couldn't assume that Risk was the only one who had access to it.

Dunja opened her computer and launched her email client. But her inbox didn't appear; instead, the program asked for a password. She typed in "Shawarmapie55"—a password she used in far too many places and ought to change as soon as she had time.

Incorrect password

She tried again.

Incorrect password

441

Had that bastard already managed to get her password changed? If he had, she could only think of one person who could have helped him.

"Yes, this is Rønning..."

"Did you change my email password?"

"Well hello there, sexy. Listen, I'm kind of busy," he whispered. "I have company and we're almost finished with our sushi—"

"Mikael, for Christ's sake," Dunja interrupted. "This is important. Are you the one who changed it?"

She could hear him sigh as the theme from *Titanic* played in the background.

"I heard you quit."

"The Sleazeball didn't give me a choice, and I have to get into my mail."

Another sigh.

"He came over as soon as you were gone and ordered me to change it. Technically, from a legal perspective, it isn't really your email."

"Mikael, it is extremely important for me to log onto my email right now. Not later. Now. Understood?"

"Why?"

"The less you know the better, so you'll just have to trust me. All you have to do is give me the new password."

"I'm sorry, I really can't. Sleizner is almost definitely going through your inbox this very second and he'll notice right away if another IP address tries to get in. As soon as he realizes it belongs to you, he'll know that I helped you."

He was right. Shit.

"But...I had a feeling you would call, so I made a copy of your entire hard drive before Sleizner could get his hands on it. I can put up a Dropbox folder."

"Perfect, and preferably right away."

"Sure. My visitor and exercise ball seem to have found a way to each other during this conversation."

442

Twenty-five minutes later, Dunja was able to transfer the picture of the killer to a USB stick. Fifteen minutes after that, she had cleaned the dried ink from the cartridges and printed it out. Ten seconds later, she left her apartment on Blågårdsgade and hurried toward Nørreport Station.

84

"THE JAIL?" TUVESSON REPEATED.

"Why not? It would only be for the weekend," Klippan said. "It's already under guard, and then we wouldn't have to wait for Malmö to send people over. On Monday we can decide if there's a better solution."

They had left the grill and were following Rundgången to the right; they could see both the prison and the police station on the other side of the street. Tuvesson hadn't decided what she thought of the idea of sending the class to the jail. It would certainly be a drastic solution, and wouldn't exactly be uncontroversial, but maybe, in the end, it was the least terrible idea.

"Let's be honest — it's the obvious thing to do. What choice do we have?" Klippan said, as if he were reading her mind.

"Do you know how much shit we'll have to take for this?"

"It'll be nothing compared to how much shit we'll have to take if we don't act and keep letting him pick them off one by one."

Klippan was right. They had every reason to believe that the perpetrator might strike again at any moment and that he had no intention of stopping until the whole class was wiped out. The main point in favour of the plan was, in fact, time. If they started now, and if everything went smoothly, they could gather everyone during the night. The main point against it was the plan itself.

"Didn't Risk take his car home?" Lilja pointed at Risk's car, which was parked outside the police station.

"I guess not," Klippan said. "He's probably still not in any condition to drive."

"Okay, let's do it," said Tuvesson. "We'll bring the rest of the class in over the weekend. In order for this to work, we have to make sure we keep as low a profile as possible and tell people only on a need-to-know basis. We have to keep this from leaking to the press at all costs—the whole plan depends on it."

SOMEWHERE, HIS SON WAS lying with hands and feet bound in a space as narrow as a coffin—and the oxygen might run out at any moment. Maybe it already had. The image of Theodor locked in that room was etched into Fabian's mind; he couldn't stop thinking about what his son was going through, not just right now but during all his years in school. How could he have failed to notice? Had he really been that self-absorbed? What about Sonja? If she'd known, she would have told him, right?

He remembered one occasion when she had said she was worried about Theodor after he came home with two broken ribs and a concussion. He'd thought she was overreacting and believed it was a normal part of growing up—boys Theo's age got in fights. He had even bragged a bit, saying that he once broke a rib by coughing when he had a bad cold.

But Sonja hadn't given in; instead, she'd had a serious talk with his teacher and attended classes to get a picture of their son's situation at school. Everything had seemed perfectly normal, just as Fabian and Theodor had said all along. In the end she let it go and agreed that she had overreacted.

He had been so wrong—so terribly wrong.

But now it was time to pay the piper—and he was the only one who could do it. He would pay up, no matter what the cost. He would perform whatever task he was assigned. If there was still any chance he could save Theodor, he was prepared to throw everything else overboard. Neither the investigation nor his own life mattered any more. Being too late wasn't an option.

445

He was following every order to the letter—he'd used the most direct route to drive to the station, parked away from other cars, and kept the baseball cap on the entire time. The perpetrator, or Torgny Sölmedal as Fabian now knew he was called, could see and hear the same things as him. But all their communication was via text: the Danish policewoman had called him, but he'd been forbidden from answering his phone.

None of his colleagues were in sight when he stepped through the entrance, which was illuminated in the dark. There was no Florian Nilsson behind the reception desk, so he was able to swipe his access card through the reader, enter the code, and walk in. He needed to get to Ingvar Molander's lab. He had never been there, but he knew it was somewhere on the bottom floor. He'd asked the perpetrator what he should do if it turned out Molander was there, and he received a swift answer:

Take care of it.

TECHNICAL INVESTIGATION I: MOLANDER read the sign beside the closed door. Fabian stuck his hand in his jacket pocket to make sure that his service weapon was ready, opened the door, and walked in. The room looked like a large garage: the floor and walls were made of concrete and there were a number of well-lit islands that functioned as workstations. Molander was nowhere to be seen.

Stand in the middle, turn around once. Slowly.

Fabian did as he was told, realizing that the perpetrator didn't know what he was looking for either. It was clear the killer suspected that Molander had found something, which was what Fabian was here to find out.

Take a rag, go over to the Peugeot.

Fabian's eyes had been so focused on the demolished silver-grey BMW that he hadn't even realized that the Peugeot was there until he got the text. The Danes had finally come to their senses and shipped it over. He walked up and read the handwritten note on the windscreen.

Dear Ingvar Molander,

Fabian Risk has spoken highly of you. I hope you can find something conclusive in this car, since nothing is being done here in Denmark.

Best wishes,

Dunja Hougaard

Homicide Unit of the Copenhagen Police

So the Danish woman was behind it. As soon as this was over—if he survived, that is—he would get in touch to thank her. The value of a useful contact on the other side of the Sound couldn't be overestimated.

Get in the driver's seat and look around.

Fabian opened the driver's side door, sat behind the wheel, and scanned the interior of the car. There were small pieces of tape with arrows and numbers on the dashboard, around the glove compartment, and on the gearstick, to mark places where Molander had found and secured fingerprints. Was that why the car was so important to the killer?

Remove the markers—wipe everything.

Fabian removed the pieces of tape and started wiping down the panel. Now and then he received a reprimand telling him to wipe more thoroughly or aim the camera in a different direction. Twenty-two minutes later, he was allowed to step out of the car.

Go get the prints.

"Unfortunately I have no idea where they are."

Find them.

IT'S PROBABLY BETWEEN NINE *and ten, maybe nine thirty but definitely not quarter to,* Astrid Tuvesson thought, although she didn't really care. No matter what they did, she couldn't shake the feeling that they were a step behind, that in some incomprehensible way this had all been planned and predetermined. But Klippan was right: it would have been seriously irresponsible not to offer the rest of the students from the class temporary, secure housing.

She lay down on the sofa after drawing the curtains and turning off all the lights. Unfortunately, it wasn't as dark as she'd hoped—about fifteen blinking diodes made sure of that. She didn't understand why electronics manufacturers still insisted on putting diodes everywhere, and decided they must have watched too much science fiction when they were kids.

Earlier she had spoken with Ragnar Palm, who was in charge of the jail, to explain their situation. He had only been able to offer her two empty cells, which could provide space for four of the ten at the most. A group cell would have been perfect, but as far as she knew there were none of those in Sweden. Instead, Palm had offered to block off parts of the detainees' common areas, where it would be no problem to fit ten beds. They would have access to the TV room, a kitchen, and a small library, which would help them feel less like prisoners.

Lilja and Klippan had offered to call around to inform everyone of the plan, so Tuvesson could use the time to get some rest; something told her this was her last chance. Unfortunately, her brain was refusing to take a break and seemed to have decided to speed up while the rest of her was trying to hit the brakes.

Ingela Ploghed swirled into her thoughts. That fragile little woman had felt so unwell and hadn't wanted to come for a ride in her car. In fact, she had tried to refuse, but Tuvesson had chosen not to listen to Ingela Ploghed or the doctor. Instead she'd pushed her as hard as she could, and felt that Ingela's memories had come back to her when they were by the tracks. She believed the sound of the train had sparked the woman's subconscious. It had lit up in the darkness with a bright, orange light.

The sun was making her sweat. The warmth was radiating throughout her body, causing her pulse to race and pump all that orange light around. She loved heat and couldn't get enough of it: thirty, thirty-five degrees, a chaise longue, and the sound of waves hitting the beach in Koh Chang. What could be better? As soon as she could afford it, she would leave the Nordic darkness behind for good. She didn't know where she would grow old. All she knew was that it didn't really matter as long as she had good food and a pleasant climate.

But she would never be able to convince Sten to move. He was like a grumpy old sunfish who vetoed everything. She took another sip straight from the bottle and found that she was having trouble focusing, but she could see him coming straight at her. That goddamn bastard...having the gall to say she should put down the bottle. He should talk. She shouted that she hated him so much and threw a bowl, which shattered against the wall. He tried to stop her and she swung at him with the bottle, heard it break, but kept hitting...

Her phone's ringtone penetrated all the way through her deep sleep, and Tuvesson realized that she wasn't on a beach in Thailand or at home in the kitchen with Sten—she was on the sofa in her office.

"Finally. You weren't sleeping, were you?" Molander said on the other end.

"No, no. Hi Ingvar. Have you found anything?"

"Quite a bit. But nothing of interest to us."

Tuvesson sat up. "Are you sure?"

"Astrid—"

"I know, but...are you sure you're in the right building?"

"Didn't you say furthest on the left from the gate? It says KRIGSHAMMAR on the door."

"That's the one. I'm sure I saw a scalpel."

"You did. But it wasn't used to remove a uterus—it was used to build and modify *Warhammer* figures."

"*Warhammer*? What's that?"

"It's the nerdiest game in existence, but you have too many breasts and too little penis to get it. A more detailed explanation would prompt your mobile carrier to discontinue their flat rate, so we'll worry about the description another time."

"You searched the whole building?"

She heard a deep sigh on the other end. "Well, it's not exactly huge."

"What about the other buildings?"

"The warrant is only valid for this building. You'll have to talk to Högsell again."

"Right...Well, crap."

"By the way, has Lilja had time to check the database?"

"Huh? Do what?"

She heard him sigh again. "I found prints in the car and I sent her an email asking her to run them through the database."

"I don't think she's had time to check her email yet. We went out for a bit and now she's with Klippan, calling—"

"Okay, well, can you make sure she reads it right away? I'm going to sleep for a few hours."

"Wait, hold on—what kind of prints?"

"It's in the email. Good night."

She heard a click. Tuvesson was surprised that Molander had hung up mid-conversation. She'd been hung up on plenty of times before, but never by Molander.

She left her office and had to squint through the bright fluorescent light in the corridor on her way to see Lilja, who was sitting on the mattress in her office, talking on the phone.

"Okay, good...I can't answer that at present, but I'll get back to you as soon as I know more. Just make sure we can reach you at this number." She hung up and looked at Tuvesson.

"How many have you reached?"

Lilja ostentatiously held two fingers up.

"That's all?"

Lilja nodded. "Jafaar Umar and Cecilia Holm didn't answer, and I was just about to call Stefan Munthe. Nicklas Bäckström and Helene Nachmansson are set, anyway. How's Klippan doing?"

"No idea. But I just spoke to Molander and apparently he sent you an important email."

Lilja gave her a quizzical look and stood up. She went to her overloaded desk, and turned on her computer.

From: ingvar.molander@polisen.se
Subject: Important!

I think I found and secured perp's prints in the car. I also suspect he might be in the database. Needs to be checked right away. Two-fer sent me on an assignment in Ramlösa, so I'm counting on you. You'll find the prints in the usual place. /I

"You better check that out right away. I'll take over and call Stefan Munthe," Tuvesson said.

Lilja nodded and pulled on her worn Converse. "One last thing: Seth Kårheden will be landing in twenty minutes, so we'll see if he keeps refusing to turn on his phone. If he does, it will probably take him at least two hours to make it home to his landline."

Tuvesson nodded. "What will we do about Cecilia and Jafaar?"

"Let's hope they're just at the movies or something."

"Okay, we'll hold off for a bit and then I'll try again."

"Nachmansson was wondering if she's supposed to drive over to the prison herself or if someone will pick her up."

"I think Klippan and I will each take a car to get them. I don't want to involve any more people than we have to."

Lilja nodded and headed for the door.

"Hey, wait. *Two-fer*? Is that what you call me?"

Lilja grinned and vanished.

FABIAN RISK HAD LOOKED in every box he could find. He'd gone through the entire archive cabinet, which was full of folders from old, closed cases. He'd even searched the wardrobe full of Molander's work clothes, and the large metal cabinet filled with technical equipment. But he couldn't find anything that even resembled fingerprints.

"There's a possibility they're not here. He could have taken them home or given them to someone else."

His phone buzzed.

Call him. Say you have to meet.

Fabian racked his brain to find a way to get out of this, but he couldn't see anything but massive, impenetrable cliff walls. There was nothing he could do but confront Molander face to face. He was just about to call him when the door opened.

He looked quickly around the room for a place to hide, but it was too late. Lilja had already seen him.

"Fabian? What the hell are you doing here?"

He didn't know what to say, so he remained silent.

"I thought I saw your car in the car park. Aren't you supposed to be at home resting?"

"I won't be able to rest until this case is solved. You know me... Well, no, you don't, actually, but anyway, that's the kind of guy I am." He added a laugh to make him sound reasonably relaxed, but judging by Lilja's expression she wasn't buying his act.

"Fabian, be honest. What are you really doing here?"

He felt his phone vibrate again.

Molander asked you to run the prints through the database.

He looked Lilja in the eye and took a few steps toward her. "Don't ask me why, but Molander called me of all people, to ask for a favour. Maybe he thought the rest of you were too busy and that I wouldn't be able to handle just lying around resting. I don't know." He stopped speaking, realizing that he was babbling. The words were just pouring out in a desperate attempt to hide the obvious. He waited for Lilja's reaction, but none was forthcoming. She just stood there staring at him. To keep the silence from becoming too uncomfortable he had no choice but to continue. "He secured some fingerprints from the Peugeot, which might be from the perpetrator, and he wanted me to run them through the database."

She shot him a suspicious look. "Weird. Because that's exactly what he asked me to do."

Fabian shrugged. "He probably just wanted to make sure it got done. The problem is, I can't find them."

"I'm sure they're in the usual spot, but of course you don't know where that is."

"No, how could I? I haven't been working here that long."

"Right, exactly."

Fabian's phone vibrated.

ALmost2oVer

He switched back to his phone's browser and typed in the new password. Once again he could see Theodor trapped in the narrow room. This time he didn't lift his head: it looked like he didn't have the strength, but at least he was still alive. Fabian could see his chest rising and falling with each breath, but he was breathing much more rapidly this time.

"Fabian, why do you keep messing with your phone?" Lilja asked. "You can go home. I'll take care of it."

He shook his head. "No, it's better if I do it, so you can keep working on your own thing. I'm sure you have an awful lot to do."

"What's going on? Did something happen?"

"No, Molander just asked both of us to do the same thing, and it's best if you let me take care of it."

"We both know I can't let you do that."

"Why not?"

He tried to look as confused as possible. She responded with an indulgent, almost sad, smile.

"Because Molander didn't contact you. If he had, you'd know where they were. Wouldn't you?"

All Fabian could do was nod and admit his mistake as he put his right hand into his jacket pocket to grip his gun. Lilja tried to back away from him, but there was no space, only a wall. She raised her arms to protect herself. He forced them away to uncover her head—surprised at how strong she was—just as he felt something hard against his leg. He lost his balance. Lilja was on top of him, shouting something about how he had to calm down.

The blow of his handgun landed perfectly, and she collapsed on top of him. Blood welled out of the wound and dripped onto his shirt. He rolled her onto the floor and stood up. Now he knew where to look. She had glanced up at the light fixture and given herself away. He pulled up a chair, climbed onto it, and reached for the fixture, discovering the folder containing the prints on top of it.

He stuffed it into his waistband, climbed off the chair, and looked around to make sure he hadn't left anything behind. At last he turned his head toward Lilja, thinking that this would appear perfectly natural. He extended his right arm beyond the scope of the camera and scribbled something on an envelope. His phone vibrated.

Show me what you're doing with your right arm!

Fabian obeyed the order and turned to look at the envelope. I'M SORRY. HE'S GOT MY SON. HIS NAME IS TORGNY SÖLMEDAL was written in messy letters.

The response came immediately.

If you care about him at all, you know what to do.

85

HE COULDN'T BELIEVE THAT he was actually awake. It still felt like he was in a dream. Several minutes had passed before he'd started to suspect that he really wasn't asleep, that what he saw and felt was reality in its most brutal form: dark, hard, and above all cramped. He had tried sitting up, but he hit his head so hard he'd felt blood running into his right eye. He tried to wipe it off, but his hands were tied together and fastened to a rope binding his feet.

Then the panic had struck. In a fraction of a second his body temperature lowered by several degrees and made him damp with sweat. He screamed as loudly as he could, right out into the darkness. It wasn't until his lungs were emptied of air and he was quiet that his thoughts had room to move around.

He had been sitting at his desk at home, writing in his journal. He was writing out all the rage that pumped through him, about to blast him into bits. He'd been listening to Marilyn Manson, ignoring the fact that it was far too loud. Dad wasn't home anyway. Then he saw something out of the corner of his eye, but he didn't react. It was a barely noticeable movement in the reflection on the window, like the shadow of a shadow. He looked up, right at the window, and saw someone coming into his room.

His first thought had been that Dad was coming in to turn down his music and have another pathetic "talk," but there was something strange about the clothes. In the summer, his dad generally only wore light colours. These clothes were dark, almost military. By the time he'd turned around, the man was already there, pressing a rag over his face.

At certain points, the little room was bathed in such bright light that he had to close his eyes. He'd assumed a hatch was being opened; a sign that he was about to be released from this prison. But no one ever came to loosen his entwined hands and feet, and after it happened several times he realized that nothing was opening; it was just a bright light someone was turning on and off.

Once, he heard someone nearby—at least he thought he'd heard someone. The sound had come through the walls, distant and muffled. He yelled as loudly as he could, screaming and banging with his elbows. But whoever it was, they hadn't noticed; no one came to let him out. He wondered if it was the man in the military clothing.

Since then, he hadn't heard a single sound other than his own pulse and breathing. Is this what it felt like to be buried alive? It wouldn't have been much of a problem to just close his eyes and go to sleep. But he couldn't do that. Not again. The next time he heard something—if there was a next time—it might be his last chance to free himself.

This time he'd be more prepared; he wouldn't just shout and bang his elbows bloody against the stone wall. A few hours ago, he managed to wriggle down a little bit until he felt something cold and metallic against his feet—a hatch.

Hope had sparked within him. Maybe he would survive after all. He banged his feet against the hatch. Although it was locked, it sounded like a bass drum and would be impossible to miss if someone were nearby. But no one came, and the silence started to seem more and more permanent. His hope diminished as the oxygen grew thin.

At first he didn't realize. He didn't understand why he was having a harder and harder time focusing his thoughts, or why he dozed off at ever-smaller intervals. Not until he figured out that he was breathing like he'd just run a 10K did it dawn on him that he was slowly suffocating.

He'd thought he would never do this, never ever, but he did it anyway...

He clasped his hands and prayed.

86

SHE HAD TO LOOK away from the bright, blinding glow that came from the overhead lights. A dull pain penetrated her left temple when she moved her head. She ran her fingers across the bump above her ear and felt coagulated blood in her hair. The pain was nothing serious, but this was the first time she'd been taken down by a colleague—Risk had knocked her out.

She'd had her suspicions about him ever since she read about the incidents in Stockholm, but it came as a total surprise that he'd go so far as to hit her.

And now he had disappeared with the prints.

It couldn't be him, could it? No, he just couldn't be the killer—right?

She grabbed one of the workbenches for support, stood up, and left the lab. On her way back to the unit she tried to call him but it went to voicemail.

"NO, STEFAN, OF COURSE we're not arresting all of you. This is just the only way we can protect you right now," Tuvesson said, holding the phone at quite a distance from her ear. She rolled her eyes at Klippan, who was on his own phone across from her.

"Great. We'll come pick you up a bit later. It's hard to say what time exactly, but we'll call beforehand. Bye." Klippan ended the call and stretched.

"No, we certainly haven't given up. We're moving full speed ahead on the case, but our assessment is that you're all in danger, which is why we…Right…Exactly. I'll get back to you as soon as I know when we'll be there. Bye." Tuvesson hung up and let out a long, extended sigh. "What an idiot. He should be grateful we're trying to help him."

"Every building has its bad neighbour," Klippan said, yawning just as Lilja came in.

"Oh my God! Irene, what happened?" Tuvesson walked up to Lilja to get a closer look at the wound on her temple.

"I ran into Risk down in Molander's lab."

"Risk? What was he doing there?"

"He was after the same prints as I was, and claimed that Molander asked him to run them through the database."

"What? Why would he do that?"

"That's what I wanted to know, too. Then this happened," Lilja said, pointing to her injury.

"He hit you?"

"Yes ma'am."

"But…are you okay?"

"I was out for a little bit, but I'm fine now."

"I don't understand…Do you?" Tuvesson turned to Klippan, who shook his head.

"Have you tried calling him?"

"He isn't picking up."

"This might be far out," Klippan said, "but just to put it out there. He can't be…He couldn't be…"

The others exchanged glances, not saying anything.

"There has to be some explanation. There just has to be," Tuvesson said, sitting down again.

"The thought did occur to me," Lilja said.

"Come on, give it up, you two."

"Well, what if Risk planted the class picture at the first murder scene? It got us to bring him in, and in turn gave him full insight into the case, which allowed him to guide us in any direction he wanted. Even when he was working on the

459

investigation, he wasn't exactly a wizard at letting the rest of us know what he was up to. Then he kept searching for the killer even though you removed him from the case; suddenly he 'finds' Rune Schmeckel as if he has the magical ability to sniff absolutely everything out, while remaining above suspicion."

"What about the boy in the class picture?" Klippan asked. "Who's he?"

"You mean the hair?" Lilja shrugged. "Who knows, but who pointed him out to us? And whose yearbook did we copy the picture from? I'm just saying."

No one spoke for quite some time. It was as if each of them needed to go through the entire case from the beginning to check and see if Lilja's suspicions could really be valid. After several minutes, Tuvesson looked up and met the others' gazes.

"No, it just can't be true."

"Why not?" Klippan asked. "It wasn't so long ago we decided that no idea was too far-fetched."

"Klippan, I don't know who the killer is, but I refuse to believe it's Risk. When would he have had the time? Think back to when the girl from the petrol station called: Risk was with us at Molander's."

"True. But Risk took the call. We have no idea if that girl really called, or whether she was already dead."

"*Someone* ran over that Danish policeman while Risk was with us. Can we at least agree on that?"

"Maybe there are two of them working together," Klippan said.

"There has to be another explanation. Irene, aside from the fact that he hit you, did you notice anything strange?"

"I don't know him all that well, but he didn't seem like himself. There was something about his eyes, almost like a look of fear or panic. I don't know how to describe it. And he kept checking his phone, like he was…"

"Like he was what?"

"I'm not sure how to put my finger on it."

"Maybe he's in contact with the perpetrator," Klippan said. "Even if Risk isn't an accessory, perhaps the killer has some sort of hold on him that he was able to use to get him to confiscate the prints."

"Well, there's at least one thing we can be sure of," Tuvesson said. "Molander's suspicion that the perpetrator is in the database must be correct, otherwise he wouldn't have gone to all this trouble. And since he accidentally left his prints on the car, he might have done the same elsewhere."

"You mean made other mistakes?" Klippan said.

"Nobody's perfect."

Lilja realized that Tuvesson was right. There was at least one other place where the perpetrator might have left his fingerprints.

And she knew just where it was.

87

ALTHOUGH IT WAS STILL the first half of July, it was already growing dark earlier each day. It wasn't noticeable enough to worry about yet, but it was just the right amount to remind a person that summer would soon be a distant memory.

Fabian Risk cut the engine and looked at the time: it was 10:13. His instructions were to park on Östhammarsgatan, a cross street of Motalagatan, where Torgny Sölmedal lived at number twenty-four. Fabian was now in Husensjö, a residential neighbourhood full of private homes, most of them from the first half of the twentieth century. He had heard the name mentioned throughout his childhood, but he'd never known anyone who lived there, so never had any reason to visit. This was his first time.

He turned his head to look down to the right, so the camera in the cap would register him picking up the folder from the passenger seat. His phone instantly vibrated with another text. But this time it wasn't yet another order. Instead, it was a gift—a chance to act.

Where are you? What did you do to the camera?

"I'm here. I'm just locking the car," he said, testing whether his suspicions were correct.

I assume you are aware of the danger of not following orders.

He quickly responded to the text: *Almost there. Batteries might be dead*. He took off the cap and placed it on the floor in front of the back seat. Then he opened the glove compartment to take out two Sig Sauer P228 magazines that were hidden under the car manual.

He really didn't like to carry weapons at all, and did his utmost to avoid it. He had managed to never fire a shot at anyone. Contrary to what most people thought, that type of situation was very rare in his line of work. The last time he had been in such circumstances was the previous winter. He should have fired his weapon, but he hadn't—he still couldn't explain why. Two colleagues died and he was to blame. He could still vividly remember the sound of their screams. It was as if they had lost track of him when he moved back to Helsingborg and had only now caught his scent again, chasing after him like hyenas. The screams, snuffling and desperate begging and pleading for their lives.

And with them came the memories of his colleagues being forced to their knees in the underground room. The captors had asked where he was, but received no response from his co-workers. They didn't know how close he had been and that he could have made a difference with the weapon in his hand. But he couldn't manage to pull the trigger.

He heard people shouting in English that they had come too far and seen too much. They raised their pistols toward his colleagues. Fabian took aim, he tried to shoot—to save them—but he couldn't do it. The shots echoed. They collapsed onto the shiny new tiles, which turned red. The screams had stopped for a little while, but he could hear them again now—louder than ever.

Would he fail this time too?

Fabian smacked his own head in an attempt to force the memories away. He inserted one of the magazines into his pistol. He left the car with the keys in the ignition and walked along Östhammarsgatan toward Motalagatan, where he took a right and crossed the street to get to the side with the even-numbered houses. He walked up the pavement. After a few metres he

463

tripped over an uneven spot on the pavement and nearly fell down headfirst.

"You have to watch out. It's awfully bumpy around here," said a man in sweatpants out walking his dog. Fabian forced himself to smile at the man, and realized that parts of the pavement had been repaved in a manner that left quite a few things to be desired.

"Yes, to say the least," Fabian said, as he moved to keep walking.

"Don't ask me why they insist on patching and repairing it. It looks like an intern did the work."

Fabian felt his phone vibrate.

I'm not the one who's running out of time.

"Last winter, Kerstin in number five fell down and broke her hip. If you add that to the cost, it would have been cheaper to just replace the whole thing."

Fabian nodded dutifully and hurried on. He arrived at number twenty-six, where the yard was so overgrown it effectively blocked the entire view from the street. It was almost impossible to see the house behind all the plants. Sölmedal lived at number twenty-four, which was the opposite of the house next door and of Fabian's expectations. It looked open and inviting, almost as if Sölmedal wanted surprise visitors. A low, white fence surrounded a neatly mowed lawn in front of the perfectly visible house; there was a garage on the right and a tall, thick hedge to the left.

Fabian couldn't make sense of it. Could this really be where this guy lived? It was very open, with neighbours quite close on either side. The mailbox said T. SÖLMEDAL, and there were lights on in the window facing the street. He stopped and pretended to tie his shoe in order to form a clearer picture of his surroundings. He quickly realized that his first impression required some modification: the sense of inviting openness only applied to the front of the house itself—the rest of the lot was a different story. A fence and the tall hedge effectively kept anyone from peering in.

He stood up and kept walking, taking a left on Växjögatan. The lights were on in the first house on the left, and he could see shadows moving inside, likely a Friday-night dinner with guests and a bottle of wine. The next house was dark and the driveway was glaringly empty. He walked alongside the house to the backyard, where there was a set of patio furniture arranged so rainwater would run off, as well as a barbecue that must have cost a month's salary. Fabian walked diagonally across the lawn and arrived at a wall of rosebushes; he pulled his hands into the sleeves of his jacket, and used his arms to push aside the branches, forcing his way through the thorny wall.

He reached the very corner of Sölmedal's lot. The house was larger than he had initially thought: there were several additions at the back, and it must have been twice as large as it had been originally. He sneaked along the edge of the yard, hidden by the cover of darkness from the rosebushes, until he came to a storage shed. He could make out a lawn mower, a pair of cross-country skis, a few rolled-up rugs, and a pile of dentist's equipment through a dirty window.

His phone buzzed in his pocket again. But this time it wasn't a text—it was a call from Irene Lilja, which meant she had regained consciousness. Tuvesson and the others would soon find out what had happened. He let his voicemail pick up and kept moving along the back of the shed. Once he reached the corner, he judged the distance to the house to be about five metres.

Five metres across the lawn with no cover.

His adrenaline was pumping as if he were about to run a hundred-metre sprint. He had no idea what awaited him and his mind was hesitating. But his body had made its decision, and he had no choice but to follow it across the lawn, up to the wall of the house, and around the next corner, where a set of steps led up to a terrace with a few deck chairs. Fabian drew his weapon and cocked it before he went up the stairs.

By the time he reached the terrace, his heart was beating so loudly that he could hear the blood pumping through his veins. The sound reminded him that he was still alive—that he could still make a difference. He took a few steps toward a sliding glass door; he could see right into the living room because the lights were on. There was a grand piano in the middle of the room. A bookcase that reminded him of the one in his parents' home took up a whole wall. At the other end of the room was a corner sofa in front of a large flat-screen TV, and...

He heard a sound—one as unobtrusive as it was life-changing: a barely audible little creak. Anything could have made that sound, except in this particular situation. Fabian whirled around toward the deck chairs.

"Fashionably late I've heard of, but is it fashionable to come sneaking around the back? That's new."

"Where's my son? I just want him back." Fabian aimed his pistol at the shadow that was rising from the chair and pulling some type of gun with a silencer on him.

"I suggest we go inside before the coffee gets cold."

"What the hell have you done with my son?"

"We'll get to that. Like I said, there are a few other things we have to work out right now, and *I'm* not the one who slowed us down." He approached Fabian with his free hand in front of him. "So I suggest we try to keep all of this civilized. Give me your gun. You can have it back when we're finished."

Fabian hesitated; he couldn't take his eyes off the man in the darkness in front of him. Had he seen him before or was this the first time? Had they really been in the same class, or was that all just a game?

"Anyway, you don't want to shoot me before you find out where little Theodor is."

He didn't recognize the man. Or did he? Maybe it was just

too dark. It felt like this was the first time they'd met, but at the same time something seemed familiar, like déjà vu.

He gave up trying to remember, handed his pistol over, and let himself be led into the living room. Wagner's *The Valkyrie* was playing in the background. They walked through a few hallways into a kitchen, where a table was set with two mugs, a French press, and a plate of cookies.

"Have a seat."

Fabian forced himself to sit on one of the chairs, although his whole body was screaming at him to attack the man, beat his head against the table, and force him to confess where he had hidden Theodor.

Torgny Sölmedal sat on the chair across from Fabian, placed his gun in his lap, and began to slowly lower the plunger through the coffee. "I'm sure you're wondering why."

"I'm not wondering anything. All I want is for you to let Theodor go. He has nothing to do with this."

"Not that it's my main motive, but by taking the lives of several of our classmates I have helped make the world just a little bit better, which is a minor, positive side effect we should all rejoice in." He smiled as he continued to press the grounds to the bottom of the carafe.

"My son! Where is he?"

"When I started mapping everyone out, I was pretty much disgusted by how unintelligent they were. You might think I'm exaggerating, but take that car ride with Jörgen, for example. It was one of the worst experiences of my life. I swear, an amoeba would have a higher IQ."

The plunger finally reached the bottom, and he poured the coffee into the mugs.

Fabian struggled not to break down as he studied Torgny Sölmedal's face in the light. He could see why no one had recognized him. His face was so ordinary and anonymous that there was no particular feature to remember him by: his nose, cheeks, mouth, eyes—all of them just looked *normal*, down to the tiniest detail.

"Go ahead and look at me: nothing will stand out in your memory. If we passed each other on Kullagatan in a week, you wouldn't recognize me."

Fabian realized that he was probably telling the truth, but it didn't matter. It wasn't important now. He took out the folder of fingerprints and placed it on the table. His sweaty hands left a number of dark spots on the folder. "Here are your prints. Now I want my son."

Torgny Sölmedal didn't even look at it. "Milk?"

"Can you explain to me what my children have to do with this?"

"Milk, or no milk?"

"Answer me!" Fabian struck the table with his fist and coffee splashed out of the mugs.

Torgny Sölmedal shot him a look and wiped up the mess with a floral napkin. "I'll take that as no milk." He handed the black coffee over to Fabian and took a cookie. "Unfortunately—and I really do mean that—you've arrived too late. As I told you all along, I didn't know how long the oxygen would last, but hindsight is twenty-twenty, and I have to admit that it lasted longer than I expected: forty-six hours and thirty-three minutes isn't bad for such a cramped space. He gave up at seventeen minutes past ten." He pushed a tablet across the table; it showed the same image Fabian had seen earlier. The only difference was that Theodor was lying perfectly still now.

Not even his chest was moving.

88

INGVAR MOLANDER WAS SURE that he hadn't been asleep. He thought he had been lying awake on the cot in the basement— so that he didn't wake Gertrud—going over and over the events of the past few days in his mind. And yet he had just woken up to the sound of his phone ringing.

It was Lilja. He didn't feel like answering. All he wanted to do was pretend that he hadn't heard it, and keep sleeping. But that would be way too obvious: everyone at the station knew he was a light sleeper and that the tiniest sound would wake him, no matter how tired he was.

"Molander speaking."

"Hi, it's Irene. Did I wake you?"

"Let's hope it's important."

"The fingerprints you found in the Peugeot are gone. Risk took them and he's probably handed them over to the killer."

Molander sat up. "What the hell are you talking about?" he managed, although he had heard her perfectly well.

"I'll explain later. The important thing is that the prints are gone and we have to—"

"Hold on. Was he in the database?"

"No idea. I didn't have time to check before they vanished."

"But how the hell could they just vanish?!"

"Like I said, Risk took them, but it doesn't matter right now. Priority number one is finding more prints as soon as we can."

"How the fuck are you planning to do that?" Molander felt a

bad mood rolling in like a German invasion, and he had no way of combating it. Not only had he been woken from a slumber he dearly needed, but they had also managed to lose the prints that were supposed to identify the perpetrator: evidence that their Danish colleague had risked her job to allow him to obtain.

"I was thinking since he obviously got sloppy in the car, he was probably sloppy other times too, right?"

"Sure, or maybe not. Even if he was, there's still a small but important question: Where?"

"At Glenn's house."

"What?"

"Glenn Granqvist. You know, the second victim."

"Yes, of course I know who he is. But why…"

"Well, Glenn hit the back of his head on the shoe rack and started bleeding, didn't he?"

She was right. His memory began to wake up from its cryo-sleep.

"You were the one who showed me that the perpetrator had used a rag to clean up the blood in the hallway, and that he'd even rinsed and wrung it out so it wouldn't drip."

"Right. So?"

"Don't you think he took off his gloves to rinse it and wring it out?"

Lilja was right. The odds were good that he'd taken off the gloves and accidentally left a print or two in the closet. "Let's head over right away."

89

HIS CLOTHES WERE STICKY with sweat even though he was shaking from the cold. His blood vessels were constricted, redistributing his blood to only the most vital organs. He was in shock, and his body was acting accordingly. Everything that had seemed so important earlier felt diffuse and fuzzy. All he wanted to do was curl up into a ball and cry, but he couldn't—not right now.

He put his hands on the table as if to stand up, but he changed his mind when he realized that he didn't have the energy. "Where is he?"

"Ironic that you're suddenly asking so many questions about your son."

"Ironic?"

"Yes, that you suddenly seem to care about him. I don't have kids myself, but I would say that your actions are probably a little late. I assume you've read at least parts of his diary. A person can't help but wonder, 'Where are his parents?' I'm sure you would ask the same thing, if you weren't the parent in question. Wouldn't you?" Torgny Sölmedal searched his face for an acknowledgement, but Fabian didn't move a muscle. "Well, we can at least agree that your beloved son was wondering, up until half an hour ago, where his parents were."

Fabian wanted to jump on the man across the table and beat his jeering face to a pulp, but he fought against it; he wanted to remain in control at all costs.

"Instead, let's talk about why you're here in the first place. You weren't even part of the original plan. You lived in Stockholm, and were only going to contribute to the death toll toward the end. Aside from you and Lotta Ting, everyone still lived here in Helsingborg. But then you moved back down. Don't ask me why, I've never understood the point of returning to the scene of the crime. But suddenly you were here and I figured I might as well pull you a little deeper into my plan. To be perfectly honest I wasn't worried about you at all: you haven't exactly accomplished an impressive list of achievements. I didn't consider you an immediate threat, which turned out to be a serious miscalculation—it has been my biggest mistake so far, and it came close to costing me this entire operation. So cheers to you and your, how should I put it, 'cop instinct.'" He stopped talking for a moment and drank his coffee. "The situation with the car was truly impressive. I've been trying to figure out how you managed to find it, but I haven't succeeded. And don't tell me, because I'll think of it eventually. By the way, your coffee's getting cold."

"Let it."

"It's up to you. Your little triumphs forced me to make some changes to the plan and, frankly, it's so much better now that you're the crowning glory instead of Monika Krusenstierna. Remember her? Our teacher, who always wore a plaid skirt and looked away the second anything uncomfortable happened? A little bit like you, actually. I bet there have been a number of times when you could tell your son wasn't doing so well, but just like Monika, you chose to turn your back on him."

Fabian couldn't restrain himself any longer. He flew out of his chair, overturned the table, and threw himself at Torgny Sölmedal, who lost his balance and fell to the ground. Fabian saw his own gun sliding across the floor, managing to stop it with one hand, only to feel his body start to cramp up. A burning pain spread from his abdomen.

472

Torgny Sölmedal turned off the Taser and wriggled out of Fabian's grasp. "Is this what you call civilized?"

Fabian couldn't respond—he was on the floor, shaking with spasms. His mind was present, but his motor skills were not. From the corner of his eye he could see Sölmedal picking up the guns and placing them on the counter; he opened one of the kitchen drawers and took out a pair of meat shears, and retrieved a syringe from the refrigerator. Fabian tried to say something, but all he could manage was a weak moan.

Meanwhile, Sölmedal inserted the shears into Fabian's shirt collar and cut a large hole in the fabric to expose his neck. Fabian tried to resist, but his body refused to obey him. Sölmedal had no trouble feeling his way to his carotid artery.

90

IRENE LILJA DROVE SLOWLY so that she didn't wake the sleeping neighbourhood, and for once she was first on the scene. She pulled over and stopped: this was probably the first time she'd ever had to wait for Molander. He was always on time and was always a step ahead of the others, ready with a solution.

But today she was the one who was a step ahead; she had come up with an idea that was so great it couldn't be put off until the next day. Was that why he was taking so long and making her wait? She toyed with the thought of just going in and gathering the prints, but decided it was too big a risk: Molander might be offended and angry for real. Besides, he had the keys to Glenn's house.

She cut the engine and the wipers stopped in the middle of the windscreen, which was one of several features of her car that she found annoying. She had developed the habit of switching off the wipers before she turned off the car, but she had forgotten this time. She must be too tired. She didn't even have the energy to be annoyed.

Instead, she reclined her seat back a few notches and looked out of the window at the rain. It had only started to come down a few minutes ago, and the precipitation was as gentle and badly needed as it was unexpected. The summer had been so hot and cloudless that she had almost forgotten there was such a thing as rain.

The raindrops landed on the windscreen and grew into small irregular pools. Pretty soon it was no longer possible to see out, and the glow of the lone streetlight became distorted, forming a hypnotic blend of reflections and colours. She was sinking deeper and deeper into sleep, trying to figure out how many hours of rest she'd managed in the past week.

Twelve minutes later, her eyes opened. She looked around, but didn't see anything other than the rain hammering at the metal of her car so violently that she was worried it would leave marks on the paint. But that wasn't what had woken her: a few seconds ago she'd thought she heard a loud banging sound. Then she heard it again, right next to her. Someone was standing outside, but the water was distorting her view so much that she couldn't tell who it was.

She rolled down the window and saw Molander's wet face looking back at her.

"Do you think I'm having fun standing out here waiting for you?"

"Oh, so now you're the one who has to wait?" Lilja asked, but Molander was already on his way up to the house. She stepped out into the pouring rain, opened her umbrella, and hurried to catch up with him. "Why didn't you bring an umbrella?"

Molander grunted as he tried key after key in the lock. "Who the hell marked these damn keys?"

"Hold on, let me help." Lilja took over and Molander didn't hesitate to take the umbrella, holding it in a position that allowed her to experience the wetness of the rain.

"Here. It's 'GG,' as in Glenn Granqvist," she said, unlocking the door.

Molander handed back her umbrella without a word and vanished into the house. As she let the water run off her onto the doormat, Lilja wondered whether he was being efficient or was just in a bad mood, although it didn't matter either way.

When she arrived at the cleaning closet, Molander was already busy dusting the light switch. Despite making every effort to hide it, she could see his barely noticeable smile.

"You sure were lucky. There are several prints here, both on the faucet and by the switch."

"Lucky? You mean 'right'?" Lilja said, receiving a stony silence in response. "And you're sure that they're his and not Glenn's?"

He gave her a weary look and took out the print lifters.

91

HE WIPED UP THE coffee on the floor. The mug had survived. He just had to wash and dry it along with the other one, and put them in their place in the cabinet. He took one of the cookies and popped it into his mouth. He tossed the rest into the rubbish bag and tied it closed. Although he would never return, it seemed important to leave the house clean and tidy. He turned off the refrigerator and freezer, unplugged the toaster and coffeemaker, then turned out the lights and left the kitchen. The other rooms were already prepared. All he had left to do was say goodbye.

He had lived there for nearly eighteen years. It was a good house, and for the most part he'd enjoyed it very much. But now the house had been sold; it was the end of an era. The new owners would take possession in early October, which would leave plenty of time for the police to finish their examination. He could already picture them presenting all the evidence he'd so carefully planted.

He turned up the volume of *The Valkyrie*, which would make a great soundtrack for their arrival, opened the front door and stepped outside. It had started to rain. So far it was still sprinkling gently, but he knew that it was supposed to get worse, so he opened his umbrella, locked the door, and left.

His car was parked a fourteen-minute walk away, where Köpingevägan crossed Malmögatan. He was in no rush, so he strolled at a leisurely pace. Everything had been going his way for the past few hours, and for the first time in several days his plan was right on schedule. The only thing that made him walk faster was the rain, which was starting to beat against his umbrella. The last thing he wanted was to get wet. He had a change of clothes in the car, but he had specifically chosen the ones he was wearing for tonight, and he wouldn't have a chance to change before he was finished and on the boat.

He dropped his house key into the storm drain, and turned right onto Jönköpingsgatan, right near Tycho Brahe School. Whenever he found himself in the vicinity of his old secondary school, he started thinking about how he had graduated with a perfect 5.0 grade point average, the highest in his class, and was still forced to watch as the scholarship went to Claes Mällvik, who only had a 4.63. It still upset him to think about it. Everyone had been so overly conscious of how difficult life had been for Claes, and they'd given him the scholarship as a consolation prize.

He couldn't deny that Jörgen and Glenn, not to mention Elsa and Camilla, had all been absolutely horrible to Claes in compulsory school, and they deserved what they got, but that didn't change the fact that he had disliked Claes ever since they started the first grade. Claes had literally got all the attention.

It had probably been more or less involuntary back in compulsory school, but in their upper years Claes had learned to take advantage of it—no one laid a finger on him there. And yet he made sure everyone knew what a hard time he'd had, and reminded them how goddamn sorry they should feel for him. The scholarship ceremony had been the last straw—he had promised himself never to end up overshadowed by Claes again.

It was a promise that reaped consequences only a few weeks later. He had just been accepted to the engineering school at Lund University, and found out a day or two later that Claes would be going to Lund as well. He decided then and there to scrap his university plans and start his own business instead. His school-level engineering degree would have to do.

His idea had been to have a sort of inventor's workshop, where he could build specially designed machines. He wasn't flooded with orders at the start, but he'd been able to pay the rent. Once microprocessors took over on a large scale, he'd ploughed through all the books he could find on the subject and worked fifteen hours a day. He loved it. A few patents later—including one for a knife-sharpener that IKEA sold all over the world, as well as the feed device on most bottle-return machines—he was financially comfortable.

He realized later on that he'd never been as happy as during that time. Even Claes was out of the picture. He'd had no idea at the time that Claes would show up again a few years later, only to cause him such pain that just thinking about it brought everything vividly back to life. His only real problem back then had been the same one he'd struggled with throughout his youth.

The loneliness.

It started raining harder and he had to hold the umbrella with both hands to keep from getting wet. He took a left onto Malmögatan and could see his car. He glanced at his watch and calculated that he still had plenty of time. Everything was coming up roses for him, and he even had enough energy left over to laugh about the time he'd been so desperate to meet someone that he'd created a profile on an online dating site, which was so fucking pathetic.

He'd met a few different women, but it had never gone further than having coffee. Each time he'd had to swallow his humiliation when they made excuses about why they had to leave early. Those white lies were meant to spare him, but they only made things worse.

He'd had an especially hard time getting over one woman in particular. She hadn't even bothered to come up with an excuse and just got up to use the bathroom in the middle of their conversation and never came back. He'd sat there waiting for forty-three minutes before he realized what was going on and had to pay the whole bill. Nowadays, he didn't understand why he had taken it so hard, why he couldn't just swallow his pride and move on.

He'd had to get closure, so he decided to contact the woman again and demand an apology. But she had blocked him, so he created an entirely new profile in which he presented himself as an art director at an ad agency and claimed to work as a model as well. He used a picture from an ad for Stenströms shirts. It didn't take long to reconnect with the woman, and he got her to agree to meet him at Le Cardinal.

He made sure to arrive fifteen minutes early. He took a seat in an out-of-the-way spot at the bar that gave him a full view of the door; he watched as she came in, her eyes scanning the room for her date. He watched her in peace and quiet as she was shown to a table, ordered a glass of red wine, and looked at the clock. She grew more and more uncomfortable sitting alone, and told the waiter for the third time that she wasn't ready to order dinner, only another glass of wine and a bowl of nuts. He enjoyed every second as if each one were a drop of fancy champagne that had just been rescued from an old shipwreck.

Fifty-eight minutes passed before she paid and left the restaurant, unaware that she was being followed. Her steps were brisk and irritated as she clip-clopped down to Knutpunkten and boarded a bus; he easily got a seat directly behind her. Like everyone else, she hadn't noticed him. She got off at Adolfsberg and he kept his distance while he followed her to her building. Five minutes later, he went in and rang her doorbell.

He arrived at his car. The rain was so heavy that he didn't collapse his umbrella until he was inside the vehicle. He placed it on the floor of the passenger seat and closed the door; then he turned the key in the ignition and let the car idle to clear away some of the fog.

It had taken her just over a minute to answer the door, but he remembered it as one of the longest minutes in his life. She gave him a quizzical look; he didn't know whether it was because of his stubble or his anonymous face. She asked who he was and what he wanted; he reminded her of their little date.

She tried to close the door but he was quicker and forced his way through the crack. Then he raped her. He took her right there on the hallway rug—not because he wanted her, he just wanted to degrade her.

The way she had degraded him.

She reported him, of course, and he was called in for interrogation. They fingerprinted him and tried to force him to confess. He adamantly denied that there was ever any rape. He acknowledged they had absolutely had sex, and that maybe it got a little violent, but it was nothing she hadn't consented to. Finally, after several days in jail, there was nothing they could do but let him go.

He programmed the address into his GPS, put the car in gear, and pulled out onto Malmögatan, heading for Södra Stenbocksgatan. In eighteen minutes he would arrive at the first home.

92

"IT DOESN'T GET ANY better than this." Ragnar Palm threw one arm out toward the prison's common area, which had been placed at their disposal.

Tuvesson's eyes scanned the room. "It still feels pretty jail-like."

"Maybe because that's exactly what it is."

She sighed. "How many bathrooms do they have access to?"

"Two. And what's the gender breakdown?"

"Five and five."

The ten cots were lined up across from each other along two walls, with a few metres between them. There were chairs between the cots, which were meant to act as nightstands. Tuvesson sat down on one of the cots and asked herself whether she would have agreed to sleep here, even if it was only for one weekend; although truthfully, they had no idea how long they would end up staying.

Palm sat down on the cot across from hers. "Do you think it'll work?"

"It has to work. There's nothing else we can do."

"I hope you realize that if this gets out—"

"Ragnar, it can't get out under any circumstances, not before the killer has been caught. How many of your people know about it?"

"Only those who need to know: my boss and some of the staff, who are definitely not a problem. They have to abide by confidentiality. But the prisoners don't."

Tuvesson's phone started ringing. It was Klippan.

"I've called everyone and I'm going to start picking them up now."

"Did everyone agree to it?"

"Yes, but they all have a bunch of questions I can't answer. How are things at your end?"

"I'm at the jail and...well, let's hope that they don't have to stay very long."

"Did you get hold of everyone?"

"Everyone but Seth Kårheden. He was supposed to land at Kastrup two and a half hours ago, so he should be home any time now."

"He still hasn't turned on his mobile?"

"No, it doesn't seem like it."

"Where does he live?"

"Domsten. I'll start picking up the others, and I'll keep calling. If he doesn't answer I guess I'll just go over there." Tuvesson hung up, got up from the cot, and headed for the exit.

FABIAN RISK HAD BEEN absolutely certain that he was about to die just like his classmates, but he'd just come to, albeit with a bad headache, so it looked like it wasn't his turn to go—yet. Waking up felt like a punishment even worse than death: a waking nightmare, where he was alive and Theodor was dead.

He could hear a faint, barely audible buzzing, and felt his head vibrate slightly. Then the vacuum-like silence returned. He tried to move, but he realized that he was bound to an old dentist's chair. His feet, legs, and arms were held down with straps, and his head...he couldn't see how it was fastened, but when he tried to move it, the pain at his temples increased. Whatever the contraption was, it stuck out on both sides of his face, like two blinders that prevented him from looking in any direction other than straight ahead. All he could see was a dark screen hanging on the wall in front of him that curved round to the right.

The faint buzzing returned and he felt his head vibrate again. At the same time, the screen in front of him lit up with a black-and-white portrait of a young Torgny Sölmedal. The picture must have been taken sometime during his middle-grade years; they had been done by a photographer in a real studio, with professional lighting. Sölmedal was sitting on a tall stool with his hair neatly parted down the middle and was wearing what looked to be his nicest shirt; he looked straight into the camera with a warm smile.

How could he never have noticed him? Fabian didn't understand. How come no one in the class had noticed him, not even their teacher, Monika Krusenstierna? And now he had been forced to take her place in the windowless little room with its curved, dark-curtained walls, where the only light came from the screen. He heard the faint buzzing once again. This time, minor as it was, he noticed that his field of vision had shifted slightly to the right.

Fabian had figured out what was happening. Torgny Sölmedal was right: he was guilty of the very same thing as Monika.

But the victim was his own son.

IRENE LILJA SAT BEHIND Molander and watched as he scanned the fingerprints and checked them against the database. Her exhaustion seemed to have vanished; the same went for Molander's bad mood. Clearly both of them had the feeling they were close to a breakthrough, but it might take anywhere from a few minutes to several hours before they knew the answer.

"Is there anything we can do to speed up the search?" Lilja asked.

"Yes—limit it to look for men born between 1965 and 1967."

"And how long will that take?"

"You tell me," Molander replied. He dropped a pillow to the floor, stretched out on it, and closed his eyes.

Lilja knew that Molander was doing the right thing, but she would never be able to fall asleep now, not when they were so close. She couldn't take her eyes away from the screen, where the database of stored fingerprints was flickering away as if it would never stop. But she could feel it. She could feel it in her bones.

Any second now, the flickering would stop.

93

HE HAD ARRIVED HOME at quarter past one in the morning and had been there no more than fifty minutes, yet his phone had already rung at least five or six times. He certainly wasn't about to answer it. He hated unknown numbers. In his opinion, if you weren't willing to make your identity known, you didn't deserve an answer.

So instead, he had a shower and a shave. He'd let his beard grow out while he was on vacation, so he had to give it a once-over with the trimmer before going at it with a razor. He kept the moustache. He'd had it as long as he could remember and was extremely proud of it. Despite the changing fashions over the years—everything from pencil moustaches to full beards—he had never altered a single whisker of his moustache, aside from trimming it twice a week.

It was probably just Kerstin calling. She was the only person he knew who blocked her number. She had started doing it a few years ago, claiming that it was because he never answered when she called, as if he were more likely to answer these days. If only she would stop calling, period, and let him come home in peace and quiet.

He tried to shake off thoughts of Kerstin; he pulled on his pyjamas and walked over to the fireplace, where he crumpled some old newspaper and a few wood chips into a ball and arranged three logs above it. As always, one match did the job.

He didn't feel tired in the least, and was looking forward to reading *Helsingborgs Dagblad*, which was due to arrive in his hallway soon. It was probably what he'd missed most during his trip: sitting in front of the fire while everyone else was asleep, reading the morning paper. Kerstin had never approved of the habit—in fact, she was always annoyed that she had to read an "old" paper once she finally dragged herself out of bed.

She had probably tried to call his mobile phone, too. There was no way for her to know he'd got rid of it. He had planned to keep it turned off throughout the pilgrimage, and to his surprise it hadn't bothered him to go without it in the least. Quite the contrary; it had been an absolute joy to be unreachable. One day, when he was looking out over one of the deepest valleys of the Pyrenees, he just did it—he threw it in. For the rest of his pilgrimage, he enjoyed silence as his only companion.

Other pilgrims had tried to reach out and talk to him but he hadn't responded. He didn't care what people thought. He wasn't going to break his silence, which felt more and more important each day. And after a while they appeared—his very own thoughts, fragile and newly hatched. He couldn't remember the last time he'd been able to think through his own ideas without being interrupted by his boss, or Kerstin, or…

More ringing. But this time it wasn't the phone; it was his front door. Who could it be at this time of night? The phone was easy to ignore—you could even pull out the plug—but a doorbell was different. He walked to the door and opened it. A man he had never seen before was standing outside under an umbrella.

94

HE WAS BREATHING, BUT it didn't feel like he was getting any air. Or maybe he wasn't breathing? Maybe his body had stopped working, and the notion that he was breathing was no more than one last residual thought before his brain blinked out, like the flailing leg of a spider after it's been ripped off its body.

Was this what it felt like to drown? He'd heard it was supposed to be one of the most painful ways to die, but this didn't hurt at all. He could hardly feel a thing, not even the metallic hatch against his feet. He had the vague impression that he was slowly fading away and disappearing.

But then came the opportunity he'd spent several days waiting for, or maybe it was only hours. He had no idea; his sense of time had deserted him long ago. He could hear a dull sound coming through the walls: a distant door opening and closing, and someone shouting. He couldn't hear what the person was saying, but it was definitely someone shouting, unless it was just another desperate attempt on his behalf to refuse to accept the facts—a hallucination that help was on the way.

He decided that it didn't matter. If he was dead, so be it, but if not, this was his very last chance. He mustered all his strength and lifted his feet into the air. At least, he thought he did. The important thing was that he tried to bang them against the hatch and make as much noise as he could. He tried to yell, but all that came out was a whisper. His feet sounded like dull, blunt drumbeats striking the hatch.

He managed to kick the hatch three times, but couldn't push any further than that, no matter how hard he tried. The suffocating silence was back, and he felt like he was holding his breath for a long time.

He'd heard that the world record for holding your breath was over seven minutes. How long would he manage? How many minutes was he up to? He didn't really want to die, not right now. For a few years he'd spent all his time thinking about how nice it would be to give up, stop fighting, and float out into nothingness instead.

The darkness surrounded him like a cosy, warm hug. If only he had known it would be so simple. He wouldn't have had to fight it, to be so scared and beat himself bloody. He sank deeper and deeper and finally…

Finally, he saw the light.

95

HIS FACE FILLED THE whole screen. Although he had a full, neatly trimmed beard, he looked so anonymous that Irene Lilja finally understood why no one had noticed him. She sat there staring at his picture, forgetting to blink until her eyes teared up, feverishly searching for something to remember him by, but there was nothing. No tiny asymmetry, no large—or small—nose. His eyes weren't even a particular colour. She tried to form a mental picture of the face behind the beard, but all she came up with were two eyes, a nose, and a mouth. He was so normal and average that the face just passed by and disappeared.

He didn't look like the sort of person who could cut off the hands of a victim who was still alive, or cut someone's throat and make a Colombian necktie either. He looked more like someone who...well, what *did* he look like? She gave up. After all, she would never be able to describe him, at least not beyond the fact that he had a beard and looked incredibly ordinary.

But there was something about the name Torgny Sölmedal that seemed familiar. She knew she'd heard it before.

"What the hell? Did the computer find a match?" Lilja, who had completely forgotten that Molander was asleep on the floor at her feet, nodded mutely. Her thoughts were preoccupied with digging deeper and deeper into her memory until she came up with the connection.

Meanwhile, Molander got up and read the words on the screen out loud: "*Torgny Sölmedal. Detained in 2005 for rape...*"

"But freed due to lack of evidence. Not to mention, he turned up earlier in the investigation. Claes Mällvik, or Rune Schmeckel, as his name was at the time, operated on his prostate in 2004 and happened to leave two plastic clips behind in, well, you know... They made a pretty big deal of it in the papers and he even had to take a leave of absence from work for a while."

"Oh right, I remember. It hurts just to think of it."

ASTRID TUVESSON HURRIED THROUGH the pouring rain, phone to her ear, as she helped Lena Olsson into the back seat. "And you're sure it's him?"

"As sure as we can be," Lilja answered. "There's only one person listed with that name, and he lives at Motalagatan 24 in Husensjö."

"In Helsingborg?"

"Yes. Molander and I can be there in ten minutes."

"Not without the SWAT team," Tuvesson said, trying to wrestle Lena Olsson's bag into the boot. "Call Malmö and wait for them."

"Astrid, come on. We can't wait for Malmö, it'll take them over an hour and a half. We have to go now."

Irene's right, Tuvesson thought as she yanked the unwieldy suitcase back out and slammed the boot, but she didn't want to lose two of her best colleagues to a potential ambush.

"Hello? Are you still there?"

"Okay, go in alone, but I want you to be careful." She pushed the wet bag into the passenger seat's footwell and closed the door. "If you're at all uncertain, back out, understood?"

"Yeah, yeah."

"Irene, I mean it!"

"Okay, okay. By the way, how are things going for you?"

"I just picked up Lena Olsson and Stefan Munthe and I'm on my way to get Lina Pålsson."

"What about the lonely pilgrim? Has he answered yet?"

"No, I'm planning to try one last time. If he doesn't answer I'll just go and ring his doorbell."

They ended the call. Tuvesson walked around the car as she pulled up Kårheden's home number. It rang on the other end. She was opening the driver's side door to get in when someone picked up.

"This is Kårheden," said a voice on the other end.

"Hello, I didn't think you would answer. My name is Astrid Tuvesson." She wondered if she should get in the car or take the call out in the rain. She decided she couldn't get any wetter anyway.

"Excuse me, but do I know you?"

"I'm sorry; I'm a detective superintendent in Helsingborg."

"Oh?"

"I've been trying to reach you all night."

"Yes, I just got back from a trip to Spain."

"So we heard. Have you been following the news about what's been going on while you were gone?"

"No, not at all. Isn't that the whole point of a holiday? But the billboards at Kastrup were impossible to miss. Is it really true what they say? Is he after the whole class?"

"We don't know, but unfortunately we have every reason to believe he is."

"That's awful. And you don't have any leads on the killer's identity?"

"We do, but I can't discuss the details. I'm calling you because the only way we can offer you protection right now is to bring you to the prison along with your former classmates. How would you feel about me coming to pick you up?"

"Right now?"

"Yes, in about half an hour."

There was a long sigh.

"It can't wait until later or the next day? I just got home and I was gone for more than a month."

"Let me put it this way: we judge your risk to be extremely high, although ultimately it's your choice. We can't force anyone to come in."

Silence filled the other end of the line.

"Okay. I understand."

Tuvesson hung up, got behind the wheel, and turned the key. A tense, expectant mood had taken over the back seat. Through the rear-view mirror she could see them staring out at the rain with evasive looks.

She knew how they felt.

96

FABIAN HEARD A FAINT buzz and felt his head turning another little bit. He had to be up to ninety degrees, or even slightly past it. Another screen was lighting up his field of vision; it also showed a black-and-white photograph of Torgny Sölmedal. His hair was just as neatly combed and his smile was just as friendly as in the last picture, but this time he was an adult.

He wanted to be seen this way. When it was all over, the pictures would surely be spread throughout the world—and, like Fabian with his head fastened to a dentist's chair, no one would be able to look away.

But then something happened to the picture. Or was he only imagining it? No, he was sure, something was definitely happening. The space between the eyes narrowed and the nose looked different. The same went for the hair. It had grown darker and longer, and whether he was still looking at Torgny or whether this was someone else, he wasn't sure. All he knew for certain was that the face before him was transforming.

He heard the buzz and his head turned again. By now his neck was considerably stretched and straining, even if it didn't really hurt yet. He wondered how many more degrees he would survive, whether his neck would break all at once or if his path to the inescapable end would be peppered with several small catastrophic moments. He had no clue. He didn't even know which he would prefer. The thought of dying wasn't as problematic as the thought of surviving.

The face on the screen before him was still changing, and he could now decipher that it looked more and more like his son. He'd taken that picture himself last spring. It had been Theodor's birthday and the family had celebrated by eating at the Hard Rock Café, where all he could think about was how annoyingly loud the music was.

There was another buzz and, just as it had before, his head turned another little bit. But this time it was different—he could both hear and feel the cracking in his neck.

97

THE RAIN HAD FINALLY stopped, as if someone had turned off a tap, and now there were mostly just sporadic drops, but the water was still gushing through the gutters in search of a storm drain that hadn't yet overflowed. Irene Lilja shoved her feet into her boots, walked up to Molander, and helped him with his bulletproof vest. He didn't say anything, but it was clear that he hadn't the smallest desire to come along.

I'm a crime scene tech, not some fucking SWAT whore, his eyes said. The closest he ever came to using a weapon was probably when he went fishing. When Irene was finished with Molander, she pulled on her own vest.

"Okay, let's go."

They locked the car and each of them took one of Molander's equipment bags before they walked down Motalagatan, which was deserted. *Nothing odd about that*, Lilja thought. It was the middle of the night and the past hour's downpour ought to have kept most night owls inside. They arrived at number twenty-four and discovered a house that looked the same as the rest on the street. What had she expected? A crumbling old mansion with a madman playing out his diabolical fantasies on an organ?

"How are we going to do this?" Molander asked.

Lilja thought about it. Some of the lights were on, but most signs indicated that he wasn't home. On the other hand, they couldn't be sure of anything, except that they didn't have much time.

"The fastest way." Lilja hurried up the front steps, cautiously felt the locked doorknob, and made room for Molander to open it.

They each disengaged the safety on their handguns and entered the hallway. The light from the living room spread out across the floor, and they heard the notes of classical music.

"Wagner," Molander whispered behind her. "It's Wagner's *The Valkyrie*."

They walked through the hall to the living room. The lights were on and the music was playing loudly. Lilja went to enter the room, but Molander placed a hand on her arm.

"He wants us to go in, look at the lights and listen to the music. He wants to see how many of us there are."

"Can't we just turn off the music? It's stressing me out."

Molander nodded toward a fuse box and opened it. The fuses were marked with neatly written labels, one for each room of the house. He pulled out the one labelled LIVING ROOM, but the music continued to play. He tried a few of the other fuses, but nothing happened.

"He seems to have bypassed the whole fuse box. I think you'll just have to deal with the music. It's actually one of his better works."

"What if he wants us to stay out of that room and leave this anxious music playing? Maybe there's something he's trying to hide with the music. And if there are cameras in there, what's to say they're not all over the house?"

Molander walked into the living room, went straight to the stereo, and pressed stop. "Happy now?"

Lilja followed him in and looked around the sparsely furnished room. There was only a leather sofa, a recliner, a glass table, and a bookcase, which was empty except for the stereo. Once Molander was finished with the room, and had determined there were no hidden cameras or microphones, they began searching the rest of the house, which had been cleaned out and was mostly empty. Everything was pristine, down to the tiniest detail; Molander couldn't even find prints in the kitchen or bathroom. The cleanliness was marred only by a small shard of porcelain on the kitchen floor, but the basement and attic were also spotless and empty.

Molander was starting to get impatient; he thought they should go to the other address registered to Sölmedal, where his workshop was located, but Lilja wasn't ready to leave the house just yet. She had the feeling they'd missed something, but she didn't know where to look. There was no doubt that the house had been wiped of even the tiniest clue that could help them move forward.

Of course the killer had counted on the fact that they would come and had prepared accordingly. Lilja sat down on the bed while she waited for Molander to finish listening to the bedroom walls with a stethoscope. He had already made it abundantly clear that this was the last thing he would do in the house. She agreed that if he didn't hear anything suspicious, they would leave.

He turned to her.

"Nothing?" Lilja asked.

Molander shook his head. "Nope. Not even the hum from a ventilation system."

"So where the fuck is he?"

"Risk or Sölmedal?"

Lilja shrugged. "Both."

"They could be absolutely anywhere, but let's investigate Sölmedal's workshop."

Lilja nodded. Molander was right: they should go over right away. She stood up and walked over to the wardrobe, which was across from the bed, and opened the door.

"Well, make up your mind," Molander said as she looked through the boring, beige clothes on their hangers.

"Okay, let's go to the workshop now. Where is it again?"

"Frejagatan 2. It's down in the industrial area just north of Råå."

They left the bedroom and walked through the hall, where *The Valkyrie* had just started up again. They exchanged a look, left the house, and went back to the car. Lilja felt frustration bubbling up inside her. This was like playing a game of rock-paper-scissors, except that Sölmedal always knew their choice ahead of time. If they threw paper, he threw scissors. He'd surprised them with an unanticipated move every time.

She hadn't expected him to be at home or at his workshop. But all they could do was go there and hope to find something, which he knew of course. They'd thrown rock, and all he had to do was hold out paper, but what was written on it this time? Another address, in someone else's name? No, that would be too obvious. If he wanted to surprise them, it had to be something else. Something...

Lilja's thoughts were interrupted as Molander stopped suddenly at the Östhammarsgatan intersection and stared straight at one of the yards.

"What is it?"

Molander didn't answer; instead, he walked up to the electrical box that was sticking out of the pavement.

"Ingvar, what is it? What are you doing?"

"This is where it is." He bent down and placed his ear against the humming air intake beside the electrical box.

"Could you please be so kind as to tell me what—"

"I'll be damned if he didn't run it way over here so that you couldn't hear anything from the house." Molander pointed back along the pavement, where there was a half-metre-wide strip of new pavement extending all the way back to Sölmedal's house.

I knew it. I knew it, Lilja thought, staring at Molander, who was already on his way back to the house.

98

LINA PÅLSSON WAS ALREADY waiting at her front door in Norra Hamnen when Tuvesson arrived to pick her up.

"Hi, I'm Astrid. If you crowd in back there, I'll take care of your bag," Tuvesson said, opening the boot.

Lina handed over her suitcase. "I understand that you haven't caught him yet, given that you're bringing us all in, but how is the investigation going now that you know who the killer is?"

"I'm sorry, but how did you know about that?" Tuvesson asked. Lina told her about Fabian's visit that afternoon and how they'd come up with the name of the forgotten student.

Tuvesson didn't know what to say. Was that why Fabian had been acting so strange? She felt dizzy from the numerous thoughts flying around her head. She quickly realized that she was under far too much stress to calculate the repercussions of Lina's knowledge, and asked her not to mention it to the others for now.

Twelve minutes later, they pulled into the small gravel drive outside Seth Kårheden's house. None of the three former classmates had said a word during the journey. She had made a few attempts to poke a hole in the silence, which was taking up all the air in the car like an expanding balloon. She asked if they'd ever had any class reunions and told them about her own class in Malmö—she'd heard that many of her classmates met regularly. All she got were a few dutiful responses. She'd even tried to turn the radio on but soon gave up: the Bee Gees' "Stayin' Alive" didn't seem particularly appropriate.

Seth Kårheden was waiting for them with a bag between his feet and a low cap that was so faded and worn that it must have accompanied him on his whole pilgrimage. She waved at him and pointed at the empty passenger seat.

It had stopped raining, but she preferred to remain in the car where the heated seat would dry her jeans. Kårheden walked around the car and opened the passenger-side door; as he got in he did the best he could to avoid dirtying Lena Olsson's bag, which was occupying most of the footwell.

"Hi. You must be Astrid Tuvesson."

Tuvesson shook his hand, welcoming him, and thought he almost looked better in real life than in the picture they had found online. He was quite handsome, except for that horrid moustache. He turned around toward the people in the back seat. "Wait, don't tell me. You must be Lena Olsson."

Lena nodded.

"It's been years, but I'll never forget how great you were at hopscotch. No one had a fighting chance."

Lena started laughing.

Tuvesson's phone rang and she answered while she was backing out of the driveway. It was Lilja, calling to say that she and Molander had returned to the house after Molander found an air outlet a few houses down the street. Tuvesson didn't quite understand what this implied, and although she had absolute faith in Molander's instincts, she very much wanted to understand what they were up to — but she didn't get the chance to ask.

"I have to go," Lilja's voice said on the other end. "I think he found something."

"Be careful," was all she had time to say before she heard the click in her ear.

"And there's our class clown, Stefan! How are you? I heard you started your own business in your later years."

Stefan Munthe nodded and told them about his consulting

firm, which helped improve internal communications at various companies.

"Well, I haven't communicated with a single person in three whole weeks, so you'll have to excuse me if I'm babbling a bit. I have what you might call some pent-up urges."

"What about me?" asked Lina Pålsson. "Don't you recognize me?"

Seth Kårheden turned to Lina and smiled. "I was saving the best for last. Nobody forgets the prettiest girl in the class."

Lina giggled and Tuvesson smiled with relief. At least their trip to prison wouldn't seem quite as painful. She braked for a red light on Drottninggatan outside the City Theatre. It was already past two in the morning, and darkness still lay upon the street like a wet blanket; a few stray partiers were searching for a new post-last-call watering hole. She had read all the official reports, but nothing would change her opinion that legally mandated last calls were crimes against humanity and did more harm than good.

The light turned green, allowing her to drive up Hälsovägen and on to Ängelholmsvägen, which was empty aside from a few taxis. She pressed the accelerator, happy that the traffic lights were on her side.

She and Klippan both arrived with their packed vehicles at the same time. Ragnar Palm came out of the front doors of the jail to greet them. She looked around, but she didn't see any journalists or curious onlookers. Their timing couldn't have been better. Now all they had to do was get the classmates inside as quickly as possible.

She stopped behind Klippan's car and asked everyone to get out, take their luggage, and follow the others inside. They obeyed without protest, but she could see scepticism in their expressions at the tall razor-wire fence and electric gate, which was currently closing behind them; at Ragnar Palm's grim face, uniform, and weapon.

And it didn't get any better at the security checkpoint, where their luggage was searched piece by piece. "No, you can't bring these nail clippers in. You can borrow some here. But you have to let me take the shampoo…No." Followed by an obligatory "I'm sorry."

The prison officers had been informed that they would have special guests, but their attitudes were so deeply rooted that they were more or less unable to give up their usual practices. They searched the new guests down to their bare skin as if they were regular old inmates, "for their own safety." A few protested, reminding the staff they were not criminals.

Seth Kårheden was the most vocal, refusing to let himself be pushed around. He vocally declared that he had come for protection, not for punishment, and he threatened to go home. This actually seemed to help, and he was allowed to bring in his insulin syringes, even though the jail doctor wasn't there to approve them.

Tuvesson could tell that Klippan was feeling exactly the same way, but like her, he was doing his best not to let it show, pretending that this whole thing was well-thought-out and for a good reason.

They needed to convince the members of the class they weren't being locked up like prisoners.

99

HE HEARD ANOTHER ONE of the barely audible ticking sounds that preceded the buzzing and the twisting action. The first few times after he figured out what was going on, he'd tensed the muscles of his neck and tried to resist as much as he could, but then he realized that the best thing to do was relax.

His neck had already cracked a number of times, and he had survived much longer than he'd been expecting. It ought to be over soon—four more buzzes at the most. He calculated the pauses between the buzzes to be slightly over three minutes, and every fifth turn was a little bit greater, twisting an extra couple of degrees. He couldn't survive another one of those.

The screen in front of him displayed another picture of Theodor. His eyes were closed and he was sitting on the floor of his room in their new house. Fabian recognized the striped rug they had purchased at the Kungens Kurva IKEA a few years back. Theodor had wanted a plain black one, but Sonja insisted on a rug that had stripes in every colour. In the photo he was lying on it with his arms extending straight out from his body, like Jesus on the cross. Probably because he had been knocked out.

And then Fabian realized something he should have figured out a long time ago. Theodor had never left the house: he had been there all along. Carrying the body of a teenage boy out of a house wouldn't exactly have been easy, and there would have been a real risk that the neighbours or a passer-by might notice and ask questions. Why hadn't it occurred to him before? The sounds he'd heard down in the basement weren't from his neighbour—they were from Theodor.

He had been locked up in the bread oven that Sonja had discovered when they moved in. Theodor had tried to make noise, but his father hadn't heard. No, that wasn't true—he had heard, but he had ignored it. His thoughts had been somewhere else, like always.

The barely noticeable ticking started up again.

Soon there would only be three turns left.

"THERE. CAN'T YOU SEE IT?" Molander said, pointing at the baseboard.

Lilja's eyes roamed over the brown board but nothing caught her attention. "All I can see is a brown-stained baseboard."

"And above that?"

"A cable."

"Exactly. It's also stained brown, and leads into the wardrobe, right?"

Lilja nodded.

"But where does it end?" Molander continued, opening the wardrobe of beige clothing. "There's no light or anything in here."

"Maybe it keeps going to the bed."

Molander shook his head. "No, it disappears somewhere behind here. Help me pull it out."

They each took a side and tried to pull the wardrobe away from the wall, but it wouldn't budge.

"It must be attached to the floor and the wall," Molander said, trying to see behind it.

Meanwhile, Lilja sifted through the beige clothing again. There was something bothering her; she couldn't put her finger on it, but now that she was standing here for the second time, she realized that she'd felt this way when she was looking through the wardrobe for the first time. The clothes were certainly beige and boring—two pairs of corduroys, three pairs of chinos, a few shirts and polos—but that wasn't the problem.

Lilja couldn't make sense of it until she discovered a small plastic bag containing two buttons attached to one of the shirts' cuffs. She looked down at Molander, who was on his stomach, shining a torch under the wardrobe.

"These clothes are brand new."

"Okay…"

"I mean, all of them. They've never been worn—they must just be hanging here for show." She pulled them aside and felt along the back panel of the wardrobe but couldn't find a seam.

Molander joined Lilja inside the wardrobe and shone his torch along the edges. They soon discovered there was a tiny seam after all. They emptied the contents of the closet and tried to push in the back panel, but it wouldn't move. Molander started tapping on the wardrobe in different places, and was met with the same dull sound no matter where he knocked.

"You might need some sort of remote control," he said, stepping out of the closet and looking around.

"Try cutting the cable," Lilja suggested.

Molander severed the cable with a pair of pliers.

Lilja, who was still in the wardrobe with her ear pressed to the back panel, felt the air change immediately. There was suddenly a faint draught. Molander came back to help, and they managed to press the back panel in about thirty centimetres; then it moved to the side like a sliding door. A row of bare light bulbs switched on in front of them, and they could see a wooden staircase that appeared to lead straight underground.

FABIAN HAD TRIED TO distract himself by thinking of other things. He thought about Sonja and Matilda and wondered what they were up to right now, whether they were still awake or if they had gone to bed. He tried thinking about Stockholm and how brutal the winters could be there, especially the most recent one. He remembered their vacation to Thailand three years ago, and daydreamed about their new house. Nothing helped. All he could think about was the pain: it had taken over and was demanding all of his attention.

Then he heard the quiet ticking he had spent three minutes waiting for: the buzz came one second later. It would be the fourth and last buzz before it was time for the fifth—the one that would put an end to his pain, in three long minutes.

LILJA AND MOLANDER WENT down the steep staircase with their handguns drawn. The dirt-cellar feeling vanished when they reached the bottom. Instead, it was as if they were on a spaceship from the 1960s. The ceiling was weakly lit and they seemed to be in a narrow, pipe-shaped corridor that slanted slightly downhill and was covered in red, wall-to-wall shag carpeting. On one side of the wall there was a shoe rack with a pair of slippers, and a hook with a white coat hanging from it.

They stooped to avoid hitting their heads on the ceiling as they walked through the hallway. After a few metres, it branched out into a T-shaped corridor that was about five metres long in both directions. They could stand upright now; the walls were straight up and down with two doors on each side of both corridors—eight doors in all.

"You go left. I'll take the right," Molander said, opening the first door on the right-hand side. It led into a room that was painted red, with blinking diodes on the ceiling and exercise equipment spread across the floor. Lounge music was streaming from recessed speakers.

Lilja opened the first door on her side and entered a room filled with neatly hung clothes. There was a vanity table with an illuminated mirror in one corner, and several wigs were arranged on mannequin heads on a shelf. There was a ton of stuff to examine in here, but the details would have to wait. She went back into the corridor.

Molander's eyes were searching a new room that looked like a small apartment, with a neatly made bed and a nightstand at one end, and a small group of furniture with a TV at the other. The room was covered in classic Art Deco wallpaper, and a bookcase full of books and LPs took up one entire wall. There were two additional doors in this room: one was visible and led to a bathroom, and the other was hidden in the patterned wallpaper. If it hadn't been for the wall-to-wall carpeting, which had a clear path trampled into it, he never would have discovered it. He stuck his finger in the small hole and slid the door to the side. The warmth of the neighbouring room hit him unexpectedly. When he saw thousands upon thousands of diodes blinking in the darkness, he knew exactly what sort of room he had found.

Lilja turned the handle to another room, but the door was locked. She backed up as far as she could and gave the door two hard kicks, but it wouldn't give. Only on the third blow did she manage to kick the door down. She found herself in complete darkness and felt the wall for a light switch, but then realized there were three heavy curtains hanging in front of the door. She pulled them aside one by one and quickly scanned the semicircular room as she raised her weapon at the man sitting with his back to her, in what looked like an old dentist's chair.

She told him to stand up slowly and put his hands over his head, but there was no reaction: either the man was dead, or he was unable to answer for some reason. She walked around the chair and realized it was Fabian Risk. Part of her had been worried that he was in danger, while another part of her had been worried that he was behind everything. She was totally unprepared for what she saw: his head was fastened to two plates and had been twisted so far to the side that just looking at it made her sick.

She placed her hand on his extended neck—he still had a pulse. He must have passed out from the pain. She shouted for Molander as loudly as she could, but stopped as soon as she felt a faint vibration from the plates that were holding Risk's head. This peculiar device was about to twist his head off.

She stuffed her handgun into her waistband and grabbed hold of the plates to try to keep the machine from turning as she put her weight against the armrest. She couldn't get a grip and felt the device continue to turn. She wanted to hit it out of sheer rage, but she was afraid that she might do more harm than good.

Suddenly the buzzing stopped and all the lights went out, after which she had no trouble twisting the entire contraption back in the other direction. With trembling fingertips she fumbled for Fabian's pulse in the pitch-black, feeling like she was about to drown in the wave of questions she wanted to ask.

A beam of light came dancing along the vaulted wall, and she heard Molander's voice.

"I think I found the fuse box."

100

FABIAN CAME TO WITH a severe pain in his neck and a throbbing headache. He was thirsty and sweaty. He wanted to swallow, but his sandpapery mouth made it impossible. It was bright, too bright to try opening his eyes. He tried to gather his thoughts, but eventually admitted to himself that he had no idea what had happened or where he was.

He thought back through the most recent events he could recall. It had been a record-breakingly miserable summer, so they'd decided to take a last-minute trip to somewhere warm: him, Sonja, and the kids. They went to Mallorca—Illetas, in fact. He last remembered being in a deck chair by the pool.

He tried to move his head, but his stiff neck refused. He must have fallen asleep with his head in a strange position, or maybe it was sunburn. Perhaps that would explain why he was so confused. He really didn't like going on seaside holidays. This damn heat was only making his headache worse, and the screaming kids all over the place weren't helping. Couldn't they at least have an age limit in the pool area? If this were his hotel, he would have banned kids altogether.

He thought about taking a dip. Maybe that was just what he needed. Then he would have a beer to make him feel at home. The bright lights were making him squint. Where was everyone else? He could see their deck chairs and wet towels. Kerstin Ekman's *Blackwater* was lying open on Sonja's chair. She'd already made it halfway through. He must have been out for hours.

He stood up and waited out a head rush for a few seconds before approaching the pool. Children kept sneaking by and jumping in, trying to splash as much water as they could on the sunbathing hotel guests, but now it was his turn.

It was important for the dive to look decent without making it seem like he was trying too hard: people were probably watching him. He sucked in his stomach, put his hands above his head, jumped in. His legs were straight and together. The cool water surrounded his body. His hands struck something hard, then his forehead. He heard something crunch in his neck. The water turned red.

A German-speaking man tried to help him out of the pool; he wanted to get him to lie down. But he didn't want any help. He didn't want to bleed in the water. He only wanted to get away from the pool and the sticky warmth; away from Sonja and the kids; away from everything.

Someone placed a glass of water to his lips and he opened and closed his eyes. Everything was spinning out of control. He saw a familiar female face. She looked good. He was sure they had met before. Was this all just a dream? No, he could clearly remember diving into the pool, hitting his head, and noticing how the blood dripped into big splotches on the deck when the German tried to get him to lie down. He put his hand to his forehead, but he didn't feel a wound.

Was he even alive? He felt something around his neck. Then he heard a voice. He'd heard it before, but he couldn't place it. *Fabian... Fabian...* He opened his eyes again and saw the same woman. Everything was moving behind her. What was her name again? Lilja... Irene Lilja. That should mean that he was alive, unless he was dead at the same time? Theodor... he had to get home and take care of Theodor. He tried to get up, but Lilja pressed him back down onto the hard stretcher.

"You have to lie down until we get there."

"Get where?"

"The emergency room. It will only be a minute now. The best thing you can do is relax."

But he didn't want to relax, much less go to some ER and wait for hours to be helped. He didn't need any help.

"I'm fine. I just have to get home to Theo."

"It's just the anaesthetic," Lilja said, patting his forehead. "Just take it easy and try to relax."

He screamed at her, telling her she was wrong and that he had to go home to Theo, his son, but she refused to listen. She smiled calmly and repeated over and over again that he should take it easy, reminding him that everything would work out. He wasn't supposed to see it, but he did: she banged on the window to the cab of the ambulance. Then he hit her again. For the second time in twenty-four hours he hit her in the face.

She went quiet and held her reddening cheek.

Finally, she was listening.

HE COULDN'T REMEMBER HOW he got out of the ambulance and up the front steps, or if Lilja tried to stop him, or if the door was locked. All he remembered was suddenly standing in his own basement, looking at Theodor lying on the floor.

Lifeless.

A woman was straddling him, pressing her mouth to his. Who was she and what was she doing? He was *dead*. The woman rose and started rhythmically pressing both hands against his rib cage.

"Fifteen...sixteen...seventeen..." she counted in Danish.

Only then did he realize that she was the police officer from Copenhagen. What was she doing in his house? He tried to ask, but she didn't respond.

"She can't talk right now," Lilja said from behind him.

He turned around but she was already on her way back upstairs. He had no idea how long he watched the Danish policewoman try to bring his dead son back to life.

It was as if time had got stuck, and suddenly the paramedics were just there. He watched them open their bags, take out their equipment, and hook up tubes and wires of various colours. They inserted a tube attached to a squeeze bag into Theodor's mouth, cut his clothes off, and spread something gooey on his chest. The Danish policewoman was lying on the floor beside him, exhausted. Lilja squatted beside her and gave her something to drink.

He heard a loud beeping noise while two paddles were placed on that very young chest. Theo's body bowed up from the floor and fell back down, lifeless, without a pulse. One paramedic made sure that the wires were connected correctly and another squeezed the bag.

How long did it continue? Fabian had no idea.

All he knew for certain was that it was his own fault.

101

ASTRID TUVESSON HAD TO admit that Ragnar Palm had done his best to mitigate the prison atmosphere since she'd last been here. He had hung curtains on the outer wall to hide the fact that there were no windows, and he had put up framed posters from exhibitions at the Louisiana Museum on all the other walls. They were probably Palm's own posters. Tuvesson knew he never missed an exhibit.

But, despite his efforts, it was still plain as day that they were in a jail. *Hopefully it will give them a sense of security,* she thought as the temporary guests selected their beds.

It happened just as she'd predicted: the men settled along one wall, the women along the other. What she hadn't counted on was their questions. She'd been naïve enough to assume that they were just as wrecked as she was and would want to go to sleep. Instead, they asked all the questions she didn't have answers to: "How long do you think we'll have to stay here?" "Is there Wi-Fi?" "My kids are coming home on Sunday. Will they have to stay here too?" "Have you even thought this through?"

She wanted to shout one big, long "*Nooooo*" at them. This was the opposite of well-thought-out. The decision had been made quite suddenly, in what could most aptly be described as a state of panic: every wasted minute made it more likely that the list of victims would grow even longer, and that the media would make more profit and add to the myth of the unrivalled killer who baffled the police like no other.

But who was she to say that there weren't other—or better ways—to tackle the situation? Maybe she had just been too tired to think clearly.

She spoke carefully, trying to give them a somewhat reasonable explanation for why she couldn't answer all their questions, and to remind them how important it was that their location remained a secret. But as soon as the words left her mouth, she could tell how hollow they sounded. "What are you trying to say?" "I have to go and pick up my kids." "I have to go to work; I was only planning to sleep here."

Klippan finally had to climb onto a chair and drop the bombshell: "You might as well realize this now. In order for our plan to work, no one can leave the jail until further notice."

"What if we do anyway?" asked Stefan Munthe.

"Like I said, no one can leave the jail until further notice! The whole point of having you here is to keep your location secret, which means that I have to collect your mobile phones. You can have them back as soon as this is over. The daytime staff can help you make a few necessary calls tomorrow. Is that understood?"

Klippan climbed down from the chair and started walking around to collect phones. No one said a thing. Tuvesson wondered if it was because they were in some form of shock, or if they were just too tired to put up a fight. Part of her wanted to run up and stop him, to make him give the phones back and tell them they could go back home. But Klippan was right: of course there was a risk that one of them might call a family member or friend, or even a journalist, and reveal the plan.

"I know you probably can't answer this, but how long do you think it will go on?" Seth Kårheden asked, breaking the silence.

"Yes, I want to know too," Cecilia Holm said. "You can't just keep us locked up in here forever, just because you can't afford to protect us in our own homes."

"No, we can't," Tuvesson said, wondering how she should continue. "We hope and expect that this won't last too long."

"You hope?"

Tuvesson looked at Lena Olsson and noticed her dejected expression; it said more than all of their protests combined. She realized that she had to throw them a bone, otherwise they would never let her leave. She had to think of something to help them relax and go to bed.

"We don't really want to make this public, but since you're so cut off from the outside world, I can tell you that we're not quite as far from solving the case as it might seem. So without promising too much, I don't think we're talking about more than a few days here at most. If the investigation does drag on, I promise to personally ensure that those of you who want to return home can do so under police protection."

To her great surprise, most of them seemed to think this sounded reasonable.

"So, what do you know that hasn't been made public?" Kårheden asked, apparently having a harder time swallowing the bait than the others.

"For obvious reasons, I can't discuss that right now. I have to leave it at that. Goodnight, and I hope you get a few hours of sleep." She walked brusquely to the exit so she could make it out before they asked any more questions.

102

THEODOR HAD ALWAYS BEEN beautiful; even the midwife noticed it when he was born. She'd said he was one of the most beautiful babies she'd ever delivered. Fabian remembered how happy that had made him, but deep down he'd thought that was what they said to all new parents, something they learned in a class. Not until the midwife called in her colleagues did he realize that his son really was something special. And he remained beautiful as he grew. His curly blond hair always hung down in front of those blue eyes with their rather mysterious, introspective gaze. He had prominent cheekbones and that soft skin, which as far as Fabian knew had never had a single pimple.

But now his hair was dyed black and kept mostly hidden under a hat. Both of his eyebrows were pierced, and he had basically done everything he could to appear ugly, although he hadn't been particularly successful. Theodor was still one of the most beautiful people Fabian had ever seen.

A few years ago, Sonja had suggested he contact a modelling agency to make a little extra money, but she'd received only a grunt in return. Beautiful seemed to be the last thing he wanted to be, as if it were the most shameful thing in the world.

And now he was lying in bed, eyes closed, perfectly relaxed, and Fabian couldn't help thinking that he was staring at death — death at its loveliest. He wanted nothing more than to cry, but he couldn't get any tears out.

Fortunately, his son wasn't dead, but he'd come so close that he had been declared dead for a few moments before his heart agreed to start beating again. Now he was in a drug-induced sleep, hooked up to a whole bunch of machines that were keeping an eye on him.

If it hadn't been for Dunja Hougaard, he would be dead. Because of her CPR, Theodor's blood had received oxygen that pumped throughout his body. She had been fired for helping the Swedish police, but had crossed the Sound to give Fabian Risk the picture of Torgny Sölmedal. He wasn't home and hadn't answered her calls.

He must have forgotten to lock the door, so she'd walked in and called out his name. It was the middle of the night, and she hesitated for a moment before shouting again—louder than before, and even louder the third time. There was no response, but she heard sounds coming from the basement.

Unlike Fabian, Dunja had realized that the sounds weren't coming from the neighbours' house but from something inside the wall. By the time she managed to drag Theodor out, he wasn't breathing and didn't have a pulse. But she didn't give up; instead, she started first aid and didn't stop until the paramedics arrived, nearly a whole hour later. How would he ever be able to repay her?

Fabian was sitting as close to the bed as he could, holding Theodor's hand. If it were up to him, he wouldn't let go until Theodor woke up. However, the threat against him was judged to be so severe that he couldn't remain at the hospital. He protested and tried to use his neck injury as an excuse, but when the X-rays showed that nothing was broken, the doctors gave the okay for him to leave the hospital with a neck brace and a bottle of pain pills.

A nurse came into the room and handed him a phone. He knew exactly who it was; he'd been trying to think of what he would say, but hadn't come up with a single idea.

"Hi."

"Hi."

"Did Irene tell you?"

"Yes."

He didn't say anything; she didn't either. For once, their silence didn't feel uncomfortable. He could hear her breathing, and the sound of her exhales calmed him. He closed his eyes and imagined she was there, lying close to him, breathing in his ear. He missed her so much.

"Sonja, I...I had no idea."

"We're coming down tomorrow. We'll talk then about what to do."

"Okay."

He heard the click in his ear, and handed the phone back to the nurse, who passed Lilja on her way out.

"Are you ready?"

Fabian nodded and stood up. He kissed his son's hand and followed Lilja out of the room.

103

BLACKSBURG, KAUHAJOKI, BAILEY, MONTREAL, Jacksboro, Red Lake, Cold Spring, Red Lion, Erfurt...The list of school shootings was infinitely long. They'd each had their moment in the limelight, but these days they all shared the same fate: forgotten in the deep abyss. Nobody remembered the schools on the list any more—no one but those who mourned.

This was different in every way and would never be forgotten. It would be etched into millions upon millions of minds, and no one would ever be able to forget his name. The process was already fully underway. The news of the spectacular murders had spread far beyond the borders of Sweden, and had been one of CNN's top stories for the past twenty-four hours.

And that was when they only knew about six dead members of the class. What would they do when they heard about the next five deaths, which would soon be a reality? How would they react when they realized that nobody was safe, not even those who left Skåne and settled in Oslo, or happened to be on vacation abroad?

He was closer to his goal than he'd ever dared to dream. During the past several years he had persuaded himself that there was no alternative but success. It was all the result of his meticulous preparations. Until now he hadn't dared to let himself admit how naïve he had been and how bad his odds actually were, but at this point complete success was more or less a given. He was in the home stretch and the finishing line was in sight.

He had nine left to go: nine people who, according to the original plan, had been scheduled to receive a night-time visitor, one by one. He'd calculated that it would take five hours, including travel time, but things had changed completely.

All nine of them were now locked in the same room—with him.

He tried to look like he was asleep, but he had a hard time hiding his smile. This was almost too good to be true. It was like God had been testing his patience and decided to reward him by rolling out the red carpet.

No one even seemed to suspect that he wasn't who he said he was. The moustache had done the trick, and the coagulated blood plus the contact adhesive he'd found held better than he had hoped. He had also done a good job playing his role and was surprised how easy it was, considering that he didn't have any time to prepare.

The obvious way to act would have been to lie low and make as little fuss as possible, to stay in the shadows and let the others do the talking the way he'd always done. But as soon as he got into the car he felt like doing the exact opposite. He felt like talking. And for the first time, they listened. He'd spoken more with his former classmates in the past few hours than he had during all his years at school.

Back then, they had hardly responded when he spoke. Now it was different. Now they were happy to talk about themselves: their kids and marriages; divorces and cheating; the career that took them close to the top of the Ericsson hierarchy, only to end in a pink slip, forcing them back to school to learn how to write a resumé; their shattered hopes and depression; the new outdoor bathtub; home-loan interest rates.

They all thought they knew who they were talking to, but really they hadn't the foggiest idea. And he was enjoying it so much. The pathetic little failures of their lives were like music to his ears, and hearing about them was like a remedy for his years of jealousy—jealousy of their success and of everything they'd had that he would never be able to partake in.

He'd always wondered how everyone else could be so secure in their roles—everyone but him. But everything was different now: the roles were reversed. They were no more than extras in his own biopic—a gang of losers—a vapid, grey mob with lives so uninteresting that he was surprised they could even bear to discuss them, much less live them.

There could be no doubt that he was doing most of them a favour by ending their days on earth. Several of them would probably thank him afterward if they could. Now, at least, their insipid little lives would come to a meaningful end. They would be transformed into another check in a box, a number added to the others to form a sum that no one would ever be able to beat—no one had ever killed their whole class.

No one.

Nine more, and he would be done.

Twenty out of twenty.

Most of them wouldn't even feel a thing; a tiny poke, and a few seconds later it would be over. Some of them would probably try to put up a fight, but that wouldn't change anything. The end result would be the same.

Twenty out of twenty.

For a few hours it would look like only nineteen out of twenty had been killed, as if one had managed to defend himself and had stuck the syringe in the killer and survived. This hero would be Seth Kårheden. Before the police managed to sift through the chaos and discovered that Kårheden was dead too, he would be far away. He hadn't yet decided whom he would select to be the killer...

Everyone had turned off their bedside lamps, although he could hear someone opening the lid of their retainer case and someone else pulling off their socks; a third punched a pill out of a blister pack. They would all be asleep within fifteen minutes. His watch said it was twenty past three, and he could feel his energy returning with every tick of the second hand.

He heard someone jangle their keys and he couldn't figure out why, until he heard the heavy metal door opening. He opened his eyes and saw two prison officers carrying in another bed; they placed it in the row across from his. Was there one more person? He was confused. Everyone was already here.

He watched as they made the bed and put a chair beside it. He wondered if one of the guards would be sleeping here, which wouldn't be such a big problem. He would just have to wait for at least half an hour more.

But his suspicions turned out to be wrong. Instead, a man was led in, but it was too dark for him to make out his identity. It wasn't until the man took off his jacket and revealed his neck brace that it dawned on him who it could be. Was it possible that Fabian Risk was sitting on the edge of the bed and glancing around the room?

There was no way he could have managed to escape on his own. The only plausible explanation was that the police had found his hiding place, which in turn meant that they had identified him. He couldn't figure out how they would have managed it: he had taken care of the prints from the car. But maybe there had been others.

He closed his eyes and tried hard to hide that he was wide awake, his heart beating double time. He really just wanted to run over there and stick a syringe in that bastard and end him once and for all, but he knew he couldn't—not yet. Instead, he had to keep his eyes closed and consider his options. He couldn't risk stumbling at the finishing line—not right now. He had come too far.

The fact that they had identified him didn't necessarily hurt him that much, considering that he would be making his own identity public in just a few hours. The process had already been set in motion, and at least a hundred people were working on it at this very moment. So, upon review, there wasn't really any reason to worry.

But he was concerned about this uncertainty. It was the last thing he needed right now. What else had they figured out? Did they know he was in the jail? And if so, did they know he had taken on Kårheden's identity? Is that why Risk was here? Or did they think joining the others was the safest option even for him?

He realized that the police likely had no idea. If they even suspected he was locked up with the remaining members of the class, they would have sent the SWAT team in ages ago and brought each of them in for questioning. The more he thought about it, the more certain he was.

They definitely had no idea.

At least Tuvesson and her colleagues didn't know. What was going on in Risk's head, however, was another question entirely. Fabian Risk existed under completely different laws of nature to his colleagues.

Risk should have died a little more than two hours ago but there he was, sitting on a bed across the room, gazing at the ten sleeping people. Nothing surprised him any more about this man. There could be no guarantee that Risk didn't suspect he was here. He might have inexplicably managed to figure out exactly what was going on and then decided to spend the night there. If he did, he should have informed his colleagues; the operative word being "should." This wouldn't be the first time Risk didn't do what he was supposed to. It was equally likely that he had decided to keep his suspicions to himself. Or perhaps he didn't suspect a thing, and was only hoping to get a few hours of sleep in the safety of the jail.

He turned onto his side, trying to make it look like he was moving in his sleep. No one could see his smile when he started the timer on his watch.

Thirty minutes, and not one second longer.

He had found his killer.

104

THE PICTURE WAS NEARLY perfect. Unlike the archival image they had been using, he wasn't sporting a wild beard, and his facial features, anonymous though they were, were all visible. This was what Torgny Sölmedal looked like today.

"And you were fired because you wanted to forward this to us?" Tuvesson asked. Dunja Hougaard nodded.

"Yes, and because I sent you the car," Dunja said, trying to sound as Swedish as possible.

Tuvesson shook her head and exchanged glances with Lilja, Klippan, and Molander. She didn't know what to say. She'd met Kim Sleizner a few times, and had always thought of him as a stuck-up, bullying type. Bullies were far from scarce in the police system, on both sides of the Sound. Like everyone else, she had heard stories about Sleizner and assumed they were just rumours. But the fact he would put up roadblocks to hinder an investigation in Sweden for his own personal gain was something else.

"And he has no idea you're here?"

"No, he doesn't even know I have the picture. That psychopathic fucking arsehole blocked my email right after he fired me."

Tuvesson and the others looked at one another.

"Sorry," Dunja said. "What I mean is, he's—"

"I think we understand," Tuvesson said. "But how did you get hold of the picture?"

"I have a good friend in the IT department."

"You can never have too many of those," Klippan said.

"Just so you know, you can count all of us as friends," said Tuvesson. "Without you, we wouldn't...I don't even want to think about it."

"I just can't understand why Sleizner doesn't want us to have the picture," Lilja said.

"My guess is he wants to present it himself at the press conference in a few hours," Dunja said.

"It's all about getting the credit."

"And taking the focus off his own mistakes," Klippan added.

Tuvesson paused for a moment, but her mind was already made up. Sleizner would be furious and would likely raise Cain to ensure that the relationship between the Swedish and Danish police forces became even more strained, if that was possible.

"Let's put out an APB right away."

Dunja felt the lump in her stomach start to dissolve. Finally — she was with a unit where the police put the case first.

"I'll upload it to the server," Molander said and then vanished.

Klippan and Lilja were already calling around to the morning papers.

"Dunja, if you want something to eat or drink, the kitchen's over there. Make yourself at home," Tuvesson said. "And if you want to rest, we have a—"

"What if I want to help?"

105

SINCE JUNE 16 SHE had only passed by the house, and it felt very strange every time. She hadn't delivered the paper for three and a half weeks, which was like an eternity for Kårheden. In nearly ten years of delivering newspapers, she couldn't remember a single time he had suspended his subscription for so long. Now that she thought about it, she couldn't recall that he had ever suspended it before.

To be completely honest, she missed him, even though she didn't know him. She hardly even knew what he looked like. But she knew one thing—he eagerly awaited the newspapers she delivered. It was probably the highlight of Kårheden's day.

But now the dry spell was over. She would deliver his newspaper, and order would be restored. She got off her flatbed moped, took a copy of *Helsingborgs Dagblad*, and folded it up as she walked toward the house. Smoke was coming from the chimney as usual, even though it was the middle of summer. Sure, it had rained quite a bit overnight and the old house must be damp, but Kårheden clung to his routines. She had figured out that much.

Halfway to the door, she changed her mind and went back to pick up a *Dagens Nyheter* and a *Svenska Dagbladet* as a little welcome-home present. It was the least she could do to show her appreciation. At the door, she folded up *Svenskan* and carefully pushed it through the letter box. She wondered how he would react. Would he assume she had delivered the wrong paper and quickly open the door, or would he accept it with curiosity and see it as a little adventure for today?

But nothing happened.

The newspaper plopped to the hall floor and stayed there, as if no one cared. No hand reached for it. She hurried to fold *DN* and pushed it through the slot.

Nothing.

What did this mean? She knew he was home; maybe he had just fallen asleep. Out of sheer impulse, she rang the doorbell as she pushed *HD* through the letter box. She watched it fall and land on top of the other papers. Something felt wrong but she didn't know what to do. Should she leave and pretend everything was fine?

She probably *should* have done that, but instead she turned the door handle. It was unlocked. She stepped inside, but left the papers on the floor. Just as she had imagined, there was a comfortable reading chair in front of the fireplace, in which wood was smouldering.

Where was Kårheden? She didn't hear the sound of a shower. She said hello, but didn't get a response. He wasn't home. Why wasn't he here and who had lighted the fire? She knew it didn't really matter and that whatever was going on was none of her business. She told herself that she should leave the house, go back to her moped, and continue on her route. Kårheden wasn't the only one who needed his paper, after all.

She walked into the living room and looked around; one door was ajar, which appeared to lead to the bedroom. Maybe he was just in there sleeping? She had no idea where he'd been during the long subscription break. It was possible he was just jetlagged.

She kept telling herself to leave, but kept going further into the house.

She pushed the door open with her foot and found him in bed, wearing pyjamas. He wasn't sleeping. He was dead, hands and feet bound to the bed frame.

She was bewildered; then she thought of all the books she had read and how many clues could be found at the scene of a murder. She had to take a closer look, even though it was against her better judgement. This was the first time she'd ever seen a dead person in real life, other than the time she passed an overturned car on Highway 111. The ambulance had already been on the scene, and she'd slowed down to catch sight of the sheet-draped stretcher. Today was entirely different.

She pressed her index finger to his bare foot. It felt cool, and the pale spot remained. She wondered if that revealed anything about how long he'd been dead. She thought about what she had read in her favourite crime novels. How much of what the authors wrote was based in reality? Did your body really start to grow stiff as soon as you died?

Her eyes moved along his arm. His pyjama sleeve was rolled up, and she could see some dried blood that had run down his forearm. She took a closer look and discovered a small red spot in the crease of his elbow. Someone had stuck a needle in his arm and poisoned him. Her heart started to race. She was really good at this.

However, she couldn't understand his face. When she'd first stuck her head into the room, she had assumed he had a moustache, but now that she saw it close up she realized it wasn't hair at all: his moustache had been removed—cut off, skin and all—and what remained was a swamp of coagulated blood.

106

KIM SLEIZNER WOKE IN a cold sweat; the sheets on his bed were damp. It was only ten past four. He could sleep for two more hours and still have time for a long shower and a good breakfast before the press conference.

He could hardly wait. At last the spotlight would be aimed at what truly mattered: the real criminal—the killer who had taken the lives of six Swedes and two Danes.

Soon the papers would have something serious to write about, instead of dwelling on his private life. He gazed out of the window and looked east. It was still dark, unusually dark for July, but the sky wasn't quite as dim over near Sweden. No matter what, today was a new day full of possibilities.

He watched a ship pass along the canal on the way to Langebro. He got carried away in a fantasy where he raced to the garage, took the car to the bridge, and hopped onto the ship's deck so he could leave all this shit behind and start a new adventure, never to return.

His heart was still pounding, but he didn't understand why. He hadn't had a single cup of coffee all day yesterday, and everything was going as planned. Dunja was out of the picture and soon he would be going public with a news item that would silence the criticism around him in one blow. He ought to feel confident, but he only felt anxious.

He took a few deep breaths before bending down as far as he could and standing up again, taking another deep breath; he extended his arms above his head and brought them down in a circle, just as he'd seen Viveca do when she was practising yoga in front of the TV. He tried again, but the movements didn't seem to have any effect on him.

He gave up and walked over to his desk, turned on his laptop, and checked to see if he had received any new emails.

Three of them had managed to make it through the spam filter.

July 10, 2010, 2:12:40 a.m.
viveca.sleizner@gmail.com

Talked to the agent, who will be by to look at the apartment at one o'clock today. I expect it to be nice and clean, and for you to stay away.—V

July 10, 2010, 3:32:51 a.m.
jens.duus@politi.dk

The picture has been printed, framed, and uploaded to our server with the password Kb48Grtda7.
See you!
Jens

Sleizner had no idea why Jens Duus always insisted on using such complicated passwords. In just a few hours it would be passed along to every journalist in the country so they could log in and download the picture, and he knew that at least a third of them would type in the wrong combination of letters and numbers.

July 10, 2010, 3:51:10 a.m.
niels.pedersen@politi.dk
http://politiken.dk/

The message didn't contain anything other than a link to *Politiken*. Sleizner looked at the clock and realized that this email had just arrived. Who was Niels Pedersen? He didn't think he knew anyone by that name. He clicked on the link.

He couldn't believe his eyes; he was flummoxed, absolutely flummoxed.

They had already got a hold of the picture he had made sure to have framed and prepared so that *he* was the one to make it public.

HERE HE IS!

The Swedish police have released a picture of the Class Killer, Torgny Sölmedal, and say they are hot on his trail. A source tells us, "He should soon be in custody."

Sleizner went to *Berlingske*'s website and discovered the image there, too.

THE SWEDISH POLICE HAVE MADE GREAT STRIDES IN
THE HUNT FOR CLASS KILLER TORGNY SÖLMEDAL!

They had even identified him! Dunja must have leaked it—it couldn't have been anyone else. But how the hell had she done it? She was worse than a fucking cockroach. No matter how hard he stomped on her, she just kept running around. He had made sure to block her email account, of course, and yet she had managed to get her hands on the picture that was the centrepiece of his entire press conference; the counterpoint to all the rumours that he was going to announce his resignation.

He would have to cancel, which would mean a major loss of prestige. Hammersten would start to wonder what was going on, but he had no choice. Without the picture he had nothing to bring to the table, and the whole discussion would end up revolving around his potential resignation. No matter how he looked at the situation, he came to the same conclusion: that filthy fucking little whore had won and he was down for the count.

But he had got up before. He wasn't out of the running just yet—not by a long shot.

107

"AND DON'T FORGET..."

"What?"

"He is incredibly dangerous."

He heard a click, and the call ended. He picked up his coffee cup, but his hand was shaking so much that he had to hold it in both hands. The coffee had grown cold, but with any luck the sugar would give him the energy he needed. He felt an instinctive reluctance, but he knew he had no choice—if he hesitated in the slightest they might end up with even more victims. He heard a toilet flush and his colleague emerged from the bathroom with a newspaper in hand.

"What is it? You look totally...what the hell is going on?"

"Sh-she called from the c-crime unit, you know, that T-Tu-Tuvesson lady."

"Okay? What the hell did she want?"

"He's here. The C-C-Class Killer."

"What the fuck are you talking about? What do you mean, *here*?"

"S-Seth Kårheden was found dead in his home," he replied, relieved that the nervousness in his voice was finally starting to let up.

"Are you suggesting that the killer is lying down in there with everyone else, disguised as Seth Kårheden?"

He nodded and felt himself starting to calm down. Now that there were two of them, it all felt so much better.

"Fucking A."

"They're working on getting us backup, but you and I have to go in and get him before he can do any more harm. We can't wait."

"Okay. Let's go—if you're up to it, that is."

"Of course I am. Why wouldn't I be up to it?"

His colleague punched him lightly on the shoulder. "Wow, this is so cool. You and I get to be the ones to take down this fucker."

They quickly checked their gear and left the guardroom. When they arrived at the locked door that led to the sleeping area, they stopped and exchanged glances.

"Ready?"

He nodded. His colleague turned the key as gently as he could, then pushed open the door.

"Maybe we should take off our shoes so we don't wake anyone up."

"Good idea."

They removed their shoes, entered the room, closed the door behind them, and waited for their eyes to adjust to the darkness. They knew exactly where to look: the killer was the guy who had done most of the talking and the majority of the protesting when faced with the idea of sleeping in the jail. He'd been right in front of them the whole time. Talk about a cold-blooded bastard. But soon he would be in custody. He didn't even feel nervous at all any more. It would all work out—he was sure of it.

A few minutes later, they started moving toward the next-to-last bed on the left-hand side. His colleague was ready with the handcuffs. Taking off their shoes had been a brilliant idea because it was impossible to hear their steps as they crossed the room.

When they arrived at the bed they discovered him asleep, lying on his stomach. His head was turned away from them, and his right hand was under the pillow while the left was beside his body. It didn't look very comfortable, but in his seventeen years as a night guard he had seen the most peculiar sleeping positions first-hand.

They were as ready as they would ever be.

He raised his left knee in the air and shoved it forward just as he bent down over the sleeping man; his plan was to jam his knee into the man's back and pull both of his arms behind him — a move that was second nature for any prison officer and one he had performed more times than he could recall.

But just as his knee was about to land, the man slid away and twisted around, and he suddenly felt a stabbing pain in his left thigh. He tried to locate the pain but he didn't have time because the man shot up out of the bed and grabbed the neck of his colleague, who dropped to the floor without a sound.

Then he realized that he was also lying on the floor. His legs must have fallen out from under him. Why couldn't he feel anything? He tried to get up again, but he couldn't move his legs. He tried to use his arms, but he couldn't move them either.

He couldn't even breathe.

108

THE DOORS CLOSED, ONLY to open again, which was typical for this time of day. There was always some waffler standing there to keep them from closing as he shouted to one of his buddies who had collapsed against one of the pillars on the platform.

Sievert Sjödal remembered being that age and leaning against the very same pillar with the same amount of alcohol in his bloodstream back in the mid-1980s. He was sure it had been more fun back then. He recalled the night Lustans Lakejer played their farewell concert at Ritz. He had stood at the very front and even got Johan Kinde's autograph afterward.

He had waited for the train that night. The atmosphere at the station reminded him of this evening; the only difference was that this time he was waiting for the train to leave so he could jump onto the tracks with his bucket and brush, a ladder over his shoulder.

He had to be careful where he put his feet, although he'd been doing this job for so many years now that he would have no problem performing the whole procedure blindfolded. He didn't feel like he would be missing out if he couldn't see: the ads he had spent the last few years pasting up were so hopelessly boring and stupid that he was certain not one of the millions of passengers who took the subway paid any attention to them. Even the 1980s campaigns had been better, like Gevalia's "Unexpected Visitor" series, or the one from Nokia that no one had understood and kept trying to figure out.

But the campaign he was in the process of putting up right now was actually kind of unique, and he couldn't help but wonder what it was actually an ad for. It featured the portrait of a man who looked incredibly ordinary, with five words written at the bottom of the poster in red letters.

IT WAS ME.
— TORGNY SÖLMEDAL

109

THE FEELING OF HIS own pulse woke Fabian up. He was out of breath; he must have been dreaming again. Normally, he never had dreams, but for the past day they had come as soon as he closed his eyes—sick, twisted plots that didn't seem to have anything to do with his real-life experiences. He couldn't remember his dream tonight, but he was sure he'd had one.

Or had something else woken him up?

He sat up and saw the row of beds along the wall across from him. He remembered he was sleeping in jail along with his former classmates. He picked up his watch from the chair: 4:23 a.m.

He was tired, far too tired to get up after just a few hours of sleep. He looked around at the other beds, but everyone seemed to be asleep. Why was he awake? He didn't usually wake up in the middle of the night. He needed to use the bathroom. Maybe it was just the pressure of his bladder that had roused him.

He got to his feet and walked toward the bathroom door on the other side of the room. He opened it as quietly as he could, and felt along the wall for the light switch, but decided not to flip it. Otherwise he wouldn't be able to see a thing on the way back.

It was pitch-black inside the bathroom, and he had to feel his way forward with both arms extended. There was a drawn plastic shower curtain to his right. He ran his hand down it until he felt something cold and hard—the edge of a bathtub. Maybe he would be able to take a bath tomorrow.

He moved further in and passed the sink before he came to the toilet. He felt for the cool, slightly sticky porcelain edge. He pulled up the seat, relieved himself, and flushed. It was louder than he'd expected, and he hoped it didn't wake anyone. He found the tap and the soap dispenser and washed his hands.

He couldn't find a towel to wipe his hands with, so he turned back to use the shower curtain. His foot touched something on the ground that rolled across the tiles. It sounded hard and metallic. He bent down and groped at the floor to find out what it was.

At last he found it next to one of the walls and, sure enough, it was made of metal and shaped like a hemisphere, a centimetre or two in diameter. He could feel some sort of pattern in relief on the rounded side, and there was a little loop sticking out on the other. He realized what it was.

A button.

The button from a uniform.

Suddenly everything fell into place. He knew why he had woken up and why the shower curtain was pulled across.

He walked over to the bathtub and stuck his hand in—his suspicions were immediately confirmed. He could feel a leg and a hand; a foot, but no shoe; two necks and two faces.

Two guards—both dead.

He was here.

Torgny Sölmedal was here. Of course he was. Where else would he be? The thought hadn't even occurred to Fabian, nor apparently to anyone else.

But who was he? He probably wasn't Jafaar or one of the women. Stefan A or Stefan M? Seth? Nicklas? It had to be one of them.

Fabian left the bathroom and walked back through the sleeping area as quickly as he could without raising suspicion. He went past his bed on his way to the exit. The door was locked, and he couldn't find an alarm button. He didn't have a phone, and probably none of the others did either. He rubbed his temples; he felt far too tired to deal with all this. Could the killer have used one of the guards' keys? Had he already left?

He walked back to his bed, looking around at the others while he did so. There was a person in every bed, except for his own. Sölmedal was still here. He opened his toiletry bag, carefully popped out the mirror inside the lid, and walked over to the row of beds across from his own.

There was a man lying on his back with his mouth open in the first bed, furthest to the right against the outer wall. Although he'd gained a lot of weight, Fabian immediately recognized him as Jafaar Umar. He crouched down beside the bed and thought of how entertaining Jafaar had always been during Student Hour in school; he'd always talked about becoming a comedian. He held the little mirror close to his mouth and tried to remember if he'd ever seen him or heard about him, but he couldn't think of a single time.

There was no fog on the mirror.

To be safe, he gently pressed Jafaar's carotid artery.

Nothing.

Jaffe was already dead, and Fabian wasn't surprised. The only question was how many of the others he'd already got to.

He walked to the next bed, where Stefan Andersson was lying on his side. He held the mirror against his mouth and didn't get any fog either. Shit. He was too late. He hurried to the next, where Seth Kårheden lay: there was no mistaking that moustache. He'd had it as long as Fabian could remember. He held the little mirror above his mouth and discovered the same results. He wiped the mirror against the leg of his pants and tried again, but the mirror was still unchanged.

Could he really have had time to kill everyone? And if so, why was Fabian still alive? Had he only woken up because the murderer had been in the process of visiting all the beds across from him? Fabian was too tired to think clearly, and he felt powerlessness spreading like a virus. He really just wanted to give up: to go back to his bed, lie down, close his eyes, and wait for his turn.

He placed his hand on Seth Kårheden's carotid artery to confirm what he already knew, but there was something else that wasn't quite right.

The moustache.

It was crooked. Almost as if it were...He cautiously felt it, and sure enough, it wasn't attached at all. He looked at it closely in his hands and discovered that it was incredibly well made for a fake moustache, until he realized that it wasn't a fake at all. He dropped it as if it were contagious and looked back at Kårheden, realizing that the dead man in the bed in front of him wasn't Seth Kårheden.

It was Nicklas Bäckström.

He tried to figure out what was going on, but he couldn't think straight; he sensed something moving on the floor on the other side of the bed, but he couldn't see what it was. In the next instant he felt a sting on his left shin. He tried to get away, but he couldn't move. The hands under the bed had already caught hold of his ankles, and were pulling at him.

Fabian fell to the floor, his neck brace hitting the edge of the bed where Stefan Andersson lay. He saw the arms slinking out from under the bed like two tentacles. While he was trying to kick himself loose, he noticed the syringe sticking straight out from his shin. The person attacking him wanted this syringe, but he couldn't reach it; it was too far down. All he could do was keep kicking and putting up a fight.

He made contact with something hard and felt the eager hands loosen their grip. He tried to pull his legs up toward his body, but they didn't move. If he didn't escape soon, those hands would be back. He turned onto his stomach and tried to get up on all fours, but his legs refused to obey him. Soon the hands would reach the syringe and inject the poison.

He reached for the leg of Andersson's bed, but couldn't quite get there. Just another few centimetres...He wriggled around and heard the bed behind him overturn. He got a grip on the bed leg and tried to pull himself toward it using all the strength he could muster.

He dragged himself across the floor with his arms, trying to get away from whatever was behind him. He needed to get to the door at any price. He was losing more and more feeling, and although he didn't believe he would make it out before it was too late, he continued to methodically slither across the shiny linoleum floor. Was he the only one left, or were some of the others still alive?

He filled his lungs to scream, but at that very second he was pulled back and turned around: Torgny Sölmedal stood up, with one leg on either side of him, smiling. Sölmedal jumped straight into the air. Fabian realized what was about to happen and tried to roll away, but he could no longer move; Sölmedal landed knees first, right onto his chest.

He heard several of his ribs crack, and felt an intense pain spreading through his lungs. He coughed and tasted blood. He gasped for breath but couldn't get any air. Sölmedal's smile grew bigger as he leaned toward him and whispered into his ear: "There's no point in fighting any more. It's over."

He was right. There was nothing left to do but watch as Sölmedal reached for the syringe in his leg. What was he waiting for? Why hadn't he injected him with the poison already, during the struggle? Fabian coughed up more blood, and he could hear a whistling in his chest every time he tried to inhale.

Sölmedal's hand trembled as if it were struggling to reach the syringe. Sölmedal's other hand was up at his own neck, trying to loosen a belt that was getting tighter and tighter. Who was strangling Sölmedal? His face was growing paler and had almost turned blue, but he continued to struggle, as if he refused to accept that it was only a matter of time until it was over.

Fabian couldn't tell if the battle went on for seconds or minutes—it seemed to go on forever. Lena, Cecilia, and Annika were behind Sölmedal, pulling on the belt, and at times it looked like they wouldn't succeed. Fabian heard them screaming for help, but he didn't see anyone coming. Instead, the colour returned to Sölmedal's face, and with it the strength to reach the syringe. Fabian made one last effort to move his leg away, but he could no longer move.

Instead, as if out of nowhere, another hand appeared and yanked the syringe from his leg. Fabian was perplexed—but it was Lina. A moment later she injected it into Sölmedal's neck.

It was finally over. He lay there—dead—tongue hanging from his mouth.

They all helped to drag the body off Fabian's chest. Then the ceiling lights came on and he heard someone running across the room. He had to close his eyes. The light felt like needles. He saw more blood, and heard agitated voices shouting over each other.

Tuvesson, Lilja, and Klippan were there. Someone put a hand to his throat and shouted something in Danish. He didn't know what it was, but it sounded serious. She shouted again, but he wasn't sure anyone was listening.

He coughed. He could taste blood in his mouth and felt it flowing down his neck. It didn't hurt any more. The pain was fading away, just like the voices.

At last it was just quiet—dark and quiet.

110

IT WAS STILL EARLY morning, but the sun was shining and nudging the temperature quite a bit past twenty degrees. It looked like another day of record heat. The traffic could still be considered sparse, but it was growing heavier by the minute and the ferry terminal already had a long, winding line of cars packed for vacation.

The first beachgoers were already arriving down at Fria Bad, putting their blankets out on the sand to secure the best spots and enjoy a few final minutes of peace. In another few hours, the beach would transform into a cacophony of yelling families, with kids dropping their ice creams and exhausted parents.

The stores along Kullagatan wouldn't open for a while yet, but the girls at Fahlmans Konditori on the corner of Stortorget were already busy putting out tables and chairs.

Yesterday's billboards were still posted outside convenience stores; aside from the murders on the E6 highway and at the library, they boasted sunscreen tests and tips for avoiding arguments while on holiday.

On the whole, it was a perfectly normal Saturday morning in mid-July. Except for one thing: everyone was talking about the same story, all throughout the country.

The face hadn't yet made it onto the front pages, but they all saw his face as soon as they left their homes—on buses and bus shelters, advertisements and commuter trains.

Those who had already been online were able to explain the whole situation to anyone who was curious. It wasn't some peculiar ad campaign: the face belonged to Torgny Sölmedal.

It was him.

111

FABIAN RISK SHUDDERED AND realized that his eyes were closed. He was alive. He tried to move his toes, but he didn't know if he'd succeeded. He really ought to be happy and relieved, but all he felt was a big black hole of sorrow. He thought about the numbers again; numbers that refused to give him any peace.

He was shaking from the cold, even though he was tucked under a thick blanket. He tried to think of something else, but the numbers were stubborn; like an obsession, they came back and repeated themselves ad nauseam.

Lina, Cecilia, Annika, and Lena had saved him: four people had survived. There were five including him — five out of twenty-one. Sixteen of his former classmates had lost their lives, if you counted Ingela Ploghed — seventeen, if you counted their teacher. It was an unparalleled catastrophe. There were question marks next to the three people who were far from Skåne, but Fabian didn't hold out much hope for them. For the most part, Torgny Sölmedal had succeeded in what he'd set out to do.

Fabian himself had failed in every imaginable way.

Twenty people were dead if you included the Danish police officer and the two guards.

And that wasn't even counting Mette Louise Risgaard.

He opened his eyes and saw a ceiling with fluorescent lights and perforated tiles that were the same colour as a smoker's teeth. It looked familiar. He had been here very recently. He turned his head as far as the pain would allow and saw Theodor in the bed next to his. He was awake; he looked back and made eye contact—neither of them said anything. It was as if silence were the most precious thing they had right now and it mustn't be broken under any circumstance. There was so much yet to be said, but it would all come in good time. So many meaningless apologies. So many strained explanations. Promises that would never be fulfilled.

Theodor extended his hand; as Fabian took it in his own he felt the warmth spread through his arm and into his body.

EPILOGUE

ANDERS ANDERSSON WAS STILL on holiday with his family at an all-inclusive hotel in Alcudia, Mallorca, eight days after the incidents in the Helsingborg jail. Although he hadn't read a single newspaper, it had been impossible to miss the news of what had happened back home. Everyone was talking about it, and it took only two days before everyone at the hotel knew that he had been in *that* class and started saying things about guardian angels and blessings in disguise.

Anders himself didn't believe in that sort of thing, but what did he know? *Maybe they're right*, he thought, and ordered another beer from the bar. He opened the last pack of *snus* he had brought along, unaware that it had been penetrated with a syringe three weeks earlier.

Despite the doctors' heroic measures, he died shortly thereafter.

Three days after Lotta Ting's holiday was officially over, she was found locked in a box in her attic at Colbjørnsens gate 12 in Oslo, arms and legs bound behind her. According to the forensic investigation, it had taken fewer than five days for her to die, thanks to the high summer temperatures.

On Sunday, July 11, Christine Vingåker and her husband left the house they had been renting in Lysekil to go home and back to work for a week before an island-hopping holiday in Greece with their children. Christine got into her Nissan Micra early on Monday morning and drove to her office, which was on Drottninggatan in Helsingborg. She had brought along the bottle of supplements she took each morning and evening. She couldn't actually afford them, but she hadn't been sick once since she'd started taking them, just as her friend had promised, and she was in her fifth year of good health.

No one else was injured when the driverless car ran into one of the concrete pillars in the parking garage under Knutpunkten.

People ripped down Torgny Sölmedal ads or sprayed nasty words over them. An increasing number of voices joined the appeal to take the posters down and replace them with something else, but it was easier said than done in the middle of the holiday season, so Torgny's face continued to adorn Sweden for the two remaining weeks of high summer.

Thanks

Mi

For all your help and thoughts. Without you and your belief that it was unquestionably possible, it never would have been happened. I love you for that and all the rest.

Kasper, Filippa, and Sander

For putting up with it all these years.

Peter and Mikael

For your time, and for your opinions. It meant more than you know.

Jonas, Julie, Adam, Andreas, and Sara

For your fantastic energy and professionalism down to the tiniest detail.

Café String and Lilla Caféet in Söder

For all the times you let me sit in my corner and make a cup of tea last until it was long since cold.

THE NINTH

GRAVE

STEFAN AHNHEM

PUBLISHED JANUARY 2017

PROLOGUE

June 14, 1998–November 8, 1999

IT WAS SO DARK he could barely see right in front of him. The prisoner transport vehicle lurched forward so vigorously on its way through the difficult terrain that the letters he was trying to write were almost illegible. But that couldn't be helped. It was his last chance to record his story of the love affair that made him leave everything behind before the pool of blood under him got too big. He would describe how he was shot down and captured by his own people and how he was now on his way to an almost certain death.

He had found the pen in the Israeli military camp at the Huwwara checkpoint in the uncontrolled part of the West Bank. The paper came from some empty diary pages he had found in Tamir's backpack, along with a used envelope he could turn inside out.

Once he was finished writing, he folded up the pages of the letter with his bloody hands, slipped them into the envelope, and sealed it as best he could. He had no stamp — or even an address. All he had was a name. But he didn't hesitate to push the letter out through the thin crack in the truck and let it go. If it was God's will the letter would get there, he thought, giving in to fatigue.

The envelope didn't even have a chance to hit the ground before it was sucked up by the strong winds and pushed higher and higher into the black, starless sky, where a storm was threatening above the Nablus mountains. The time between dull rumbles and flashes of lightning diminished and the promise of rain hung in the air. In only a matter of seconds, the rain would hammer the envelope down to the ground and transform the dry earth to wet clay. But no rain ever came, and the bloodstained envelope continued its journey over the mountains and across the border towards Jordan.

SALADIN HAZAYMEH WAS LYING on his sleeping pad looking up toward the sky, where the light of dawn was making its first hesitant attempts to peak out. The strong winds from the night's storm had finally calmed down and it looked like it might be a beautiful day.

It felt as if the sun had decided to clean up the sky for his seventieth birthday. And though his birthday was the whole reason for this ten-day long hike, Saladin Hazaymeh was completely occupied by something else.

When he first noticed it up in the sky, he thought it was an airplane at an altitude of several thousand metres, but then decided it must be a bird with an injured wing. Now he had no idea what was floating down to the ground some fifty metres ahead of him, glistening in the light from the sun.

Saladin Hazaymeh got up and noticed his usual morning back pain was gone. He hurried to roll up his sleeping pad and put it in his backpack. Something was about to happen—something of great significance—and he felt full of energy.

It could be nothing other than a sign from the god he had believed in for as long as he could remember, telling him that he was on the right path. For this birthday, he'd retraced the steps of Jesus all the way from Jerusalem to the Sea of Galilee.

Yesterday, he had visited the holy grotto in Anjara and had hoped to spend the night there, just as Jesus had done with his disciples and the Virgin Mary. But the guards had discovered him and he had been forced to sleep under the open sky. But there was a meaning to everything, he thought, hurrying off with a light step across the uneven land toward the olive tree, where the sign from God was caught among the branches.

When he got there he saw that it was an envelope. An envelope? He thought.

As much as he tried he could not come up with a logical reason to explain its origins. He finally decided that heaven would have to do. And perhaps that wasn't completely wrong. His inner voice kept repeating how important it was that he took care of it, like a mantra. It was how things were intended. That—and nothing else—was the real point of all his wandering.

After a number of attempts, he managed to hit the envelope with a stone and catch it before it hit the ground. It was dirty and full of small tears; it looked as if it had survived the end of the world against all odds. It was also heavier than he'd expected.

All doubt had now blown over. God had chosen him. This was not just any old envelope.

He inspected both sides for clues, but found nothing other than a name written in small, sprawling letters: *Aisha Shahin*.

Saladin Hazaymeh sat down on a stone and laboriously sounded out the name, but it meant nothing to him. After some hesitation he took out his knife and carefully slit open the envelope. Unaware that he was holding his breath, he pulled out and opened the letter, examining the long rows of handwriting.

It was Hebrew, that much he could tell. But he could barely read Arabic, so how would he be able to understand this?

What was God trying to say? Was he punishing him because he never learned to read? Or was the letter not intended for him at all? Was he only an insignificant middleman whose sole purpose was to pass it along? He tried without success to dismiss the disappointment while he folded the letter and put it back in its envelope. He continued his wandering northward toward Ajloun, where he reluctantly put the letter into a postbox.

MANY WOULD THINK THAT Khaled Shawabkeh had behaved shamefully and was deeply immoral. He, on the other hand, did not feel guilty at all when he picked up the envelope without a stamp, sender, or complete address. Letters where the sender had failed to do their part became his property. It was a practice he had applied, without exception, during the forty-three years he had worked sorting post.

At home he had many boxes filled with stray letters, one for each year. He liked nothing more than fishing one out at random and studying the contents that were meant for someone else. This particular envelope was something out of the ordinary.

The oxidation confirmed that the journey itself must have been an adventure. Moreover, someone had already slit the envelope open, but left the contents inside—for him and no one else.

Exactly ninety-eight minutes earlier than usual, Khaled Shawabkeh arrived home and locked the door. He had skipped afternoon tea, even though he'd brought harissa cakes, and jogged the whole way home from the bus. Now he was really out of breath and could feel the sweat trying to penetrate his tight polyester shirt. Dinner could wait. Instead, he poured a glass of wine from the bottle that was hidden behind the books on the bookshelf, sat down in the armchair, took out the envelope and solemnly coaxed out the letter.

Finally, he said to himself, reaching for the wine, blissfully ignorant of how the blood clot, which had been building up in his left leg for several years, had loosened and was following the blood flow all the way up to his lungs.

EVEN THOUGH IT HAD been more than a year since Maria's

uncle died from a lung embolism, she still hadn't set foot in his house. Her two brothers had challenged the will and done everything they could to pressure her to refuse the inheritance. Even her own father tried to convince her otherwise, arguing that Khaled Shawabkeh had gradually lost his mind over the years and had left his house in disarray. He also didn't think women would ever be cut out to own and manage property.

But Maria held her own and now, finally, she could put the key in the lock and go inside. In the negotiations, she'd become estranged from her brothers and parents. The house would be cleared out and sold, and with the money she could afford to quit her job at the tailoring shop, move to Amman, and start working her dream job at the Jordanian National Commission for Women.

IT SHOULDN'T HAVE BEEN possible. There was really nothing to suggest that the letter would ever reach its recipient. There were so many obstacles that the probability was so slight it was impossible to even calculate.

Yet that was exactly what happened.

One year, four months, and sixteen days after the letter had been pushed through a crack in the prisoner transport vehicle and had been taken hold of by the winds in the black night, it ended up in Maria Shawabkeh's hands. A few hours later, she had succeeded in piecing together most of the missing information.

Three sleepless nights after reading the horrific story from the letter, she made a few Internet searches, put a stamp on the envelope, wrote down the complete address, and left it at the nearest post office—without any idea of the consequences.

Aisha Shahin

Selmedalsvägen 40, 7th Floor

129 37 Hägersten, Sweden

Part I

December 16–19, 2009

Many people will be horrified by the things I've done. Some will see them as revenge for all the injustices that have been committed; others as an unlikely game to trick the system and show how far one person can go. But the vast majority will believe that these are the actions of an extremely sick person.

All of them will be wrong.

1

Two days ago

SOFIE LEANDER WAS SITTING in the waiting room at Stockholm South General Hospital waiting for an ultrasound. She was browsing through a well-thumbed copy of *We Parents* filled with page after page of beautiful, happy mums and dads and she wanted nothing more than to be one of them. But after so many fruitless rounds of IVF, she'd started to doubt that her egg production would ever get started.

This was her absolute last chance. If the procedure didn't work this time, she would have no choice other than to give up—something her husband already seemed to have done.

He had promised to be by her side when she needed him, but he'd missed today's appointment. She turned her mobile on and read his message again: *Have a conflict and unfortunately won't make it.* He treated the whole experience like it was shopping for milk on the way home from work. He hadn't even said "good luck."

She had hoped that the move to Sweden three years ago would revive their relationship, especially since he had even chosen to take her surname. She'd seen it as a declaration of love; proof the two of them were united, no matter what happened. Now she was no longer so sure, and she couldn't escape the feeling that they were slipping farther and farther away from each other. She had tried to bring it up, but he persistently avowed his love for her. She could see it in his eyes though; or, more correctly, in the way he avoided her eyes.

Now, the man who had once saved her life, suddenly had "conflicts" and hardly looked in her direction. She wanted to call and confront him, to ask if he'd stopped loving her or if he'd met someone else. But she didn't dare. Besides, she was sure he wouldn't answer anyway. He almost never did when he was working, and especially not now when he was in the middle of a new project. Her only chance was a positive report from the doctor. If she could just get that, surely everything would be fine again. She would finally be able to give him the child they always wanted and he would realize how much he really loved her.

"Sofie Leander," she heard her name being called. She followed the midwife through the corridor and was shown into a small examination room with closed blinds, a large computer-like apparatus and a hospital bed.

"You can hang up your coat on the hook and then lie down on the bed. The doctor will be here at any moment."

Sofie nodded, and took off her coat and boots, as the midwife left the room. Once on the bed she pulled up her blouse and unbuttoned her pants. She decided to try her husband anyway and ask what was so important that he couldn't join her. As she was reaching for her handbag the door opened and the doctor came in.

"Are you Sofie Leander?"

Sofie nodded.

"Good. I'll have you start by lying down on your side with your back to me."

Sofie did as she was told and could hear the doctor opening some kind of plastic packaging behind her. She couldn't put her finger on it, but there was something about the whole situation that didn't feel right.

"Excuse me, I'm here to have my ovaries examined."

"Absolutely. We just have to take care of this first," the doctor said, while pressing on her vertebrae.

Suddenly she felt a prick in the middle of her back.

"What are you doing? Did you just stick me with a syringe?" Sofie turned around and saw something slip into the doctor's pant pocket. "Now I demand to know what—"

"You don't need to worry. This is just purely routine. Are those your things?" the doctor said, pointing to her coat and boots, but he didn't wait for an answer and set them by her feet. "We don't want to forget anything, do we?"

This wasn't the first time Sofie had been in for an ultrasound of her ovaries, so she knew that this was definitely not routine. She had no idea what this was. All she was sure of was that she no longer wanted to be part of it and wanted to get away from the doctor, the examination room, and the whole hospital.

"I think I have to go now," she said, trying to get up. "I want to leave, Do you hear me?" But her body refused to obey. "What's happening? What have you done?"

The doctor leaned toward her, smiling, and stroking her cheek. "You'll understand soon."

Sofie tried to protest and scream as loud as she could, but the respiratory mask that was stretched across her face suffocated all sound. Before she knew it, the brakes of the bed had been released, and she was being wheeled out of the examination room and into the corridor.

If only she could grab something, anything at all, and pull herself out of the bed to make everyone realize what was happening. But she couldn't. All she could do was lie there, stare up toward the ceiling, and watch as the fluorescent lights passed by and doors opened.

She saw so many faces: pregnant mothers and soon-to-be fathers, midwives and doctors. They were all so close, but still so far away. She heard voices and the sound of elevator doors closing behind her. Or were they opening? She was disoriented.

Then she was alone with the doctor again, who was whistling a tune that echoed between the hard walls. It was the only sound she could hear other than her own breath, which was starting to remind her of the asthma she had as a child. At that age, she had felt completely helpless when she had to stop playing to gasp for air. Now she felt both helpless and small, and wanted nothing other than to collapse and cry. But she couldn't even do that.

The fluorescent lights on the dark concrete ceiling ended, and then she saw first her legs, and then her upper body, lifted onto a stretcher. *You'll soon understand*, the doctor had said. How could she understand? All she could think of was that plastic surgeon in Malmö who had injected something into his patients so they couldn't resist when he raped them. But why would anyone want to rape her?

She was pushed backwards into the ambulance and tried to focus on the sounds. She heard the driver's side door close and the engine start. They started moving and turned west on Ringvägen and then continued along Hornsgatan toward Hornstull, where they left the city along Liljeholmsbron. She had no problem following the route initially, but it got worse when they went round a roundabout. After that she lost all sense of direction.

About twenty minutes later they finally stopped. She had no idea where they were, but she heard a garage door open. The ambulance went in about thirty metres before the engine was turned off.

The ambulance doors opened, and she was pulled out and carried away on the stretcher. New fluorescent lights chased each other in the ceiling. The pace quickened, and doctor's steps echoed against the hard floor until they abruptly stopped. She heard keys and a beeping sound, and then an electric motor starting.

She was rolled into a dark room, and it sounded as if

something was closing behind her. A strong lamp in the ceiling was turned on and was shining right down onto a rectangular table. She couldn't see any windows, or figure out the size of the room. She could only make out the lamp and the table with a number of devices around it. She was pushed forward and could now see that the table was covered with plastic and had a number of straps and an inch-wide hole right below the mid-point. There was a smaller metal table alongside the rectangular one that had various surgical instruments lined up on a white towel.

Once she saw the scissors, tongs and scalpels, she understood exactly why she'd been taken away—and what was coming.

Can't wait to read the rest?

If you're addicted to Ahnhem, tell us in no more than 140

characters why you loved *Victim Without a Face* and you could

win an exclusive early copy of the next book in the Fabian Risk

series, *The Ninth Grave*.

Tweet us **@hoz_books** using hashtag **#FabianRisk**

or email **competition@headofzeus.com**

for your chance to win.